WRITTEN IN RED

A Selection of Recent Titles from Annie Dalton

For children

ANGEL ACADEMY: LIVING THE DREAM
CHERRY GREEN, STORY QUEEN
FRIDAY FOREVER
INVISIBLE THREADS
LILAC PEABODY AND HONEYSUCKLE HOPE
NIGHTMAZE
WAYS TO TRAP A YETI

For adults

The Oxford Dogwalkers' Mysteries

THE WHITE SHEPHERD *
WRITTEN IN RED *

* *available from Severn House*

WRITTEN IN RED

An Oxford Dogwalkers' Mystery

Annie Dalton

Severn House Large Print
London & New York

This first large print edition published 2016
in Great Britain and the USA by
SEVERN HOUSE PUBLISHERS LTD of
19 Cedar Road, Sutton, Surrey, England, SM2 5DA.
First world regular print edition published 2016 by
Severn House Publishers Ltd.

British Library Cataloguing in Publication Data
A CIP catalogue record for this title is available from the British Library.

ISBN-13: 9780727894960

Severn House Publishers support the Forest Stewardship Council™
[FSC™], the leading international forest certification organisation. All
our titles that are printed on FSC certified paper carry the FSC logo.

Typeset by Palimpsest Book Production Ltd.,
Falkirk, Stirlingshire, Scotland.
Printed and bound in Great Britain by
T J International, Padstow, Cornwall.

Acknowledgments

Grateful thanks to Fiona Ferguson, Jeanette Johnston, Jane Darby and Tim Couché for generously sharing their expertise, and to local dog-walking friends Trish Mallett, Sarah Nash and Marjorie Guichard for walks, talks and ongoing support. Also huge thanks to the real Tim Freemantle and to Helen Vallier, who kindly lent their names to two of our characters.

Prologue

James Lowell emerged into a chilly December dusk relieved to have given his last but one tutorial of the Michaelmas term. Though his rooms were only a few hundred yards away, he was still recovering from a chest infection so he had been forced to wrap up like some old buffer in a tweed coat, cap and muffler. All he needed was a blasted stick, he thought.

Teaching increasingly tired him nowadays, even when he was well, but to his surprise James actually felt reinvigorated by the lively discussion he'd had with his tutees. While he was bundling himself back into his layers, two girl students had come up to wish him a happy Christmas, then rushed off on their bikes to sing carols at Carfax Tower. Older people loved to complain about the young, but each time James saw those fresh young faces looking back at him, he saw himself at their age, exuberant and clueless as a puppy; dangerously clueless, in his case. The thought produced the familiar ache around his heart.

Passing under one of the college's many medieval archways, he set off up the steep stairway to his living quarters, noticing, as he always noticed, the tight bend where countless unknown

1

scholars before him had steadied themselves against the same solid oak beam. This simple action, repeated across the centuries, had worn a satin-smooth depression in the shape of a human palm. Such a small thing, yet it moved him every time.

Living in an Oxford college, you were constantly reminded that you were just a fleeting presence in a vast historical continuum. Some people disliked Oxford for that reason, chafing against its self-importance and outmoded traditions. But to James, Oxford stood for everything that was humane and good. It was his home, his shelter from the storms of the outside world, his second chance.

He'd first arrived at Walsingham College as an undergraduate to read history and politics. He had somehow achieved a first, despite the fact that he was certainly having some kind of break-down at the time. Then, after confused years of wandering, James had found his way back and never left. In his early thirties, he had written a book on medieval thought which had earned him the respect of his peers. Since then there had been at least a dozen other well-received books. Currently he was immersed in writing a study of seventeenth-century English radicalism which he believed to be his best work yet.

The thought of the almost-completed final chapter waiting on his laptop made James hurry up the last few stairs. He could almost feel ideas and sentences forming as he felt for his door key. It was the old-fashioned kind with wards, more suited to Bluebeard's chamber, he thought, than the apartment of a celibate old academic. A tall, straight-backed man, even in his late sixties, he had to stoop to insert it in the lock.

Already mentally at his desk, he almost failed to notice the envelope sticking out from under his door. In the semi-twilight of the landing, the pale paper seemed to glimmer. James picked it up, rubbing his thumb over the expensive stationery, puzzled by the fact that it bore only his name. Post normally entered Walsingham College via the porter's lodge and was kept in the recipient's pigeonhole until it was collected. This had obviously been delivered by hand. Equally puzzling was the careful calligraphy. Who bothered with beautiful handwriting nowadays? It was most likely to be some kind of tedious invitation. James loved Oxford but had developed a phobia of hot rooms filled with braying academics.

Without turning on any lights, he dropped the communication unread on a cluttered coffee table on his way to rescue the fire which had burned down almost to ashes. Something felt subtly different about the room, though he felt sure it looked the same as when he'd left. Exactly the same in fact, he thought, down to the familiar and well-loved smells: wood-ash, old leather-books and ancient timber mixed with liberal quantities of wax polish, and that unique composite fragrance which was the signature scent of Walsingham itself.

Crouching by the hearth, James took small logs from a basket and threw them on to the faintly glowing embers. Still uneasy, he glanced around

3

the small apartment. At the far end were two further doors. One led to a galley kitchen with rudimentary cooking facilities, the other to a monkish little bedroom with bathroom attached. It was ridiculous to think someone had been in his rooms. 'You're going gaga,' he told himself irritably. He wasn't normally given to nervous fancies. In bed at night he'd hear the medieval building creak and shift but the sounds never bothered him. If any ghostly scholars were watching over him as he went about his solitary routine, they probably recognized him as a fellow lost soul, he thought. Once again, he felt that familiar sorrowful ache.

One of the logs caught with a loud crackle. Fresh flames leapt, illuminating his surroundings with their orange flicker. It was a few minutes past six, but it might have been midnight. This time of year, his rooms, with their tiny leaded windows, were almost dark by two in the afternoon. With the lights off, the only visible sign of the twenty-first century was the blinking light on James's laptop. As an historian he knew it was ridiculous to imagine that life in medieval times had been somehow simpler or nobler than his own, yet the fantasy persisted: a childish dream of a golden time and place where he could have been the man he'd always longed to be, a good and honourable man.

Hauling himself to his feet, James went around switching on lamps. Like some Dutch old master, the subdued lighting tenderly picked out domestic details here and there: the gilded titles on the spines of books, the gleam of a button on the cardigan cast over the back of the old chesterfield, the metal trim on his Dansette record player kept for sentimental reasons since he now owned a state-of-the-art music system.

He was safe at home with everything he held dear, yet he still felt strangely on edge. He decided it must be the mysterious letter. Putting on one of the several pairs of cheap reading glasses he kept around his apartment, James seated himself by the fire and slit open the envelope, drawing out a sheet of folded cream-coloured paper.

The shock of the words inside robbed him of all sensation. He sat numb, unseeing, as the letter slowly slipped from his hand. He'd persuaded himself that the danger had passed. Fifty years had gone by. In a few years, he would die of some tedious old person's ailment and his secret would die with him. He had hidden himself away in this most cerebral of cities. He had lived, or tried to live, a blameless but intellectually productive life. Now some fiery whirlwind out of the Old Testament had torn off the roof from above his head, exposing him as a hypocrite and a sham. For an instant, he saw himself as a tiny squirming figure, a terrifying vortex of divine wrath overhead.

James stood up, dazed, and went to pour himself a whiskey, but all he could see were those patiently executed words, like something one might copy out for a child who was learning to read – assuming you wanted to give them nightmares. *You must Cleanse this Foul Darkness from Your Soul, or You will Burn in Hell for Eternity.* In the style of an old illuminated manuscript, each of the capital letters was inscribed in red as if to underline the theme of purgatorial fire.

Still standing, James took a burning gulp of his whiskey. He had never told another soul what had happened that day. The only people who knew were James and Tallis.

Tallis. After all this time, the name still held its old ambiguous charisma. It was not impossible that he was still out there somewhere, lurking in the shadows. But though Tallis might conceivably still be alive, James couldn't believe he'd written the letter. Tallis had made James feel that his guilty conscience was a pathetic indulgence, a weakness. As an individual, James was utterly insignificant, Tallis had said. The important thing was to limit the damage, or James would have destroyed everything their group had been working so hard to achieve. By this time James was doubtful if they'd achieved anything at all, but he was still recoiling from the terrible thing he'd done, and so he'd agreed to let Tallis clean up his mess.

James felt the gooseflesh rise on his arms as he remembered the chilling efficiency with which Tallis had acted to do just that . . .

He set down his glass and went to his desk. The surface was littered with notebooks and papers, crucial references for the last leg of his book, the book he'd hoped might be his legacy and which now seemed pathetically unimportant. Bending to open a deep drawer James pulled out an old leather-backed album. He took the album and the glass of whiskey to a small table beside the chesterfield. About to sit down, he abruptly changed his mind, and went to search through his stash of LPs. He found the one he was looking for, slid it out of the tattered sleeve, placed it on the turntable of his ancient record player, selected the track and softly lowered the needle.

The twanging opening chords of 'Time Is on My Side' filled the room, and instantly he was back in the stale little booth in the music shop, the two of them sharing one set of headphones.

It was the closest he'd ever been physically to a girl. He had both wanted it to last for ever and also to immediately flee back to his room so he could process the devastating, soul-wrecking sensation of first love. She had been comically horrified that he'd never heard of the Stones, while James had been stunned that a girl – *this* heart-stoppingly beautiful girl – could relate to something so savage, so raw. With typical generosity – she was carelessly generous to everyone she allowed into her inner circle – she'd bought him the record as a gift.

'Someone's got to drag you into the twentieth century, James, darling,' she'd said mischievously. Helplessly smitten, he'd played the song whenever he was alone in his room, to re-evoke the pleasurable torture of loving her.

Sitting on his chesterfield, his glass in one hand, James turned the pages of the album with the other, leafing past pictures of smiling young people in sixties' clothes. The pictures were just old black-and-white Kodak snaps, yet whenever he looked at them he always saw their real colours. How formal young people had looked then: the boys in tweeds and cords like headmasters in training, the girls with matching twinsets and backcombed hair. He smiled at the photo of Isadora in an unflattering fluffy sweater failing to look relaxed in a punt. With one of her endearing hoots of laughter, she'd confessed that she didn't know how to swim. How touchingly young she was then; the youngest undergraduate of her year. Their paths had crossed of course over the years. Oxford academia was a small and incestuous world. Once he'd looked up feeling her eyes on him from across the room. But they'd never once spoken. Tallis had seen to that.

He turned a page and his hand stilled. It was the only photo he possessed of them all together. Piers had acquired an old London cab of which he was enormously proud and in which he tirelessly drove everyone around. In the picture they'd all taken up poses against the taxi's gleaming black flanks, except for Piers who hung out of the driver's window, waving and grinning at the camera. The photograph captured the ebullient confidence of the times so perfectly it could have been for a sixties' photo shoot.

James turned to the next page and felt his mouth go dry as he came to the photograph that always brought such mixed joy and pain. Random sensations assailed him: her gentle fingers stroking his hair, exploring his skin, the scent of her perfume mingled with the cigarette smell that had gradually impregnated everything he wore. She smoked, so James did too. If he couldn't win her love he could at least earn her approval.

It hurt to see her so young and lovely. She'd

been the first of the girls to grow her hair long, not artfully layered the way long hair was styled today but falling like a pale straight curtain around her face, with a thick fringe that hung almost in her eyes. He remembered how the smallest movement could bring that silky curtain swinging across her cheekbones, veiling her feelings from view. In the picture she was wearing a simple shift dress that she'd bought on one of her mysterious disappearances to London. Almost as soon as she'd got it she gave it away to Catherine, one of the other girls. 'I've gone off it,' she'd said abruptly. 'Here, take it!'

'But it's by *Mary Quant*,' Catherine had said in awe.

She'd had extraordinarily lovely blue-grey eyes, lovely yet utterly enigmatic. As if her brows and lashes weren't already dark enough, she would outline them Cleopatra-style with some sooty cosmetic. A year later all the girls were doing it. She'd been ahead of her time, he thought, rushing recklessly into some magical future of love, peace and universal freedom – a future that never came. James had been too young then to understand the damage that ran through her like a fault line. The things she did. The risks she took. He'd imagined he could save her, cherish and protect her, but instead . . .

'You'll come running back,' Mick Jagger threatened. 'You'll come running back to *me* . . .'

James felt an infinitesimal change in the air of his room. At the same moment he heard a faint creak. Too late, adrenalin surged as something smashed down on the back of his skull, followed

9

by agonizing pain that penetrated right to the roots of his teeth. Doubled over by the impact, half blinded by the blood streaming into his eyes, James looked up at the indistinct figure that was suddenly standing over him and he knew that the letter-writer was right.

It was time for him to pay.

One

It was a few minutes after eight on a bright frosty
morning and Anna Hopkins was walking her dog
on Port Meadow. She was dressed in her old
parka, jeans, muddy boots and a knitted scarf
with a repeat motif of Jack Russell terriers. It
had been given to her by her friend Tansy 'as a
ridiculously small thank you for letting me stay
at your place till I sort myself out!' All the terriers
were bright pink, except for one tiny black Jack
Russell that faced stubbornly in the opposite
direction. Tansy had watched anxiously as Anna
unwrapped her gift from its layers of tissue. 'It's
meant to be a joke?' she'd explained. 'Because
of us being the dog walking detectives? Don't
feel you have to wear it. I know you're more of
a monochrome girl.'

It's true that Anna had once seen herself as
monochrome. Her palette of caramels and char-
coals had seemed like the safer choice; the same
with living alone. For sixteen years, just surviving
had used up so much energy. There'd been little
left for engaging with the outside world.

And then she'd risked a change, such a small
unthreatening change, or so she'd told herself.
She'd adopted Bonnie, a White Shepherd who
carried the hidden scars of her own traumatic
past. And in a matter of weeks Anna's monochrome life had transformed into chaotic

11

full-spectrum colour. Terrible and wonderful things had happened. And now here she was, wrapped warmly in a shocking pink scarf, her honey-coloured hair tucked under her grey slouchy beanie, boots crunching on frost, breath smoking in the midwinter cold, as Bonnie ran around her in joyous circles.

Port Meadow was an easy walk from Anna's home in Park Town, a space where she could let Bonnie run off her excess energy; and so Anna had recently resumed their walks here. She wondered whether she would ever be able to see a young woman out jogging without feeling her heart leap in the irrational hope that it was Naomi running towards her, glowing and alive.

Someone was coming towards Anna, in fact, but she wasn't glowing so much as puffing with effort. Dressed in a shapeless coat and leggings, a young woman was toiling over the uneven ground behind an enormous off-road buggy. The faint wails from inside the buggy grew louder. Drawing level with Anna, she stopped in her tracks. She threw Anna a despairing look. 'You wouldn't like to swap your beautiful dog for my baby, would you? You might have more luck getting him to sleep.' She jiggled the buggy back and forth on the frosty grass.

An intensely private person, Anna had been unprepared for the startling intimacies she elicited from complete strangers when she started walking Bonnie. Tansy said it was the same when she'd been minding her friends' poodle, Buster. But Tansy wouldn't see this new mother as an intrusion, Anna thought. She'd see a sleep-deprived young woman longing for contact with another adult, any adult, and so Anna reluctantly stepped up. 'I'm sure you're doing a much better job than you think,' she managed.

The woman threw her a grateful look. 'God, I really hope so,' she said fervently. 'If I'd had any idea how hard this would be, I never would have dared.' She had to raise her voice as the yells from the buggy increased in volume. 'My husband's away on business and last night I broke all the baby book rules and took Louis into bed with me.'

'Did it work?' Anna asked.

The woman shot her an exhausted grin. 'For two and a half hours. Suppose it's got to get better at some point?'

'I'm sure it will,' Anna said, striving to be upbeat.

'Oh, well, I'd better get back. Enjoy your walk.' The woman set off trudging behind her buggy, watched warily by Bonnie. The White Shepherd had come to sit at Anna's feet as soon as she saw the woman approach. This worrying new behaviour, dated from the night when intruders had broken into her flat with the intention of adding her to their list of undiscovered homicides; a list that included Naomi Evans. Trying to save Anna's life, Bonnie had almost died herself.

'We're probably more likely to win the lottery than run into another psychopath,' Anna told her dog as they continued on their way. 'We were just really unlucky. I think we should view that as our lifetime's quota and move on, sweetie.'

Bonnie appeared to give her suggestion serious

thought, gazing up at Anna with the luminous intelligence that made her resemble a white wolf out of a fairy tale. 'Come on, lazybones,' Anna told her. 'You're here to let off steam! So go, go, *go*!'

Bonnie didn't need telling twice. She shot away at top speed, looping back to Anna, before zooming away again like an exuberant puppy. She couldn't move quite as fluidly as she had before her injuries, but she certainly wasn't letting it slow her down.

There were other dog walkers dotted over the wide open space. Her grandfather would love this scene, Anna thought. A talented artist, who'd only discovered his gift late in life, he'd know how to render the hats and scarves in streaks and blobs of pigment, the sooty shapes of rooks circling and tumbling overhead, the colours of the different dogs against the sparkling frost.

Anna was getting to know some of the other dog walkers by sight. There was the strident woman who treated the meadow like her personal boot camp for her misbehaving Border collies; the slow-moving man in the tweed cap with his elderly liver-and-white spaniel. One day Anna had heard him coax, 'Come on, old girl, just a bit further then you can go home and snooze.' And she'd realized that he had been tenderly adapting his pace to his valiant little spaniel's so as not to tax her joints.

She was oddly fond of the spaniel man, even though they'd never spoken. Other people Anna had disliked on sight, like the forty-something woman who was always raging tearfully at someone on her phone (an ex, Anna had decided, or a soon-to-be ex), as her West Highland terrier pattered stoically beside her. Seeing her now, Anna swerved discreetly in the opposite direction. She spotted another Port Meadow regular in the distance: a stocky young man walking a cream-coloured Staffordshire bull terrier on a short lead. The first time Anna had encountered him on the path he'd quickly stepped aside with his dog to let Anna and Bonnie pass. She'd thanked him and he had stopped, shy but friendly, to make the usual jokes about Bonnie, asking if she wasn't really a wolf.

'I'd love to let Blossom off for a run,' he'd said wistfully. 'But when you're out with a Staffie you can't afford any misunderstandings.' He'd gone on to relate Blossom's short but painful history so far as he and the vet had been able to piece it together. Apparently kept for breeding purposes at what must have been a particularly hellish puppy farm, she'd been found dumped, heavily pregnant and in need of medical attention, by the side of the motorway.

Every rescue dog came with a story, Anna thought now as she returned the young man's friendly wave, and some of those stories really made her loathe her fellow humans. She decided it was time to go home. Today was also Tansy's day off, and Anna had left her weighing out ingredients for a batch of muffins. 'Experimental Christmas muffins,' she'd confided.

Like Anna's, Tansy's life had recently changed for the better. She'd ditched her waitressing job

15

at the vegan cafe, found a job she loved at a friend's art gallery and, after years of dating 'losers and abusers', in Tansy's words, had become romantically involved with the young police sergeant they'd met during the investigation into Naomi's murder. 'I'm not counting chickens,' she'd told Anna. 'Liam's so sweet and normal. I've never done sweet and normal before. How do I know that something won't suddenly trip my switch and turn me back into Mad Maxine McVeigh, the gangster's daughter?'

Anna had been faintly puzzled by those chickens; Tansy was always coming out with these funny little proverbs. But she'd just said soberly, 'You *don't* know.' She understood Tansy's fears too well to wave them away. That's why her inbox was filling up with unanswered emails from Tim Freemantle.

Tim belonged to Anna's old life, her lost life; the life in which her parents, her two brothers and her little sister were still alive. But now, for the first time since her teens, Anna felt she had a future. She couldn't risk getting sucked back into that nightmarish black hole where she'd existed for so long.

After she and Jake had come back from their trip to the Lake District and he'd driven off to Heathrow, she'd done some soul-searching, forcing herself to acknowledge that she'd probably never know what happened that terrible summer's night. If she was going to move forward, she was going to have to accept that. Harder still, she was going to have to act on it.

And so that's what she'd done. She'd stopped

16

her obsessive online searches. She'd stopped trying to track down Max, her long-ago teenage boyfriend. She'd cancelled every single Google alert relating to the Hopkins family murders. It felt as if she was being torn into a million panicky pieces, but she did it. It was true that she still occasionally found herself in her study, her hand hovering over the drawer where she kept the key to her antique armoire but so far she'd managed to leave the key untouched.

As with any recovering addict there were nights when Anna woke up sweating, in the grip of her old compulsions. But then she'd raise herself up on her elbow and see Bonnie asleep in her basket and her own breathing would deepen and slow and she'd remember that what she had before was not a real life but just a recurring bad dream. That's why she refused to let herself read Tim's emails, or anything else that might feed her obsession with the past.

Anna was halfway home when her phone started buzzing in her pocket. She saw the caller ID and her heart lifted. 'Jake? Where are you? Any idea when you'll be back in the UK?'

'Real soon, I hope,' he said. 'Just got some last-minute meetings lined up.'

'Don't leave it too long to book a flight,' she reminded him.

'Why, are you missing me a little?' Jake's warm southern accent still made Anna go a little weak at the knees.

'Fat chance!' she said, with a laugh. 'I have an extremely extrovert flatmate now, remember?'

'It must be quite cool though, having her stay

with you for a while?' Jake said. *Tansy and occasionally Liam*, Anna thought but didn't say.

Instead she said, 'You know Nick and Leo decided to come back early? They missed their dog! I never would have understood that before I had Bonnie. Not that Buster in any way compares with Bonnie, obviously!'

'Buster always struck me as kind of light on personality,' Jake agreed. 'Must have been a surprise for Tansy though, when they just rocked up out of the blue.'

'It was. She thought she still had months to find somewhere to live.'

'How's it working out, anyway, sharing your space?'

'We just survived our first quarrel,' Anna told him.

'Seriously? You guys quarrelled?'

'I might be exaggerating very slightly,' she said. 'We just found out that we have incompatible ideas on Christmas tree decoration. Luckily, Isadora turned up before things got too tense and we let her have the final say on what went where.'

Anna's friendship with Tansy and Isadora had quickly become such a major part of her life, it was hard to remember they'd only known each other slightly less than three months. One sunny September morning, Anna, Tansy and Isadora had been separately walking their dogs on Port Meadow, when Anna's White Shepherd suddenly took off across the spongy wet ground, still attached to her lead. With Anna grimly hanging on, Bonnie had half dragged her over to some

18

bushes. Sensing that something was wrong, Isadora and Tansy had hurried to Anna's aid and found her staring down at the blood-soaked body of Naomi Evans. For reasons Anna still didn't fully understand, the harrowing circumstances of their first meeting had become the basis of a firm friendship between these three very different women.

'Isn't Isadora Jewish?' Jake was still pondering Anna's remarks about the Christmas tree.

'She is. She also has an alarmingly random approach to hanging up baubles. Tansy and I practically had to sit on our hands until she went home and we could rearrange them all again!'

'And how's our Bonnie?' Jake said. 'Is she behaving herself? She hasn't started digging up the next door neighbours' gardens?'

He was referring to Bonnie's behaviour on the shore at Ullswater, something which Anna and Jake had witnessed with mixed amazement and relief. Since the night of the break-in, Bonnie had lost confidence; but Anna hadn't realized how badly until they set off to drive to the Lake District. A few miles outside Oxford, Bonnie had begun panting and salivating, obviously distressed at being away from familiar surroundings. In her short life Bonnie had survived all manner of dangers, but it seemed that being savagely attacked in her own home had traumatized her. Jake and Anna had agreed that they'd abandon their plans and take her home the next day if this upsetting behaviour continued once they reached the Lakes.

By the time they'd arrived at Ullswater,

Bonnie's chest and belly, together with the fleece blanket she was sitting on, were saturated with drool and Anna's nerves were shredded. This was not how she'd imagined the start of their holiday. Trying to lighten the mood, Jake had suggested they took Bonnie down to the lakeside to stretch their legs before they checked into their hotel.

The instant Bonnie felt loose shingle slipping and sliding under her paws, she became a different dog, racing around them in circles, then for no obvious reason she stopped dead, let out a single ringing '*wuff!*' and began to dig with such ferocious energy that Anna and Jake were sprayed with a shower of tiny stinging stones. If they hadn't forcibly removed her she'd probably still be there, frantically digging in a crater of her own making. But some inner transformation had occurred on that stretch of shingle, because when they'd returned to the car, Bonnie had jumped calmly into the back apparently without a second thought.

'No,' said Anna, wondering if Jake could hear the smile in her voice. 'She hasn't tried to dig up anyone's garden. I think digging is Bonnie's special holiday thing.'

'The digging cure,' Jake said in a musing tone. 'Shame there's no way to market it.'

'Shame it only works for dogs,' Anna added a little wistfully.

'Hush,' Jake told her. 'Like my aunt Mimi used to say, "We're all works in progress."'

When Anna adopted Bonnie, she'd only been told that she'd belonged to an old lady who had died. Now she knew that this lady had been Jake's Aunt Mimi who had been minding Bonnie for her adopted nephew, Jake McCaffrey, a former US Navy SEAL. Jake had found Bonnie in Afghanistan, where she'd been injured in a roadside blast. At that time she was little more than a gangly puppy. He'd tended to her wounds and named her after the first dog he'd ever loved. He'd also taught her excellent canine manners, plus one or two party tricks, like how to open a refrigerator and fetch him a beer. When he'd received a posting to the Philippines, Jake had sent Bonnie to live with his recently widowed Aunt Mimi in Oxford until he could give her a settled home. But Mimi had unexpectedly died and so the White Shepherd had been sent to a rescue shelter. The first time Jake met Anna he'd explained that he had no intention of subjecting Bonnie to yet more upheaval and distress by taking her back; he was just happy to know she'd found such a good home.

Before Anna met Jake, the very thought of love – the terrifying risks involved in loving or being loved – would have made her run a mile. But through Bonnie, she and Jake had immediately found common ground. They loved the same dog, a dog who adored them in return. On that basis they'd quickly grown to be good friends. Yet despite their mutual attraction neither of them had tried to take things a stage further.

'You don't think you and Jake have got stuck in the Friends' Zone,' Tansy had suggested when Anna confided in her. 'Like, you've might have missed your window?' Though she was only her early twenties, Tansy had appointed herself as Anna's more worldly wise agony aunt.

'What happens if you miss your window?' The thought that her flatmate's explanation held more than a grain of truth was depressing.

Tansy had given her a beaming smile. 'You just wait until it comes around again, you daft muppet!'

'But what if it doesn't?'

'It will,' Tansy had said with utter confidence. 'Trust me, you two are meant!'

Even though Anna didn't yet know what she and Jake were to each other, she had decided she was grateful; grateful to feel alive again, to laugh again, and even flirt again. She tried not to think too much about the future, just taking things day by day.

'And don't you worry about Christmas, OK? I'll be with you if I have to steal a plane and fly it myself!' Jake told her as he was about to ring off.

'Well, that's a reassuring thought to end on,' she said laughing.

Jake's voice had kept her company almost to her front door. After Anna's grandmother died, her grandfather had signed his Georgian town house over to Anna before moving into a nearby retirement home. Anna now occupied the lower two floors. The two other flats she rented out to a banker that she hardly ever saw, and Dana, a trauma and orthopaedic surgeon at the Sir John Radcliffe.

Letting herself into the hall, Anna was met by the smell of baking wafting up from the kitchen.

22

She could hear Tansy singing along enthusiastically to Sam Smith's 'Stay with Me'. Before Tansy came, this flat had been Anna's place to hide from the world. Tansy's presence had changed all that and Anna was still figuring out how she felt about it.

She hung up Bonnie's lead with her parka next to Tansy's coat, then snuck a peep through her sitting room door in case Tansy had made some unofficial alteration to their Christmas tree. But it was just as she'd left it, magical, shimmery and flawlessly symmetrical, exactly the way a Christmas tree ought to look.

Anna suddenly found herself smiling. She quite liked this new Anna Hopkins who had let another person move into her space, a person who painted stars and rainbows on her nails, sang happily off-key and filled the air with the orangey smell of fresh-baked muffins.

She went downstairs to the kitchen, still her favourite room in the flat. Part conservatory, with a view into the courtyard garden, it gave the impression of being bright and airy on even the gloomiest winter day. Today, with frost glittering on the flower pots and sunlight streaming in, it would have looked perfect if it wasn't for the almost empty shelves on the dresser. *It doesn't matter*, Anna told herself for the umpteenth time. *It's just stuff.*

Wagging her tail, Bonnie went straight to Tansy to let her know they were home. 'Hi! I didn't hear you guys come in. How was your walk?' Tansy glanced up from the dishwasher where she'd been stacking the pans she'd used for baking. Her glossy black curls, inherited from her Trinidadian mum, were pulled into their usual careless topknot.

'Good.' Anna refilled Bonnie's water bowl at the sink. The minute she'd set it down, Bonnie began drinking with the single-minded concentration only a thirsty dog can manage. 'Jake called,' Anna added. 'He sends his best, also asked if you'd been on any exciting stakeouts!'

Tansy straightened up from the dishwasher. 'Well, next time you tell him from me that joke is getting *old*!' Her delicate heart-shaped face suddenly registered concern. 'He's still coming for Christmas, isn't he?'

'Yes, he's still coming. He says if necessary he'll steal a plane and fly it himself.'

'Can Jake actually fly a plane? Silly question, of course he can! He could probably build one from scratch!' Tansy gestured to the tray of muffins cooling on the counter. 'Ta-da!'

'They smell amazing!' Anna said. 'What's in them?'

'Orange zest, cranberries,' Tansy said. 'Shall I make us some coffee?' Tansy had been a dedicated vegan and a health-nut besides when they'd first met, drinking only filtered water and herbal teas. But since she'd got together with Liam her determination to eat only pure foods had flown out of the window. 'He *seduced* me with a bacon sandwich!' she'd told Anna one morning, only half joking. 'I just don't know who I *am* any more, Anna! I drink espresso with you. I eat bacon with him. You'd better hope I never run into Hannibal Lector!'

24

Anna gave a yearning look at the muffins. 'I'd love some,' she told Tansy. 'But I think I left my iPad at work. I was just going to collect it. Can you hold off till I get back? I shouldn't be long.'

'Sure,' Tansy said mischievously. 'Wouldn't want Nadine to give you a demerit for leaving your things lying around the office.'

Anna tipped some kibble in Bonnie's food bowl and was about to speed back upstairs when she noticed the envelope lying on the table. Tansy had posted all her other Christmas cards days ago except this one.

'Shall I post this for you while I'm out?' Anna asked. 'I've got some stamps.'

'I haven't decided if I'm sending it yet.' Tansy was instantly tight-lipped. It was like she'd slammed a door between them and Anna knew to back off. Tansy's feelings about her dad were complicated to say the least. 'Anything you need from town?' she asked in her most neutral voice. Tansy just shook her head. 'Well, text me if you think of anything.'

Twenty minutes later Anna was walking through Oxford's city centre, heading towards the college where she had a job-share as an administrative assistant. Soon the students would disappear home for the holidays, but for now Anna could still enjoy them as part of the scenery.

Oxford felt genuinely Christmassy now, she thought; the crisp December air, the kitschy Christmas songs blasting from doorways, the strings of little twinkling lights and festive decorations everywhere. It was a long time since Anna had actually looked forward to Christmas, half her life-time in fact, but this year she felt as giddy as a five-year-old.

She still hadn't bought Jake a present, she remembered. She mentally scrolled through possibilities (Jake travelled a lot, he still didn't have a permanent home, so nothing too cumbersome). She'd almost reached the gates of Walsingham College before she noticed the emergency vehicles parked up on the pavement. There was an ambulance, as well as two motorbikes, the kind used by first-response paramedics, and what looked to Anna like an entire fleet of police cars.

She felt her happiness wobble. The previous Christmas one of Walsingham's most promising female undergraduates had taken a fatal overdose. Anna wasn't working at the college then, but she'd heard about it from her colleague Kirsty. She should know, if anybody knew, how hard the Christmas holidays could be for someone who was already struggling to keep afloat. Suppose it had happened again?

Then a stab of fear went through her, and she thought, *Oh, God, what if something's happened to Kirsty – or Paul?* Anna's life had taught her that absolutely anything could happen to anybody at any time. She went in through the gates of the porter's lodge where the senior porter, Mr Boswell, was visibly grey with shock.

'What's happened?' Anna asked though she was dreading the answer.

'It's Professor Lowell. Brenda found him when she went in to clean. The poor man must have been lying helpless all night.' Boswell shook his head.

Caught up in her own alarming imaginings, Anna had forgotten that people sometimes collapse from natural causes. 'Was it his heart?' she asked, wondering if Kirsty had been told. Kirsty had a soft spot for Professor Lowell.

Boswell's expression became grim. 'No, miss, I'm sorry to say he was attacked in his rooms. Beaten to a pulp, Brenda said he was.' The porter rubbed a meaty hand across his face. His chin quivered. 'I mean, what kind of heartless thug would want to harm that lovely old man?'

Anna heard fresh police sirens outside. 'I should let you get on,' she managed. 'You've got enough to deal with.' She fled through the gate, hurrying along the covered stone walkway that led to the administrative offices. The first time she'd entered these ancient walled gardens, she'd felt a fleeting sense of peace and calm enclose her as if nothing could ever harm her here.

With a jolt she spotted Tansy's boyfriend, Liam, with his boss, Inspector Chaudhari, on the other side of the gardens. They were talking to Walsingham's shocked-looking principal. Seeing Anna, Liam discreetly raised a hand in greeting. She just nodded and continued on her way. She'd attracted plenty of voyeurs in her time, people who got off on other people's tragedies, and she didn't want Tansy's boyfriend to think she was like them.

Unexpectedly her way was barred by a ruddy-faced police constable. 'Stand aside, please, miss, if you wouldn't mind. They need to bring the stretcher out.'

She hastily moved out of the way. Three

paramedics emerged from a doorway at a run, one on either side of the gurney, one holding up some kind of drip. Anna caught a shocking glimpse of the professor, his eyes closed, his blood-streaked face pale as vellum beneath the oxygen mask, bloodied bandages around his head.

She was suddenly somewhere high above herself, like a bird, or one of Walsingham's stone gargoyles, looking down at the whirling blue lights and the concerned faces of the paramedics as they loaded Professor Lowell's ominously still form into the ambulance.

Two

Anna could never remember afterwards how she made her way to her office. She just found herself on the claustrophobic little landing outside. Nadine's voice was unpleasantly audible through the not-quite-closed door. 'I'm sorry, Paul, but this is simply *not* good enough for Walsingham College. *Someone* needs to put up a notice on the door of Professor Lowell's tutorial room right away letting his students know the tutorial has been cancelled.' As usual, Nadine was turning someone else's misfortune into her personal drama.

'Nadine, since you immediately emailed everyone on the professor's tutorial list *and* posted a notice on the College website, I honestly don't see that anything else needs to be done.' Their senior administrator's normally mild tone was acquiring an edge. 'The tutees concerned are all third years and living in halls. They'll have already heard the news, and the porters will have enough to do this morning of all mornings without dashing around sticking up notices.'

Anna really couldn't take Nadine today. She'd have to pick up the iPad during her next shift. She was about to retreat when her boss emerged on to the landing. 'Anna!' Paul said, obviously startled to see her. 'Are you OK? Come in and sit down.'

Seeing her escape cut off, Anna felt herself break into a sweat. She opened her mouth with absolutely no idea what she was going to say. 'I – I forgot my iPad.'

She heard Kirsty call, 'Is Anna here? Oh, God, has she heard?' She came rushing out of the office. Anna caught a glimpse of her shocked hazel eyes and coppery curls, before Kirsty enveloped her in an embrace. 'Have you heard about Professor Lowell? I can't believe it.'

'Yes, I heard.' Some people find it comforting to have people around them in a crisis. Anna found it unspeakably stressful. Her overriding instinct was to run and hide. But she'd grown genuinely fond of Kirsty so she let herself be drawn into their airless little office.

Nadine appeared not to notice Anna's arrival, and was instead engaged in extremely theatrical typing. Officially Nadine and Anna now shared the job that Nadine had once done full-time. Unfortunately Nadine's inner control freak had

29

not accepted this change of status. Her eyes fixed stonily on her screen, Nadine activated the office printer which began to emit clicking and whirring sounds.

'He was *such* a duck,' Kirsty was still clinging on to Anna's hand. 'Such a brilliant, *brilliant* man, but he never talked down to anyone, not like some of them. He always used to ask me about Charlie – I mean, *attacked* in his rooms, Anna! I can't believe it! It's like *nobody's* safe anywhere, even here!' She gave an involuntary glance at her little boy's photo on her desk. 'It'll be some crazed druggie looking for something they could sell. The professor must have surprised him and he flipped!'

It was an all-too-likely scenario, Anna thought. The professor's injuries had been savage as if they'd been inflicted in a kind of frenzy.

The printer spat out a single sheet of paper. Nadine rose majestically from behind her desk as if to remind everyone whose desk it really was. Somewhere in her early fifties, she was dressed in an electric turquoise two-piece that made Anna think of cruise-wear. ('Nadine's very matchy-matchy,' Kirsty had commented once.)

'I'm not quite sure why you're here, Anna,' Nadine said in a frigid tone, 'but I'm afraid neither Kirsty nor I have time to chat. My morning was already looking like the morning from hell. Now on top of that I have to personally take this notice over to Professor Lowell's tutorial room!'

'I don't believe you do, Nadine, as I've already said.' Paul was still standing in the doorway. He attempted a smile. 'Pre-Christmas tutorials are usually just an excuse for mince pies and a glass of mulled wine!'

'We can't just send out emails in a situation like this!' Sometimes Nadine sounded like a bad actress who was playing the part of an administrator. 'This is Walsingham College! We simply cannot let this unfortunate incident impact on our standards.' Snatching her notice from the jaws of the printer, she swept out in a blur of turquoise.

Paul ran his hand distractedly through his hair. He looked as if there was a great deal he wanted to say but being Paul was too professional to say it out loud.

Kirsty had no such qualms. '"Unfortunate incident",' she mimicked bitterly. 'That poor man's fighting for his *life* and she's worried about Walsingham's ancient fucking *standards* or whatever.' She abruptly covered her face. 'I was so happy on the bus this morning,' she said in a muffled voice. Kirsty had recently gone through a particularly unpleasant break-up; for a time it had looked as if she and Charlie might be made homeless. When he learned that Kirsty and her little boy were in need of accommodation, Paul had offered to let Kirsty rent his annexe until they found a more permanent home.

'I told Charlie we could buy our tree this afternoon when he comes out of nursery. I promised him he could help decorate it.' Kirsty took her hands away from her face. 'And all the time, poor Professor Lowell was lying all by himself, hurt and scared, and I feel like I should have been able to *stop* it happening!'

31

Paul whipped off his spectacles, often a sign that his emotions were running high. They were subtly stylish, new spectacles, Anna noticed. In fact his general appearance, previously stuck at 1990s geek, was also subtly more up to date. Kirsty seemed to have been doing a little strategic styling.

'You couldn't have known though, Kirsty.' Paul tentatively lifted a hand as if to touch her shoulder then let it drop. Conscious of being Kirsty's boss and now her landlord, he was careful never to do anything that might seem to be taking advantage, but his protective body language gave his feelings away; at least, it did to Anna.

'You absolutely couldn't have known,' Anna agreed. She walked across to the desk she shared with Nadine and opened the drawer designated for her personal use. As she'd hoped, Nadine had placed her iPad inside for safekeeping. She stowed it in her bag before she straightened up and looked at Kirsty. 'Professor Lowell wouldn't want you to feel guilty. He'd just be touched to know that you think so kindly of him.'

'Do you think so?' Kirsty said, swallowing.

Paul nodded. 'Anna's right, he'd be touched.'

'I always think he has *such* sad eyes.' Kirsty's eyes brimmed and she quickly fumbled for a tissue. 'Sorry, it's been a tough few days.'

Kirsty had had a tough few years, Anna thought. Not only had her husband, Jason, thrown Kirsty and her small son over for his ex, it had emerged that he'd been having a clandestine affair with a sixteen-year old who was now expecting his baby. The girl's father and big brothers were after

32

Jason's blood, and his ex, quite sensibly, had dumped him. Kirsty knew she'd had a lucky escape, but it still hurt. 'I just feel so stupid for ever imagining that he loved me and Charlie,' she'd told Anna the last time they'd talked over lunch. 'It's like he's dragged us into his squalid Jeremy Kyle world. It's humiliating.'

Allowing herself to be hugged by Kirsty one last time, Anna left the office, denying Nadine the satisfaction of ignoring her twice in a row. When she emerged on to the High Street she saw that there were now only two police cars parked outside. The urgent lights and sirens had all moved on to the next emergency.

Anna made her way back to the Cornmarket along streets hung with Christmassy stars, swooping angels' wings, and, more surprisingly, flying umbrellas. She found herself wishing she could take her own advice. It wasn't Kirsty's fault Professor Lowell had been attacked, why should Anna think it was hers. 'Believe it or not, Anna, everything is not always all about you!' her mother used to say, exasperated. But this horrifying attack in her workplace had stirred up all her old shame and guilt. *She* had let it in. The violence had followed her. It kept on following her.

On the bus back to Park Town, she tried to soothe herself by imagining the small pleasures she'd been anticipating before her morning took such a violent turn; taking her grandfather to midnight Mass on Christmas Eve, cooking him Christmas dinner with all the trimmings, helped by Tansy and Isadora who would both be with her for Christmas Day. It was sickening what had happened to Professor Lowell, but she had to try not to let it devastate her.

When Anna let herself into her flat she was surprised to see Bonnie waiting for her by the front door. She bent to stroke her. 'What are you doing up here all by yourself, you funny girl? You can't have missed me that much already!' There was something in her dog's physical presence that always made Anna feel calmer, safer, more real. She wondered whether all dog owners discovered this magical side benefit to dog ownership, or if she just had an incredibly special dog?

She glanced in through the sitting room door. Aside from a lick of fresh paint, Anna had done little to change this room since her grandparents' day. She liked the calm Georgian space exactly the way it was, with its wooden shutters, faded kelim rugs and old sofas, and her grandfather's eclectic collection of paintings. Now, with Christmas baubles softly shimmering on the Norwegian spruce that she and Tansy had chosen for their tree, the room seemed to be almost holding its breath. There had been so much grief and sorrow in this house, but Anna didn't want to be that grieving woman any more.

Needing to banish the image of Professor Lowell's broken and bleeding face, she walked over to the Christmas tree and flicked a switch so the fairy lights sprang to life. Fairy lights had been the one aspect of Christmas tree decoration on which she and Tansy had been in complete agreement. No intermittent flashing, no hideous LED colours, just simple, starry white. 'Let's have our coffee and muffins up here!' she called to Tansy.

Hearing Anna's voice, Tansy came hurrying up from the kitchen. 'Isadora's here,' she said in a low voice. 'Something really terrible has happened but she can't seem to tell me what.'

Anna followed Tansy downstairs. The kitchen still held the warm scents of spice and orange from Tansy's baking. The French doors stood slightly open. Isadora was outside, smoking a roll-up with the single-minded intensity that marks out the serious smoker.

'I never knew Isadora smoked,' Anna whispered to Tansy.

'She said she found the tobacco in a drawer,' Tansy hissed back. 'It's got to be rank by now.'

Isadora's eleven-month-old puppy, Hero, was on the other side of the door, her breath making tiny smudges on the cold glass, and looking equally appalled by her owner's behaviour. Anna had never been able to figure out what breed of dog Hero was. 'Half dog, half goblin?' Tansy had suggested with a grin, when Anna had finally asked, and explained that Hero was the result of an illicit liaison between a cocker spaniel and a Tibetan terrier. 'Hence the disturbing combo of cute floppy ears with manic Bettie Page fringe!'

'I've made coffee,' Tansy told Anna in a more normal tone. 'Do you want some?'

'Yes, thanks.' Anna was still watching Isadora. Her long, wiry black and silver hair had been pulled back from her face with a raggedy scarf. Her trousers looked as if they'd been fished out of the dirty laundry hamper. Over the trousers Isadora had thrown a shapeless black garment that seemed part coat, part horse-blanket. Anna had only once seen the colourful Isadora all in black and that was at a memorial service.

Bonnie joined Hero at the window, as if in silent solidarity. *Even the dogs know something is wrong*, Anna thought.

Isadora stubbed out her roll-up and came indoors. 'Anna, you're back,' she said in a depleted voice utterly unlike her usual actressy tones. 'I'm so ashamed to just descend on you like the Madwoman of Chaillot. I do actually feel as if I might be going mad, you know.' She tried to laugh but her eyes had a wild haunted look. 'I simply couldn't stay in my house with all these terrible thoughts going round inside my head.' She darted a glance at Anna. 'I tried to think of somewhere I would feel safe and it was here with you two.'

'You were absolutely right to come,' Anna said.

Isadora let herself be coaxed up to the sitting room, where she lowered herself stiffly into the nearest chair, looking dismayingly old and frail. Numbly accepting a mug of coffee she immediately set it down again. She slipped her hand into an inside pocket, as if checking that something was still there.

'Isadora, what's made you so upset?' Tansy reached out to squeeze their friend's hand.

'Oh, darling,' Isadora said. 'There's so much you don't know about me, so much I can never

36

tell anyone.' She had come out without make-up, another alarming first. The stark contrast between her haunted dark eyes and her pale unmade-up face made her seem almost a different person.

'I had a phone call from a friend,' she began. 'She was upset because one of her colleagues had just been rushed into hospital. Of course she couldn't know what a devastating impact her news would have on me. She has no idea that I know him. Nobody knows. Nobody was ever supposed to know.'

Anna was beginning to wonder if Isadora might be having some kind of breakdown. 'So this person who was rushed to hospital was a good friend of yours?' she asked, hoping to get Isadora back on to firmer ground.

Isadora shook her head. 'He was far more than a friend. Oh, we weren't ever lovers,' she added quickly, 'though we loved each other deeply. You see James and I came to know each other in what I can only describe as extremely heightened circumstances.'

'You don't mean like – a war?' Tansy said, struggling to make sense of this.

'It was a war in a way,' Isadora said. 'Or that's what we believed – for a time. We were so idealistic, you see.' She began fiddling nervously with her earlobe as if she'd expected to find one of her pendulous earrings hanging there. She gave an apologetic laugh. 'I know everyone thinks their generation is unique, but those of us who lived through the sixties have more reasons than most to believe it.'

Isadora's hand surreptitiously slipped back

inside her pocket. 'James is woven into every one of my most precious memories of that time. To lose him would be like . . .' She took a deep breath, and seemed to regain control of her emotions. 'My friend had confided that James might die. When I put down the phone, I knew I had to go to the hospital to be with him. What was some stupid secret compared to the death of someone so – *essential* to my life? Suddenly I didn't care about anything except getting to James's bedside before it was too late. He'd never married; never lived with anyone. I wanted him to know he wasn't alone; that I still thought about him – *cared* about him.'

Isadora touched her throat. 'Excuse me.' She took a couple of sips of her coffee. 'That's better,' she said slightly hoarsely. 'And then the postman came and after that I couldn't think. I just grabbed my car keys and . . .' She looked horrified. 'I don't know what I was thinking driving in that state, with Hero in the car.' Hearing her name, the little dog came to sit by Isadora's feet, looking up anxiously through her fringe. Isadora didn't seem to see. She was breathing hard as if she'd been running.

Anna and Tansy exchanged glances. They'd never seen their friend like this.

'What happened?' Anna asked her.

Isadora withdrew her hand from her pocket and held out a crumpled sheet of paper. 'Someone's sent me an anonymous letter.'

Three

Isadora's words produced a stunned silence in which her harsh breathing was the only sound.

At last Tansy said, 'You don't mean like a poison pen letter?'

Isadora's hand crept up to the scarf she'd used to bundle back her unusually unkempt hair. She untied then rather fiercely retied it. She avoided looking at either Anna or Tansy.

Catching Anna's eye, Tansy mimed pouring out a drink.

Anna nodded and Tansy went to pour out a large tumbler of brandy, then wordlessly exchanged the tumbler for Isadora's letter.

Isadora took a deep gulp of her drink. 'Read it aloud please, Tansy.' Though she was still avoiding their eyes, her tone had all the authority of the professor who'd terrified generations of Oxford undergraduates.

Having unfolded and smoothed it out, Tansy's eyes were already swiftly travelling down the letter. 'Is this some kind of sick *joke*?'

Isadora shook her head. 'I'm afraid not.'

Tansy started reading in a scornful tone that conveyed exactly what she thought of Isadora's correspondent:

Everything is Known. Nothing is Hidden from my Eyes.

Death is but a Door, and Time is but a Window.

You chose Traitors for Friends. Your Friends you left to Die.

Now the Day of your Calamity is at hand when your Nakedness shall be Uncovered and your Shame shall be Seen.

This is the Law: An Eye for an Eye, a Tooth for a Tooth, a Hand for a Hand, a Foot for a Foot, a Burn for a Burn, a Wound for a Wound, a Bruise for a Bruise.

A LIFE FOR A LIFE

And I shall Bathe my Feet in the Blood of the Wicked!

Tansy turned the letter round so Anna could see the handwriting. 'Note the bonkers red capitals.' She made a twirling gesture with her finger, Tansy shorthand for loony tunes.

Anna took the letter and understood why Tansy had raised her voice with the words *A life for a life*. They were the only words written entirely in red.

Anonymous letter writers often claim privileged information, but this writer seemed to be claiming intimate knowledge of Isadora's soul. The letter, with its hellfire capitals, read as if it issued directly from the hand of God, an extremely pissed off, unforgiving god at that, if with superb penmanship. Anna had no idea what to think about the content. She had lived among the mad and she'd read her share of bizarre ramblings; she'd even written some. But she'd never read anything quite like this.

40

'Seriously, it's bollocks,' Tansy told Isadora. 'It's like a bad episode of *Miss Marple*. 'You can't possibly take this seriously.'

'You don't understand!' Isadora jumped up, making Hero scoot backwards in fright. She began to pace, setting the Christmas tree baubles tinkling. Anna heard her mutter, 'It's been fifty years. Surely I'm allowed to tell it now?'

She swung to face Tansy and Anna. 'He said we could never tell!' she said in a despairing tone. 'We must never speak or write to one another. We must forget we'd ever met!' Isadora seemed to be in the grip of some internal conflict.

Anna said, 'You don't have to tell us *anything*, Isadora. Not if you're not ready.'

'It's not like Anna and I are ever going to judge you,' Tansy said gently.

As if released from a spell, Isadora let out a little gasp, making proper eye contact for the first time. 'You – you dear girls,' she stammered. She returned to her chair, gathering Hero into her arms and bent her head over her little dog, murmuring into her fur. 'Did I frighten you, sweetie? I'm so sorry.' Her storm of emotion had given way to an exhausted calm.

Anna took the opportunity to help herself to a muffin. It felt like a long time since breakfast, but she hadn't liked to eat when Isadora was so upset. *Fifty years*, she thought. Isadora had said she'd kept her secret for fifty years! How had Isadora Salzman, the Queen of Indiscretion, who talked about her sexual adventures at the drop of a hat, managed to keep a secret – *any* secret – for fifty years?

41

Her mind flashed back to the evening she'd spent with Isadora in the Eagle and Child. Isadora had lured Anna there with a promise of an old-fashioned open fire but really she'd just wanted to get hammered. As the vodka glasses had stacked up, Isadora had held the other customers spellbound with her stories. She'd shown no sign of ill effects from alcohol, unless one counted sparkling eloquence as an ill effect, until they'd emerged into the cold night air, when she'd crumpled, weeping, into Anna's arms. Anna hadn't been in the best of shape either that night. Even so she'd felt the tidal pull of an immense, unspoken grief.

Isadora was looking around Anna's sitting room, properly taking in her surroundings for the first time. 'Your tree worked out beautifully, despite your differences.' She took a breath. 'I am going to tell you both,' she said abruptly. 'I want to. I don't really know if I'll ever be ready. I think it's more that the secret is ready to come out. Like a rotten tooth,' she added with one of her dark hoots of laughter. Knocking back the rest of her brandy, she held out her glass for a refill.

Tansy shot a covert grin at Anna and Anna suspected they were sharing the same thought. Though she was not yet her old high-octane self, Isadora was on the mend.

Sipping at her brandy, she began to tell her story in an ironic, oddly formal tone which Anna later realized must have been the only way Isadora felt able to break her long silence.

'Once upon a time there was a young girl. Don't

42

make the mistake of thinking she was just any girl. She was, her parents never tired of saying, their 'little miracle'. By the time her mama and papa had made their way to this country, they considered themselves too old for starting a new family. They had both lost their first loves in the death camps. There had also been lost children but their names were too precious to be spoken aloud, and so they existed only in the grieving silences between her parents' words. These nameless brothers and sisters had not been miracles. They were just ordinary children, but what had happened to everyone in the camps was so extraordinary that all the sweet daily ordinariness of human existence had been driven from her parents' world for ever . . .

'It wasn't an easy role, being Mama and Papa's miracle child. Everything she did that merely ordinary children do – walking, talking, learning to read and write – was greeted by them with a frenzy of delight that sometimes made it difficult for her to breathe. Still she loved her mama and papa and she perfectly understood what they needed from her. Miracles! The more the better!

'Taken separately these miracles were fairly small: making her parents laugh, rubbing away Mama's headaches, learning to master simple tunes on her Papa's violin. But the joy these tiny triumphs inspired in her parents was immense. So the girl made a silent promise that she would excel at absolutely everything she attempted. In this way, she would save her parents – and herself – from the silent reproaches of those other nameless children.

43

'Imagine Mama and Papa's excitement when the girl was offered a scholarship to read English at Oxford just a few days after she'd turned seventeen! Now imagine how strange this seventeen-year-old daughter of impoverished émigré eccentrics must have appeared to her fellow undergraduates in her shabby unfashionable clothes. For the first time in her life our miracle girl felt she was failing. Not at her studies. Studying had never been a problem. It was Oxford's social whirl which made her feel so hopelessly out of her depth. She knew about books, ideas and music. Until now, books, ideas and music had comprised her whole life! But she didn't have the least idea how to behave at parties, or which of the many strangely shaped forks to use at dinner. And she daren't so much as glance at the god-like dons at High Table, quoting Latin and Ancient Greek to each other across a glittering forest of silver candelabras.

'Then, barely a couple of weeks into the first term, she – she met someone, and everything changed.'

Isadora stopped talking and looked into her glass. It was empty. 'I'm going to take a break,' she said abruptly and left the room. They heard her make her way downstairs.

'We should go with her,' Anna said. 'I could do with some air.' She went into the hall to retrieve her coat and scarf.

Tansy followed her out. 'This is really intense, isn't it?' she said in a low voice. 'I'm a bit scared of where Isadora's story might be going, to be honest.'

Wherever it's going it's not anywhere good, Anna thought.

They found Isadora in the kitchen feverishly making another roll-up.

'Mind if we keep you company?' Tansy asked.

The dogs followed them out into the little courtyard that led up to the garden proper. This time of year only evergreens were visible and the more stalwart herbs, sage and thyme. The few tiny splashes of colour came from the scarlet berries on a glossy little holly tree that had almost outgrown its terracotta pot. The high walls made the courtyard a sheltered spot, but Isadora still shivered in her horse-blanket coat as she puffed at her unsavoury roll-up.

'Here, have this before you turn completely blue.' Unwinding her scarf Anna gave it to Isadora.

Bonnie brought her favourite ball hopefully to Isadora's feet. 'Not just now, you darling dog,' she said. 'Too busy polluting my body. Addictions are so bizarre,' she said to Anna. 'I haven't wanted one of these for decades. Smoking disgusts me! Now suddenly—' she gestured with her malodorous roll-up.

'One more day of being a smoker won't kill you,' Anna said. She threw the ball up the steps for Bonnie who immediately went hurtling after it, watched with some puzzlement by Hero. Why exert yourself to bring back a ball only to have to go galloping after it again?

Isadora wrapped Anna's scarf more closely around her, continuing to smoke as she resumed telling her story. 'One day, I'd been into Blackwells

45

to pick up a book I'd ordered. When I came out a man fell into step with me and started talking as if we'd known each other for years.'

Anna noticed that Isadora had dropped her fiction that her narrative was about 'a girl'. Now there was no question that this was Isadora's story. She had been that miracle girl, forced to compete for her parents' love with all those unknown dead children.

Isadora exhaled a cloud of smoke. 'I still remember the first thing he said to me. He said, "I *am* right, you are Isadora Salzman, aren't you?" When I admitted, rather startled, that I was, he said, "I knew it had to be you. I was told you had the most beautiful Pre-Raphaelite hair".'

'*What* a pickup line,' Tansy said laughing. 'Did it work?'

'I'm embarrassed to say it did. I'd been longing for a man to say something like that my whole life. He asked if I had to rush off to a lecture or could he buy me a cup of coffee so we could talk more privately.'

'And what did he look like, this smooth-talking guy?' Tansy seemed to have forgotten her fears that this would end badly and was now caught up in a 1960s' True Romance.

'Darling, even after all these years, I find that an impossible question to answer. He wasn't particularly good looking, or not in a conventional way. There was just something mesmerizing about him. He was older than me by a good few years, which of course made him deliciously exciting.'

'So you went?' Tansy said.

46

'I went. Blast the stupid thing!' Isadora's roll-up had gone out. She relit it and sucked in a fresh lungful of smoke. 'So, yes, we went for coffee, sitting in an intimate little booth – he seemed very keen that there shouldn't be any eavesdroppers – and he explained the real reason he'd approached me. He said I was a person of considerable interest to the people he worked for. Apparently, as a fluent Russian speaker I'd been on their radar as soon as I'd arrived at Oxford.'

'Fuck!' Tansy's eyes went wide. 'Your mystery lover man was in Intelligence! Holy shit, Isadora!'

'When was this? 'Sixty-four, 'sixty-five?' Anna remembered that relations between East and West were particularly strained in the early sixties.

''Sixty-five,' Isadora said. 'Europe was still recovering from the horrors of the Second World War only to be threatened with all kinds of nightmarish new scenarios, thermo-nuclear war among them.' She stubbed out her roll-up. 'He said that I could – that I *should* – help him and his people to make the world a better, safer place. He said his department was concerned about the activities of certain radical groups both at Oxford colleges and in the town. He said I wouldn't be in any danger. I'd just go along to meetings, keep my eyes and ears open for anything that suggested undue involvement with the Soviets, and report back. And so, I – I agreed.' Isadora's eyes were tracking a tiny toy-like plane making its way across the sky.

Tansy sounded disapproving. 'You agreed to spy on people they suspected of being communist?'

47

Isadora was still watching the plane. 'Yes, Tansy, I agreed. After what my parents went through, the idea of another world war filled me with horror. In a way, I felt as if I was doing this for them, and for my dead brothers and sisters.' She gave her arms a brisk rub. 'As I said, I was very young.' She drew a sharp breath. 'I spent all the time I wasn't in college either at meetings or cycling to meetings, endless tedious meetings where young men – it was almost always men in those days, pompously set other young men straight on points of procedure, or criticized their "analysis of the situation" – God, how that phrase made my heart sink! When I think of the hours I spent sitting on a bottom-numbing chair, listening to some opinionated boy sharing his unique insights into dialectical materialism while my stomach rumbled with hunger. I hardly ever had time to eat in those days. Then every couple of weeks I'd meet up with my handler at a greasy spoon off the Cowley Road and report back and if I was lucky he'd buy me a plate of egg and chips!'

'But what were they planning to do with all this information?' Tansy had always slightly hero-worshipped Isadora, and seemed to be struggling to get her head around this reckless young woman who'd been willing to invade people's privacy for individuals and purposes unknown.

Isadora gave her a sad smile. 'I don't blame you for disapproving.'

'I don't mean to be all judgey,' Tansy said awkwardly. 'I suppose I just don't get why you'd do it.'

48

'Tansy, darling, I was seventeen! I'd been feeling so lost and out of place, a Jewish ugly duckling, and this man had not only singled me out as beautiful: at one stroke he'd given my life meaning! He'd practically ordered me to help him save the world. Sweetie, at that point I'd have followed him through *fire*!'

Isadora brushed a few dead leaves off the garden bench before she sat down. Hero immediately hopped up beside her. 'Up till this point, I'd naively imagined that I was the only person he'd approached in this way. Then one afternoon when we met for our usual catch-up off the Cowley Road, my handler told me that he had a different kind of assignment for me. He asked if I'd heard about the society ball that was being held at Blenheim Palace. I said yes, I'd heard some of the real socialites in my year talking about what they were going to wear.

'"Well, you'd better start thinking what *you're* going to wear, Miss Salzman," he said smiling, "because we've arranged for you to be sent an invitation!" He said a girl called Tatiana, who had some vague family connection to the current Russian ambassador, was going to be there, partnering the chinless young aristo whose twenty-first birthday this ball was to celebrate. Tallis said it was the kind of situation where important information might be exchanged and he was going to introduce me to some other undergraduates who would also be going.'

'You were going to be spying at a *ball*? That's outrageous!' Tansy was half laughing.

'Sounds bonkers, doesn't it?' Isadora said, 'He

49

made it clear that we were just being brought together for this one event. We were to pair up and attend the ball as if we were normal couples, but really we'd be there as his department's eyes and ears. He told me to go to the Randolph Hotel on a particular day and he'd introduce me to the other members of his group, and I'd be assigned my partner for the ball.' Isadora's voice became brisk as if she needed to get this part over with. 'And so I went and I met them. The partner assigned to me was James Lowell.'

Anna stared at her, finally understanding what she should have realized from the start. Isadora's friend James, the one who'd been taken to hospital, dangerously close to death, was James Lowell, the elderly academic Anna had seen being rushed through the college gardens on a gurney.

'James was my Prince Charming,' Isadora explained, fighting tears.

In the kitchen, Anna's phone started to ring. She was torn. She was desperate to hear the rest of Isadora's story, but there was the chance it might be someone from Bramley Lodge calling about her grandfather. Though she wanted to believe he was immortal, he was almost ninety and rationally she knew the call could come at any time.

'Just answer it, darling,' Isadora said, dabbing her eyes. 'To be honest, this is rather taking it out of me.'

Anna hurried into the house, snatching up the phone just before the answer phone kicked in. 'Anna Hopkins!'

'Hi, Anna. I'm really hoping you won't hang up on me.' The male voice was husky and uncertain. 'This is Tim, Tim Freemantle.'

Anna felt the blood leave her face. She heard him swallow. 'It's taken me so long to get hold of your number and you didn't respond to my emails. Perhaps you didn't read them? I honestly don't mean to be like your stalker but I need to talk to you. I've finally got a lead on Max.'

Four

Anna woke in darkness to find a perplexed White Shepherd peering down into her face. She was chilled through to her bones. For some reason her neck hurt – a lot, she realised, when she tried to move.

She put out a groping hand and discovered hard floorboards where her memory-foam mattress was supposed to be. For a moment she stayed where she was, feeling Bonnie's warm breath on her cheek, wondering what the hell they were both doing in her study. It took a further sixty seconds to register the busy whoosh of water through the pipes. *Shit!* It was morning!

Anna shot upright, rapidly prioritising her panics. Last night Tansy had told her she wanted to go for a run before work. She'd offered to take Bonnie. But Bonnie was here, shut inside Anna's study with Anna, where they'd been since – since whenever it was she'd decided she wasn't going to be able to switch off her bedside light and fall asleep as if this was just another night.

She scrambled to her feet. If Tansy had ever wondered why the fiercely minimalist Anna kept an enormous French armoire in her extremely small study, she'd been too polite to ask. Tansy and Isadora knew some of Anna's history, but Anna would be mortified if her flatmate knew that last night she had finally crashed into merciful black oblivion only after she'd stretched herself out beside her cupboard of horrors, her fist clenched around its key.

Anna crept to the study door. If she was quick, she could be inside her room before Tansy emerged wide awake and ready for her run. She softly opened the door. Bonnie immediately went rattling down the polished wooden steps to the kitchen, keen to use her dog flap.

The instant Anna was back behind her bedroom door, the nagging voice started up: *You go on and on about how you're going to be Miss Super-Sane from now on, and then you pull a stunt like that.*

In one of the more questionable therapy groups she'd attended over the years, they'd had to go on an inner journey to meet, and supposedly overcome, their inner critics. Other group members came face-to-face with critical parents and teachers, bitchy older siblings and other blighting authority figures. On her journey Anna had been confronted by an entire hockey team of narrow-eyed Anna clones who took it in turns to verbally rip her to shreds. But that was then.

'Back off!' she muttered, as she headed for her

shower. 'I *have* changed. I didn't open it.' Every nerve in her body had been screaming but she'd resisted. She'd just needed to know that her old safety valve was there if she needed it.

It was hearing Tim Freemantle's voice that had tipped her over the edge; the shock of hearing someone say Max Strauli's name after so many years. She'd immediately flashed back to the grubby interior of Max's biscuit-coloured Ford Fiesta, thick with the fug of skunk and cider mixed with the faint teenage odour of Max himself. She saw his grey-green eyes quickly flick away from hers as he said the last thing he ever said to her. 'I think you're a great girl Anna and I really like you . . . I'm just not, you know, in *love* with you. Is that cool?' Sexy, scruffy, devious Max, who'd dropped out of sight after her family's murders and had never been seen since.

Tim's phone call, on top of everything else that had happened that day, had been one trauma too many to process. *This doesn't have to be a drama*, Anna told herself. She'd survived without sleep plenty of times before. A scalding-hot shower and a couple of cups of strong coffee inside her and she'd be able to function.

Thanks to Tansy taking Bonnie out on her run, Anna had time to regroup. She showered, dried her hair and put on her work clothes before going down to the kitchen to make coffee.

Lately, and Anna found this weirdly difficult to admit, she almost looked forward to work days. She'd taken her admin job as a means to an end; a way to give her life structure while the real business of her life, as Anna had seen it then, went on behind the scenes. Though she hoped she'd never develop Nadine's unnatural passion for all things admin, Anna had been surprised to discover that she found genuine satisfaction in resolving a student's problems, or smoothing out misunderstandings between departments. She also liked looking up from a tricky phone call with the bursar, a famous bore, to see Kirsty miming an attack of narcolepsy. She liked that she and Kirsty had started going out for a sandwich and a gossip at lunchtime. Just little unimportant things, but together they added up to something that Anna had never imagined she could have: a *life*.

She'd had a life before obviously, but it had been largely make-believe. *She'd* been make-believe. She'd gone through the motions of going out to work, or to visit her grandfather, but inside she was secretly longing for that moment when she could shut herself safely behind her front door and stop pretending. *I was in hiding*, she thought, *in my beautiful flat with my granny's beautiful china*. She glanced across at her dresser shelves empty except for one exquisite china cup. The rest of her grandmother's precious Limoges tea set had been smashed to pieces as Bonnie tried to defend Anna from their would-be killers.

When Anna had eventually returned with her friends to clear up the mess, she'd immediately started to sweep up all the broken crockery. Tansy had made her stop. While Anna and Isadora had scrubbed away at Bonnie's bloodstains, Tansy had sifted through the fragments, until she'd located five eggshell-thin pieces that originated from the same cup. Taking them home she'd painstakingly glued them back together. The salvaged cup, with its visible hairline fractures, gave Anna a bittersweet feeling each time she saw it. Anna wasn't a fan of motivational sentiments but that one about 'becoming strong at the broken places' had struck a chord. She had become stronger these past months. She didn't need everything in her life to be beautiful and flawless before she could feel OK. And one bad night didn't mean she was going bat-shit crazy.

Impressed to be having these kinds of positive thoughts on ninety minutes sleep, Anna took down the jar filled with Tansy's home-made granola, poured some into a bowl and added a dollop of yoghurt. Despite no longer being a strict vegan, Tansy was still big on what she called 'clean eating', making home-made soups and stews, and insisting they buy their bread from her friend Leo's bakery in the covered market. Anna was still sitting at the kitchen table, crunching granola and contemplating a second cup of coffee, when Tansy came back with a happy, panting Bonnie.

Bonnie went straight to Anna and pressed against her knees, giving her the foolish doggie grin that Anna now unquestioningly accepted as a genuine heartfelt smile. 'Did you have a good time?' Anna asked her. 'Did Tansy meet Mr Darcy?' Meeting Mr Darcy on Port Meadow had been their recurring joke since the week they'd both been off sick with flu and Anna had made Tansy watch all her favourite screen adaptations of Jane Austen.

'No fictional heroes in sexy wet shirts today, sadly!' Tansy took a loaf of sourdough bread out of the bread bin, and slotted two slices into the toaster. 'I saw Blossom and her man. I think Blossom's man is actually quite lonely.'

'How can you tell?'

'Not sure. It's just a vibe.' In the middle of pouring herself a glass of pink grapefruit juice, Tansy gave an anxious glance at the clock. 'Better get a move on. I'm supposed to be helping to organize a private view. Did I tell you, I'm going to look at a studio flat later?'

'Promise you won't take it if it's grim,' Anna said, really meaning it. 'I'm not *that* desperate to get rid of you.'

'I know that,' Tansy said cheerfully, 'but I also don't want to outstay my welcome.' She snatched her bread slices out of the toaster as they started to scorch. 'So how about Isadora's big reveal yesterday?' she added in a Tansy-type segue. 'My Secret Life as a Chain-smoking Spy?'

'She never did the big reveal though,' Anna pointed out. 'She never told us what happened at the ball.'

Emotionally shattered after her phone call, Anna had gone to rejoin her friends only to find Isadora zipping her tobacco tin into her bag, getting ready to leave. 'I need to go home and rest now,' she'd told Anna. 'I need to be by myself. I can face it now, thanks to you and Tansy.' She'd enveloped them both in a hug and

Anna had smelled her musky perfume overlaid with the raw sweetish scent of rolling tobacco.

'You didn't finish your story?' Tansy had protested. Isadora had given her a weary smile. 'It will keep for another time, darling girl.'

'You've got to admit it's weird though.' Tansy had a quick swallow of her juice. 'The three of us meet for the first time at a murder scene and each one of us turns out to have secrets!' She slid an involuntary glance at her unstamped Christmas card still lying on the counter. 'I mean, what are the chances?'

'Probably quite high.' Anna absently rubbed the bruise on her palm left by the antique key she had clutched all through the night. 'Probably everybody has secrets, if we only knew.'

'Not Liam,' Tansy said with a sunny smile. 'What you see is what you get with Liam. That's one of the things I like about him.' She waggled her eyebrows at Anna. 'I've just got to persuade him to dive into a lake in his shirt and he'll be bloody perfect!'

On her stop-start bus journey into work, Anna found herself going over her phone call from Tim. She'd cut herself off from his family so completely that it had felt dangerous even to think about them. Now for the first time she found herself feeling almost nostalgic. She couldn't remember how her parents and Tim's had first become friends; in her memories they seemed always to have been there. The two families were in and out of each other's homes so often that she'd come to consider Chris and Jane as her second set of parents; a far superior set, she'd thought at the time. More extrovert in temperament than Anna's parents, Tim's mother and father had a way of infusing everyone around them with their infectious *joie de vivre*. The happiest holidays, the liveliest parties and excursions were the ones they'd shared with Tim's family. Her more reserved parents had blossomed in the Freemantles' company and Anna had had Tim for her partner in crime. Nine months younger than Anna, he'd been closer to her in age than Dan and Will, her brothers. But it wasn't only proximity that had made her regard Tim as her friend. He was a kind, good-humoured boy who had once devoted almost all of one half-term holiday to teaching Anna all his best moves so she'd be able to shine at her first school dance. They'd been pretty cool moves too, she thought, for an eleven-year-old.

As she stepped off the bus, Anna had a sudden vivid memory of the silky fabric of the dress she'd worn for the dance. She had felt so wonderful in that dress! Tim had phoned her the next morning to check how it had gone. 'I knew you'd be fine,' he'd told her. 'I mean, once you've learned from the best . . .!'

Until his phone call Anna hadn't spoken to Tim since that summer, sixteen years ago; the summer her life fell apart. She'd seen him at the funeral beside his parents, white-faced, in an unfamiliar suit. Tim's mother had cried and tried to embrace Anna, but she'd brusquely extracted herself and walked away, unable to forget that she'd once childishly preferred Chris and Jane to her own mother and father; a preference she doubted she'd tried to hide. The only parents she'd wanted just then were her own, and since she couldn't have them she would just have to get on with the business of being a bona fide orphan.

Anna made her way down the High towards Walsingham College, still lost in her thoughts. Inside the porter's lodge, Mr Boswell was explaining something to do with the log book to a young trainee porter who had just recently started working at the college. The older man briefly broke off to greet Anna, telling her she had post. She collected her bundle of mail, then passed through the medieval archway into the walled gardens. In the distance, two gardeners were patiently working their way along the rose beds. The drab colours of their clothes made them appear timeless, almost part of the gardens, as if these same two elderly men had always been here, patiently tending Walsingham's roses.

As she was thinking this, a familiar figure emerged from a doorway. 'Hello, Anna. How are you?' Inspector Chaudhari greeted her. 'Apart from finding yourself in unfortunate proximity to another violent crime, obviously.' He gave Anna a wry smile, as if trying to soften any implied criticism.

'Apart from that, I'm very well, thank you,' she told him. She could never really get a satisfactory fix on how old Inspector Chaudhari was. Apart from a slightly pouchy look around the eyes, he gave the impression of a man confidently in his prime.

'Policemen are supposed to be inured to this sort of thing,' he said, shaking his head, 'but I find it hard to think what that poor old man could have done to provoke such a savage attack.'

'I think everyone here feels like that,' she said.

The inspector passed his hand over his glossy black hair and Anna felt her heart sink, sensing that he was getting ready to broach something uncomfortable. She was fairly sure she knew what this might be. 'I imagine you've been wondering if a date has been set for the trial?' he said, then before she could answer, he said apologetically, 'It'll be a good few months yet, I'm afraid. But my sergeant tells me you've got some good friends supporting you?'

She nodded. 'I have. I'm very lucky.'

'Well, if you should need anyone extra for backup, my wife asked me to tell you that she cooks a mean—' Anna was almost sure he was going to say 'curry', when the inspector flashed her a sly grin and said, 'Sunday roast. Alisha's lasagne is also extremely popular in our house!' he added.

'That's really kind of you both.' Anna could tell he was trying to make up for their rocky start after she'd found Naomi's body.

'She means it, you know.' Inspector Chaudhari's expression took on a sudden solemn intensity, as if he thought Anna doubted his wife's intentions. 'You would be made very welcome.'

She felt herself turning pink. 'Thank you,' she managed awkwardly.

They turned as Liam Goodhart came hurrying up from the porter's lodge, talking into his phone, and Anna had a surreal sense of her two worlds colliding. A couple of days ago she'd run into

Tansy's boyfriend in his boxers on her landing and here he was being an official policeman. Liam gave her a neutral wave as if he had just remembered the same encounter and Anna gave a neutral wave back, before continuing on her way to the admin block.

A few minutes later she was at her desk trying to figure out a tactful way to remind certain college tutors to check the central departmental database and upload their end-of-term marking, if they hadn't already done so. (In fact, none of the tutors she was writing to had done so.) It seemed like a simple task but Anna was finding out that very little in academic life was ever simple.

Everybody hated checking these databases (except possibly Nadine), and nobody liked uploading on to them. Some of the more antiquated professors were downright phobic about it. Then there were the inevitable one or two who considered themselves far too important to faff about with these kinds of tasks. It was Anna's job to explain that this was not some Kafkaesque requirement devised specifically to upset academics' lives; it originated from the lofty heights of the Dean's committee. Everyone, without exception, was now expected to comply with the new Best Practice Guidelines as laid down by the UEIA (University Excellence in Action). '*If you have not yet complied,*' she typed, wondering if it would be too cheeky to emphasize 'not', '*may we remind you that with very few days to go till the end of the Michaelmas term this is now a matter of some urgency.*'

Partway through the morning, Anna was cheered to discover an email from Jake saying he'd switched a few meetings around and hoped to be heading to the UK sooner than he'd thought.

At lunchtime, she and Kirsty went to Georgina's in the covered market for coffee and a bagel. The popular upstairs cafe was a relaxed, sometimes downright noisy, venue where it could sometimes be hard to hear yourself speak. Periodically Anna had to put her head close to Kirsty's to hear her latest instalment of her life post-Jason. She had finally taken Anna and Paul's advice and gone to a solicitor to initiate divorce proceedings. 'I should have listened to you guys earlier,' Kirsty said. 'I feel so much better for getting everything started.' Anna offered to treat them both to dessert but Kirsty said she was on a mission to secure this season's all-important toy for Charlie.

'The trouble is, every other parent of a pre-school boy is going to be after the same toy,' she said, buttoning her winter coat. 'So this could get ugly. I'm thinking, concealed nail file up my coat sleeve, what do you reckon?'

Anna laughed. She couldn't picture herself ever being prepared to fight to the death to acquire some trashy piece of mass-produced plastic, but possibly Kirsty hadn't been able to picture it either, pre-Charlie. Love changed you in ways you could never have imagined.

She arrived back at the office to find Paul sitting by her desk, looking oddly blank. 'Paul? Is everything OK?' Her voice pulled him out of his reverie and he shook his head.

'I just heard that Professor Lowell has died. He never regained consciousness, poor old guy.'

Anna saw again the professor's blood-streaked face, parchment-white under the oxygen mask. 'Oh God, how awful!' She began hunting for her phone. She needed to tell Isadora.

Paul took off his glasses, passing a hand across his face. 'Now he'll never finish his book. That sounds like a stupid thing to say, but his writing meant everything to him. I think it had become his life.'

'The poor man,' Anna said as she punched in Isadora's number. 'Sorry, I need to tell somebody, someone who is – was – a close friend of his,' she explained.

'No problem. I'll leave you to it.' Paul got to his feet. 'Can I leave you to tell Kirsty as well?'

'Yes, of course,' Anna said, waiting for Isadora to pick up.

'*Anna?*' Isadora's voice was audibly shaking. 'Oh, Anna, I've been hoping you'd ring. I've had such a strange and terrible day.'

Anna's heart sank. 'You've already heard. I wasn't sure if you knew.'

'About James, you mean? Yes, my friend called and told me.'

'Would you like me to . . .?' Anna paused, then rephrased her question as a statement of intent. 'I thought I'd come over to see you after work.'

Isadora sounded ready to weep with gratitude. 'Oh, darling, *would* you? I'm rather floundering to be honest. I just don't know what to do or think.'

Anna arrived at Isadora's home in Summertown

63

just as Sabina, one of Isadora's new lodgers, wheeled her bike out through the gate, nibbling a piece of what looked like dry toast. Isadora's decision to take in lodgers was originally prompted by the need to pay for repairs to her rambling red-brick house. Anna suspected Isadora had secretly hoped for late-night suppers while they all engaged in the lively debates she remembered from her undergraduate days. Instead she'd found herself sharing her home with a shy mathematician from South Korea, and an equally reserved girl from Geneva who was studying International Business Management at Oxford Brookes.

Wrapped in a sky blue pashmina, her hair braided into a long strawberry-blonde plait, Sabina gave Anna a preoccupied half-smile before she rode off on her bike, still nibbling hamster-like at her toast.

Isadora opened the door accompanied by Hero. 'The kettle's on.' Isadora looked and sounded terrible. James Lowell's death had obviously hit her hard. Her little dog followed them through into the kitchen, where she positioned herself under the table, staring fixedly at Anna through her Betty Paige fringe.

Isadora hadn't made too many concessions to her lodgers, Anna thought, glancing around her friend's kitchen. Apart from the counters, which were always pristine, every available surface was heaped with books, papers, and other fascinating detritus, including, Anna noticed, a kit for building a birdhouse. 'Earl Grey?' Isadora asked in a lifeless tone.

'Lovely,' Anna said, noticing the vodka bottle

on the table and wondering how much of its contents were now inside Isadora. She had known Isadora for several months now. She'd seen her tenderly covering a dead woman's face with her own silk scarf, she'd seen her convulsed with laughter, and drunk and grieving, but Anna had never seen Isadora like this. All her life force, all her passion, had gone out of her, leaving behind a ghost of her former self.

Anna cleared some books off a chair so she could sit down. 'I brought food.' She'd made a point of stopping off at Marks and Spencer on the way back from work. 'But you probably don't feel much like eating?'

'Maybe later, darling.' Isadora managed a wan smile. She sloshed boiling water into the tea pot, spilling a fair amount on the floor. Definitely been knocking back the vodka, Anna decided. Seeing Isadora bearing down on her with the steaming tea pot, she quickly made space. She couldn't tell if Isadora actually wanted her there.

Isadora poured their tea and Anna waited, nursing her cup between her hands, inhaling calming bergamot fumes and wishing that Tansy were here. Tansy almost always knew the right thing to say. 'I'm really so sorry about Professor Lowell,' she tried awkwardly, but was silenced by Isadora's incredulous look.

'This isn't just about James! Did you think this was just about James?' Isadora jumped up and went out of the kitchen, coming back with a large padded envelope. 'First that terrible letter, and then, this morning, I found this in my postbox.' She gingerly slid out a pile of handwritten pages.

65

They were photocopies, marred with fuzzy lines and smudges. Isadora looked down at them in a kind of mute horror.

'What is it?' Anna said.

Isadora swallowed. 'It's an excerpt from Hetty's journal.'

Anna said, puzzled, 'Sorry, who's Hetty?'

Isadora collapsed back into her chair. 'Who was Hetty Vallier?' she said with one of her dark laughs. 'Darling, that's the kind of question which only someone who never knew Hetty would ask!' She began furiously stuffing the pages back into the envelope as if she couldn't bear to look at them for another second. 'Who could possibly have sent this to me? Who would do such a thing?'

Feeling out of her depth, Anna tried tentatively, 'Maybe Hetty wanted you to see it for some reason?'

Isadora went so white that Anna thought she might faint. She grabbed at Anna's hand across the table, and Anna felt her friend's terror go jolting through her own body. 'That's simply not possible. Hetty was murdered fifty years ago.'

Five

18 January, 1966

I'm sitting on a train in the middle of nowhere. We're stuck somewhere between Bath and Cheltenham and nobody seems to know why.

These are not the life-changing sentences with which I'd hoped to start my brand new diary but I'm trying to discourage the unwanted attentions of the man sitting opposite. I can only assume he's just been released from an extremely long prison sentence, since I'm not looking remotely feminine, being bundled up like an old babushka in just about every garment I own (not counting the three stolen ball dresses which are squashed at the bottom of my suitcase). I'm wearing my Persian carpet coat (that's what Felix calls it, in his delightfully belittling brotherly way!) also stolen from the attic at Daddy's, over the darling little dress that Maeve bought me at the start of the holidays, over two pairs of woollen tights. Under the dress, I am wearing two thermal vests. Over my coat, I am muffled in a long woollen scarf that my little stepsister Phoebe knitted me for Christmas. Despite this, and the fact that my fingers and possibly my nose are now turning dangerously indigo, the man is still giving me alarmingly lecherous looks. So I am now madly scribbling in my book doing my best to look like a budding novelist who has been seized with a sudden fit of inspiration and is absolutely not to be interrupted!

I am actually feeling a little bit like crying. I was exactly the same when I had to go back to school after the holidays. I think it's this frightening inbetweenness that I can't stand. In theory, you see, there's nothing to stop me getting off at the next station and hitching a lift back to Daddy and everyone at the Mill House. I could give up the entire project of studying for a degree. I could run away to London, rent a room in South Ken or somewhere, and find myself a job, something fun, like designing theatrical costumes.

The thing is, I'm not actually sure Daddy has even properly taken in that I'm up at Oxford. It's hilarious when you think about it. I'm about to start my second year, and Daddy still hasn't noticed that I've taken to disappearing for eight weeks at a time! (This would also explain why he never gets around to paying his share of my grant. Maeve has promised to talk to him for me. I can't bear to seem needy and whining. Daddy loathes people who are needy and whining. He says he has to block it out or he can't work, and painting for Daddy is like breathing to everyone else . . .)

My father does this wonderfully convincing impersonation of someone who is listening with passionate intensity to everything you say, when in fact he's several millions of miles away envisioning his current painting and hasn't heard a word. I seem to remember that he was in the middle of his big triptych at the time I got the letter, plus I think it was about then that he had started to get serious with Saskia, so it's perfectly understandable really if one of his daughters getting into Oxford didn't quite make it to the top of his list of concerns. Also unlike normal fathers, Daddy has very little time for formal education. He believes in art and foreign travel. I honestly think that if I told him I'd decided to drop out, he'd just say, 'Do whatever makes you wake up smiling, Hetty my darling.'

Did I ever wake up smiling? I'm not sure

68

anyone does that in real life, do they? Not after the age of three or four? Not even Daddy and, apart from the rare days when his painting is going badly, he's the happiest person I know. It's strange that someone as warm and lovable, adorable really, as Daddy can also seem so detached from the very people who love him. It really is one of life's riddles.

As I was writing that last sentence the conductor just went striding past our compartment with the kind of hunted expression that positively defies you to ask what's wrong! I noticed him blink slightly at the sight of me in my Persian carpet coat. Needless to say I hadn't planned to wear it in public in its current state. It still has dozens of moth holes which I eventually plan to embroider into exotic flowers and birds – but just now I need it to stop me freezing to death. My feet were already blocks of ice from waiting so long in the (unheated) station waiting room at Exeter. Now I can't seem to feel them at all.

I've lost my thread. Yes. Inbetweenness. Every time I have to leave the Mill House it feels as if I'm physically tearing myself free from some powerful magnetic field. It's an absolutely terrifying sensation, as if, deep down, I'm not sure I'm capable of surviving outside it.

But then, as I get closer and closer to Oxford, I can feel the equally strong magnetic pull of my new life, with my dear little room at Lady Margaret Hall, and my friends. So, though at this moment I am longing to just jump off the train and hitch home to Devon, I also know that as soon as I walk in through the porter's lodge at

LMH I'll feel that excited bubbly feeling of being back in Oxford, in the glorious glittering centre of things. (Not to mention the occasional illicit adventure to keep me on my toes!) But at this moment, stranded like a little stray iron filing between my two worlds, I feel lost, as if my life has absolutely no point.

Rereading those last lines, I have JUST remembered why I gave up keeping a diary!! It always makes me depressed! I end up writing things that even I don't understand (for instance, comparing myself to a lonely little iron filing!). So I shall stop writing about my boring feelings and write about my fabulous Christmas holidays with my father's chaotic and ever-increasing ménage.

I actually get on really well with all Daddy's ex-wives and girlfriends, though 'ex' is not a term that anyone has ever heard my father use. The thing about Daddy is, he never subtracts people, he just adds – and adds! He delights in big family get-togethers where he can gather together all the people he cares about under his roof, and this Christmas just about everybody was, apart from my mother – she's still in an ashram in India somewhere. My favourite ex-stepmother Maeve was there, with Felix and Bella, who I feel every bit as close to as my real sister, Carrie, even though Felix seems permanently grumpy these days. Lalla was there, with my two half-sisters, my two stepbrothers and her new husband, Raphael. Nina typically got hopelessly lost on the way, finally rattling up the drive in her Morris Traveller well after midnight, minus one of her headlights, her exhaust pipe trailing by a thread and a crate of *Veuve Cliquot* in the back (more of that crate later!).

Obviously Saskia was there, with the new baby, Effie, who is just a perfect little pearl of loveliness. Saskia never has much to say for herself, but wafts around in fetching assemblages of camisoles and Victorian petticoats, apparently oblivious to the freezing temperatures. One time Maeve said, exasperated, 'Saskia, please do put some proper clothes on over those amazing breasts of yours or I'm going to fling a blanket over you myself!'

The Mill House is always cold but it was exceptionally freezing this Christmas. Daddy said he'd forgotten to order logs, but Felix reckons he still owes for the last two loads and they've quite rightly refused to deliver any more until Daddy coughs up. Luckily, Felix and I found some dry logs in a forgotten wood-store and wheeled them back to the house in a squeaky old barrow. Clem and Felix also chopped up a wormy old blanket chest, so we were able to have a fire last thing on Christmas Eve and on Christmas Day itself but after that we just had to endure the steadily deepening cold.

On Boxing Day, seeing us all turning blue and morose in our coats and scarves, Daddy said, 'Oh, for fuck's sake, you lot! Where's your fucking spirit of enterprise?' Whereupon he shepherded us all into the ballroom, made Felix, Clem and Toby help him set up a net, and got us all playing indoor tennis! Everyone took turns playing, even the little ones, and we all ended up warm and glowing and laughing. Even Felix agreed it was

71

the best fun he'd had in ages, and Felix can be darkly resentful of Daddy sometimes. I just loved seeing Daddy at the centre of everything, like a tangle-haired but still wonderfully handsome Father Christmas, with everyone adoring him. He's in his fifties now and still has more energy than people half his age.

I've talked about the lack of heat. I should probably mention the food which was the usual mad mix of feast and famine. Lalla lives in France now with Raphael, and they had generously loaded up their car with stinky cheeses and pâté and bottles of wine for everyone. This was lovely of them but not terribly Christmassy. Someone had given Daddy a brace of pheasants which Maeve cooked beautifully with bacon and some of Lalla's wine but in the end there were so many people crowded around the table that no one got more than a couple of mouthfuls.

Luckily Lalla had made bread for everyone a day or two before. (Lalla is into artisan bread-making.) No one had fancied it previously (it is extremely worthy bread) but late that night when all the littlies were asleep and the older ones had staggered drunkenly off to bed, Felix confided that he was suffering such violent hunger pains that he might have to stab himself in the eye with one of Daddy's paintbrushes to distract himself. So Carrie and I went to investigate Lalla's bread but to our dismay it had become absolutely rock-like. We agreed that it might just be tolerable if it was toasted, but toast was obviously impossible without a fire. Then Phoebe said, 'The lumber room! We could chop up those old chairs!' So

Felix and Clem sneaked up to the lumber room and brought down three broken kitchen chairs that have been up there waiting to be mended forever, and smashed them into pieces and got a beautiful blaze going in the fireplace.

Carrie and I managed to saw off slabs of Lalla's rocklike bread and we all took turns to toast them over the flames. There wasn't any butter to be had, sadly, but clever Phoebe found a jar of home-made quince jelly. It had become so solid with age we virtually had to chip it from the jar but it tasted delicious! We sat around the fire (the parts of us nearest the fire scorching, every other part chilled to the bone), eating lumps of toasted bread spread with quince jelly, and then Felix suddenly remembered the case of Veuve Cliquot which everyone else had apparently forgotten and all us Vallier offspring got rip-roaring drunk, because while there is never enough food in our father's house you can almost always find plenty to drink!

I'm thinking of Daddy's Christmas present to me now, snuggled in between the stolen ball dresses. It's the most extravagant and wonderful thing he's ever given me. We all got madly extravagant presents this year, but I love mine the most – a tiny but genuine Picasso sketch of a horse. When Felix saw it, he went into one of his dark moods. Later he said, 'You're not seriously going to keep it? Hetty, just sell it, for fuck's sake! You're completely broke. All of us are completely broke!' I couldn't explain that I would never dream of selling one of Daddy's presents, even if I had to live off raw potato peelings to survive

73

which fortunately, being in halls, I don't. Whether they are wildly extravagant like the Picasso, or silly and funny like that Ze'ev caricature of the snail, I treasure every one of my father's gifts to me like stardust . . .

Hurray, the train is moving again and the lecherously staring man has gone off to the bar . . .

20 minutes later

Our train has just managed to crawl into Cheltenham station. Now we are sitting helplessly in our icy cold carriages waiting to find out what will happen next. An engineer has been sent for, but apparently we could be stuck here for hours. Several of the more prosperous passengers have chummed up with each other to share taxis to wherever they're going. I shall simply have to wait until either the engine problem is resolved or another train comes along.

I thought I might as well occupy myself by describing an unusual event that happened last term. Earlier I mentioned 'illicit adventures'. I'm not supposed to tell anyone about these things, but I feel one should be allowed the odd indiscreet entry in one's private diary. (This isn't Stalinist Russia after all.) About three weeks before the end of the Michaelmas term, I got a typically enigmatic summons from Tallis to go to the Randolph for what he described as an 'unrepeatable opportunity' to meet 'kindred spirits'.

Tallis has a way of making quite innocent things seem thrillingly cloak-and-dagger, but I did think this sounded positively shady! However, since this meeting was taking place at the rather stuffy and grand Randolph, I decided to take it on trust that he wasn't trying to lure me into some kind of secret sex club and set out with a distinct frisson of excitement!

I was hoping to write about my evening in full but my hands are so cold that I'd need to write with my woolly gloves on and it's almost impossible to write with thick woolly fingers, the horrible woolliness sets my teeth on edge. So I will just say that I liked almost all of my fellow guests at the Randolph, particularly the beautiful James, but the person who intrigued me most of all was a painfully shy girl called Isadora. The rest of my news I shall have to save until I get back to my cosy little room at LMH.

Six

'. . . It is my privilege to have been asked to conduct this ceremony composed of words and music which reflects the life of James Lowell, particularly the music he loved. While this is an immeasurably sad day, let our ceremony today not only be an opportunity to say goodbye to James and to grieve for him but also to remember and celebrate his life and all that he did.'

The heating in the chapel seemed not to be working. Anna was grateful she'd thought to put on an extra layer under her not very substantial

75

black dress. She and Isadora had found vacant seats at the end of a row. Appalled at the notion of a humanist funeral ('But James was a practicing Roman *Catholic*! Why did he want some soulless service in a crematorium!'), Isadora had warned that she wanted the option of simply walking out if things got too dreary. Anna had mentally translated this as, *If I get too upset.*

On Tansy's instructions, Anna had arrived at Isadora's house three-quarters of an hour earlier than arranged, to vet their friend's outfit for stains, dog hairs and general suitability. Since James's attack Anna and Tansy had been alarmed to see their friend's appearance slide past 'eccentric' and edge perilously close to 'bag lady'. But when Isadora opened the door she was dressed with the kind of head-to-toe glamour that could have taken her to the funeral of a minor royal. 'Wow, Isadora! You look like you've stepped off the cover of *Vogue*!' For the first time in weeks it seemed, Isadora had given her a ghost of a smile. 'I thought I should make an effort, if only to counteract this hideously brutal venue.'

Knowing that James had no close relatives, Anna had imagined that attendance at his funeral might be sparse, but the chapel was almost full of soberly dressed academics. The only person there under sixty, not counting Anna, was the celebrant, a tall fair-haired woman in her middle years. Isadora had already shot several withering looks in her direction. Anna suspected she was longing for the celebrant to say something sick-makingly trite or worse, split an infinitive, so she could despise her along with this shabby excuse for a funeral.

'I appreciate that some of you may be more accustomed to a different form of service,' the celebrant said with a smile, as if she'd divined and sympathized with Isadora's distaste, 'so there will be a reflective time later which you may choose to use for private prayer.' She paused, looking around the assembled mourners, including them all in her steady gaze. 'When someone dies so violently, and, to all intents, pointlessly, it's not surprising if we struggle to deal with the shock. We can rage at the waste, the unfairness, the loss of all his friends' and colleagues' hopes for him, but from what I have learned about James Lowell, the last thing he would have wanted is that we spend our time together today feeling sad or angry . . .'

Isadora unfastened then refastened both of the buckles on her bag, then began twisting her antique silver rings around her fingers. On the way over she'd talked nonstop about anything and everything except the funeral they were on their way to attend. Her son, Gabriel, and his wife, Nicky, were off to Australia to spend Christmas with Nicky's family. Isadora didn't know if she should take their gifts round before they left. 'I still make up Christmas stockings for them, just silly little gifts. I used to love doing stockings for Gabriel. I simply couldn't bear to give it up. For years I've been telling myself I should stop. I know it just makes him even more embarrassed by his ridiculous mother. But then last year Nicky announced that she'd finally

77

embraced the whole stocking concept, and then she emailed me – *emailed* can you believe! – their fucking *wish list*! I'm talking cashmere bed socks, Jo Malone candles!'

Needing all her attention for negotiating Oxford's ring road, Anna had confined her responses to sympathetic noises, knowing that Isadora needed to keep talking so as not to raise the one topic that was uppermost in both their minds: would any of the surviving members of the group, which Anna had privately christened the Oxford Six, turn up to the funeral? Isadora had admitted to Anna and Tansy that since the advent of the Internet she'd several times googled her friends' names hoping to discover what had become of them. She'd learned that Piers Courtenay had died, far too young, of a heart attack. Robert Keane was still very much alive; he had gone on to marry money, not to mention earned huge amounts on his own doing something in the City. Catherine Hetherington, however, had apparently disappeared without trace. Isadora had been unable to find her in any UK records. 'What about your handler bloke?' Tansy had asked her curiously, 'Didn't you ever think to look him up on the internet?'

'Given his line of business and the fact that he undoubtedly used a false name in all his dealings with us, I think I'd have more luck looking for the Scarlet Pimpernel. Besides, he's probably in the ground by now,' Isadora had added with one of her dark laughs. 'He must have been ten years older than me at least, *and* he smoked like a blast furnace.'

Anna sneaked a surreptitious glance around the chapel. There were a number of unfamiliar faces but none of them looked as if they might qualify to be the Scarlet Pimpernel, she thought, and had to fight a nervous desire to giggle.

The celebrant had finished her introduction. 'Elspeth Gildersleeve from Walsingham's music society, of which James Lowell was an active member, will now play "The Lark Ascending" by Vaughan Williams,' she told them. An elderly woman rose from her seat. Anna heard the soles of her shoes squeak faintly as she went to stand by the coffin. She lifted her violin from its case, checked the tuning, adjusted a couple of pegs, then she closed her eyes and began to play.

While Anna listened, another part of her drifted back to the puzzle of Hetty Vallier's diary. Isadora had sent Anna away with the photocopies, saying brusquely, 'You girls can read them, if you like. I simply can't bear to have them in my house.'

That evening when Tansy arrived back home, Anna had told her about the diary excerpts, saying she wasn't sure if they should read something so personal. Tansy had looked at her as if she was nuts. 'How can you not want to read diary entries by Isadora's mysteriously murdered best friend?'

'You're right,' Anna had admitted sheepishly. 'I do want to. I only feel like I shouldn't!'

She and Tansy had curled up in opposite corners of the largest sofa swapping photocopied pages between them as they struggled to decipher Hetty Vallier's somewhat eccentric handwriting. As she read, Anna could almost hear Hetty striving to maintain her larky upbeat tone as she described her Christmas in her father's haphazard and over-crowded household.

'I wish whoever it was had sent Isadora the whole diary,' Tansy had commented, frustrated, when they'd finished. 'Hetty sounds like a real character. I loved the stolen ball dresses! Her father was a prize shit, though, and I'm the world expert on shitty fathers!' She'd briefly returned to Hetty's last entry. 'Can you honestly imagine a "painfully shy" Isadora?'

Once upon a time, Anna would have agreed. The Isadora they'd met three months ago had seemed like a confident woman of the world. But these past weeks had taken a heavy toll, bringing that insecure younger self dangerously close to the surface.

The violin soared and soared. Anna saw Isadora dab at her eyes. It seemed she wasn't finding this funeral so soulless after all. Anna caught herself imagining how she'd describe the event to Jake, and how she kept sneaking hopeful looks around the chapel in case a member of the Six burst in to make a Hollywood-style last-minute arrival.

Anna suspected that Jake would tell her she was using Isadora's troubles as a distraction from the Max issue. Having arrived safely in the UK, he had managed to fit in a flying visit to Oxford. It had been lovely to spend time with him, but Jake was not a man to tiptoe around a tricky subject. 'You should absolutely meet up with him,' he'd said firmly, when she'd told him about her call from Tim. 'You've said yourself he's a decent guy.' Anna knew this to be true. These days, Tim worked as an investigative journalist.

He could have sold her family's stories to the tabloids any time he wanted, but he hadn't.

Anna heard the squeak of the violinist's shoes as she returned to her seat. The Principal of Walsingham College, a tall, thin, balding man who always reminded her of a heron, delivered a short eulogy, regretting both the shocking manner of Professor Lowell's death and the loss of one of the finest minds he'd had the privilege to know, but insisted that his books would be his legacy to future generations. After the Principal, a procession of colleagues and acquaintances came up to relate their memories. After enduring four or five of these, Isadora hissed, 'Who *is* this dull old fart they're all talking about? James wasn't some tame old academic. He *burned*, Anna, he burned with love and hope.' Anna could feel Isadora being torn between her long-ago promise to keep silent and an almost overwhelming need to leap up and declare her connection with this dead man.

The celebrant had returned to the front, holding a faded orange paperback. Anna could see a strip of bright pink paper marking her place. 'I'm going to read a poem by Robert Frost, which had powerful associations for James Lowell.'

In one of those super-lucid, out-of-body moments that she associated with extreme panic, Anna knew even before she heard the title that it would be same the poem Tim's mother had attempted to read at Anna's family's funeral. Jane Freemantle had collapsed sobbing before she reached the end. Tim's father had helped her back to her seat, then taken his wife's place at the

81

lectern to read the remaining lines in a trembling voice.

Doped up on tranquillisers, Anna would have sworn she hadn't taken in a word that was spoken, either inside that church or later by her family's gravesides. Yet, maybe five years afterwards, she'd gone to a screening of the *Outsiders* in whatever city she was living in at the time, and had had to flee from the cinema when Ponyboy began to read the same poem.

Now Anna felt each word pierce her heart until she felt as if she couldn't breathe. Somehow she forced herself to stay in her seat until the last line had been spoken, then she whispered to Isadora that she was going out for a minute.

The chapel gardens still glittered from an overnight frost, as if some invisible confectioner had sifted icing sugar over them. Anna walked along the paths, blindly at first, then, as her heart rate slowed, she began to register the memorial plaques and floral tributes. She could still hear Robert Frost's words. *Nothing gold can stay.* She pictured her little sister, Lottie, her brothers, Will and Dan; so full of noise and mischief. She hadn't considered them as golden or even particularly precious. They were just her family. She'd assumed they'd be around to annoy her for ever. At sixteen she'd had more important claims on her time; Max Strauli, for instance. The night they were murdered she'd stormed out to a friend's. She had known she was missing her little sister's birthday party, yet she hadn't felt a flicker of guilt.

Anna made herself stop and read the words on

the nearest plaque, as a way of bringing herself back to the solid physical present.

Beryl Harris
1922–2005
Beloved Mum and Gran. Never Forgotten.

Not *'Beloved Wife'*, Anna thought. She let herself imagine the life of this unknown woman, widowed, divorced or simply abandoned, valiantly bringing up her children alone.

Calmer now, she became aware of other people wandering through the gardens in ones and twos. They'd probably arrived early for the next funeral. The celebrant had explained the necessity to keep to a strict timetable and Anna had felt Isadora bristle at the implication that James's funeral service was just one on a continuous conveyer belt of death.

Anna noticed a young woman, her cheeks pink with cold, pushing an elderly man in a wheelchair towards her. She noticed wheelchair users now because of her grandfather, but she thought she would have noticed this striking white-haired old man regardless. Dressed all in black, with a matching fedora, he emanated world-weary elegance. An actor, Anna thought, or an old jazz musician. With his leather-gloved hands clasped together on his lap, he endured his rattling progress along the paths with a bland expression that gave nothing away. Yet, as they passed each other, he surprised her with an ironic tip of his hat.

Sufficiently composed to return to the chapel, Anna managed to slip discreetly into her seat.

83

Isadora whispered, 'You're just in time for the Bach. James *adored* this piece.'

The violinist was still playing as the coffin began slowly sliding out of sight. Anna heard Isadora say softly, '*Shalom*, darling boy,' then she covered her face with her hands.

People were buttoning up their coats, getting out of their seats, the start of a civilized exodus. Anna heard the Principal thanking the celebrant, inviting her back to Walsingham, 'So we can all raise a glass in memory of Professor Lowell. Our chef always puts on an excellent buffet. You'd be very welcome.'

'Do you recognize anyone at all?' Anna whispered to Isadora.

She looked up, her eyes red-rimmed. 'You know the really sad thing? Even if any of them were here I probably wouldn't recognize them, any more than they'd recognize this saggy old bag as Isadora Salzman.'

'You're not a saggy old bag,' Anna said fiercely. 'Don't talk about yourself like that.' She glanced around the almost empty chapel. 'People will be waiting to come in. Do you want to go back to Walsingham with the others, or would you rather go home?'

Isadora felt she should go to Walsingham. 'I owe it to James.' She laid her hand on Anna's. 'You don't have to come. I can easily get a cab.'

'Don't be silly,' Anna said. Though Isadora had been the only member of the Six to show up at James's funeral, it was still possible that one of the others might make it to his wake.

When they arrived outside the college buttery which had been co-opted for the occasion, Isadora said, 'Can you point me in the direction of a cloakroom? I need to touch up my ghastly visage. Maybe you could go and find us some drinks.'

Isadora was gone so long that Anna wondered if she'd changed her mind and slipped off home. When she eventually appeared, Anna hurried over to put a glass of red wine in her hand and caught a tell-tale whiff of tobacco. Isadora must have smoked a crafty roll-up to calm her nerves. As Isadora's fingers closed around the stem of the glass, Anna heard her sharp intake of breath and a good half of its contents slopped on to the floor.

'I'll get you another glass,' Anna said. But Isadora seemed not to notice her spilled wine or the woman who swiftly arrived to mop up the mess.

'Isadora?' Anna said, touching her arm.

'Robert's here,' Isadora said in a faint voice. She was gazing in wonder and dismay at a well-dressed, clearly well-fed man, standing with his back to the buffet table. With a half-empty glass of brandy in his hand, he seemed to be surveying the room, though without any real interest. He had a faint smile on his face as if entirely satisfied with his own thoughts. Seeing him, it was easy to imagine that this was Robert Keane's habitual pose in social situations.

Isadora knocked back what was left of her drink. '"A sixty-year-old smiling public man,"' she quoted in a hoarse whisper. 'Hetty always thought he'd go that way, but sometimes people can surprise you.' From the flicker of sorrow in Isadora's eyes, Anna knew just how much she'd been longing to be surprised.

Robert seemed to sense he was being watched. He suddenly glanced in Isadora's direction and Anna saw startled recognition in his face. 'He's coming over,' Isadora hissed. She was visibly shaking. 'Oh God, Anna, I don't think I can do this!'

Robert was already hurrying towards them. 'Isadora? Isadora Salzman?'

'Hello, Robert,' Isadora said.

He patted his waistline with a laugh. 'There's considerably more of me than there was the last time we met! I'm flattered you recognized me. But look at you! You've hardly changed at all! You still have those amazing dark eyes and that fabulous Pre-Raphaelite hair.'

Isadora gave a brittle laugh. 'How wonderfully tactful of you to edit out all the rest of me! But how are you, Robert? Are you well?'

'I'm very well, thank you,' he said in his big hearty voice. 'My wife finally left me. My children hate me. My grandchildren hardly know me. But life still goes rolling merrily on, ha ha ha!' Robert seemed to realize that this was an inappropriate comment for a wake, adding hastily, 'Still in shock about poor old James, obviously. What a dreadful thing – you just can't imagine that anything like that could happen here inside these hallowed walls.'

He was drunk, Anna thought. Still upright and articulate but lacking any kind of social filter. His slightly unfocused gaze suddenly locked on to Anna. 'But you must introduce me to your young friend, Isadora darling!'

Isadora introduced Anna, tactfully omitting the unfortunate circumstances in which they'd met, and they exchanged polite inanities. Anna wondered if Robert Keane was a habitual drunk, or if he'd just needed a few stiff drinks to help him get through this rather unique ordeal. Like Isadora, Robert had defied their handler's instructions in order to honour James's memory. Perhaps this was as painful for him as it was for her? Anna sensed something dark and desperate beneath Robert's persona of the jolly drunk. Depression seeped from him like stale body odour. Possibly Isadora felt it too, because she said in gentler tone, 'It's good that you came, Robert. I did wonder . . . well, I hoped, that some of us – you know, might feel it was time . . .'

'Well, Cathy Hetherington obviously did!' Robert's expression darkened. 'She doesn't call herself that now, obviously. She's Sister fucking Mary Catherine or something equally godly.' He let out a humourless laugh. 'I presume she eventually gave herself to Jesus because, apart from yours truly, he was the only male left who hadn't already had a poke!' The raw anger in his voice made Anna want to take a step back.

Isadora stared at him. '*Catherine?* Catherine's here?'

'Over there by the window,' he said in the same aggrieved tone. 'She's the one dressed like Katharine Hepburn playing a missionary.'

Anna followed Isadora's gaze to a tall, rather-too-thin woman. Catherine was dressed exactly as Robert had described, in a long shapeless skirt and jacket that didn't suit her, would not have suited any woman, in fact. Her expression was as you'd expect a nun's to be, composed and calm. All at once her tranquil expression became oddly fixed. Anna followed her gaze and saw the young pink-cheeked woman wheeling the elderly man she'd seen in the memorial gardens, now without his rakish fedora. Catherine went hurrying across to talk to them.

'No!' Robert said in a harsh voice. 'Fucking hell, *no*! That can't be him.'

'It is,' Isadora almost whispered. She was suddenly ashen under her make-up.

Robert gulped the last of his brandy. 'He needn't think I'm going over to talk to him, the old bastard.' For all his aggression, he sounded shaken, almost frightened.

'Who is that man?' Anna asked, although she was almost sure she knew.

Isadora didn't answer. Catching hold of Anna's hand, she pulled her through the crowd, galvanized by some furious energy, though whether it was anger or simply excitement, Anna couldn't tell. But when they finally caught up with Catherine she had returned to stand by her solitary window, and the man in the wheelchair had vanished.

'Catherine?' Isadora said. 'I can't believe it's you after all these years! How *wonderful* that you came!' For a moment she was the old actressy Isadora, her voice rich with warmth and affection.

Catherine might dress like a dowdy

88

headmistress but she was still lovely, Anna thought. Close up, with the winter light from the mullioned window falling on her face, she had that almost painful beauty which Anna associated with saints in old paintings. 'Hello, Isadora,' she said coolly. 'Actually I'm Sister Mary Catherine now.' The words were obviously meant as a reproof.

Isadora looked as if she'd been slapped. This was how the seventeen-year-old Isadora Salzman must have looked, Anna thought, as she blundered through her first weeks among Oxford's great and good. But Isadora was older and tougher now. Making a lightning-fast recovery, she went on the attack. 'I saw you talking to Tallis! Why was he here?'

Catherine's response was so swift that it almost didn't seem like a lie. 'I haven't seen Tallis since the nineteen-sixties, Isadora. You must have seen me talking to my old teacher from LMH.' She gave an involuntary glance across the room, before briefly returning her attention to Isadora. 'It's good to see you again. I really was so sorry to hear about James. But I'm afraid I can't stay, they're expecting me back at the Mother House.'

She hurried away leaving Isadora looking after her in dismay. 'He *was* here. I know it was him. You saw him, didn't you Anna?'

'If you mean that man in the wheelchair, yes, I saw him,' Anna said. 'And I saw him earlier in the memorial gardens.'

'And Robert most definitely saw him.' Isadora seemed to be trying to convince herself.

But when they tried to find Robert to ask him, he had also disappeared.

'It's so ridiculous. *I'm* so ridiculous,' Isadora said in despair, when they'd returned to her house in Summertown. 'But whenever I pictured meeting any of them again, I'd always imagined it would be just like it was; that we'd simply resume that wonderful effortless connection. But they could have been two utter strangers. Robert is just a drunken old banker and Catherine looked at me as if she hated me.' She tried to laugh. 'Not very nun-like of her, I have to say!'

They were sitting on opposite sides of Isadora's kitchen table. Anna was drinking coffee. Isadora was nursing a glass of vodka. A large manila envelope lay on the table between them. Isadora had taken out a handful of photographs none of which she'd yet shown to Anna. She fanned them out, keeping them face inward like a hand of cards that she wasn't quite ready to reveal.

'It's not just that I wanted to see my old friends, Anna. I wanted – I *needed* – them to see *me*. Nobody knows me now the way they did. It makes me feel so alone, so bleak – I can't even describe it. And Catherine made me feel as if I was going insane!' Isadora extracted two photographs from her fan, pushing the others into a pile. 'I don't intend to bore you with hundreds of tedious photos. In fact, I have hardly any from those days. I just want to show you these two.'

She showed Anna a picture of the six friends posed against a lovingly polished London cab. Anna examined it with interest. 'That's *such* a

90

sixties' picture! Is that Piers Courtenay driving the cab?'

Isadora's expression became fond. 'Yes. He was so proud of it. He was always lovingly polishing and valeting it! He'd go off to fetch it for one of our jaunts, and we'd hang around on the corner, saying, "Don't worry, a cab will come along in a minute!" then Piers and his cab would appear around the corner and we'd all flag him down! It sounds silly now, but at the time it seemed like such fun!'

'It certainly looks like you're having fun in the picture!' Anna was still studying the photograph. 'And that's Catherine leaning on the bonnet.' Her face already had that painfully exposed look as if she'd been born without the normal human defences. Catherine definitely belonged in a Renaissance painting, Anna thought, not out in the world, grappling with the mess and muddle of real life.

'So I'm guessing that lovely girl with the long blonde hair must be Hetty?' Anna said, though she'd seen at a glance that Hetty was far more than simply 'lovely'. She had that luminous quality which the camera loves but which is impossible to pin down.

'She was *extremely* attractive to men,' Isadora said unnecessarily.

'Was she a bit of a wild child?' Anna asked.

'*Was* she!' Isadora said, with one of her great hoots of laughter. 'Oh, my goodness, that girl!'

But though Hetty's body language said 'sixties' wild child', her beautiful eyes held a great deal of hurt for someone so young, Anna thought.

'James absolutely worshipped her,' Isadora said.

'James was very handsome when he was young,' Anna commented. 'Don't you think he looks like the young Dirk Bogarde?'

Isadora leaned in to examine James's features more closely. 'So he does! You know I've never seen that till now. I probably didn't appreciate him as much as I should have,' she added in a wistful tone.

'You didn't even have a little tiny crush?'

'No,' Isadora said, with a faraway look. 'I somehow never saw James in that light.'

'What about Catherine? Did she have a thing for James?'

Isadora shook her head. 'Catherine was one of those women who seem doomed to have huge unrequited passions – for Piers, for instance.' She passed the second photo to Anna.

'That's you at a ball!' Anna said, delighted. 'Is that the one where you were partnered with James?'

Isadora shook her head. 'This was in my second year, when we all went to the May Ball. This wasn't taken at the ball but afterwards. What they call "a survivor's photo".' She let out a yelp of laughter that threatened to turn into tears. 'We should have got someone to take one at James's wake. Me, Catherine and Robert. The three elderly survivors of the Oxford Six!'

Anna looked at the six young unused faces smiling back at the camera and tried to imagine how it must feel to see them through Isadora's eyes; so much shining potential, so many broken dreams. *Somehow this all goes back to Hetty*, she thought. James's violent death, though terrible in its own right, had reopened old wounds caused by Hetty's murder, an event which had obviously traumatized Isadora so badly that she still wouldn't – or couldn't – tell Anna and Tansy the full story.

From her long experience of trauma Anna knew better than to press her. She drained the last of her coffee. 'I'm going to have to go back now, Isadora. Tansy's having a pre-Christmas thing with her family and Bonnie is due for another walk.' She picked up her bag, feeling guilty to be leaving Isadora alone with her sad memories.

'I have to say that is one decided benefit of having a very small, *extremely* lazy little doggie.' Isadora's voice was suddenly falsely bright. Gathering Hero into her arms she covered her startled furry face with kisses.

And that's how Anna left her, cuddling her dog and sorting through her envelope of old photos, a half-full bottle of vodka at her side.

Seven

In her office a few days later, with the rain hammering against the windows, and the smell of her and Kirsty's wet coats drying out above the radiator, Anna was struggling to concentrate.

Like most people, Anna had learned to switch channels when she came into work, shutting off personal concerns in order to focus on the steady flow of requests and complaints needing her attention, but this morning Nadine's to-do list seemed more than usually mind-numbing. Anna found her thoughts straying to Professor Lowell's funeral and the strange puzzle of the Oxford Six. Had the elderly man in the wheelchair really been Tallis, their former handler? Isadora and Robert obviously thought so. But then why would Catherine lie? What might it take to make a *nun* lie?

Part way through the morning, she heard Kirsty ask, 'Are you *trying* to melt a hole in it?'

Her amused voice pulled Anna back to the present with a bump. 'Sorry?'

'You've been staring so intensely at that wall,' Kirsty explained. 'I was scared you might accidentally create a portal into another dimension.'

'With my amazing superpowers?' Anna suggested.

'Or something along those lines!' Kirsty agreed, straight-faced.

Anna laughed. 'You know, for a minute there I thought you'd been possessed by the spirit of Comic-Con Paul! Portals? Other dimensions? Seriously?'

'I don't think of it as being possessed, so much as being open to exciting new ways of thinking,' Kirsty said demurely. She gave Anna a naughty smirk. 'Can you imagine Nadine's expression if she came in this afternoon and found her office had sprung a leak into another dimension?'

'Can you imagine the Post-its waiting next time I come into the office?' Anna said darkly.

'You *do* understand the meaning of the phrase "duty of care", Anna!' Kirsty mimicked. 'I've already got the To-Do List from Hell without running around saving Walsingham's students from flesh-eating zombies!'

Their mutual teasing went a long way to lightening Anna's mood. Even so, she was relieved when it was time for her to leave the office. There were times when half a day as a university administrator was more than enough.

On her way out, she stopped inside the porter's lodge to drop off some post.

'Afternoon, Miss Hopkins. You off home now?' asked Tate, the new porter.

'Yes. I'm going to take my dog for a good long walk so I hope the rain eases off! Are you all on your own today?' Anna hoped she had managed to keep the surprise out of her voice. Though Tate appeared cheerful and hardworking, she and Kirsty had noticed that Boswell still seemed to be keeping him on an extremely tight leash.

Tate gave her a grin. 'Yeah, Mr Boswell had an emergency dentist appointment and Mr Phipps has gone down with flu. So what kind of dog you got?'

'A White Shepherd,' she said.

'First thing I'm going to do when I can afford my own place,' he confided, 'get myself a dog. A working cocker like old Roop's and get her trained as a gun dog.'

'Roop's?' Anna wondered if she'd heard correctly.

'Roop's one of the gardeners. He's got a lovely little spaniel. She's getting on now but her tail never stops wagging.' His smile became wistful. 'I love dogs. They're the most loyalest creatures on earth. A human will always betray you if the price is right, but a dog will stick by you through thick and thin.'

By the time Anna had reached home and made a hasty toasted cheese sandwich, the rain had slowed to a misty drizzle. Grateful that Jake wasn't here to see her in her hideous fishermen's waterproofs, Anna set out with Bonnie for Port Meadow. She should really make the effort to find some new walks, Anna thought. Port Meadow was just so convenient that she'd unthinkingly fallen into a routine. She let Bonnie off her lead as soon as they were safely inside the gates. At the start of a walk she could almost feel her young healthy dog's pent-up energy longing for release. Gathering her snowy limbs together, Bonnie shot away across the water-logged grass then stopped, looking back at Anna with an expectant expression.

'Oh, you want a race!' Anna said laughing.

They ran, chasing each other in and out of trees, sloshing through the temporary streamlets that often appeared after heavy rain, and Anna felt some of the stress and sadness of the past weeks falling away. At last, she came to a breathless standstill, bracing her hands on her knees, as she gulped in air. This was the true pleasure of living with dogs, she thought. Regardless of mud, cold or rain, they were ridiculously joyous – and it was catching!

They walked back to her flat at a more sedate pace. Once Anna glanced down and caught Bonnie looking up at her with her soulful dark-rimmed eyes. 'You are a lovely dog, you know that?' she told her.

Lovely, but disgustingly muddy. Anna whisked Bonnie down to the kitchen, and was in the middle of cleaning her off with an old towel when the doorbell rang. Anna hastily sloughed off her trawler-man outfit and hurried upstairs to answer the door.

When she saw the strangely familiar dark-haired man standing on her step, she was initially too stunned to react, and then she thought her heart was going to jump out of her mouth. Confusion and terror robbing her of all social graces, she went to slam the door in Tim Freemantle's face. Before it could close, he said urgently, 'Anna, please, I found Max Strauli. He agreed to talk to me. He's told me all about that night.'

She froze, still gripping on to the door handle. She didn't know which freaked her out more, the arrival of her childhood friend still recognizable after so many years, or the news that had brought him here to her door. After the night when Anna had arrived home to find her family bloodily slaughtered, like in a scene from a revenge tragedy, her boyfriend, Max, disappeared off the map and she'd never been able to find him. She managed to say, 'You've talked to Max?'

'Yes, for a couple of hours. Can I please come in and tell you what I've found out?'

Tim must have had a growth spurt in his late

teens because they now stood exactly eye to eye. He'd always been skinny; that hadn't changed. His clothes still looked rumpled, but they were nice, slightly hipster-ish clothes. She could see fine dark stubble on his chin, the same colour as his short curly hair.

Every protective instinct implored Anna not to let him in, yet like a sleepwalker she found herself stepping back from the door. 'OK. But first I've got to finish drying off my dog.'

Tim followed her down to the kitchen where Bonnie was drinking noisily from her bowl, surrounded by a decorative frieze of muddy paw prints. She turned briefly to inspect Tim, decided that he didn't pose an immediate threat and went back to gulping down water.

'Coffee?' Anna said.

'Coffee can wait until you've dried your dog.' Tim cast an awed glance at Bonnie. 'I can see there's quite a lot to dry.'

Anna was relieved to be able to delay the moment, to take the time to rub down Bonnie, followed by the near-automatic process of making coffee. Her heart hammered inside her chest, but she could just about breathe. She could deal with this. She hoped she could deal with this.

With a flicker of alarm, she noticed Tansy's unsent Christmas card still lying on the table and quickly slid it behind the toaster. Very few people knew that Tansy was Frankie McVeigh's daughter and Tansy preferred to keep it that way. When Anna returned her attention to Tim she found him covertly studying her face. 'What?' she said.

He gave an apologetic laugh. 'Sorry, I just haven't seen you since that summer, and you look so uncannily like your mum. Even that little thing you do when you're nervous.'

'What little thing?' she said immediately suspicious.

He touched his hand to the back of his neck. 'That little thing.'

Anna, who almost never cried, for a moment felt close to tears. Her grandfather was the only other person left who knew her from that time and he had never said outright that she looked like his daughter Julia, her mother. She swallowed. 'You also look uncannily like your mum,' she told him. 'Neither of us looks anything like our dads.'

Tim went to stand by the French windows, looking out into the rainy courtyard. She wondered if he'd noticed the empty dresser shelves and what he'd think if he knew how near Anna had come to joining her brothers and sister wherever dead people end up. 'So do you live here alone?' he asked.

'I did for a while. Now I'm sharing with a friend, just until she finds a place of her own.' Anna carried their mugs over to the table. 'I don't know if you take sugar.' She let out a nervous laugh. 'I seem to remember you used to pig out on Flying Saucers and jelly beans.'

Tim came to join her. 'And you used to be able to fit five cream crackers in your mouth at once,' he said with a grin.

'Dan always beat me though,' she said. 'He had jaws like a hippo, that boy!'

It hit them both at the same moment that she was joking about her murdered brother.

Tim picked up his mug and took a rapid swallow of his too-hot coffee. 'I didn't mean to upset you with my phone call the other day. I feel especially bad about it, because I kind of schmoozed your number from your grandfather, talking about all the good times my brother and I had with your family. He thought – well, bless him, he said, he thought it might be good for us "young people" to talk.' He flashed Anna a humorous look. 'I guess we must still seem quite young to someone who's almost ninety?'

'You *are* still young,' Anna said. 'You've hardly changed, except for the stubble.'

'Ditto,' he said, 'apart from the stubble obviously! Though, in my earliest memories of you, you're always upside down.' It was Tim's turn to give a nervous laugh. 'Seriously! You were either standing on your head or dangling from a tree branch. And then you grew up and became the coolest girl at Cherwell.'

'I might have made it into the cool set. I doubt if I was ever the coolest girl,' Anna objected. 'Plus, how would you know how cool I was? You were miles away at Marlborough.'

'Being a swot and a nerd and counting off the days till the holidays.' He took another gulp of his coffee. 'And there's Dad telling me these were the happiest days of my life, Jesus! Running the school newspaper was about the only thing that kept me sane.' Tim shifted in his chair. 'I'm really sorry to just turn up on your step like the Ghost from Christmas Past. But you didn't reply

100

to any of my thousand and one emails and I just didn't know what else to do.'

They'd stopped circling around each other now. Anna felt a flicker of fear. Now Tim was going to tell her why he was here.

'My wife suggested sky writing.' He flashed a nervous grin. 'I thought that was a bit too Spike Jonze.'

'That's why you've been emailing, because you found Max?'

'Actually, he isn't Max Strauli these days,' Tim said. 'He's into shamanism now. On his first shamanic journey he was told he had to pick a new name for his new life, so now he goes by "Dagon".'

Anna stared at him. '"Dagon"? You're sure he wasn't just joking around?' Max had been an outrageous, not to say cruel, joker.

Tim shook his head. 'Nope, he was deadly serious. It's the name of a Babylonian fertility god. I looked it up on my phone when I got back into my car.'

Anna tried to imagine what heavenly thunderbolt could have turned egotistical upper-middle-class Max into the kind of person who went on shamanic journeys.

'So he's just – Dagon now? He doesn't have a last name?'

'I don't think you need a last name do you, if you're a god?'

Anna felt a hysterical fit of giggles fighting to escape. 'So I'm guessing he's not working for Microsoft then?'

'He's not working full stop. No computer, no

mobile phone. He's living in a van with a New Age Traveller community in mid-Wales. Permanently stoned, as far as I can tell.'

'And he sees himself as some kind of fertility god?'

'There were crowds of little feral kids in and out of his van. I don't know if any of them were his. There was a pretty girl hovering silently in the background, or she would have been pretty if someone would give her a few vitamins. She didn't look more than sixteen.'

Anna felt an all too familiar rush of fear. 'And Max told you about – about the night my family . . .'

'He didn't tell me much,' Tim said quickly. 'But he did say that he was completely off his face the night it happened. He told me that someone called Dominic—' He noticed Anna flinch. 'You knew him, yeah?'

She gave a tight nod. 'Yes, I knew Dom.'

'He said Dominic had given him an eighth of black and a wad of cash to take you out for the night, get back in your good books, whatever that meant.'

'We'd broken up,' Anna explained. 'He'd dumped me, just a few days before.' That's what they'd fought about in his Ford Fiesta. It had ended with her jumping out of his car, and walking all the way back to North Oxford in the early hours. Stoned and drunk, filled with raw teenage hurt and rage, it had seemed to Anna that her life was over. She closed her eyes wishing she could go back in time and shake some sense into that silly self-absorbed girl.

102

'Anyway, Max – sorry, "Dagon",' Tim corrected, 'commented that he'd never known Dom to be generous with his drugs and he thought that was just a little bit suspicious, or at least he did once he'd sobered up.' He slid an anxious glance at Anna. 'So did you know that Dominic's back in the country?'

Anna gave another tight nod. 'I've known for a while.' It was before she'd cancelled all her Google alerts. The trail had gone cold. Max had apparently dropped off the grid. Dom had allegedly disappeared to Argentina to work in his uncle's vineyard.

And then, in a peaceful Oxfordshire churchyard, a few weeks after she and Bonnie had almost lost their lives, her phone had sounded that heart-stopping *ping*. Fighting for calm, she'd gone straight to the nearest newsagent to buy a copy of *Tatler*. Back home, she'd frantically scanned pages, until she found the three-line news item tucked away in 'Bystander', the *Tatler*'s gossip column.

Anna had ripped it out and run with it into her study. Half blind with distress, she struggled to fit the key into the lock of her armoire for what must have only been seconds but had felt like a screaming eternity.

That had been a bad night, her worst since she'd got Bonnie. Almost the worst part about it was that she'd half-convinced herself it was all over! She was going to be like Naomi Evans. She was going to embrace life and possibly fall in love! But that single *ping* on her phone had been enough to send her hurtling back into the dark . . .

'So have you spoken to him?' Tim said.

'Dom? I can't get anywhere near him,' Anna said. 'I don't know how much you know about his family, but Dom's always been pretty much untouchable.'

Tim drained his coffee. 'He does seem quite disturbingly well connected.'

Anna was still trying to absorb what he'd told her. 'I was surprised when Max was suddenly so desperate to see me again,' she admitted. 'I mean, seeing as he'd been so keen to break up just a few days previously.' Surprised and flattered, she thought, not to mention smug in that way of sexually confident teenage girls. *He still wants me.* Now it seemed Max hadn't wanted her at all. He'd just wanted his eighth of black. What had Dom wanted though?

She glanced across at Tim. He remembered her dangling upside down from trees. She remembered him patiently teaching her his dance moves. For years they'd been inextricably part of each other's worlds. But that was long ago and in another lifetime. Unlike Anna, Tim still had the parents and sibling that he'd started out with. And now he had a wife and a successful career in journalism. For the first time it occurred to her that he might even have children.

Without realizing, Anna folded her arms defensively across her chest. 'Why are you actually here, Tim? Why are you raking up all this stuff after all these years?'

Bonnie picked up on the new edge to Anna's voice. Stepping out of her basket, she silently placed herself between Anna and Tim.

'It's OK,' Anna told her. 'Tim's not going to hurt me.' But Bonnie kept her eyes warily fixed on Tim.

Tim was dismayed. 'Why would she think I was going to hurt you?'

'Some men broke in to my flat,' Anna told him. 'They – hurt us both. Since then Bonnie has been a bit distrustful of strangers.'

'Fucking hell, Anna, I should think that's all you bloody needed!' Tim's voice was husky with emotion. 'I'm so sorry. I had no idea.'

'So why exactly are you here?' Anna repeated.

'I was just going to get around to that,' Tim said. 'It kind of has to do with Alice.'

'Is she your wife?'

He shook his head. 'Alice was my girlfriend. We met on our first day at Bristol Uni. It was wonderful. *She* was wonderful. We were inseparable all that first term. And then Alice found someone else. Someone she found more – exciting, intriguing, challenging; I think those were the words she used when she dumped me.'

'That must have been quite crushing,' Anna said, privately wondering where Tim was going with this.

'It's much, much worse than you're thinking,' he said. 'Three months after Alice left me, she was found strangled.'

'Oh God, *Tim.*'

'She'd been thrown down into the Avon Gorge, you know under the suspension bridge?' Tim swallowed. 'Anyway, it was just two years after your family . . .' He passed his hands across his face. 'Given what you've been through, Anna, I don't want to do a self-indulgent song and dance about how your family's murders affected me. But they did have – quite an effect. And then, what happened to Alice, and the disgusting self-serving web of lies and false alibis her killer wove to keep anyone from finding out the truth . . . well, I suppose it made me quite – *angry*!' He gave a grim laugh. 'And I thought, I could either let this anger corrode me from the inside and turn me into a complete nutjob, or I could become the kind of person who tries to find out the truth.'

'It was the exciting new boyfriend who killed her, wasn't it?' Anna said.

Tim nodded. 'It took a long while to prove but in the end it all came out, that he'd attacked two previous girlfriends and badly frightened several other girls with his mood swings.'

Anna felt a pang of guilt. If she'd stayed in touch with the Freemantles, she would have known about this harrowing time in Tim's life. She could maybe have helped. *Unlikely*, she reminded herself. Anna couldn't even help herself back then. But that didn't stop her feeling ashamed.

Tim ran his hands through his hair. 'So, to answer your question, I'm not here to stir things up, or to get a sensational story. I suppose what I really want is your blessing. I want to help you solve this mystery that screwed up your life – and, to some extent, mine.'

For the first time Anna felt a flicker of irritation. Exactly how had Tim's life been 'screwed up'?

106

'Anjali, that's my wife, thinks I'm "crazy-pants".' He made quote marks in the air. 'She said I should let sleeping dogs lie – if Bonnie will forgive the phrase.'

'Your wife could be right.' Anna took a deep breath. 'Tim, we've been out of touch a long time, so you can't even begin to know what it – what my family's murders – did to me. I've driven myself almost mad trying to find out who could have broken into our house that night, I actually accused a completely innocent person and had a restraining order taken out on me. I've spent time in mental institutions. I put my entire life on hold, while I tried to track their murderers down, and – it *damaged* me, Tim. It's taken me over sixteen years, but I've finally reconciled myself to the fact that I may never know if Max or Dominic were involved. I just can't let myself go back to that bad, obsessive place, I just can't!'

Tim didn't answer her for a moment. 'I can see that,' he said at last, 'and I wouldn't ask it of you. What I'm asking is for you to let *me* do the tracking.'

After Tim had gone, Anna put their mugs in the dishwasher then she mopped the floor, erasing Bonnie's muddy paw-prints. It had been surprisingly pleasant and heart-warming to spend time with Tim. But some instinct told her he hadn't been entirely straight with her. She wished Tansy was home so she could run her and Tim's conversation past her. She tried to call Jake but his phone was switched off so she left him a voicemail. Then Anna went upstairs, shut herself into her study and unlocked the armoire that functioned as her murder cupboard.

She opened out the two doors, and ran her finger along one of the taut red strings that crisscrossed countless photographs, witness statements, newspaper cuttings, until she found the scrap of paper she'd torn from the gossip column in *Tatler*.

'*After an enviable life trajectory which has taken him from the highlands of Argentina to high-energy New York, Dominic Scott-Neville has brought his beautiful wife, former model and well-known socialite, Ghislaine, back home to the family estate in Oxfordshire, following the sudden death of his father, Ralph Scott-Neville.*'

Eight

At six thirty a.m. the next day, Anna was making coffee in the chilly kitchen, moving around as quietly as possible so as not to disturb Tansy, when the phone shrilled, startling her out of her wits. She threw herself at it, knocking it out of its cradle. '*Grandpa?*'

'Oh, Anna, I'm so sorry, how thoughtless of me. I didn't mean to give you a scare at this unearthly hour. I honestly didn't think you'd pick up. I only meant to leave a message.'

It was Isadora. Anna's knees went weak with relief. She knew that one day the phone would ring at some weird time of day, and it wouldn't just be a friend wanting to leave a message. She took a long breath. 'That's fine, Isadora. I've actually been up a while. Are you OK?'

'The police came to see me late last night,' Isadora said. 'Robert Keane committed suicide.'

Barely awake after a turbulent night, it took a few seconds before Anna's brain caught up. *Oh, fuck*, she thought, *Robert Keane*. 'I don't know what to say,' she said, stunned. 'What an unbearably crap few weeks you're having.' She recalled his words at James Lowell's wake. *My ex-wife finally left me. My children hate me. But life goes rolling merrily on, ha ha ha*. Now another member of the Oxford Six was dead.

'I don't know what to say either – or what to *think*.' Isadora gave a bewildered laugh. 'At the moment, I think I'm in that state of shock – which you will recognize only too well, Anna – when the only way one can keep afloat is by doing mindless physical tasks.'

Anna heard the boiler make its familiar *wumph* as the heating finally kicked in. Her bare feet were freezing. She should have put socks on. She'd been in too much of a hurry to put some distance between herself and her bed, herself and her dreams.

'Have you been awake all night?' Anna watched Bonnie nosing hopefully in her bowl, hoovering up tiny specks of yesterday's kibble.

'Not all night,' Isadora said. 'I knocked myself out with a couple of diazepam with a whiskey chaser. Then I got up and scrubbed the tiles in my bathroom. Now I'm making bread.'

'Tansy and I will come over,' Anna said.

'Darling, you know I always love to see you both, but I'm honestly not asking you both to leap into action. I just wanted to let you know as you met Robert at James's wake. I'm really fine. I've thrown out the last of the tobacco.'

'I can hear that you're fine,' Anna said truthfully. 'But we'll come over anyway. You can give us breakfast.'

An hour later, Anna, Tansy and Bonnie were in Anna's Land Rover heading for Isadora's house. Groggy from her rude awakening, Tansy was still struggling to piece the sequence of events together. 'What were you doing up at that hour though? It's your day off.'

Anna kept her eyes on the road. 'Bad dream,' she explained briefly.

It had started innocently enough with Tim and Anna watching their younger selves down by the seashore. Then Tim had nudged her with his shoulder. 'Do you think we ought to tell them? It seems so wrong that those little kids don't know what's up ahead.' And suddenly Anna was outside her family home, struggling to open the front door with a key that kept splintering into ever smaller pieces, as her little sister, Lottie, screamed and screamed on the other side of the locked door for Anna to come in and save them.

'Dreams are bastards, aren't they,' Tansy said sympathetically. 'The really bad ones leave this kind of evil residue that haunts you all the rest of the day.'

'They do.' Anna glanced across at her flatmate, still sleepy in her fleece-lined parka, her curls

110

pulled up into a kind of messy fountain. After a late date with Liam, Tansy had been dead to the world when Anna knocked on her door, yet the instant she'd grasped the situation she'd sprung into action.

'So how did Isadora seem?' she asked, yawning.

'Eerily calm,' Anna said, 'given that her old friends are dropping like flies. She's making bread apparently,' she added a little uncertainly.

'Oh. OK.' Tansy gave a small shrug. 'Whatever gets you through the night.'

In the long minutes it took Isadora to answer the doorbell, Anna couldn't help wondering which version of Isadora Salzman they'd find inside. Had she been making bread in her pyjamas, her hair in uncombed witch-locks? But when Isadora eventually opened the door she was dressed in a pair of well-cut trousers and a pretty Fair Isle cardigan that Anna hadn't seen her wear before. Her hair had been brushed and tied back with a jade silk scarf. 'Sorry to keep you waiting,' she said slightly breathlessly. 'My hands were sticky with bread dough, and I had to sluice them off. Come in, it's blissfully warm in my kitchen.'

'What are you baking? It smells amazing.' Tansy said as they followed Isadora along the long corridor to the back of the house.

'I've got cinnamon rolls already in the oven and a couple of loaves still proving,' Isadora said over her shoulder. 'I may have gone a little overboard.'

Isadora wasn't exaggerating about the warmth. The heat emanating from her range cooker was positively equatorial. Beside the cooker, two loaves had been set to rise on a wooden stool. The dough was already visibly pushing up from under the red-checked cloth Isadora had used to cover them. Tansy lifted a corner of the cloth. 'Ooh, yum, onion seeds!'

'I know this must seem like a bizarre reaction.' Isadora suddenly sounded defensive. 'But I suddenly had this – *compulsion* to do something useful and real. I've never really seen myself as a Jewish mother, but *in extremis* I seem to have a choice: either I go to pieces, or I cook and clean!'

Tansy went to Isadora and put her arms around her. 'You are *awesome*, Isadora,' she told her fervently. 'You're one of the most awesome women I know.'

'I don't understand why the police came to tell you that Robert had killed himself.' Anna had been pondering this in the car.

Isadora threw up her hands. 'Because the poor man named me as his next of kin! It's insane! Until the other week we hadn't seen or spoken to each other for fifty years!'

'Robert named you as next of kin?' Anna said, astonished.

'According to his solicitor. Apparently Robert changed his will a few days ago.'

'He must have changed it after he saw you – after Professor Lowell's funeral,' Anna said.

Isadora didn't seem to hear. 'I just feel so terrible for him. How lonely must he have been to name someone he hadn't properly talked to since the sixties? It's as if all the years since then

112

– his family, his financial success – were just dust and ashes at the end.'

'He said his kids hated him.' Anna was leaning against the counter next to the cooker. Bonnie sprawled by her feet, eyes half closed, savouring the warmth.

'There could have been a good reason for that,' Tansy pointed out. She'd collapsed into Isadora's wicker chair and looked as if it wouldn't take much to make her drift back to sleep.

'I realize that, Tansy. Robert was no angel and I'm sure he disappointed his family in all kinds of ways.' Isadora's voice was tart. 'But ex-wives can be extremely vindictive, especially when their ex-husbands are as wealthy as Robert – and to cut him off from his children – it's just too spiteful. *Shit!* I almost forgot the rolls!'

Watching Isadora slide out the tray of soft pillowy little rolls, delicately gilded with sugar and egg, Anna wondered if Isadora would forever associate the smell of freshly baked cinnamon rolls with Robert's suicide.

Isadora transferred her rolls to a cooling rack then picked up her thread where she'd left off. 'Men from my generation, Englishmen that is,' she corrected quickly, 'can find it hard to admit to uncomfortable emotions. When I think of that frightful smug persona Robert felt he had to put on, when inside he was just . . .'

'Sorry to ask this, but how did he—?' Tansy asked.

'Carbon monoxide poisoning,' Isadora said. 'The housekeeper arrived for work and heard the car engine running inside the garage. The police found a note on the passenger seat. *Forgive me. I just can't bear this nightmare any—*' Breaking off, she whisked away the tea towel in a sudden panic, peering anxiously at the rising loaves underneath. She gave an apologetic laugh. 'Sorry, I don't seem to be doing very well at multitasking.'

'I'm not surprised,' Tansy said. 'Why don't I put the kettle on and make everyone a hot drink while you get the loaves in the oven?'

'First James, now Robert,' Isadora said half to herself. 'I can't help feeling we're all being punished for Hetty.'

Hetty again, Anna thought. Was Isadora saying that James's death and Robert's suicide were somehow linked with the long ago murder of Isadora's friend? 'So as next of kin do you have to go and ID the body?' she asked.

'Technically I don't have to. One of his colleagues or his housekeeper could do it. But I said I'd do it.'

'Isadora, *why*?' Tansy's eyes were wide. 'Why *do* that to yourself if you have a choice?'

'Because I need to, darling,' Isadora said. 'I told the police I'll go down to the John Radcliffe later this morning.'

Anna could see Tansy steeling herself to do the right thing for Isadora, however horrifying. 'Well, OK,' she said bravely. 'I still don't think you should, but if you really have to, Anna and I will come with you, won't we?'

'What about your job at the gallery?' Isadora said.

'It's my day off,' Tansy said confidently, then

114

shot an alarmed look at Anna. 'It *is* my day off, isn't it? I fell out of bed in such a hurry I'm not entirely sure which day this is!'

'We *both* have today off,' Anna told her. 'So we can both come with you, Isadora. But right now I need you to show me where you keep Hero's lead. I'm going to walk the dogs.'

'Oh, you darling girl, *would* you?' Isadora said at once.

Anna kept both dogs on their leads as they made a quick tour around the streets. It was just past eight o'clock and people were emerging from their houses, to drive to work or drop their kids off at school. Every few yards Hero stopped in her tracks to look back at Anna with an affronted expression, apparently thrown by this change in her routine. Bonnie calmly kept pace with Anna, occasionally sniffing the air, clearly as relieved as Anna to be out of doors.

Anna had experienced a sudden, urgent need to get out of the house. The violence of events, old and new, the vicious murder and then a suicide, the reappearance of Max and Dominic – had all conspired to make her feel suffocatingly hemmed in. It wasn't exactly the run up to the season of peace and goodwill she'd been hoping for. Anna still hadn't spoken to anyone about Tim's visit. She hadn't wanted to get into it with Tansy on the drive over – given the circumstances, she'd felt they should be concentrating on Isadora – and she still hadn't been able to get hold of Jake.

Logically she knew there could be all kinds of reasons for him not to get back to her, but her nerve endings weren't convinced. 'He'll call,' she told Bonnie, as if saying it out loud would make it true, 'Jake always calls,' and Anna experienced the secret pleasure of seeing Bonnie's ears prick up at the sound of her favourite man's name.

She arrived back at Isadora's as Tansy was clearing some of the clutter from the kitchen table, making space for a plate of warm cinnamon rolls. They were just sitting down when Isadora's lodger Sabina wandered in. Today, her hair was confined under a knitted beanie, making her look more like a student from the twenty-first century and less like a romantic Heidi of the mountains. 'Oh, I didn't know you have visitors, Mrs Salzman,' she said coolly.

'Perhaps you'd like to join us?' Isadora suggested. 'I've made far too many of these delicious little rolls, so you'd be doing me a favour.'

Without turning round, Sabina carried on with extracting a loaf of anaemic sliced white bread from a shelf in Isadora's fridge. 'This morning we have an important test. I will just make my toast and eat it on the way.'

The three women made slightly awkward conversation while Sabina toasted two slices of bread to her satisfaction, then went on her way with an airy, 'Goodbye, ladies!'

'That's all she ever seems to eat, toast,' Isadora said. 'I'm starting to think she has some kind of disorder. Still, at least she comes in to use the toaster,' she added plaintively. 'Myung-Hee never comes in the kitchen at all except to use the washing machine, which for some reason she seems to do at dead of night. Gabriel thinks I

116

scare them off by being too intense.' She suddenly covered her face. 'Oh dear, life never quite works out the way you hope, does it?'

'I wouldn't take it personally,' Anna reassured her. 'Sabina and Myung-Hee are just young and self-absorbed. Things will get better, Isadora, seriously.'

'And you and Tansy really don't mind coming with me to the mortuary?' Isadora said. 'You don't have to come *in* with me. I'd just be so grateful if you could accompany me as far as the door. For some reason I find that hospital particularly daunting.'

The Sir John Radcliffe turned out to be not just daunting but vast. As Anna stood with her friends in the brilliantly lit foyer, staring up at the bewildering map of departments, a woman's voice said, 'Anna? I *thought* it was you! Do you need some help?' It was Dana, who rented Anna's top-floor flat.

'My friend needs to go to the mortuary to identify a body,' Anna said, keeping her voice low. 'Could you point us in the right direction?'

Non-medics might have launched into expressions of sympathy. Dana just said, 'Why don't I just take you there? I've got a clinic in thirty minutes though, so we'll have to walk fast!' She sped off along the gleaming corridors, exchanging greetings with passing nurses, only stopping once to allow a porter to manoeuvre a cumbersome trolley into a lift.

Anna mainly knew Dana through her choice of break-up music – Van Morrison, played at such high volume that Anna could sometimes hear faint strains of it in her garden. Somehow she'd never really taken on board that Dana was also a real live doctor. But here she was in a dazzling white coat, stethoscope parked neatly in her top pocket, finding her way through this vast sterile maze like a female Virgil in a particularly modern hell. Dana accompanied Isadora right up to the desk, saying, 'I believe this lady is expected.'

'Suppose Isadora changes her mind and needs us to go in with her?' Tansy whispered to Anna.

'I'll go in with her, don't worry,' Anna said.

But Isadora remained adamant that she wanted to go in alone.

Tansy and Anna took seats outside and waited. Tansy kept fidgeting with her nails. She'd painted them just the other day in her favourite Van Gogh Starry Night style, but now there seemed a real danger she might peel it all off. 'I think I've seen too many procedural dramas on TV,' she confided to Anna. 'I'm getting horrible visuals of what's on the other side of that door. Bodies in drawers, labels on toes, a grim-faced pathologist staring down into someone's open skull and simultaneously eating his lunch.'

'Now I'm getting horrible visuals,' Anna told her.

The door opened and Isadora came out, looking strained but resolute.

Tansy jumped up. 'Are you OK?'

'Yes, darling, I'm fine. Everything that wasn't really him was completely stripped away and there was . . .' Isadora tightly pressed her lips together, in an attempt to control her emotions. 'There was just poor, dear Robert.'

They set off back towards the enormous hospital car park. They had finally found Anna's Land Rover when her phone began to ring. She unlocked her vehicle for Isadora and Tansy to get inside. 'I just want to take this,' she told them.

'Hi, kid!' said Jake's familiar voice. 'I hope you haven't been trying to get hold of me? I dropped my phone in the bath,' he explained sheepishly. 'Totally killed it. I've been running around like an idiot trying to organize a new one. Are you and Bonnie both OK? And your grandfather?'

'We're all fine.' It was a dull winter's day with clouds lowering over the city, yet hearing Jake's voice Anna felt as if the sun had just come out. 'Well, I say we're fine,' she amended, 'but poor Isadora's just had to ID a dead friend at the hospital mortuary. We're leaving the hospital now.'

She heard Jake take a breath before he said, 'I'm really sorry to hear that. Was it a close friend?'

'More like a comrade,' Anna said, 'Back in the days when Isadora was a teenage spy.'

There was another longish pause before Jake said, 'This is going to be one of these two-cups-of-coffee stories, isn't it?'

'You should probably aim for three,' she said. 'Three *big* cups.'

It was crazy, she thought, how the mere sound of his voice made her feel calm and safe. At some point he'd phone again and she'd tell him all about Isadora and Tim. But right now it was enough to know that she and Jake were OK.

119

Nine

'So that 'was another bizarre first,' Tansy said, stifling a yawn. 'Anna, Tansy and Isadora visit the morgue.' They were in Anna's car heading back to Park Town, having dropped Isadora off at home. Tansy leaned back against the head rest. 'God, I'm shattered.' She blinked as if she was trying to get the world properly into focus. 'Hey, Isadora's lodger is a pretty little thing, isn't she?'

'Not the warmest bunny in the world,' Anna said.

'True, but that's probably an advantage in international business or whatever?' Tansy shook out her ponytail and began redoing it. 'There hasn't been time to tell you,' she said abruptly. 'Liam texted to say he's coming over after work. I hope that's OK?'

Anna slowed to avoid a cyclist. 'You should know by now you don't have to ask. Liam's always welcome.'

'I know, but I don't want you to feel we're taking advantage. Anyway, he's offered to cook us all a curry,' Tansy said.

'Even better! Assuming Liam can cook?' Anna added, belatedly registering Tansy's doubtful expression.

'He's not a bad cook,' Tansy said. 'He's just – well, you'll see . . .'

'OK, *now* you're making me nervous!' Anna told her.

Liam turned up promptly at seven, wearing a pea coat over his jeans, his hair still damp from the shower, a bag of groceries in each hand. 'Got to love the Cowley Road,' he said, as he followed Anna down the stairs to the kitchen. 'Almost as good as Leeds for food shopping – note the "almost".' He pulled three bottles of Tiger beer out of one of the bags, popped the tops, and smilingly handed one each to Anna and Tansy. 'Now you two just chat among yourselves and I'll get everything prepped!' Twenty minutes later Anna and Tansy had to retreat to stand by the open French doors. 'Try not to look!' Tansy hissed, as fumes of scorching chillies filled the kitchen. 'Liam's like the Cat in the Hat. He causes total devastation but he always gets it all cleaned up at the end!'

Anna did her best to follow Tansy's advice but couldn't help an awed glance at her kitchen counters now littered with every pan, dish and kitchen implement that she owned.

Tansy abruptly ducked out into the winter darkness, triggering the security light, and retrieved a well-gnawed tennis ball. She tossed it up the garden steps for Bonnie to chase. 'I don't want Liam to think we're talking about him,' she whispered as Bonnie raced after the ball. 'I hate when women do that snide under-mining thing when men cook. I mean, we all have to learn, right?'

Anna suppressed a flinch as behind them Liam threw some new ingredient into a pan triggering

121

tremendous crackling and spitting. 'That oil is seriously too hot, though,' she whispered.

'I *know*. Plus, did you *see* how much green chilli he was putting in?'

'Drop it,' Anna told Bonnie firmly. Reclaiming the ball, she flung it into the garden. 'Just be grateful he brought all those beers,' she said under her breath. In the middle of taking a swig from her bottle, Tansy burst out laughing, spraying beer down her top.

But when Tansy's boyfriend eventually called them to the table to eat and Anna saw the colourful array of dishes covering the table, she was surprised and impressed. He might have wrecked her kitchen but he had produced a real feast. 'This looks amazing, Liam!'

'It really does,' Tansy agreed giving Anna a grateful smile.

'Hopefully everything will taste all right,' Liam said a little anxiously. 'Well, dive in, everyone. Help yourselves.'

When everyone had loaded their plates, he raised his beer in a toast. 'Well, thank God it's Friday, eh?'

'Bad week?' Anna said.

'More like frustrating,' Liam said.

'Remember how you promised you wouldn't talk shop at the table?' Tansy said in a warning voice.

Liam gave her an entirely unapologetic grin. 'I did, didn't I. Must have slipped my mind!'

'Sorry, Tansy,' Anna said. 'Can I just ask Liam one quick work-related question?'

'So long as it's just one,' Tansy said sternly.

'I just want to know if the police are any closer to figuring out who's responsible for attacking Professor Lowell?'

Liam shook his head. 'We haven't got any strong leads. Unfortunately our lack of progress is making the college authorities edgy, which is making the chief superintendent super-edgy, and unfortunately it all ends up at the boss's door.'

Seeing Anna about to help herself from one of the many dishes on offer, Tansy managed a discreet mime of fatal choking and Anna surreptitiously limited herself to a polite spoonful.

'It's been a tough few months for the inspector really, all these murders,' Liam said. 'Well, for all of us really; feels a bit like we've stumbled into an old episode of *Inspector Morse*!' His eyes briefly clouded then, possibly mindful of his promise, he said in a more cheerful tone, 'Anyway, what have you girls been up to on your day off? Something fun?'

'We went to the morgue,' Tansy told him, giving Anna a wink.

Liam almost choked on his mouthful of *paratha* and took a hasty swallow of beer. Tansy solicitously patted him on the back. 'We had to take Isadora to ID a body,' she explained.

Liam put down his beer. Anna could see he didn't know whether to believe her. 'Seriously?'

Anna nodded. 'One of Isadora's old friends from her undergraduate days. He killed himself a couple of nights ago.'

'The banker bloke?' Liam said. 'I heard about that.' He frowned. 'Wasn't Professor Lowell an old friend of Isadora's too?' They both nodded.

123

'That's really rough,' he said, shaking his head. 'How's she holding up?'

Anna mentally paged through her recent encounters with Isadora. She pictured her puffing agitatedly at her stale roll-up, dressed in her designer finery for James's funeral, looking pale but resolute after identifying Robert's body. 'That depends,' she said cautiously. She could feel Tansy avoiding looking at her. They had begged Isadora to tell the police about her anonymous letter but she only repeated that she would when she was ready, and she insisted that she still wasn't ready.

'We're going with her to Robert Keane's house tomorrow – that's the banker bloke. He named her as his next of kin.' They'd got back to Isadora's from the hospital to find a small package waiting for her from Robert's solicitor. It contained an explanatory letter with directions to a house in Boars Hill, a set of keys and Robert's alarm code. Isadora had silently read the note before telling them, 'Apparently Robert wants me to organize his funeral. He's left detailed instructions for me at his house. The solicitor seems to feel this is a breach of some kind of protocol, but says he feels he has to comply.' She'd abruptly stopped talking to gather her little dog into her arms. 'I'll drive out there tomorrow,' she'd added before burying her face in Hero's curly black coat. 'Darlings, I didn't sleep at all last night,' she'd told them, 'and I'm suddenly very tired. If you don't mind seeing yourselves out, I'm going to go upstairs to take a nap.'

Isadora had shown no sign of resenting this

124

startling imposition by a man she'd lost touch with so many years ago, but Anna could see how much it was costing her. Exchanging glances with Tansy, she'd said, 'Would you mind if Tansy and I came along? We could pick you up around ten, if that's OK with you?' Already part way up the stairs, Isadora had half turned to give them an infinitely weary smile. 'That would be an act of great kindness, thank you.'

Keen to move the conversation away from violence and death, Anna said, 'Liam, this is really lovely. Can I help myself to some more?'

'Of course! I've made plenty!' Carefully avoiding the dish with the industrial amounts of chilli, Anna refilled her plate. Liam turned to Tansy, a mischievous glint in his eye, 'Did you tell Anna who we saw at Freud's last night?'

'No! Anna woke me at bonkers o'clock to go over to Isadora's and I completely forgot!' Tansy gave Anna a broad grin. 'We only saw Dritan Lika! Well, it was Liam who spotted him. Oh, my God, Anna! I know Dritan's a really bad boy and everything, but talk about sex on legs!' Dritan Lika was a notorious local gangster who had come to Anna and Tansy's attention when they were trying to find out who had murdered Naomi.

'He was wearing a really beautiful leather jacket,' Tansy added with a sigh. 'And I bet you his shirt and boots were handmade.'

'If you want, Tansy will draw his entire outfit for you,' Liam said wryly. 'She gave him quite a thorough looking-over!' A less secure man would make this sound barbed, Anna thought, but Liam seemed genuinely amused. 'So, talking

125

of gangsters, Ms Lavelle . . .' He gave a meaningful glance at the Christmas card which was currently propped up by the toaster.

'No, I haven't posted my father's card!' Tansy blazed. 'I may *never* post it! Stop bugging me about it, Liam, OK?'

Anna felt as if all the oxygen had suddenly been sucked out of the room. She knew something of Tansy's past life. She'd even met Tansy's gangster dad in person and understood exactly why she felt so sensitive about him around Liam. All the same it was a shock to see the normally sweet-tempered Tansy obviously spoiling for a fight.

Liam took a leisurely swallow of his beer. 'OK, Tansy,' he said amiably, 'but just a simple "No, actually, I haven't posted it yet, Liam," would have sufficed.'

After what seemed to Anna a long tense moment, Tansy gave him a slightly ashamed grin, though she couldn't resist a mocking, '*Sufficed?* Get you, Liam "I'm studying for my inspector's exams" Goodhart!'

He just grinned back at her and Anna saw Tansy suddenly let go of her anger. 'Can you believe how laid-back this man is?' she said to Anna. 'He should really be a Zen master.'

'How do you know I'm not?' he asked calmly. 'You need all your Zen powers in today's police force, believe me!'

Gradually all the food was eaten. Liam polished off the dish with extra chilli then rather hastily knocked back the last of his beer. 'Think my hand might have slipped with that one,' he said a little hoarsely. 'Now, you girls take your cups of coffee or whatever upstairs and I'll clean up.'

Anna and Tansy took a pot of camomile tea and two mugs up to the sitting room, followed by Bonnie. Bonnie settled at Anna's feet and began gracefully washing one of her front paws.

'*Exactly* like the Cat in the Hat? Do you swear?' Anna whispered to Tansy. 'No pink ring? No turmeric stains?'

Tansy reached across to pat her arm. 'It'll be fine! You did a good deed tonight, Anna Hopkins.'

'It was Liam who did the good deed. I couldn't have faced cooking tonight. If it was down to me we'd live off toast like Sabina.'

'Yes, but you let him loose in your lovely pristine kitchen and you hardly panicked at all – that was very brave,' Tansy teased.

'Just tell me I'm anal, why don't you?' Anna was trying and failing to close her mind to the alarming crashing and clattering downstairs. 'I should probably go down and show him where I keep the dishwasher stuff?' she suggested anxiously.

'Hey, he's a detective,' Tansy said. 'He'll figure it out.'

Eventually they heard the dishwasher start to thump and churn. Soon afterwards Liam popped his head around the sitting room door. 'OK, I'd better get off. I've got to drive up to Leeds tomorrow and I didn't get too much sleep last night.' He gave Tansy a fond look.

'Actually, I didn't get too much sleep last night either, so I'll be off to bed now,' Anna said feeling she should give Liam and Tansy space to say their goodbyes.

'If Isadora doesn't mind putting off going to Boars Hill till Monday, I could drive you all there, give you a hand?' Liam offered. 'It's not going to be much fun, is it, going to some house where some poor bloke just committed suicide?'

'Aw, that's really thoughtful, Liam,' Tansy said, 'but I think Isadora just needs to get it over and done with.'

She glanced at Anna for confirmation and Anna nodded. 'So she can get back to normal.' Anna wasn't sure what 'normal' consisted of these days, but she liked to imagine a peaceful stretch of time in which nobody they knew was black-mailed, fatally stabbed or horribly bludgeoned to death. 'What are you doing in Leeds?' she asked Liam.

'My dad's having his sixtieth birthday bash.' He smiled at her. 'Well, technically he's my foster dad, but to me he's just my dad.'

Anna dimly remembered Tansy mentioning this family gathering. Liam had asked Tansy to go with him but she'd flown into a panic. 'It's too soon!' she'd told Anna. 'Suppose they hate me on sight! Suppose I hate *them*? How is Liam going to feel about me then?'

'Have a safe trip,' Anna told him. 'And if I don't see you before, I'll be seeing you at Christmas!' From the way Liam and Tansy were looking at each other, she seriously doubted that Liam was going to get his early night. She made a discreet exit with Bonnie following on her heels.

Ten

'Do you think that tree arrived pre-decorated in a box from Harrods? Or do obscenely rich people seriously pay other people to come and decorate their Christmas trees?' They had just let themselves into Robert's house, a monstrous red-brick temple surrounded on two sides by dank-looking woodland. Tansy had focused her immediate dislike of their surroundings on the first thing they saw when they came in the door: Robert's towering silver Christmas tree.

'His wife had recently left him.' Isadora reminded her, her voice echoing around the oak-panelled hall. 'And he worked in a notoriously unforgiving industry, don't forget. He'd still have been expected to return his colleagues' hospitality, maybe host a pre-Christmas party.'

The three women stood staring up at the tree. Its frosty silver branches, hung with sapphire and white ornaments, added to the feeling of Arctic chill that pervaded Robert's house. Anna was glad they hadn't let Isadora go alone.

Tansy stuck her hands in her coat pockets, shivering. 'This has to be the ugliest house I have *ever* seen.' Lack of sleep made her seem slightly snappish. She'd told Anna that Liam had finally left somewhere around three in the morning. 'Oh! Except that staircase.' Her tired face suddenly lit up. 'The staircase is *really* cool! You could dance down it like in those fabulous old movies!'

'There's a gym and an outdoor swimming pool – and, bloody hell, a cinema!' Anna had found a brochure for a high-end estate agent on the hall table. 'It looks like Robert had put it up for sale.'

Tansy and Isadora came to look over her shoulder. Isadora frowned. 'Hmm, I think using "impressive" three times in the first paragraph was a distinct error of judgment. Tutankhamun's tomb is "impressive" but you wouldn't want to live there.'

'Plus who the fuck calls their house "Ormidale"?' Tansy gave a snort of laughter. 'It sounds like somewhere elves live in *Lord of the Rings*!'

'Shall we have our coffee before we get on?' Anna suggested.

'What, here in the hall?' Isadora said anxiously.

'Are you serious?' Tansy said. 'We'll have it in the kitchen like staff!'

'If we can find it,' Isadora said.

Anna held up the brochure. 'It's OK. There's a floor plan.'

They set off in search of the kitchen. Oak-panelled rooms opened into yet more oak-panelled rooms, each with its own picture-perfect arrangements of sofas, tables and lamps. Lacking even the smallest signs of daily wear and tear, they resembled those mock-ups of real rooms that you saw in department stores, Anna thought, only less inviting.

Tansy opened a door and said, 'The kitchen's in here!'

'Oh dear, more oak,' Isadora said. 'I hate to

130

think how many innocent trees were felled to build this horror.'

They had brought flasks of coffee with them. In unspoken assent, they drank it standing by a kitchen counter. All the cupboards were pale oak and all the counters were dark and glassy. Tansy experimentally touched one with a fingertip, instantly creating a smear. 'These would be a bastard to keep clean,' she commented.

'Have you noticed,' Isadora said, 'we're the only colourful things in this house!' Anna hadn't noticed this until Isadora had pointed it out, but sure enough Tansy's knitted snood in a warm pumpkin shade, her own pink scarf and the tiny glints of green and orange in Isadora's tweed coat formed the sole splashes of warmth and colour in a house otherwise devoid of either of these things.

A dull wintry light filtered in through drawn Venetian blinds. Isadora went to peer out through the slats. 'There's a garden.'

'I feel like we shouldn't be here.' Anna was warming her hands around her cup. 'Like we're intruding.'

'It's this house,' Tansy said. 'It disapproves of us. It disapproves of everybody who doesn't have an offshore bank account!' She opened the fridge which contained five lemons, and several bottles of tonic. Robert's freezer was similarly empty, except for a single drawer that was half filled with frozen meals from a high-end catering company.

'The house can think what it likes,' Isadora said, turning round. 'Robert wanted me to come.'

131

'Don't you think it's just a bit odd that he's asked you to do all this?' Tansy hesitated then decided to risk speaking her thoughts out loud. 'Robert obviously wasn't in a good mental state. You don't think he could possibly have sent you that weird letter?'

'No, Tansy, I don't.' Isadora's voice was sharp. 'Robert was many things but he was not the kind to send anonymous threats.'

'Could he have sent you the extracts from Hetty's diary though?' Tansy persisted.

'Possible but unlikely,' Isadora said in the crisp tone she had once used to quell her students. Unlocking the back door, she took a few steps into the garden. It stretched away into the distance, all lawn and clipped box hedges. 'Not a flower anywhere,' she said, half under her breath.

'It feels as if nobody has ever laughed or sung inside this house ever,' Tansy said, 'or cooked and enjoyed a real meal, or even had a good therapeutic quarrel.'

'. . . Or made love, proper love,' Isadora said coming back into the kitchen. Her expression was wistful. 'I know I shouldn't, but I can't help hoping that Robert had a little pied-à-terre somewhere that he shared with a warm-hearted woman.'

'If he had a woman somewhere, why would he name you as next of kin, though?' Tansy said.

'I know that really, darling, I just can't bear the thought of his life being so lonely.'

'Shall we have a snoop upstairs before we go hunting for your letter?' Anna asked.

Isadora was first to ascend the sweeping

132

Hollywood-style staircase. When Anna and Tansy joined her at the top, they found her examining a display of framed family photographs that took up part of one wall. There were dozens of photos of Robert's three children recording the usual stages of upper-middle-class childhood including various sporting triumphs; then rather fewer pictures of these children as adults with babies and toddlers of their own.

Anna stopped in front of a picture of a fair-haired woman in her thirties leading a pony with a tiny helmeted child mounted on its back. Judging from the woman's clothes and hairstyle the photo had been taken sometime in the 1960s. 'Is that Robert's ex?'

Isadora gave a tight-lipped nod. 'Yes, that's Cornelia.'

'So he married a nice working-class girl, then!' Tansy said drily.

Isadora gave one of her wicked hoots. 'Cornelia would have a stroke if anyone ever thought she was working class!'

'Were you and Cornelia both at Oxford at the same time?' Anna asked.

She nodded. 'But not the same college. Cornelia was at St Anne's. God knows how she got in! All she ever talked about was her dog. She always said she never wanted a family, just horses and dogs.'

'Before going on to give birth to three incredibly unattractive children,' Tansy pointed out. Either Robert's house or lack of sleep seemed to be making her increasingly waspish.

'They do rather seem to take after their mother,'

Isadora agreed. Her smile gradually faded. 'I was appalled when I googled Robert and found out who he'd married. We all knew Cornelia had a thing for Robert, but he always insisted that she was ghastly.'

'Didn't you say she had money?' Anna said tentatively.

'Robert was no saint,' Isadora said, 'but he wasn't the kind of man to marry just for money.'

'Maybe not when you knew him,' Tansy suggested.

'You know, none of this makes any sense!' Isadora gestured towards a photograph of Robert at his golf club, triumphantly holding up the winner's cup. She looked distraught. 'It's as if he became everything he was trying to leave behind. Everything he most despised.'

Anna wandered further along the landing. She stopped in front of a small framed sketch. 'Is this a real Matisse, do you think?'

Isadora came to see. 'Heavens, I think it is!'

Anna suspected that her grandfather would faint from excitement if he ever found himself in close proximity to a genuine Matisse. Was Robert a true art lover like her grandfather, she wondered, or had he simply recognized a good investment opportunity? They'd seen other paintings as they walked through the house but there had been many more empty spaces where paintings had obviously once hung. Maybe Robert's wife got them as part of her divorce settlement, or Robert had sold them off to help pay her maintenance?

The women looked into four or five bedrooms

before they found the master bedroom where Robert had been sleeping. On his bedside table was a stack of recent Man Booker winners seemingly unread. In the wardrobe they found shelves of identical blue-striped shirts, rolled socks, beautifully folded underclothes. Robert's housekeeper must have been coming in until quite recently, Anna thought, peering in at the perfectly pressed handmade Saville Row suits and rows of gleaming Italian leather shoes. Each new discovery intensified her sense of a lonely castaway marooned on an island of privilege.

'Where's his home cinema?' Tansy asked.

Anna consulted the floor plan. 'In the basement, along with the gym and the sauna.'

Nobody was interested in the gym, but Tansy fancied seeing inside Robert's cinema. 'This is the one decent room in the house!' she announced when she saw the luxurious seating arranged around the enormous screen. She plonked herself in the front row. 'Try it, Anna, this is *so* comfy! Wonder what the last movie was that he watched?' Tansy picked up Robert's tablet, lightly tapping the screen which immediately sprang to life.

'*Don't!*' Anna warned. 'For all you know, he could have been watching porn!'

Tansy did a little smirk. 'So he could! I'm surprised I didn't think of that!'

But when the movie screen lit up it only showed the final frame of a Humphrey Bogart movie.

'I remember all six of us going to an all-night Humphrey Bogart screening.' Isadora's eyes were misty with nostalgia. 'We eventually emerged, blinking like moles, into the most marvellous sunrise!' She seemed to wilt, as if she'd suddenly reached the end of her reserves. 'Have you found the study on your floor plan, Anna? I think I'd like to find that letter now and go home.'

To get to the study they had to pass through what Anna assumed was the main sitting room where corporate-style Christmas cards, several featuring gaudy-coloured pheasants in snow, were displayed along a pale marble mantelpiece. Possibly Robert's housekeeper had put them there in an attempt to give his house a more festive air. Anna couldn't imagine a suicidal Robert doing it.

After so much sterile perfection, it was almost a shock to walk into Robert's study and see his waste bin overflowing with crumpled pieces of paper. Tansy lifted out the piece nearest the top, carefully smoothing it out. 'Oh, my God,' she said. 'I think these are, like, his first attempts.'

'You mean at a suicide note?' Isadora suddenly looked pale.

Tansy nodded. 'And there's a ton of other stuff underneath.'

'We should probably take a look,' Anna said.

Tansy tipped up the basket and they started to sort through the crumpled papers. Some of them had been ripped across several times, but it wasn't difficult to piece together Robert's increasingly dire predicament: demands from banks, credit card companies, his firm of solicitors, letters about deals that had gone sour, letters from furious investors.

Anna pictured Robert, alone in his study, at

one end of this cavernous house, a house that it seemed his bank had already taken into its possession, as he struggled to find words to express why his life had become unendurable. 'I'm going to get a bin bag,' she said. 'I don't think anyone else needs to see this, and the police will have photos of the evidence by now.'

'I agree.' Isadora looked strained.

Anna found some bin bags in a utility room off the kitchen and they bagged up the distressing contents of the waste basket.

'Did Robert say where in his study he'd left the letter about his funeral?' Anna asked.

Isadora shook her head. 'I assumed he'd have left it on his desk, somewhere that was easy to spot.' But apart from a heavy crystal tumbler that still smelled faintly of whiskey, Robert's desk was empty.

'Top drawer maybe?' Tansy suggested.

They hunted through all the desk drawers without success.

'We haven't looked in the filing cabinets,' Tansy pointed out.

'We'll need a key,' Isadora said.

Tansy tugged experimentally on a top drawer which immediately slid open. 'Apparently not!'

Taking one stainless steel cabinet each, they embarked on a systematic trawl through the drawers.

'Any other bright ideas where we might find this letter?' Tansy asked once the filing cabinets had been exhausted.

'Perhaps the bookshelves,' suggested Anna. They began taking each book down, flicking through the pages in the faint hope that something would fall out.

'I don't get it.' Tansy looked up from her search through the kind of heavyweight volumes that invariably end up stacked on bottom shelves. 'Why would Robert ask you to come and find a letter but not give you a helpful hint as to where to find it?'

'It does seem rather perverse,' Isadora agreed.

'He's got a huge number of art books,' Anna said.

Isadora straightened up, rubbing her back. 'No need to sound so surprised. Even a banker is allowed a soul, you know.'

Tansy sat down cross-legged, and started to flick through a leather-bound album. 'Look what I found. Happy photos of Robert!'

The album offered a glimpse of such a different Robert to the man she'd met that Anna was tempted to ask Isadora if he'd had a twin. All the photographs seemed to have been taken on a foreign holiday of some kind. One picture showed him at a table in a vine-covered courtyard relaxed with other smiling men and women. Two of the women wore long floaty skirts. Everyone was drinking red wine.

'Where was he do you think?' Anna asked. 'Italy? South of France?'

'Definitely somewhere Mediterranean,' Isadora said. 'I wonder who all those other people are.' She turned a page. 'I didn't know Robert painted!' The photographer had caught him unawares, with an expression of deep concentration as he added a fresh brush-load of colour to his canvas. In the background, Anna could see a glimpse of one of the floaty-skirted women and the corner of someone's easel.

'And I found this little sketchbook, look.' Tansy held it up to show them. Anna's grandfather had a similar pocket sketchbook, which he carried everywhere. The first pages of Robert's sketchbook were crammed with tiny vigorous drawings: a slack-jawed man sleeping on the Tube, a flower stall in a street market, a side view of a woman at a bar. It was a beguiling visual diary of a particular time in Robert's life.

Isadora merely glanced at the first few pages before resuming her search for Robert's letter, but Anna kept flicking through. Robert's art holiday must have inspired him because he'd drawn in his miniature sketchbook every day for almost six months. The last picture, dated May 2006, was a self-portrait, in which a stiffly smiling Robert in his business suit, was looking into a mirror at a shabby homeless man who was also Robert. After that, there were only blank pages.

Isadora found the box file in a bookcase next to an elaborate marble fireplace. She lifted it up and placed it on Robert's desk. 'I feel as if we're opening Pandora's box.' She gave a nervous laugh. 'Though did you know it was originally a jar that held all the evils of the world, not a box? I suppose Pandora's jar doesn't sound so ominous?'

Tansy was already investigating the contents. Her expression changed. 'Oh shit. She handed Isadora a cream-coloured envelope addressed in a familiar flawless longhand.

139

Isadora said very quietly, 'So there was something evil in here after all.' With an expression of extreme distaste, she laid it aside unopened.

'Don't you want to know what it says?' Tansy asked.

'No,' Isadora said with emphasis. 'I don't and I shall burn the ghastly thing the first chance I get.'

Underneath the letter was a large manila envelope. Isadora cautiously opened it, sliding out a pile of grainy photocopies. Anna looked over her shoulder. 'That looks like it's from Hetty's diary.' Hetty's chaotic scribble was unmistakable.

Tansy scanned the first entry. 'These aren't the same as your ones, Isadora. These are new.'

'Oh, this is just unbearable!' Isadora said angrily. 'Who is *sending* these things? And *why*?'

Under the envelope, they found more copies of the same pictures of the Oxford Six that Anna had seen in Isadora's kitchen: everyone posed around or inside Piers's lovingly maintained black cab, the survivors' picture after the May Ball, with Isadora and Hetty in 1920s-style evening gowns, a picture of a young Isadora in a punt wearing a fluffy sweater that made Anna itch just looking at it. Tansy carefully took the photographs from the file and laid them out on Robert's desk the way Anna had once seen her lay out tarot cards, then glanced into the now almost empty file in case there was anything she'd missed. 'There's a folder.' Tansy gently shook out the contents on to Robert's desk alongside the photographs.

'Oh, Isadora,' she said softly.

The desk was covered with pictures of a young Isadora Salzman. There were sketches on paper napkins, one from the Randolph Hotel, pages torn from a school exercise book, one sketch dated June 1992 had been ripped out of a Filofax. Clearly drawn from memory, it was an exquisitely tender drawing of a teenage Isadora smiling at someone the viewer couldn't see. There was an electric silence in which Anna saw the colour drain from Isadora's face.

Out of all this morning's discoveries – Robert's dire financial situation, the second anonymous letter, the new extracts from Hetty's diary – Isadora seemed most overcome by the drawings. 'I didn't know,' she said, stricken. Her hand went to her face. 'I never caught him drawing me. I never saw him draw anyone. Until you found that little sketchbook, Tansy, I didn't know he could.'

'You must have known he had feelings for you?' Anna said.

Isadora shook her head. 'No.' She unconsciously traced along her cheekbone with the back of her hand, as if seeking for the young woman she had been. 'I thought he was in love with Catherine at one time, but I never dreamed . . .' her voice trailed off.

'This was at the bottom of the file.' Anna handed a folded piece of paper to Isadora. 'I think this is your letter.'

Isadora made no attempt to read it. She looked completely numb.

Tansy abruptly sat down in the desk chair. 'Isadora, I'm sorry, but you've *got* to tell us what happened to you all back then.'

141

Isadora's eyes were wide with dread. 'I will, darling, I promise.'

'*When*, though?' Tansy insisted. 'I know you guys all made some kind of creepy vow of silence, but if you don't tell someone very soon this is seriously going to make you ill.'

'I *know*!' Isadora almost sobbed. 'And I am going to tell you! I want to. I *need* to.' In her distress, she tugged on a wiry strand of her hair as if she wanted to rip it out. 'But I simply can't speak about those things here in – in Robert's house.' Her gaze was pulled back to the napkin where Robert had secretly sketched her face the first time he'd seen her. Then Isadora buried her face in her hands and wept.

Eleven

1 February, 1966

I've been back at Lady Margaret Hall now for almost a fortnight, but what with fighting off a bout of bronchitis, ploughing my way through my terrifying reading list, staying up at nights writing essays, alternating with bleary-eyed nights embroidering over the moth holes in my Persian carpet coat, I've had hardly any time left over to write in my diary.

I've just had to stop writing to put on my pyjamas, an outgrown pair of Felix's, which Maeve kindly passed on. They're striped blue-and-cream flannel and so soft and warm I was actually purring with pleasure to myself as I put them on! Now I'm sitting up in bed with a mug of black coffee to help keep me awake while I quickly describe my intriguing evening at the Randolph while it's still reasonably fresh in my memory.

I'd imagined that I'd be meeting the others in the hotel bar, but when I arrived there was a message waiting at reception, directing me to one of the upstairs suites, which rather revived my earlier anxieties about sex clubs. But when I arrived outside I was relieved to hear the civilized clink of cutlery coming from inside. I knocked and Tallis himself let me in. He cracked some joke about me always being late for everything then he gripped my wrist just a little too hard as he whispered, 'You are not to speak about any of your previous assignments with these people, Hetty, understand? The people you're about to meet may be working for my department but they are not your confidants and to treat them as such would be a dangerous mistake.'

Then he let go of my wrist and I rubbed it a little ostentatiously, and he said, 'Sorry Hetty, my love, I didn't mean to get so intense but a lot is riding on this – for me but most of all for the British government.' In a louder voice he said, 'Come in and meet the others.' He ushered me in to the room, saying, 'Everybody this is Hetty—' I had the feeling he was about to tell them my full name and I really didn't want to go into all of that with people I would probably never meet again so I said quickly, 'Just Hetty is fine.'

There were five of them, awkwardly dispersed

around the room, looking as confused as I felt. One of the boys, a typical ex-Etonian, if ever I saw one, seemed actively hostile. One of the other girls I recognized as another second year from LMH and I saw from her startled expression that she recognized me. This was the first time I'd really understood that Tallis had at least five other young protégées apart from me. It was a rather humbling moment – for all of us, I suspect. Until now we'd probably each assumed that we were special in some way, that Tallis had identified some unique quality or skill that only we could offer . . . Now, without a word of explanation, he was showing us – what? That each of us was disposable? That he had plenty more where we came from?

Despite a rather unpromising beginning, my encounter with Tallis's other 'little spies-in-training', as Robert ironically named us, turned out to be unexpectedly diverting! Tallis had arranged the most delicious lunch and I stuffed myself like an absolute pig. I honestly thought my buttons would pop right off!

While we ate, Tallis explained why he'd called us together. It was quite a story. His people (Tallis always refers to his colleagues as 'his people') had discovered that the son of a minor aristocrat, currently up at Balliol, had become suspiciously embroiled with a girl from Soviet Russia who happens to be a friend of the Russian ambassador's family. They must have been madly determined to meet, since Tallis said that Tatiana (that's the girl's name) was under constant surveillance by the KGB, on the one hand, and Tallis's bunch, on the other. We'd all been called together because Tallis had learned that Tatiana was going to be invited to a winter ball at Blenheim Palace which was being held early in the Hilary Term to celebrate the young aristo's twenty-first.

Tallis said his people were concerned that this occasion might be exploited by the Soviets in some way, possibly for the passing of sensitive information, or for some sinister eventuality that his department hadn't yet envisaged. Our job was to attend the ball, as ourselves, partnered by other members of the group. 'And do what?' drawled the ex-Etonian whose name, I discovered, was Robert Keane.

'Blend in,' Tallis said crisply. 'Follow them, be my eyes and ears.'

'And report back the instant Tatiana's magic coach reverts to a pumpkin?' Robert suggested with a sneer.

Tallis gave him a look so withering that Robert actually flushed dark red. 'The Soviet threat is not a joke, Robert. It's most certainly not a fairy tale. Perhaps you'd rather I chose someone else for the job?'

Robert subsided sulkily in his chair. He was turning out to be almost as tedious as I'd feared, though I took to the others almost at once. Catherine Hetherington, the other girl from LMH, is far livelier in person than she'd seemed from a distance with her rather worthy-looking friends. As for James Lowell, he's just too shockingly beautiful for words! Several times I caught myself shamelessly imagining what he'd look like without his clothes. (In fact, as I quickly

145

and naughtily discovered, and as so very rarely happens in my experience, the reality was far, far lovelier than my imaginings!) The really sweet thing is he's completely unaware of how devastatingly handsome he is! I liked Piers Courtenay enormously too. He had everyone in stitches, even Robert.

The shy, slightly prickly and distinctly intriguing Isadora I've left till last; partly because I still don't know quite what to think of her except that, in direct contravention of Tallis's warnings, I have made up my mind to get to know her better. First, Isadora is ridiculously young, still just a school girl really. She told me with a slightly defiant toss of her head that she'd just turned seventeen. Also I'll admit that when I first set eyes on her, with that frizzy cloud of hair, and wearing a strange lumpy skirt with a hideous sweater that probably crackles with static every time she takes it on or off, I couldn't imagine what Tallis was thinking of, involving her in his little espionage games. And then I watched her as she was talking to Tallis and I quickly realized that he knows exactly what he's doing. For one thing, she's bright, ferociously bright, and for another, hidden beneath those lumpy clothes, I sense a fiery femme fatale longing to break free!

I decided there and then that I would be the perfect person to help bring about this magical transformation. It was immediately obvious that Isadora was terrified at the very idea of going to the ball. I asked her if she had a suitable dress, and she said (another defiant head toss) that she had, but having seen her day clothes I am deeply suspicious. I feel horribly guilty, because I'd promised her there and then that I'd go over to Somerville College (imagine getting a scholarship to Somerville when you're only sixteen!) in the first week of term to embark on my big transformation project. But what with bronchitis and struggling to keep up with course work, I've hardly had time to breathe.

6 February, 1966

I've finally met up with Isadora. We almost literally bumped into each other in the pouring rain outside the Bodleian and went into the nearest cafe to warm ourselves up over hot chocolate. I explained why I hadn't been round to see her and she said perfectly seriously, 'I simply assumed you'd decided that I was such a hopeless case that you'd very sensibly abandoned me!' And she gave one of her wonderful laughs. With less than a week to go before the ball, Isadora said she was on the verge of a nervous breakdown. I tried my best to calm her down. I told her that I have eight sisters of varying ages and am therefore an expert on absolutely everything to do with girls' hair and make-up. What I didn't say is that I am determined to get a look inside Isadora's wardrobe, as soon as is feasible, and if I detect so much as a hint of mud-coloured nylon in there I shall march her straight back to LMH and make her try on one of my stolen ball dresses . . .

As it turned out, Isadora voluntarily showed me her ball dress – just wordlessly produced this hideous thing, and held it out to me for my approval. 'As you see I do have a dress to wear for the ball,' she said rather too brightly. 'My mother got it from the bargain rail in Barkers. Will it do, do you think?' Her expression said that she knew all too well that it wouldn't, but she couldn't quite bear to spurn her mother's hideous offering outright.

I pretended to give it my serious consideration. 'I'm not sure if it would be right for this particular ball,' I said, choosing my words with care. 'But if you don't mind coming back to my room, I think I just might have a dress that would suit you perfectly.'

When Isadora saw herself in the 1920s ball gown, which once belonged to Daddy's mama, she almost cried, and I have to confess I very nearly cried myself! 'I look quite lovely,' she said in an awed voice. 'I don't look like me at all.'

'It does look like you,' I told her fiercely. 'It looks like the real you! I mean it, Isadora! No more brown nylon! Even if I have to take you out shoplifting!'

After Isadora had put her own clothes back on, I made coffee and offered her a cigarette. I'd pinched several packets of Gauloises from Lalla. Isadora thanked me and took one but made no attempt to smoke it. Still holding her unlit cigarette she wandered around my room looking at all the little things I've brought from home, not even trying to disguise the fact that she was looking. Isadora's still quite young like that. All at once she stopped in front of the little pastel drawing Daddy did of me when I was six or seven, and which I take with me everywhere. 'This looks like a Francis Vallier,' she said, surprised. I nodded, thinking, Oh, fuck it, here we go again! 'Francis Vallier is my father,' I said, bracing myself for gushing comments about how thrilling it must be to have such an amazingly gifted man for your dad, la, la, la, because that's what everyone always says. But Isadora didn't say anything. I handed her a mug of coffee, and she curled up in my spare arm chair looking sternly thoughtful and about twelve years old. Her continued silence was beginning to make me quite uncomfortable, so I said, 'So how do you feel about having James as your partner for the ball?' (Tallis had told us who our partners were to be, before we left the Randolph.)

'Fine,' she said absently. 'He's really nice.'

'And how long have you known Tallis?' This was really an indirect way of asking, 'And what do you know about him?'

'About three weeks into my first term, I think.' She frowned. 'It seems such a long time ago now. Time seems to work differently at Oxford,' she added with a laugh. 'I fit ten million more things in a day than I'd have even imagined possible at home!'

'Tallis is outrageous fun, isn't he?'

I'm almost sure Isadora blushed as she said, 'Yes.' Then she let out a charming hoot of laughter. 'It's all nonsense, though, isn't it? I pretend to take it seriously, but it's just a game.

I'm sure Tallis doesn't really believe in it either.'

I was almost certain these weren't Isadora's real feelings. Perhaps she didn't actually know what those were? She was playing it cool, pretending she could stop Tallis's 'game' any time she wanted, but secretly loving the glamour and intrigue that he manages to generate wherever he goes.

'It's quite a thrilling game though,' I said, thinking of my most recent assignment.

Isadora suddenly looked up at me with her solemn brown eyes. 'I've never smoked before,' she confessed. 'Promise not to laugh if I have a choking fit?'

I lit her cigarette and she took a tiny suspicious puff but somehow managed not to cough. Squinting at me through the smoke, she said abruptly, 'My parents know quite a few brilliant artists. Writers, painters, you know. However wonderful they are, they aren't always very easy people to live with, are they?'

And that's when I knew we'd become real friends.

20 May, 1966

I have a new and deeply troubling worry but I daren't write about it here. If I actually saw the words written down I think I might completely fall apart. I have never felt so alone in all my life.

5 November, 1966

The London train is just pulling out of the station. It's a raw lightless November day like that poem

150

I once had to learn at school. 'No sun – no moon! No morn – no noon – No dawn – no dusk – no proper time of day.' A depressing sort of day to be beginning a thrilling new life with the man I love and yet, incredibly, that's what I'm doing – and, oh, the utter RELIEF to be cutting my final ties with the old life! To be finished (after this one last assignment) with Tallis for good. Why did I ever let myself be drawn in to his web of never-ending lies? He's a conman. He's worse than a conman. He's a monster.

I am so lucky that I found S. He's the exact opposite of Tallis in every way. Simple goodness just shines out of him. All he wants is to make me happy and I am! He's promised that he is going to make everything right and I truly believe him. I do.

I just wish I hadn't done quite so many shameful things. At the time, or most of the time anyway, they didn't seem so very shameful, but when I think about them now, I feel disgusted with myself, especially at the part I played in helping Tallis to control A. I'm quite scared at what Tallis might do to him. But I can't think about that now. I've told Tallis it's over. I'm making a clean break, a fresh start.

I can't help feeling sad at leaving my friends. I behaved so badly to James. But how could I tell him that I only ever slept with him that one time because, in that moment, he was so deliciously and irresistibly lovely that I just had to take him to bed? Because to James, us going to bed with each other wasn't just a moment, it was some huge declaration of eternal love. He looked

151

so strange yesterday when I told him I was giving up on my degree and leaving Oxford and England for ever. I thought James had finally accepted that we could only ever be friends. But after I'd told him that I was going to America to make a new life with S., he went so quiet, so still, as if he'd pulled all his emotions deep inside where nobody could see. He looked like a badly treated dog that had lost its very last hope of kindness. I really hated and despised myself for putting that look on his face.

I feel almost as bad about Isadora. She's the heart's friend I always dreamed of having and I've so longed to take her into my confidence. There have been so many times when I've almost blurted out what happened to me over the summer. But each time, when it came to it, I simply couldn't. Isadora's still so young and we've led such different lives, and – this is going to sound terribly old-fashioned – she's still so unspoiled. And I can't help knowing how much she admires and looks up to me. I couldn't bear to see the disappointment in her face when she found out the sordid truth. I wish I hadn't made that big scene about Tallis last night. Isadora may be young but she's not a fool. I should have just trusted her to extricate herself in her own good time.

I'm so grateful to S. for giving me the chance to leave all my mistakes behind me, to shed the old wild out-of-control Hetty and make a fresh start as his wife. Oh, my God, I'm going to be a wife! I'm going to be a proper grown-up wife!

Twelve

It was eight thirty in the morning and Anna was unsuccessfully pretending to be still fast asleep. The reproachful sounds from Bonnie's basket were so soft as to be nearly subliminal, but behind her closed eyelids, Anna could feel her White Shepherd's brown-eyed stare boring into her brain. It was three days before Christmas. She was officially on holiday now and had been looking forward to a luxurious lie-in. Unfortunately Bonnie had a sixth sense that alerted her the moment her human made that invisible transition from sleeping to waking. Anna sat up, running her hands through sleep-dishevelled hair. Bonnie gave a tentative but distinctly hopeful wag of her tail. 'OK, OK, you big bully,' Anna said, yawning.

She gave a quick despairing look around her unfinished bedroom with the stack of still unpacked boxes that she'd only partially managed to hide behind a decorative wooden screen. 'I'll get around to it,' she told Bonnie. 'Maybe in the new year?'

Her mobile rang. Anna blearily peered at the screen and saw Jake's name pop up.

'Hi,' she said. 'What are you up to today?'

'I was just about to ask you the same question!' Jake sounded disgustingly wide awake. 'I wondered if you'd like to go to a German market with me this afternoon?'

153

Anna yawned and stretched, still fuddled with sleep. 'You want us to fly out to Germany? Today?'

Jake sounded amused. 'We could do that if you want! But I was thinking more of the German market in Oxford. Seeing as I'm only up the road,' he added.

She suddenly realized what he was telling her. 'You're in Oxford!' Jake wasn't supposed to arrive until Christmas Eve.

'I got here late last night.'

After weeks of waiting, she was finally going to get to spend some time with him. She felt a familiar mix of elation and panic. 'Where are you staying?'

'It's more like camping,' Jake said. 'At Mimi's house,' he explained just as she was picturing him shivering in a tent. 'So will you go with me, or would it be too same-old, seeing as it's practically on your doorstep?'

'I've never been,' Anna confessed. 'It's like taking tours of Oxford colleges. You only go if you have visitors, or little children,' she added, remembering Kirsty describing her little boy's surprised delight at seeing Broad Street transformed with brightly coloured stalls. 'I'll walk round the market with you for a while,' she said, 'but then I've promised to go and see someone from work.' Kirsty had invited Anna over to her new place to swap Christmas gifts.

'Would you like to meet up with me later for dinner?'

'Jake, I'm so sorry, I can't.' If it had been anything else she'd have cancelled in a

154

nanosecond. But tonight's supper with Isadora was not negotiable. She and Tansy had worked too hard to make it happen.

'Hey, don't apologize,' Jake said. 'You didn't know I was going to be here.'

'It's just that Tansy and I have a dinner date with Isadora.' Anna was doing some quick thinking. Isadora knew and liked Jake. Besides it might be a good thing to have him along on this particular night. 'Why don't I ask if I could bring you? It's not going to be anything fancy, just soup and bread, then Isadora's going to tell us about her friend who got murdered in the sixties.'

After a pause, Jake said wryly, 'You Oxford girls really know how to show a guy a good time. Will there be autopsy photos?' He was referring to their first, somewhat surreal, dinner together at Isadora's house.

She laughed. 'I sincerely hope not! Seriously, don't feel you have to come, but we've been trying to get her to talk about it ever since she got that anonymous letter.'

'Isadora's been getting anonymous letters?'

'Just the one,' said Anna. 'I'll fill you in when I see you.'

That afternoon, well-wrapped up against the cold, she took the bus into town. She'd arranged to meet Jake at the Martyrs Memorial, a useful, if not terribly cheerful, landmark for new visitors to the city. She arrived to find him already waiting at the bottom of the steps. Above the rooftops the last of the sunset was fading in colours of arctic green and rose. Midwinter afternoons in Oxford had always held a magical quality for Anna. The addition of smoky violet twilight and twinkling lights to this medieval city made her feel that anything was possible; a child could be born in a manger, a former marine just might one day come to see her as more than a friend.

She saw Jake's eyes light up as he caught sight of her. He came forward to greet her, stooping to kiss her cheek. He smelled of soap and clean linen and some subtle and elusive scent that was just Jake. She felt the winter chill on his skin and on his leather jacket. 'This city gets more beautiful every time I come,' he said. 'What time do you have to be at your friend's?'

'I said I'd be there around six, before she puts her little boy to bed.' Kirsty had wanted Anna to meet Charlie. Anna was sure that Kirsty would be thrilled if Jake had tagged along, but didn't feel up to the cross-examination that would inevitably follow.

'Do they sell door wreaths at German markets?' Anna asked as they set off walking.

Jake smiled. 'You'll be spoiled for choice,' he promised.

Each time they spoke their warm breath made little puffs of white. By the time they'd reached Broad Street, Anna's cheeks were tingling from the cold.

Against the backdrop of descending twilight, the Christmas market was a dazzle of fairy lights and festive colour. Somewhere a brass band was playing carols. They walked past stalls hung with handmade Christmas ornaments and giant gingerbread cookies iced with Christmas greetings. The air smelled of spice, sugar and chocolate.

Jake stopped at a stall selling *glühwein*. 'Shall we get some to warm us up?'

She was surprised. 'I thought you didn't drink.'

'I make an exception for *glühwein*,' he said with a grin. Despite the cold, he wasn't wearing a scarf. Maybe he didn't own one? She could buy him a woollen scarf for Christmas; there was still time.

Warming their hands around their plastic beakers of spiced red wine, she and Jake walked from stall to stall, pausing to look at hand-carved nativity scenes and Christmas-themed tea-light holders. One stall was selling beautifully made wooden toys. Anna was tempted to buy a tiny wooden tractor for Charlie, then decided that a little boy who had mastered his mother's iPad would probably be confused by any toy that didn't emit electronic noises or flashing lights. Besides she already had a gift-wrapped present for Charlie in her bag.

Glancing up, she caught Jake looking at the Christmas lights suspended above their heads, the glittering angels, stars and those puzzling celestial umbrellas. 'I know what you're thinking,' she said. 'How come nobody ever told me there were flying umbrellas present at the Nativity?'

'You're right, I was thinking that!' he said laughing. 'Maybe you could tell me your more esoteric Christmas story some time?'

Among the stalls selling *lebkuchen* and

157

traditional Christmas decorations, there was a scattering of Oxford tradespeople selling local crafts and produce. They stopped at one stall for Anna to try on some pretty felted wool hats until she suddenly became self-conscious. 'I'm really not a hat person,' she insisted.

'I'd be inclined to disagree with you about that,' he told her.

It was Anna who spotted the stand offering beautifully packaged gins from a local micro-distillery. She went over to investigate, thinking she might buy a bottle for Isadora. 'I might buy a bottle myself,' Jake said when he saw the dizzying array of gins on offer.

'So you make an exception for *glühwein* and gin,' Anna said. 'Not to forget the occasional beer that you trained your dog to fetch you and your buddies from the fridge.'

He laughed. 'I can't put anything past you girl detectives! I'm not a drinking man's drinker is all,' he explained. 'But I've hung out with enough British expats that I've learned to enjoy an occasional gin and tonic – and these gins look like works of art.'

'Or magic potions,' Anna suggested. She read out some of the ingredients. 'Blackberries, heather, wild roses . . .'

The stallholder offered them thimble-sized samples to try but Jake said all he'd be able to taste was the *glühwein*. 'I like the sound of this one though,' he said hopefully. 'Juniper, apple and elderflower with a subtle dash of citrus.'

'Sorry, mate, I've just sold the last one of those,' said the stallholder. 'But we make and sell all these gins in the Hollybush just off Brasenose Lane.'

'Thanks, man, I shall make sure to remember that the next time I come,' Jake told him, smiling. His calm assumption that Anna and Oxford were now an accepted part of his life made her feel both happy and flustered. He suddenly grabbed hold of her hand, pulling her through the crowd. 'Look, there are your wreaths!'

The stall smelled like a winter forest. Dressed in an embroidered dirndl under a warm woollen jacket, the stallholder looked as if she'd just arrived from the mountains of Bavaria. She patiently fetched down wreath after wreath for them to examine. Jake was right, Anna was spoiled for choice. Eventually she chose one for Kirsty's door, and then Jake bought Anna's second favourite for Anna's house. 'I could see you didn't want to leave that one behind.'

Anna felt her breathing quicken as she realised that there was nowhere else she'd rather be. Usually her mind raced ahead or was helplessly sucked back into the past. But in this moment, she was just *here* – in the bitter cold, breathing in the pine forest smell of the wreath stall, returning Jake's smile.

Then he said, 'So, tell me, have you been back in touch with Tim?' and she felt an almost physical jerk as all her old anxieties came swarming back again. She wanted to hold on to the magic of being in the moment but she could hear herself instantly becoming defensive.

'Not yet. I have – reservations. It's not that I think he's going to sell me to the tabloids. I just

159

have this feeling he's not being quite straight with me.'

'So you're completely ignoring him and hoping it will all just go away?'

'I'm guessing that doesn't seem like a very sophisticated strategy to a military man?' Anna was trying to keep her tone light.

Jake studied her face for a moment. 'Would you rather talk about this another time?'

She'd rather not talk about it at all, but she just nodded, relieved to be let off the hook.

He glanced at his watch. 'We've still got twenty minutes before you go see your friend. Let's get a cup of coffee somewhere out of this cold and you can fill me in on what's been happening to Isadora.'

Charlie was already in his pyjamas by the time Anna reached Kirsty's. Kirsty had warned her that her little boy might be shy, but he immediately took Anna's hand and led her to their Christmas tree, proudly pointing out the decorations he'd made at nursery. Anna waited until Kirsty's little boy was absorbed in watching his favourite DVD, before surreptitiously handing over her present for him. After careful consultation with Kirsty, Anna had bought Charlie a tiny Captain America costume. 'He'll be *thrilled*,' Kirsty said, keeping her voice low. 'He is obsessed with the Marvelverse.'

'And this is for you.' Anna produced Kirsty's wreath from its tissue wrappings.

'Oh, my God, Anna, that's so beautiful! I was longing for one of those but I'd already spent too much on Christmas.'

'It's not really a present,' Anna said. 'It's just to mark your and Charlie's first Christmas in your new home – which looks lovely by the way.'

'It still feels like a miracle,' Kirsty said. 'We both love it here, don't we, Charlie?'

Charlie briefly turned around from the TV. 'And I made those paper chains with my mum,' he told Anna, before plugging his thumb back into his mouth.

'Can you stay and have a hot drink and a mince pie?' Kirsty asked hopefully. 'Paul's coming over. I know he'd like to see you.'

'I'd love to, thanks.' Anna didn't have to be at Isadora's until seven thirty. Jake had gone off to do some last-minute Christmas shopping. 'I go to all these exotic locations,' he'd said, a little wistfully, 'but I never get to see anything except the inside of hotels and airports.'

'So what have you been up to?' Kirsty said. 'Whatever it is, it's doing you good. You look absolutely glowing!'

'I think that's probably just the cold.' Anna laughed to cover the flash of fear that had come out of nowhere. It seemed too dangerous somehow to name her happiness out loud in case some malign eavesdropping spirit overheard. Though she was perfectly capable of hexing her own happiness, she thought wryly, it's not like she needed any supernatural aid.

'Oh, good, there's Paul!' Kirsty said. 'I'll just go and let him in.' She ran to the door and Anna heard her say, 'You're just in time for mince pies!'

Thirteen

By the time Anna had finally squeezed on to one of the packed buses leaving the city centre, she was already late. Jake was patiently waiting for her at Isadora's gate, a bunch of flowers in one hand and a bottle of Veuve Cliquot in the other. 'I forgot to factor in Christmas shoppers,' she said apologetically. 'You should have just knocked and gone in. You must be freezing.'

'Do you think these flowers are OK?' he asked anxiously. 'I thought they looked like Isadora but now I'm not so sure.' The mix of purple hellebores and scented white viburnum with winter berries and evergreens was absolutely Isadora, Anna thought. 'You were right on both counts,' she told him.

He laughed. 'Funnily enough, I felt quite confident about the champagne.'

They started walking up to the house just as Isadora came out. 'What are you two doing out here in the cold?' She was wearing a Japanese-style jacket in grey silk over baggy grey silk trousers. A pair of long dangling earrings made of very solid looking silver swung from her earlobes. She had dressed up for the occasion, Anna thought, touched. She had dressed up for Hetty.

'It's lovely to see you again, Jake!' Isadora said. She kissed him on the cheek then swooped on the flowers. 'I hope this fabulous bouquet is for me!'

Jake smilingly held up the bottle. 'This is also for you.'

'How lovely!' A flicker of regret crossed Isadora's face. 'But I think I might have to save it for another happier occasion.'

'It's yours now, ma'am,' he told her. 'That means you get to choose the time and place.'

'Let me take your coats.' Isadora quickly shifted back into hostess mode. 'Everything's almost ready.'

In the kitchen all the windows had misted over with condensation. Tansy stood by the cooker, sprinkling finely chopped herbs into a gently bubbling pot. After the chill outside, Isadora's steamy, fragrant-smelling kitchen felt blessedly warm. Anna and Jake quickly shed their heavy sweaters.

'Hi, you guys!' Tansy turned around, wooden spoon in hand. 'Anna, come and taste this soup for me, tell me if it needs more salt?'

Anna helped herself to a clean spoon, dipped it into the pan and blew softly on the parsley-speckled spoonful. 'This is more like a stew,' she said. 'Are there lentils in this?'

'And white beans, and winter vegetables.'

'It's good,' Anna said, cautiously sampling from her spoon. 'It doesn't need more salt.'

Tansy silently indicated the wire rack where three enormous loaves of freshly baked bread had been set to cool. '*Three* different kinds,' she whispered.

Anna's eyes widened. 'Has she been baking all afternoon?'

'She said it was the only way she could stop herself running over to next door's builders to blag some tobacco!' Tansy whispered back. 'She's putting a brave face on, but she's completely freaked about this. It's good that Jake is here because, let's face it, he's pretty much unshockable.'

'He is,' Anna agreed.

A short time later everyone was seating themselves around Isadora's table. Isadora ladled Tansy's soup into bowls, and Tansy sawed off hunks of bread for everyone.

'I thought I should let you all eat first and then talk,' Isadora said, a little awkwardly. 'Certainly my mother would have insisted. But then I'd probably keep thinking of more reasons to put this off, so if you don't object, I'm just going to begin before I lose my nerve and hope not to spoil everyone's appetites. I'm rather regretting not opening that champagne,' she told Jake with a nervous laugh.

She closed her eyes, as if summoning her resources. 'I'm not sure exactly where to start. I don't know how much any of you know about the Cold War?'

'Just what you've told us,' Tansy said.

'Ditto,' said Anna.

'A little,' Jake said. Everyone turned to look at him. 'As well as serving in the armed forces, I've read a lot of John le Carré!' he explained with a grin. 'The Cold War was a forty-year standoff between the West and the Soviet bloc. It began after the end of the Second World War and lasted until the dissolution of the Soviet

164

Union in the early nineties, wasn't it?' he asked Isadora.

'So it was called a "cold war" because they didn't fight any actual battles?' Tansy said.

'After the invention of the atomic bomb, all the rules of military engagement changed,' Jake said. 'The bomb made the prospect of another world war way, *way* too scary to contemplate.'

'Both sides were terrified that the other side had the ability to decimate them in a nuclear war,' Isadora said. 'Meanwhile, each side continually tried to best the other in every way they could short of pressing that appalling button.' She took a sip from her water glass. 'The Cold War was a time of heightened international tension and suspicion and, at times, outright paranoia. This led to governments building up their own secret spy networks so they could find out what the other side was doing.'

Jake nodded. 'But instead of allaying governments' fears, it actually generated a kind of paranoia feedback loop.'

'That's it exactly,' Isadora said. 'All these covert intelligence activities only intensified everyone's panic, further complicated by the fact that agents occasionally switched sides, or played both sides off against each other, or just had their own private and peculiar little agendas.' She abruptly moved her untouched soup bowl to one side. 'I should have listened to my mother. I don't know why I thought I'd be able to eat.'

'I'll heat some up for you later,' Tansy said.

'I can always eat unless I'm actually under fire,' Jake said, 'and sometimes even then!'

165

'This does feel a little like being under fire.' Isadora tucked back a strand of hair that had entangled itself with an earring. She seemed to be inwardly bracing herself before she continued. 'So now we finally come on to my very small and inglorious part in the Cold War. I think it's common knowledge now that during the sixties, students at both Oxford and Cambridge were approached by intelligence agencies to spy for them.

'As Tansy and Anna know, at first I was naive enough to imagine that I was the only student Tallis had chosen to help avert a third world war. Tallis was the man who approached me,' Isadora added for Jake's benefit. She gave a short laugh. 'In fact, my missions were mostly pretty mundane. I was just to infiltrate any student groups that Tallis's people regarded as suspiciously radical. There was also a Marxist group in the town that some students were involved in. I went to meetings and then I dropped off my reports in a dead-letter box. I have to say, the first few times that part of things felt enormously exciting!' For a moment, Isadora's eyes shone at the memory. 'I probably shouldn't say that, should I?' she added quickly. 'But it's true. Of course, later I found out that Tallis had also been sending the others along to monitor these groups. He'd been rotating us, it turned out.'

'Why would he do that?' Anna said.

Isadora shrugged. 'Because he didn't trust any one person to do the job, or he didn't want us to arouse undue suspicion? Or maybe he just enjoyed the idea of his six protégées obliviously crossing each other's paths until he decided it was time for us to meet.'

'So who was Tallis working for? MI5?' Jake asked.

Isadora shook her head. 'We never knew. I think, deep down, we all had inklings that Tallis was playing some long game of his own, but he had this extraordinary ability – a *compulsion*, perhaps – to make people believe him, and so, ridiculous as it seems to me now, we did! Nowadays he'd probably be diagnosed as some kind of sociopath.'

Anna remembered the elegant-looking man in the wheelchair who may or may not have been Tallis. She pictured him ironically tipping his hat, almost insisting on being acknowledged, refusing to be some anonymous old bloke in a wheelchair.

Isadora drank some more water. 'I can't entirely hate Tallis.' Her voice became wistful. 'All those wonderful months with Hetty and the others I owe entirely to him. But then, sometimes, when I can't sleep at night, I wonder, was it all smoke and mirrors? Was *all* of it just lies?' She set down her glass. 'You've probably all seen *Midsummer Night's Dream*?'

She gave them a forlorn smile. 'That's what those months were like for me, a golden magical dream, and yet all the time Tallis was subtly manipulating us behind the scenes just like Puck in the *Dream*, making us fall in love with the wrong person, or jump at horrors that weren't actually there, or – far worse, making us blind to horrors that were!' Isadora brushed her hand

167

across her eyes as if sticky wisps of her handler's sorcery still lingered. She gave one of her dark hoots of laughter. 'And that *ridiculous* contrivance of six young strangers attending the same ball to intercept a spy! Yet Tallis made it so plausible – so *thrilling*,' she added, shamefaced.

'You never told us what happened at the ball,' Tansy said. 'Did your minor aristocrat actually try to pass information?'

'Nothing happened at the ball.' Isadora suddenly sounded bitter. 'Nothing was ever going to happen. I think Tallis was just experimenting on us, his little intellectual lab rats, seeing how deeply he could draw us into his cold-war narrative.' Her expression softened slightly. 'We were all *deeply* disappointed that nothing happened at Blenheim Palace,' she admitted. 'After all of Tallis's elaborate preparations, we'd failed in our first big mission. But then after the ball, as the sun was rising and we were about to drive back to Oxford, this man dressed as a waiter emerged from some trees and beckoned us to follow him deeper into the palace grounds. Well, he could have been anyone! He could have been taking us to our deaths! But I suppose we were all a little drunk as well as under this – this *bewitchment* that Tallis had laid on us, and so we followed him like lambs in our finery, and found a glorious champagne breakfast laid out for us in this beautiful little gazebo, all strung with lanterns. There was even a heater! Tallis had arranged it for us. Well, after that, it was almost inevitable that we'd all become friends – as he had presumably calculated.'

168

'You were already friends with Hetty,' Tansy reminded her.

Isadora got up from the table, coming back with her envelope of photos. She smiled at Tansy. 'Yes, Hetty took me *extremely* firmly under her wing from the start! But after that night the rest of us began meeting together, in cafes and parks, in punts on the river, in each other's rooms.' Isadora fanned the photographs out on the table to show Jake and Tansy. 'We went out in Piers's car to the Trout at Wolvercote. We went to London to see bizarre foreign art films. We drove to Stratford and saw David Warner's *Hamlet*, one of the best performances I've seen before or since.'

'But you were all still going along to the meetings?' Anna said.

Isadora nodded. 'We went together and separately. It was the – I won't say "unquestioned" but *unchallenged* – basis of our friendship, that we were somehow helping Tallis to save the world. It was part of what made us so special, so golden – like fairy coinage that might disappear if we examined it too closely.'

Nothing gold can stay, Anna thought.

'Tell us about Hetty,' Tansy said. 'Tell us what happened.'

Isadora touched the photo of Hetty Vallier. 'Hetty was right at the thrilling golden centre of it all. And then, at some point – I can't tell you when – everything must have changed. But to my shame it's only all these years afterwards that I realize this must be what had happened. It's so easy to lose sight of what is happening to the

169

people you love most. You get distracted by your own concerns, so that you're looking the wrong way just when you should be paying attention – maybe the person even *wants* you to look the wrong way – but of course that doesn't let one off the hook.' Her eyes were dark with pain.

'Hetty looks like a very special person,' Jake said.

'Doesn't she?' Tansy said. 'She reminds me a little bit of Marianne Faithful when she was young and gorgeous!'

Now that Tansy had pointed it out Anna could see a striking resemblance between Hetty and the former convent school girl who had hung out with the Rolling Stones and recorded songs filled with a bittersweet loss that she was officially too young to feel. Hetty's eyes held that same bittersweet look.

'Hetty was a sixties' girl before they were invented,' Isadora said. 'She chopped her skirts short, when other girl undergraduates were still wearing twinsets and pearls.'

'You said men found her irresistible,' Anna said. 'Did Tallis?' She'd been wondering about the handler's relationship with the girls in Isadora's group.

Isadora's eyes clouded. 'I suspect that Tallis recognized very early on that Hetty had qualities that could be useful to him.'

'She was sexy,' Tansy suggested.

'Extremely sexy, also beguiling, charming and unashamedly upper-middle class – a combination that men often find extremely seductive. Some weekends she'd take off on mysterious jaunts to

London. She often returned with money, which she said her stepmother had given her to help pay her bills, but then she'd use it to buy everyone presents or take us out to dinner. Once she came back with a dress – I think it was a Mary Quant? – which she immediately insisted on giving to Catherine. It was almost as if she couldn't get rid of it soon enough.'

'You think Tallis was, like – *pimping* her out?' Tansy said.

A quiver went through Isadora. 'I think it – was subtler and rather more complex than that. But I suspect there was some element of pimping, yes. The last time I saw Hetty she intimated – sorry!' She briefly covered her face, fighting to keep her emotions under control. 'Sorry,' she said again, trying to smile. 'I'm afraid this is the part that I really can't bear.'

Everybody could see how agonized she was, but nobody asked if she'd rather stop. She had borne these secrets for too long. *Isadora needs us all here to bear witness*, Anna thought. *She needs us to hold her steady while she gets rid of this poison once and for all.*

Isadora poured herself more water, gulping half of it down before she went on.

'One night, Hetty and Robert were scheduled to go to the Marxist group in the town that Tallis's people believed might be fomenting communist dissent. I would have gone with them but Tallis needed me to go to a meeting of the University's Russian Society. I'd been before countless times. It was always completely innocent, just an excuse to discuss Russian films over caviar and vodka,

171

but Tallis said his people needed me to go, so I went.

'When I got back to my room, Hetty was waiting for me. She'd come straight from the town meeting. She seemed extremely upset. That's when I realized that she hadn't been herself for a long time. I tried to think when I'd lost sight of her, the real Hetty, and it scared me that I'd let myself be fobbed off by that bright brittle facsimile for so long. She wasn't bright and brittle that night, however. She seemed angry and frightened.

'She said she had something to tell me. There was a particular person of interest to Tallis's people, someone who was a regular attendee at the town group. She said, "Isadora, it's all lies! It's nothing to do with politics and saving the world, it's all about money." She said this man had been selling British secrets to the Russians for gain and now Tallis was blackmailing him. Hetty said he'd been playing this man along for months and he'd used her to bait the trap. She could see that I didn't believe her. She was pacing my room, smoking and crying. She said, "Don't you understand! This is *dangerous*, Isadora! He's not trying to *stop* these communications with the Soviets. He's fucking *profiting* from them?"'

'What did you say to her?' Jake asked quietly.

Isadora's eyes filled with tears. 'I'm ashamed to say I laughed. I told her she was being ridiculous but underneath I was horrified. Hetty was breaking the rules. We weren't supposed to compare notes about things Tallis asked us to do. But Hetty was doing something far more

172

dangerous. She was questioning Tallis's integrity. She wasn't even questioning it; she was saying outright that he was corrupt!'

Anna had secretly feared this was where Isadora's story was leading. Through her diary entries she felt she had got to know – and like – Hetty Vallier and she felt a cold dread for this generous, quirky but deeply damaged girl.

'That was the last time I saw her alive.' Isadora's voice shook. 'She'd told me that next day she had to go up to London. Tallis needed her to sweeten negotiations with some high-ranking Russian dignitary. She said this was going to be the very last time.'

'*Russian?*' Tansy whispered to Anna. 'I thought—?'

Isadora was still talking. 'Hetty said it had just been a bit of a laugh at first. But she had found out that Tallis had a dark side, a terrible and very frightening side, and now she wanted to stop. She wanted us all to stop before it was too late. She told me that she'd met someone, someone straightforward and kind.'

'The American,' Tansy said.

'She never told me who he was. I didn't know he was American until you girls read that part of her diary. I didn't know she was planning to leave the country and make a life with this farmer or whatever he was. It sounds so unlike Hetty, it makes me wonder if she was having some kind of breakdown.'

Anna thought it sounded like the absolute opposite of a breakdown. She thought Hetty might have finally found some peace and calm, the calm of being loved by someone normal after growing up in that chaotic household where there was always champagne but never enough to eat.

'When did you know?' Jake's voice was quiet.

Isadora swallowed. 'That she'd been murdered? Tallis summoned us to some stuffy little room at the back of the same east Oxford cafe where he'd bought me egg and chips when I first started working for him. That's the place he chose to tell us. Poor James had to go out to be sick.' From Isadora's bleak expression, Anna knew she was suddenly back in that airless room where she'd first heard the inconceivable news that Hetty Vallier, once the centre of everything golden in Isadora's life, was dead. 'He said her body had been found in the Thames wrapped in a monogrammed sheet from a hotel known for dubious assignations. She'd been strangled.' Isadora closed her eyes as if she was still struggling to absorb this part of the story. 'And of course by the next day it was in all the papers.'

'Did Tallis speculate on who might have killed her?' Anna asked.

'He wouldn't talk about it. He wouldn't let us talk about it. He reminded us that we had all signed the Official Secrets Act and could be tried as traitors if we broke our silence. He said he was dissolving our group and we could never meet or talk to each other again. He said if it ever got out, the damage to his department, and to the security of this country, would be incalculable. It was like a – a banishing. He made us leave the cafe one at a time. I was afraid even to look at the others as I left, but when I got outside Robert was still there fumbling with his bike chain. His face was red and puffy as if he'd been crying, but he said, "At least they got their man in the end. That's the one good thing that's come out of this whole fucking mess," and then he got on his bike and rode off.'

'What did he mean by "At least they got their man?"' asked Jake.

Isadora lifted her hands. 'I don't know. I didn't want to know. I didn't understand how this game we'd all been playing had turned into some nightmarish film noir.' She tried to smile. 'So that's what happened. And now Catherine and I are the only people left who remember.'

And Tallis, Anna thought but didn't say.

Isadora began to collect up the soup plates. 'I know we said just soup and bread, but I did poach some pears in red wine. I thought I should give you something at least *slightly* Christmassy after subjecting you to this rather grim trawl through my past.' She was back in hostess mode, Anna saw. She'd promised she'd tell them what had happened, and now that she'd told them, she wanted to stuff all her dark secrets back into whichever mental strong-box she'd been keeping them all this time.

Tansy went to help Isadora with the pears. Anna heard Tansy say, 'Are you sure you don't want me to reheat your soup?'

'Thank you, but I don't seem to have much appetite,' Isadora said.

Jake surreptitiously nudged Anna's shoulder. 'Isadora's dog has a really, *really* disconcerting stare. She's been doing it ever since I got here.'

175

'According to Tansy, Hero's half goblin.' Anna was careful to keep her voice down.

'Are you sure it's just half?' Jake asked with a grin.

Isadora and Tansy came back with the dish of pears and a jug of Chantilly cream. Isadora began serving out the pears into pretty antique-looking bowls. When it was Jake's turn, he said politely, 'Thanks, but I'm not really a big dessert man.'

'You never eat desserts!' Isadora said in horror.

Jake smiled. 'No, ma'am.' He sat back in his chair. Anna could see he was thinking something through. At last he said, 'I'm not sure if it's OK to ask you this, Isadora, but if you and Catherine are the only members of the Oxford Six still left alive, who do you think is sending those anonymous letters?'

Isadora's smile faltered. 'Of course, Anna's told you about that. It *is* rather a puzzle, I agree. But I don't think we need to talk about that now, do we?'

'Catherine probably wrote them! I mean, it's got to be some kind of religious nut and she's the only one in the frame,' Tansy said. 'Anyway, I'm with Isadora. We should be thinking about Christmassy things, not giving any more of our energy to some anonymous letter-writing weirdo.' It was Tansy who'd been so insistent that Isadora should tell them about Hetty. Now she seemed upset and slightly scared at what they'd unleashed.

'With respect, I disagree.' Jake was polite but firm. 'I think we need to get to the bottom of it.'

At that moment Anna could see the calm pragmatic soldier he'd been. Jake saw a problem that needed solving, and he was offering to help.

Isadora slammed her fist down on the table, rattling the crockery and water glasses. Hero fled to her basket. 'I don't *want* to get to the bottom of it!' Isadora almost shouted. 'I am *terrified* of getting to the bottom of it! I feel *so* desperately guilty, Jake – I am afraid it will *destroy* me!'

'What in the world do you have to feel guilty about?' Though Jake's expression didn't change, his southern intonation had become more pronounced, the only sign that his emotions were touched.

'Because Hetty tried to warn me, and I wouldn't listen! And now Hetty and James and Robert are all *dead*!'

'But that's not your fault,' Anna said. 'None of it's your fault. There's no reason to think that these three deaths are linked in any way and there's *absolutely* no reason for you to feel responsible.' She could have cried for Isadora and she could see that Tansy felt the same.

Telling her story was supposed to help Isadora move on with her life. Instead tonight's supper had only stirred up a wasps' nest of painful memories. Of all people, Anna should have known better. It made no difference that Anna hadn't personally pulled the knife on her parents. As an angry teenager, she had wished them dead a million times, and somewhere in her mind she was still terrified that simply through not loving them as they deserved she had caused their deaths. Whereas Isadora seemed to believe that

177

she'd killed her friends through a simple failure in concentration.

Jake was right, obviously, about finding out who was behind the letters. *Damn him*, she thought, miserably. But, like Tansy and Isadora, Anna had suddenly had enough of sadness and secrets. Like them, she wanted to stuff the genie back in its bottle; at least until after Boxing Day. Glancing at Isadora's troubled face Anna hoped that it wasn't too late and they could still have the happy Christmas she'd been longing for.

Fourteen

'Anna, *Anna*! Happy Christmas! I've brought you coffee. *Very* strong coffee!'

Anna squinted at her clock radio. It was 7.30 a.m. 'Are you mad?' she said weakly. 'Go back to sleep.'

'I *can't*!' Tansy stretched out her arms. 'The sky is awake, so *I'm* awake.'

Tansy must have had quite a few cups of strong coffee herself, if she was quoting dialogue from *Frozen* at seven thirty in the morning. Anna sat up, clutching her pillow as a barrier between her and this unexpected intrusion.

'I know it might seem early to you,' Tansy explained, 'but when you've been up since five, it feels like practically lunchtime!' Gently taking away the pillow, she passed Anna her coffee.

'Why did you have to get up at five?' Anna said, confused.

'My slightly drunk and disoriented mother phoned to wish me happy Christmas at midnight Port of Spain time. They said to tell you a very happy Christmas, by the way,' she said without drawing breath. 'Then I was too wide awake to go back to bed so I took Bonnie out for a walk.'

'Oh, was that real?' Anna had a vague memory now of Tansy whispering to Bonnie in the dark. For the first time she took in Tansy's outfit, an outsize scarlet sweater with a goofy Rudolph the Reindeer on the front, over glittery black leggings. She looked like a wide-eyed Christmas elf.

'I've prepped the turkey,' Tansy confided, pulling a face. 'Haven't done that since I used to help my mum back in the day.'

'I told you I was going to do that,' Anna protested.

'It was fine! It was only half as gross as I remember!' Tansy perched herself on Anna's bed, and Anna noticed the three tiny glittery baubles threaded into her flatmate's hair elastic. 'It was a nightmare, getting it in the roasting dish, but it's in! Are you impressed?'

Anna was impressed and relieved. The organic free-range turkey Tansy had insisted on having delivered could have passed for a decent sized emu. Tansy continued to list her dawn achievements while Anna groggily sipped her coffee. 'And I'm *so* sorry I woke you, Anna,' Tansy finished up, clasping her hands together, 'but I couldn't wait another *minute* for you to open your Christmas stocking!'

'OK, OK,' Anna said, capitulating. 'But first I'll need a shower.'

'And then you'll need this,' Tansy told her with a grin. She held up a second oversized sweater with the words *Ho-Ho-Ho* blazoned across the front.

'No!' Anna said firmly. 'In fact, no-no-no!'

'Yes-yes-yes!' Tansy said equally firmly. 'These are our happy Christmas sweaters and we will wear them *all* day. Bonnie!' she called suddenly. 'Come and show Anna your gorgeous Christmas self!'

Anna's White Shepherd presented herself at her bedside with a distinctly sheepish expression.

'*Antlers!*' Anna said, aghast. 'You put sparkly *antlers* on Bonnie!'

Tansy gave her a sunny smile. 'I almost got her the fairy wings, but I thought she suited antlers better.'

Anna bent to pat her poor embarrassed dog. *It could have been fairy wings*, she told Bonnie silently. *In a way you've had a narrow escape!*

Looking up, she caught Tansy watching her with an anxious expression. 'Is it too much?' she said in a small voice. 'I just wanted everyone to have a *really* happy Christmas.'

At that moment Tansy looked so vulnerable that if Anna had been the hugging type, she would almost certainly have hugged her. *We both want the same thing*, she realized. But unlike Anna, Tansy hadn't settled for just wishing for some elusive Christmas magic. She had taken it on herself to be the slightly manic director of festivities.

And so Anna showered and obediently pulled on her *Ho-Ho-Ho* sweater, over a pair of (non-glittery) leggings, and went downstairs to the sitting room. Tansy had a fresh pot of coffee waiting with a basket of croissants from her friend Leo's bakery and they opened the little presents they had bought for each other and stuffed into Christmas-themed stockings.

Twenty minutes later, Anna was tucking into one of the croissants, hopefully watched by Bonnie, surrounded by a sea of crumpled paper and ribbons. 'So you seriously never got picked to be Mary?' Tansy said. 'I'd have thought you'd have been a shoo-in.'

'No, no, I got *picked*,' Anna said, 'but three days before the performance I went down with chicken pox. The teachers gave my part to this girl who could have easily won a prize for being the child who looked the *least* like the Virgin Mary!'

'Insensitive bastards,' Tansy said, shaking her head.

'I know! I was gutted. I'd learned the song and everything.'

'What was the song?' Tansy asked.

'"Snowy flakes are falling softly",' Anna said. 'Don't make me sing it or I'll cry!'

Tansy did her sympathetic therapist's voice. 'That memory still hurts, doesn't it?'

'Yes. It does, damn you!' said Anna, laughing. 'Now it's your turn.'

'Ah,' said Tansy. 'Well, I *also* got picked to be Mary – which was extremely forward-looking of our teachers, as all the other kids in my class were white.' She beamed at Anna.

181

'I thought you went to school in London?' Anna objected. 'Not to stereotype anybody obviously.'

'My mum and I weren't living in London that Christmas,' Tansy explained. 'Looking back, it was probably her and Frankie's first trial separation, but anyway, my mum obviously forgave him that time, because she called him up and told him I was going to be the star of the school nativity play. So he gets into his flash Merc and heads off to deepest Norfolk, driving through the fog down all those twisty little lanes, eventually finding the school with, like, *half* a minute before the curtain goes up. And when I walk out on stage with the short little white boy who's playing Joseph, there's Frankie sitting bang in the middle of the front row holding hands with my mum, both of them total bags of nerves!'

'That was so sweet of him,' Anna said really meaning it, 'driving all that way.'

'For a twenty-minute nativity play, I know! What wasn't quite so sweet was when little Joseph and I came on to take our bows at the end and my dad jumped up, pulling my mum to her feet, and gave us this long standing ovation. Talk about mortifying!'

'But that was sweet too in a way,' Anna said. 'Your dad was obviously really proud of you.'

'My dad loved Christmas,' Tansy said. 'He's from this big London family, half of them villains in one way or another, and he'd insist on having everyone over for this huge tribal Christmas meal. It was always mayhem. Dinner was always late, little kids under everybody's feet, venomous old aunties digging up some ancient family feud, and Frankie right in the heart of it all, drunk as a lord, having a whale of a time!'

'Did you always put out snacks for Santa?' Anna asked.

'Of *course* we put out snacks!' Tansy looked outraged. 'Always exactly the same snack, actually, a wedge of Christmas cake and a glass of Dad's whiskey.'

'We left a single mince pie, a glass of brandy and a carrot for Rudolph.' Having finally cracked the secret of Santa's identity, Anna had then been co-opted to help her parents to sustain this make-believe for her younger brothers and little sister, hastily consuming Santa's mince-pie for him before she went bed while her father drained the brandy.

'I forgot about Rudolph's carrot!' Tansy said. 'In the morning there'd always be a mysterious bite taken out of it! It didn't matter what size carrot you left out, for some reason poor old Rudolph never got to eat the whole thing!'

'Did Frankie do that thing with footprints?'

Tansy frowned. 'What thing?'

'Make a single manly boot-print on the hearth?' Anna said, 'Final proof that Santa had come down your chimney?'

'Ooh, cute touch! No, Dad didn't do fake boot-prints. I shall have to remember that if I have kids!'

Anna's phone beeped. Kirsty had sent her a photo of a beaming Charlie in his Captain America outfit.

'So we should probably get on with the

183

trimmings?' Tansy said. 'Jake will be used to different side dishes, won't he? Don't they have sweet potato pie in the States? Or is that Thanksgiving?'

'I don't think he'll care what side dishes we give him,' Anna reassured her. 'Jake is always perfectly happy with whatever turns up on his plate.' From the little that Jake had let slip Anna suspected that his mom had not been the sweet-potato-pie-making kind, at Christmas or any other time.

She and Tansy headed downstairs to a kitchen that already smelled deliciously of roasting turkey. Tansy opened the fridge pulling out a carton of cranberries and a bag of Brussels sprouts. Anna's phone beeped for a second time. 'Jake wants to check what time he should pick up my granddad,' she said.

Tansy tipped the sprouts into a colander. 'The turkey should be cooked about one. It has to rest, so if they can get here by – oh, fuck it!' She broke off laughing. 'I sound like those mad foodie magazines – "Countdown to Christmas!" Tell Jake to come when he's ready. He and your granddad won't mind, will they, if we're still prepping things?'

As it turned out, Jake arrived with Anna's grandfather just as Liam was parking his car.

It took a certain amount of manoeuvring to get George Ottaway out of Jake's hire car and into the house. When everyone was in the sitting room and Anna had finally remembered to introduce Liam, her granddad simply waved her away with a laugh, 'I already met Liam on the step! This is Tansy's young man!'

184

Tansy gave Liam a flirty look, 'Hear that, Goodhart? You're my young man!'

'Loving the understated knitwear, Tans,' he said straight-faced.

'Good, because there's one here with your name on!' Tansy flashed back. She turned to Anna's grandfather. 'Mr Ottaway, what kind of chair would be best for you?'

'Something hard,' Anna's grandfather said. 'If it's too soft I need a winch to get me back up! It smells gloriously Christmassy in here,' he added in a slightly wondering tone as if he thought that might have just happened by magic. In fact, Anna and Tansy had stayed up feverishly making clove oranges the night before. They had used clementines because they were smaller and took less time, tying them up with red ribbon and piling them in a shallow pewter dish which Tansy had found in a cupboard, along with nuts, nut-crackers and festive sprinkles of gold stars.

Seeing George Ottaway smilingly looking around the sitting room, Anna wondered if he felt strange being back in the house where he'd lived with her grandmother for so many years.

The doorbell rang. 'That'll be Isadora,' Tansy said. 'I'll go.'

Moments later Isadora appeared, carrying Hero in her arms. 'Happy Christmas, everyone! How wonderful to see you all!' She was wearing a fabulous knitted garment that could have been modelled on Hetty's stolen Persian carpet coat. Her earrings were large silver birds, possibly crows (a city girl, Anna wasn't good at birds),

185

hanging from silver chains interspersed with garnets and what Anna thought might be black pearls. She looked like their old actressy Isadora, only even more so. Anna felt a rush of affection tinged with relief. Isadora had not only survived their night of truth telling, she had survived it magnificently!

Tansy followed clutching a huge Fortnum & Masons Christmas cake. 'Look what Isadora brought! We hadn't even got to thinking about what to give you all for tea, had we, Anna?'

'There's a case of Veuve Cliquot in the back of my car, darling.' Isadora smilingly handed her car keys to Jake. 'Would you mind bringing it in for me?'

It was really happening! Christmas was happening here in Anna's home just the way she'd dreamed. She caught her grandfather looking at her. 'Are you OK?' she asked him in an undertone. 'Are you OK, being back here in your and Granny's house?'

'I feel *extremely* OK, thank you!' She heard delight and warmth in his voice. 'In fact, I feel wonderful! Do you know the really wonderful thing? It feels as if it's yours now.'

Immediately guilty, Anna said, 'But I've hardly changed a thing!'

'I meant, it feels like your *home*. Before, it felt as if you were just perched like a bird on a ledge, ready to take flight at any moment. Now it feels as if you *live* here.'

Liam and Jake were good-naturedly allowing Tansy to bully them into wearing the Christmas sweaters, she'd bought for them. 'I didn't buy

186

you one, Isadora,' she said. 'But perhaps you won't mind wearing these until after lunch? And then you can put your beautiful silver birds back.' Tansy ceremoniously handed Isadora a pair of earrings made from Christmas baubles. 'I didn't get you a jumper either, Mr Ottaway, but I did get you a Christmas tie.'

Anna's grandfather unfolded his snowflake-patterned tie with an amused expression. 'I haven't had to wear one of these for so many years I've almost forgotten how to tie one. Hopefully it will come back to me!'

Eventually everyone was dressed in an appropriate festive garment. Tansy had even supplied Hero with a fake diamante collar. Bonnie collapsed happily across Jake's feet, apparently resigned to her antlers, and when everyone was settled with a drink, Tansy said gleefully, 'OK, *now* we can start exchanging presents!'

'What time did she get up?' Liam whispered to Anna.

'About five,' she told him.

'I'm impressed she's held out that long!'

All the gift-wrapped parcels were fetched out from under the Christmas tree, and exchanged and unwrapped to exclamations of pleasure and surprise.

Anna's grandfather's present to Anna was a beautiful watercolour of her White Shepherd. For a moment she was lost for words. 'It's stunning,' she told him at last. 'You've caught Bonnie perfectly.'

Jake came over to see. 'That is a very fine picture of my favourite dog.'

187

'I'm glad you like it,' George Ottaway said with a smile.

Next it was Jake's turn to open his gift from Anna's grandfather. When he eventually uncovered the framed artwork inside, a slow smile spread over his face. 'You would make an excellent poker player Mr Ottaway because I did not see this coming at *all*!'

Anna's grandfather had made three charcoal sketches of Bonnie in her most characteristic poses and had them framed as a single work. 'Anna's always telling me she's your dog as much as hers,' he explained.

'These are wonderful,' Isadora said. 'I am deeply jealous and so is Hero.'

'I'll paint Hero for you if you like,' Anna's grandfather offered. 'I'd enjoy painting her. She has unusually compelling eyes.'

'I'll say,' Tansy whispered to Anna.

'She does, doesn't she?' Isadora said eagerly. 'Oh, I would *love* you to paint her, George. May I call you George?'

'The gallery where I work is going to have an open exhibition next year,' Tansy said to Anna. 'Your granddad should enter.'

'I'm always telling him he should get his work into an exhibition, but he always fobs me off,' Anna said. 'You talk to him, Tansy. Maybe you'd have more luck.'

After presents in the sitting room, they moved down to the kitchen for Christmas lunch, Jake unobtrusively assisting Anna's grandfather down the stairs. Unobtrusive was Jake's style, Anna had noticed, freshening Isadora's drink, making sure her grandfather was comfortable, chatting easily with Liam about his work, helping everything run smoothly. Now and then he'd catch her eye and give her his quick warm smile. There was no sense that he was simply carrying out a polite social duty. He seemed genuinely at home with everyone. That was Jake's gift, she thought, to make himself at home wherever he hung his hat.

Her Christmas present to him had been a soft woollen scarf in subtle gradations of wintry duck egg, caramel and grey. Anna had also given him a book, *Inside of a Dog: What Dogs See, Smell and Know* by Alexandra Horowitz. She had wanted to give him something Bonnie-related, since Bonnie was how they'd met. She didn't know what Jake had given her for Christmas. He'd slipped the flat gift-wrapped package into her hand when no one was looking and told her not to open it until she was alone.

Jake's present to Isadora, a pewter replica of a pilgrim badge depicting a hound and a hare, had sent her into ecstasies. She immediately pinned it to her lapel. 'Where did you find such a *wonderful* thing?'

'A little curios shop,' he'd said smiling. 'Anna told me you're a medieval scholar and I thought it had a kind of medieval look. I'm glad you like it.'

Tansy had planned for either Liam or Jake to carve the turkey, but they swiftly delegated this tricky task to Anna's grandfather, pleading clumsiness and inexperience. Anna doubted that he was taken in by their ruse, but he acquitted

189

himself with honour, carving the monstrous bird into perfectly judged slices that fell before his knife like a deck of cards.

'That was downright *poetic* how you carved that turkey breast,' Liam said in awe.

'When I carve, it looks like wild dogs have been at it,' Jake said.

'The trick is to slice as close to the breast bone as you can get,' George Ottaway explained. 'Of course, it helps to have a good knife!'

'I'm in love with your granddad,' Tansy whispered to Anna as they quickly laid the table with cutlery and Christmas crackers. 'Would you consider sharing him? My Trinidad grandpa is dead and Frankie's dad – well,' she gave Anna a mischievous grin. 'Better not get me started on him!'

They began to carry all the serving dishes to the table, the bowls of stuffing, the Brussels sprouts cooked to Tansy's mum's special recipe with chestnuts and red wine, the ruby-coloured cranberry sauce, the roast potatoes, parboiled and rolled in semolina before being roasted in olive oil, the acorn squash stuffed with jewelled rice (another of Tansy's concoctions), the tiny sausages wrapped in streaky bacon, a huge jug of gravy.

'This looks positively Dickensian!' Isadora exclaimed. 'You girls must have been up since dawn!'

'One of us was,' Anna told her with a grin.

When they were all seated, George Ottaway raised his glass. 'I want to propose a toast,' he said, a little shyly. 'To friends and loved ones, both here and elsewhere. May they know as much happiness as I have felt in this house today! Happy Christmas, everyone!'

Tansy, who had insisted on sitting next to Anna's granddad, gave him a little clap. 'That was so beautiful,' she told him. 'It's so wonderful to meet you finally. You really must think about putting your work in our exhibition. Would it be too cheeky to ask if I could come over with Anna some time and see some of your paintings?'

Anna felt slightly as if she was dreaming. It was Christmas and for the first time since her teens she had all her favourite people under one roof. They ate. They pulled crackers. Anna refused to wear her paper crown but Isadora wore hers with pride, even reading out the terrible joke. 'I suspect that sounds better in the original Polish,' she said laughing.

'Are you accusing us of buying knock-off crackers!' Tansy said, pretending outrage.

Tansy got slightly drunk, though that may have been partly through lack of sleep. Now and then a hopeful doggie nose would appear from under the table where Bonnie and Hero waited for the scraps they were convinced would eventually come their way.

'Well, darlings,' Isadora said, when they'd all had their after dinner coffee. 'I am sorry to rudely eat and run, but I promised a friend I'd go to this choral thing at Christchurch.'

'You can't even stay for some of your cake?' Tansy said.

'I'd like nothing better than to stay here with you all.' Isadora seemed genuinely regretful. 'But I feel I should keep my promise to Marjorie.'

She carefully removed her bauble earrings, placing them in her bag along with her medieval pilgrim badge. Tansy found her a Christmassy carrier bag for all her other gifts. 'You and I will meet again, George,' Isadora told Anna's grandfather, stooping down to kiss his cheek. 'And we will discuss you painting Hero.'

It was only when she and Tansy were showing Isadora out that Anna realized it would soon be dark. 'I should walk Bonnie,' she said.

'I'll come with you,' Tansy said. 'I could do with some fresh air to wake me up! Would your granddad like to come, do you think?'

Fortunately Jake had foreseen this eventuality and stowed her grandfather's wheelchair in the boot of his car. 'We won't be long,' Anna told him.

'Hold up!' He bent to remove Bonnie's antlers. 'I don't think we want the other dogs knowing about these, honey.'

Liam and Jake said they'd stay home to man the dishwasher. 'And drink strong spirits and talk about football,' Liam said with a grin.

Anna grabbed her old olive-green Barbour coat, Tansy threw on her fluffy black-and-white-striped faux-fur jacket, and they set off to Port Meadow with Anna's grandfather in his wheelchair. There had been a couple of hard frosts so they didn't have to worry about the wheels getting bogged down in the mud.

They arrived to find several of the Port Meadow regulars there, including the loud-voiced woman with her Border collies, and Tansy gave Anna's grandfather a running commentary on each dog walker as they came within his sight line. They got a friendly wave from Blossom's owner, who was with a couple who looked as if they might be his mum and dad. Tansy quickly filled in Anna's grandfather about Blossom's tragic history. For some reason, Anna had just assumed that Blossom had been taken to a rescue shelter after she'd been picked up wandering beside the motorway. She'd imagined that Blossom's new owner had adopted her from a shelter, the same as Anna had adopted Bonnie. She hadn't realized that he had spotted the heavily pregnant Staffie wandering by the side of the motorway and immediately pulled over. 'Can you believe Blossom was already in labour? Can you imagine someone abandoning her in that state!' Tansy sounded indignant. 'She had her first puppy in his car. He took her and her tiny puppy back to his home where she gave birth to another seven, but they were in such bad shape, two of them died almost immediately. He was able to save the remaining six. He said he never meant to get a dog, but by the time the puppies were old enough to go to new homes, he and Blossom had totally bonded. And you can see from how she looks at him how much she adores him!' Tansy finished up, slightly breathless.

Anna's grandfather was looking faintly astonished.

'People talk to Tansy,' Anna explained.

'So I see,' he said with a laugh. 'And it sounds as if every dog comes with a story.'

'Rescue dogs do, that's for sure,' Tansy agreed.

Anna's grandfather was looking around him

with obvious pleasure. 'I can't remember the last time I went to Port Meadow,' he said, innocently causing her a stab of guilt. 'I'd forgotten the beautiful horses. What a treat!'

The cloudy sky above the meadow was taking on a brooding appearance so that Anna could almost see the darkness of the coming night encroaching on the short midwinter's day.

'There's a suspicious amount of matching knitwear on show this afternoon,' Tansy commented. 'We know what they all got for Christmas!'

'I don't think we're in a position to joke about other people's knitwear,' Anna told her.

Tansy's eyes sparkled. 'You don't fool me, Anna Hopkins! You won't want to take your jumper off tonight! You'll be wearing it in bed.'

'In my nightmares maybe,' Anna said with a grin. She had spotted a slow-moving flat-capped figure with an equally slow-moving dog making their way through the gathering gloom. She was always touched by the man's tenderness to his old dog. She was about to point them out to her grandfather. Then she saw that this particular old dog was not a spaniel but some kind of crossbreed, and its owner was a man she'd never seen before.

When Anna thought Bonnie had had enough of a run around, she called her back and they set off towards home. 'Is it wrong that I'm already thinking about Isadora's posh Christmas cake?' Tansy said. 'Why is it that eating too much always makes you want to eat even more? It's like some kind of Zen ko‾an or something!'

Back in the warmth and comfort of Anna's

sitting room, George Ottaway said apologetically, 'I might have to close my eyes, now – just for a minute.'

While Anna's grandfather dozed, Tansy went to make more coffee and Anna cut slabs of Christmas cake for Liam and Tansy, the only people who felt able to eat another morsel.

It was properly dark outside now. Anna had kept the sitting room lights low, partly so as not to disturb her grandfather but also to enjoy the sight of the Christmas tree softly twinkling. She was sitting on the floor with Bonnie, dreamily watching the tree as she listened to Tansy, Jake and Liam discuss which movie they could watch, one which George Ottaway might also enjoy. All at once Anna's phone beeped inside her bag. It would be Kirsty, she thought, sending another photo of Charlie. She took out her phone and felt her smile fade.

Happy Christmas & New Year. All the family send their love. Tim. PS, Please think about what I said.

Anna was instantly back in the big family kitchen, smelling the sharp tang of lemon being stirred into toothachingly sweet royal icing. She could see her and Tim's mothers' palette knives dipping in and out of the jug of hot water, smoothing and rounding the icing as they worked or ruffling it into snowy waves depending on the design of the cake. Somehow it had become a tradition, the two families' happy, slightly boozy get-together before Christmas to decorate the cakes they later gave to friends and relations. When they were old enough Tim and Anna were

195

allowed to ice their own. She remembered the deep sense of satisfaction she felt the first time she was allowed to place the tiny plastic fir tree, just so, on her ruffled icing snow. She'd felt happy and useful standing on her chair at the counter beside Tim, both of them carefully decorating their cakes, dimly aware of their mothers chatting, Christmas music playing. What had their fathers been doing? Anna couldn't remember.

All the family send their love.

Did Jane Freemantle still make Christmas cakes every year? Did she think about Anna, the only member of the Hopkins family still alive, as she smoothed and ruffled and dipped her knife into the hot water? *Stop it,* she scolded herself. *You're alive, Anna Hopkins. You're alive – and today you celebrated Christmas with the people you like best in the world.*

'Are you OK?' Jake came to sit beside her. Bonnie immediately shifted over to lean her head on his knee. Anna wordlessly showed him her text. Across the sitting room, Tansy was expressing astonishment that Liam had never seen *It's a Wonderful Life.*

'There was – a period in my life when Tim's mum and dad were my preferred parents. I thought his mum was way cooler than my mum, and his dad was, like, the *perfect* dad, you know? The dad I was supposed to have had? God, I was a horrible little kid!'

'I doubt that.' Jake's hand found Anna's and held on to it for a moment. 'Don't be hard on yourself. You can get ambushed by all kinds of

196

memories this time of year.' Dizzy from his touch, brief as it was, Anna wondered what memories might be ambushing Jake. Memories of his parents, his time in Afghanistan?

A few minutes later, George Ottaway woke up and Tansy shamelessly lobbied for his support to watch *It's a Wonderful Life*. Anna smiled to herself as they settled down to watch. It was always going to be *It's a Wonderful Life*, she thought. The discussion had been pure formality. The classic Christmas movie had been a non-negotiable part of Tansy's Yuletide agenda, along with the cheesy jumpers, dog antlers and Brussels sprouts with chestnuts.

Once, Tansy briefly lifted her head from Liam's shoulder to give Anna a beatific smile. Bonnie was in her favourite place, lying across both Anna's and Jake's feet. Jake was sitting beside Anna, his hand resting close to hers; wonderfully, disturbingly close.

When George Bailey found the message from Clarence the angel in the film, telling him that no man was a failure who had friends, Anna's grandfather loudly blew his nose. 'Damn it, this film always makes me cry!' he said fiercely.

After the credits had rolled, Tansy packaged up some Christmas cake for Anna's grandfather. Jake had offered to drive him back to Bramley Lodge. 'I'll come back tomorrow,' he told Anna, as they said their goodbyes outside the house. 'We can take Bonnie for a long walk somewhere. Maybe have lunch?' Jake gently moved aside a strand of her hair that had come loose from her ponytail and Anna felt every cell in her body come alive. 'Don't forget to open my present, OK?' he told her.

Anna left Tansy and Liam watching *Pirates of the Caribbean*, and went downstairs to feed Bonnie and wash up the tea things. It was an old habit, deferring pleasure. She was saving Jake's present until every last cup had been washed, dried and put away; every last leftover covered in plastic and stowed in the fridge. What could Jake have bought her, she wondered, that he wanted to keep just between them? Not knowing was exciting but also unnerving. Would Jake's Christmas gift finally reveal how he thought of her, what she meant to him?

Her kitchen phone began to ring. Preoccupied with her own thoughts, she glanced at the screen without much interest and saw a number with an international code. It would be a wrong number, she thought. All over the world people in various stages of inebriation were phoning friends and families. She picked up the handset. 'Hello?'

'Is that Anna Hopkins?' The man on the other end sounded stressed. 'This is Gabriel Salzman.'

Anna was confused. Wasn't Isadora's son in Australia? 'I'm afraid she's not here,' she said apologetically, thinking he was phoning to wish Isadora a happy Christmas. 'Your mother left a few hours ago.'

'My mother is in the John Radcliffe,' Gabriel informed her.

Anna felt the blood leave her face. 'Oh, my God, has she been in an accident?'

'No.' His voice was tight, almost angry. 'She's been attacked.'

198

Fifteen

Anna hurried through the sliding doors into the hospital foyer and was momentarily bewildered to see a Christmas tree and gaudy swathes of decorations. It felt like years since she and Tansy had carefully laid the table for Christmas lunch. It didn't seem possible that this was still the same day.

She had driven to the hospital on automatic pilot. Now the significance of Gabriel's call was catching up, turning her vision fuzzy. She stared up at the map of all the different medical departments, but couldn't make sense out of any of it. Outside the hospital, she'd seen a young woman jump out of a taxi and run into A&E with her small baby, screaming for someone to help her, leaving the car door flung open and the cabbie staring after her.

Liam and Tansy arrived at Anna's side. 'Sorry,' Tansy said, breathless. 'We had to go round that fucking car park three times before we found a space.'

'Where did Gabriel say they'd taken her?' Liam asked.

'Something like the emergency medical unit?' Anna said,

'That's where people go to be assessed after A&E,' said Liam.

They were still wearing their silly Christmas sweaters. After Gabriel's phone call they had just jumped in their cars and rushed straight to the John Radcliffe. Jake had gone to Isadora's to check on Hero. Gabriel hadn't seemed to know what had happened to Isadora's little dog during the attack.

Liam led the way to the emergency unit, but when they arrived, a rather weary staff nurse told them that Isadora had just been moved to the cardiac care unit.

'Oh, my God, is something wrong with her heart?' Tansy's eyes went wide with alarm.

The nurse suddenly looked doubtful. 'I'm sorry, but are you all relatives of Ms Salzman?'

'Tansy and I are her daughters,' Anna told her without missing a beat.

'And I'm with the Thames Valley Police,' Liam said, officially sanctioning her lie.

Out in the corridor Tansy said, 'Her daughters? *Seriously?* Because obviously you and I look so much alike!'

'We could have different fathers,' Anna said.

'I don't think they need to know the exact circumstances of anyone's conception, Tans,' Liam said. 'Just saying "daughters" is enough.'

Anna tended to become quiet and withdrawn when she felt scared. Tansy chattered randomly about whatever came into her head. The thought that Isadora had worrying heart symptoms as a result of this violent attack was freaking her flat-mate out. It was freaking Anna out too.

They made their way to the cardiology unit, where they successfully repeated Anna's lie to another overworked nurse and were directed to Isadora's bay.

200

Lying with her eyes closed, Isadora looked dazed and pale in her one-size-fits-all hospital gown. She'd been hooked up to a gently beeping machine which Anna assumed must be monitoring her heart. Her right wrist was encased in plaster. Her right eye looked painful and puffy. Her right cheekbone was badly bruised. Seeing her so vulnerable made Anna want to cry and also smash her fist into whoever had hurt her so badly.

'Isadora?' Tansy said softly. 'Isadora, we're *so* sorry.'

Isadora couldn't quite manage to open her injured eye, it was too badly swollen. 'Oh, my darlings, how lovely that you came,' she said in a weak voice.

'We came as soon as we got Gabriel's call,' Anna told her. Isadora's son had sounded almost hysterical with worry but, being Gabriel, there was also the unspoken accusation that his mother had somehow timed the attack to cause him maximum inconvenience.

Isadora struggled and failed to raise herself from her prone position. 'Can someone please adjust this stupid bed?' Together Anna and Tansy helped Isadora to sit up. 'Careful with my right side, darling,' she told Tansy, wincing. 'They think I've cracked a rib.'

Propped up on her pillows, Isadora tried to smile then burst into humiliated tears. 'I've lost all my beautiful presents!' she wept. 'Jake's pilgrim badge, everything.'

'The bastard took your Christmas presents?' Liam was tight-lipped. He'd been keeping in the

201

background until now, obviously not wanting to embarrass Isadora.

'They took *everything.*'Isadora's voice rose like a hurt child's. 'My bag. My wallet with all my cards. My phone. My jewellery.' Unconsciously, her uninjured hand went to touch her left ear behind hair that was still shiny and matted with blood.

'What's happened here?' Tansy said abruptly. She carefully moved aside a bloodied strand of Isadora's hair. 'Oh, my God!' she said appalled. Isadora's attacker had savagely torn one of her crow earrings from her ear, ripping her earlobe.

'He didn't get the other one. So he didn't get absolutely everything,' Isadora said with an attempt at bravado. 'But my poor cardigan is ruined, all dirty and bloody.' Her face crumpled as she remembered.

'We'll get it cleaned, don't worry,' Anna said.

'And I can't seem to remember what happened to Hero.' Isadora clutched at Anna with her good hand. 'I remember her jumping out of the car, but after that . . .' Her voice tailed off.

'Jake has gone to your house to make sure Hero's OK.' Anna said, grateful to be presented with problems she could actually solve.

'Did you get a look at the person who attacked you?' Liam's voice was gentle.

'I don't know. I can't seem to remember.' Isadora was becoming increasingly wild-eyed. 'I think I remember taking my keys out of my bag but then after that everything is just a blank.'

'Did they say anything to you?' Liam persisted. 'Can you remember the sound of their voice?'

202

'Liam, she's still in shock,' Tansy protested.

'I know she's in shock, Tans, but in these types of situations time is of the essence.' Anna wondered if Liam knew he'd slipped into his police sergeant's voice. 'If anything comes back to you, Isadora,' he said earnestly, 'the smallest little detail, however unimportant it seems, be sure to let us know. I want to catch the scumbag who did this to you.'

Isadora was still fruitlessly trying to reconstruct the timeline of her attack. 'I don't think I'd got as far as opening the front door. If I'd opened it, Hero could have run indoors to hide, but I can't remember if I'd put the key in the lock? Oh, God! I hope they didn't hurt Hero!'

'Isadora, listen,' Tansy's voice was firm but gentle. 'I'm going to find some warm water and cotton wool. I'm going to sponge all that icky blood off your hair. You'll feel much better when you're properly clean.'

But just then the harried nurse appeared to alert them that the cardiologist had arrived to examine Isadora, and they all had to decamp to the corridor.

Liam took out his phone, checking for messages.

'I am so ashamed of myself,' Tansy told Anna in a low voice. 'We should have seen this coming. Why the *fuck* didn't we see this coming? I mean, this isn't some opportunistic robber, this was deliberate. This was personal.'

Anna felt sick. Tansy had spoken her own thoughts out loud. Isadora had been in danger and they'd just let it happen. 'You seriously think this is connected with her friends' deaths?'

'It's got to be! I mean, Jesus Christ, Anna, there were six in their little group. Now four of them are dead and whoever attacked Isadora had a really good crack at making it five!'

'How can they all be connected though?' Anna asked bewildered. 'Hetty was murdered fifty years ago and Robert committed suicide.'

'I didn't say I know *how*,' Tansy hissed. 'But we know Robert got another one of those mad letters, so it's *got* to be something to do with all this weird spy shit.'

Liam had put his phone away and was looking at them with an odd expression. 'What mad letters?' he demanded.

Shit! Anna thought. Liam had been doing his invisible cop routine again. In their distress she and Tansy had forgotten he was there. They still hadn't told Liam about either Isadora's or Robert's letters. Isadora had been adamant that they shouldn't tell the police about hers, and somehow they'd never thought to report finding a second poison pen letter at Robert's house.

Liam was still waiting for an answer. 'What letters?' he repeated with a distinct edge to his voice. 'You never mentioned any threatening letters.'

Flustered, Tansy explained about Isadora's beautifully hand-written letter warning of divine retribution for unspecified sins.

'When was this?' Liam's eyes held none of their usual warmth.

'The morning after the night Professor Lowell was attacked,' Anna said.

'And then you found a second letter while you were all at that banker bloke's house?'

'Yes, Robert Keane,' Anna said.

'And you didn't think you should maybe pass this information on to the police?' Liam lifted his hands as if to tear out his hair. Anna had never seen him so pissed off. 'You should have told us about this. You should at least have told *me*, Tans,' he said angrily.

We should have, Anna thought. And they most probably would have. But Tallis had threatened Isadora with the Official Secrets Act, warning of dire consequences if her activities with the Oxford Six ever became known. And Tansy's childhood with Frankie had left her with an aversion to telling the police anything at all if it could possibly be avoided.

Without waiting for an explanation, Liam set off towards the lifts.

'OK, so we made a mistake!' Tansy called after him. 'You don't have to bloody storm off!'

Liam turned, grim-faced. 'I'm not storming anywhere. I'm just going outside so I can phone my boss and ruin his family's Christmas for him.'

After her brief flash of defiance Tansy looked as if she might cry with shame. 'Do you really need to call him today?' she said in a pleading voice.

'He needs to know there's a pattern. Isadora's attack isn't just a one-off.'

'But Robert killed *himself,*' Tansy's voice shook with distress.

'We found a similar letter in James Lowell's room, Tans,' Liam said, exasperated. 'They all knew each other, didn't they? They were all friends back in the day? There's some weird link between them – which we might have picked up on sooner if you hadn't kept crucial information to yourselves. And then your friend Isadora might not be lying injured in this hospital on Christmas Day,' he added, as close to mad as Anna had ever seen him.

Tansy's face went ashen. 'You don't need to try to make me feel bad about Isadora.' Her voice quivered. 'I will never forgive myself for this. Never!'

Liam took half a step back towards her. He looked stressed and upset. 'I'm sorry, Tans, but you and your friends should have trusted the police to decide what is important and what isn't. You should have trusted *me*,' he added. The doors to the nearest lift slid open and he disappeared inside.

Tansy tugged miserably at a stray tendril of her hair and a tiny Christmas bauble hit the floor with a tinkle. She bent down and started picking up the pieces. 'You know that lyric?' she said as she straightened up. '"Life is what happens to you while you're busy making other plans"?'

'Yeah, I know that lyric,' Anna said with feeling. 'He'll come round,' she added, wanting to comfort her friend.

'I'm not sure he will.' Tansy's eyes were bleak. 'He feels like I betrayed him and I suppose I have in a way. I didn't play by his rules.' She gave a little shrug, refusing to feel sorry for herself. 'I'm going to see if that doctor's finished yet. I want to help Isadora clean herself up a bit. These poor nurses have enough to do.'

'I'm going to call Jake,' Anna said. 'See if he's

found Hero. Then he can send a pic to my phone and we can show Isadora she's OK.'

'Good plan,' Tansy said. 'What if he hasn't found her though?'

'He'll have found her,' Anna said.

Tansy went back into the ward and Anna turned on her phone. She was surprised to find a terse voicemail from Jake. 'Can you come to Isadora's as soon as you get this? There's something I think you need to hear.'

Anna caught Tansy up by the nurses' station. 'Tell Isadora I'm popping over to her house to fetch some of her things. She could be in for a couple of days.'

'Did Jake say anything about Hero?' Tansy called after her.

'No, but I'm sure she's fine,' Anna said to deter further questions. 'I'll take a pic while I'm there!'

Anna drove over to Summertown feeling a creeping unease. It wasn't like Jake to be so enigmatic. Could he have found a clue to the identity of Isadora's attacker? But then surely he'd have said, 'there's something I need you to *see*'?

He opened the door before she'd even pressed the bell and hustled her towards the kitchen. 'We're in here.'

Anna's mind anxiously seized on that mysterious 'we'. Hero must have been hurt after all and Jake had had to call the vet. Isadora would be distraught.

But when she walked into her friend's cluttered kitchen, she saw Hero in her basket curled into a furry black ball. With her back pointedly turned to the room, she seemed subdued, but not obviously harmed. Knowing Hero, Anna thought, she was mostly put out by this unwanted disruption to her routine. 'Hello, you grumpy little dog,' she told her. 'Isadora will be so happy to know you're safe.'

A suppressed sob made her glance up. For the first time, she saw Sabina sitting in Isadora's wicker chair, looking almost as small and woebegone as Hero. Her blonde hair hung loose around her face which was pale and tear-stained. A fluffy blanket had been draped around her shoulders. From time to time little shudders went through her. Shock, Anna thought. Gabriel hadn't mentioned who had found Isadora and called the paramedics, but it dawned on her now that it must have been Sabina.

Jake had begun to delve in Isadora's kitchen cupboards. He emerged with a somewhat dented espresso pot and an unopened pack of Lavazza. 'I don't know about you,' he said to Anna, 'but I could do with a cup of strong coffee before we get started.'

Started on what? Anna wondered. Jake's grim expression suggested that whatever it was, Anna was going to need some serious reinforcement.

Unscrewing the metal pot, he filled the lower chamber with water, put a couple of scoops of coffee in the upper compartment, carefully screwed the pot back together and put it on the smallest ring on Isadora's cooker, doing it so meticulously that Anna thought she might scream. She opened her mouth to demand what was going on, only to receive a slight shake of the head from Jake.

208

He brought the coffee pot and cups to the table, pulling out a chair for Anna. 'First things first,' he said. 'How's Isadora?'

Sabina started to cry in earnest.

'Not great,' Anna said. 'She's got a broken wrist and a possible cracked rib. She's almost certainly concussed. She can't remember who attacked her or anything that happened after she got out of her car. She's terrified something's happened to Hero.'

'Hero very sensibly ran off to hide in the bushes,' Jake said. 'She came out as soon as she heard Sabina on her phone calling the emergency services.'

So it was Sabina who'd found her. Anna turned to her. 'I'm so glad you were here . . .' she began and was interrupted by Sabina's racking sobs.

It was obviously upsetting to find your landlady bleeding and unconscious, but Sabina's reaction seemed excessive considering how remote she had always acted around Isadora.

'What's upset you?' Anna asked her. 'Did you see who attacked Isadora? Did someone try to hurt you?'

Sabina only shook her head, sobbing as if her heart would break.

'Just tell her, Sabina,' Jake said. 'You know it's got to come out.'

Tears were running down Sabina's face, but she couldn't or wouldn't speak.

Jake gave a tired sigh. Christmas probably seemed like years ago to him, too. 'Sabina's the one who's been sending the letters,' he told Anna.

'What letters?' For a moment Anna's mind was

a blank. 'Oh, fuck! *Those* letters?' Her eyes widened as she tried to absorb this news. '*Sabina* sent them? Why would you *do* that?' she asked bewildered.

'Tell her who you are,' Jake said.

Sabina swallowed. 'Hetty Vallier was my grandmother.'

Anna just stared at her. 'Oh, my God,' she said faintly. She had a dizzy sense of worlds and times colliding. How had she not seen that Sabina looked so much like Hetty?

'Tell Anna what you told me,' Jake said.

Still clutching her untouched espresso, Sabina haltingly began to fill in the gaps in Hetty's story.

In the summer of 1966, Hetty had not been on vacation or working at some underpaid holiday job like her Oxford friends but in a convent in Switzerland waiting out the last weeks of her unintended pregnancy. She had given birth to a little girl, Iona Grace, before returning to Oxford to resume her studies, leaving her baby daughter behind. Iona had very few memories of her life in the austere orphanage run by nuns. 'Most of it Mum's blanked,' Sabina said. 'My dad thinks it's like post-traumatic stress, like soldiers get?' She had to stop to wipe her eyes. 'Some of the nuns were OK. But there were two – Mum used to call them "the twisted sisters" . . .'

Sabina had dropped the stilted foreign-girl act, Anna noticed, and was talking in natural-sounding English. Anna thought she even detected a slight London accent.

'My mum said the nuns taught her three things,' Sabina said, 'embroidery, perfect handwriting,

and how to cry at night without anybody hearing.'
Her voice wobbled.

Perfect handwriting. Anna felt a shiver go
through her as she realized who must have taught
Sabina her flawless calligraphy.

'Mum had to live there in that horrible place
until she was sixteen. On her last morning, the
Mother Superior called her into her office and
gave her a package. Inside was a little baby's
nightdress Hetty had sewn and embroidered while
she was waiting for Mum to be born. There was
also a diary and a package of letters and money.
A *lot* of money,' Sabina emphasized. 'Someone
had been sending a cheque to the convent every
month since my mum was a few months old.'

'Was the money from the Valliers?' Anna asked,
interrupting.

Sabina's eyes became cold and flinty. 'No,
Mum never had anything from them.' She leaned
forward, her silky hair briefly swinging across
her face. 'Anyway, that night Mum stayed in a
hotel for the first time in her life. She was too
scared to go down to the restaurant so she called
room service. There were only two items on the
menu that she recognized: wiener schnitzel and
apple strudel, so she ordered those. The strudel
was so wonderful that my mum rang down for
a second helping. After she'd eaten she lay down
on her bed and began to read the letters.'

Sabina swallowed. 'Despite the terrible things
the nuns had told her about her mother, my mum
had always clung to a hope that one day she'd
come for her. Up in that hotel room, her stomach
full of good food, the package of letters waiting

in her suitcase, my mum thought that all her secret prayers had been answered. She had no doubt that the letters and the money were from the mother that she had never known. But my mum says as soon as she read the first letter something died inside her. No one was going to come. Her mother was dead, murdered. She'd come to a bad end just like those vicious old women always said she would.'

'Who were the letters from?' Anna asked.

Sabina gave her an incredulous look. 'Can't you guess?'

When Anna didn't answer Sabina went on with her story. 'My mum took a train to the nearest town where she found herself a room and a job doing fine embroidery for a dressmaker. She did well. She made a life. On her first ever holiday, she went to London where she met my father. Not long afterwards they got married. My father said she was ecstatic when she knew she was expecting me. She was going to be part of a real family at last.'

Sabina broke off. She suddenly seemed to notice her espresso and took a couple of sips. 'Unfortunately, the happy family thing never really . . .' She took a shaky breath and began again. 'After I was born my mum went into a severe post-partum psychosis. She was in and out of psychiatric institutions for most of my childhood. My dad couldn't cope so he left her. He left us both. Mum tried really hard to keep it together. She was so brave. She decided we'd go back to Switzerland. She thought she had a chance of staying well there. But then when I was twelve my mum had a really bad psychotic episode and my dad took me back to London to live with him and his new family.' Sabina was twisting her fingers together. 'They're OK, really. But it's never felt . . .' Her voice trailed off.

'That's why you wrote those letters?' Anna said. 'Because you blamed Hetty's friends for what happened to your mum?'

'They weren't real friends!' Sabina's eyes blazed. 'They could have helped her to keep her baby, then Mum wouldn't have had to grow up in that terrible orphanage and she wouldn't have got ill.'

It was the wrong moment to suggest that Hetty's daughter might have succumbed to mental illness regardless of her upbringing, though being abandoned to the twisted sisters had surely added to her problems, Anna thought.

'So . . . you *planned* this?' Jake asked. 'You came to Oxford, intending to seek out Isadora and the other Oxford Six members?'

Sabina gave a nervous smirk, unable to hide her pride at her own cleverness. 'Thanks to my mum I had enough info to track them down. I lucked out with my lodgings though. I couldn't believe it when I went to the lodgings office and found Isadora Salzman on the list of this year's landladies!'

Jake set down his coffee cup. 'So you insinuated yourself into her home,' he said slowly, 'and you set about secretly punishing this wonderful warm-hearted lady because, in your opinion, she'd failed to help your grandmother. You don't think that's a bit of an overreaction?' Jake's southern accent was becoming more pronounced.

'She *deserved* it!' Sabina flashed back. 'They *all* deserved it! Anyway, I was only doing the same as them!'

'How do you figure that?' Jake said.

'Playing games,' Sabina said contemptuously. 'Playing a part. Spying on people, dropping off secret messages. I was just doing it back to them.'

Anna wanted to say that this wasn't quite how it was; that, in the beginning at least, Isadora and her friends had genuinely believed they were helping to save the world from another devastating war. She was surprised to feel a sneaking sympathy for this angry girl. Sabina had chosen such an elaborate revenge against people she had never met, people she had only glimpsed in the pages of her grandmother's diary. What could have driven her to such extremes?

'You never thought of playing things differently?' she said tentatively. 'Hetty came from an enormous extended family. You could have got in touch with them. I'd have thought they'd have welcomed Hetty's granddaughter with open arms.'

To Anna's dismay, fresh tears welled up in Sabina's eyes. 'That's what I thought!' Her voice was raw with hurt. 'After I came to live with Dad, I kept reading about the Valliers in the papers and society magazines. I got a bit embarrassingly fan-girlish at the thought of being one of them. I felt like they were my real family. I'd literally dream about them.' Her tears spilled over. 'I should have left it as a dream,' she said bitterly.

Anna felt her heart contract. 'You contacted them?'

214

Sabina gave a tight nod. 'And got accused of being an opportunist and a liar.' She angrily brushed away her tears. 'They said Hetty had never had a baby. Maeve, her stepmother, was the only member of the family who could have backed me up, and she'd died just a couple of years after Hetty. I was accused of trying to capitalize or whatever out of their family tragedy. Because obviously I don't know anything about tragedy! I'm not a real person, apparently. I'm just a mistake, a nobody, like my mum.'

Here was the part of Sabina's story that had been missing, Anna thought. If the Valliers had welcomed Sabina into their family, Anna doubted they'd all be sitting in Isadora's kitchen on Christmas Day, having this painful conversation. It had been one rejection too many for Sabina to absorb. She wasn't just angry with Hetty's friends, she was angry with the whole world, a world that refused to see her.

I never saw her either, she thought, Sabina had been the toast-eating Swiss girl, a minor character eclipsed by the larger drama of Isadora and her friends. It hadn't occurred to Anna that Sabina also had a story, that Sabina was how Hetty's story had ended, the end of a long line of hurt and damage.

Sabina suddenly let out a scared whimper. 'Was it my fault that Robert Keane killed himself?' She couldn't meet their eyes.

Jake and Anna exchanged glances.

Anna took a breath. 'The truth is we don't know why he killed himself. His life was basically a train wreck, Sabina. His wife had left him. He had no relationship with his children. He was going to have to declare himself bankrupt. He'd been severely depressed for a long, long time.'

Sabina shot her a frightened look. 'But my letter could have pushed him over the edge?'

'We can't know that,' Jake said. 'Besides, that's all in the past. Right now, we need to think about what to do about you.'

The colour drained from Sabina's face. 'What do you mean?'

'First off, we've got to tell the police that you wrote those letters.'

Sabina tried to plead with him but Jake shook his head. 'If only to eliminate you from their inquiries,' he said soberly. 'So they know your letters aren't connected with all these attacks.'

Sabina looked as if she might pass out. 'I didn't hurt anybody I swear! Even though Professor Lowell *deserved* to be hurt,' she added childishly.

'What are you talking about? Why did he deserve it more than the others?' Anna could feel herself starting to lose her temper.

Sabina sat back in her chair. 'Because James Lowell murdered Hetty.'

Sixteen

It was Boxing Day, a few minutes after noon. Jake had just taken both the dogs for an overdue walk. The previous night, Anna had made a quick

216

dash over to Park Town to pick up a very relieved Bonnie and pack an overnight bag. There had been no sign of Tansy.

As Jake ushered Bonnie and Hero out through the back door, Anna had begun transferring her centre of operations into the smaller of Isadora's two sitting rooms where she'd also passed the night.

Sabina had been furious when they'd insisted that she called her father but after she'd spoken to him she'd seemed almost relieved to have everything finally taken out of her hands. Her father hadn't seemed surprised to hear that his daughter was in trouble. 'We invited Sabina to spend Christmas with us,' he'd told Anna, in the huffy tone that she thought might be habitual. 'But she said she had too much work. My wife and I have tried to do our best by her but she doesn't make it easy.' His best didn't include being able to come up until after Boxing Day, thought Anna wryly. He had made it quite clear that they couldn't expect him to cut his family Christmas short simply because his daughter was in a spot of trouble. Anna and Jake had felt they had no choice but to promise to stay with Sabina until he arrived.

Anna had insisted that she could manage on her own. Hetty's granddaughter was hardly Jake's problem and he had enough to do with sorting out Mimi's house. But he'd just said, half joking, 'I think of it as karma. I wasn't exactly an angel either in my teens.' Something else she and Jake shared.

Even so, Anna felt the responsibility for this

217

troubled girl weighing on her. She'd chosen the sitting room because it was directly opposite the stairs. If Sabina tried to creep out of the house, Anna would hear. Though Sabina had apparently accepted her and Jake as her temporary minders, Anna wouldn't put it past her to try something stupid.

Setting her coffee down on a small carved table, she dumped her little pile of photocopies next to the armchair nearest the door. Someone, Anna thought it was Jake, had pulled back the curtains and opened the old sash window a crack to let in the cold fresh air.

Anna had visited Isadora countless times but she had never been in this room until last night. At the time, her mind had been too full of the day's events, and Isadora's lighting too dim, to properly take in her surroundings. The room had just been somewhere more relaxing, though no less cluttered, for the three of them to sit after a day that already seemed to have lasted several weeks too long. Now, for the first time, Anna noticed the photographs propped haphazardly on Isadora's already overflowing bookshelves. The majority were old black-and-white photos featuring people unknown to her, their solemn or laughing faces looking back at her from a world that no longer existed. Curious, she picked up an old studio portrait of a formally dressed man and woman she assumed to be Isadora's parents. Their wedding portrait, she decided, though their stiff expressions showed no obvious signs of joy. Beside the wedding picture was a framed photo of a dark-haired little girl furiously plying her

218

bow across the strings of her miniature violin. The little miracle girl, Anna thought with a pang, who had first dedicated herself to saving her parents from their grief and after that the world.

There were several photos of an endearing small boy with sticking-out ears and two or three of a rather less endearing teenager just recognizable as Gabriel, the future accountant. There was also an intriguing photograph of a handsome fortyish man. Anna studied his face for a moment, wondering if this was the mysterious Valentin, who Isadora had once declared to be the love of her life.

Anna returned to her armchair, alert for any sounds coming from upstairs. Earlier this morning she'd had to wake Sabina from a dead sleep so that she could talk to the police officer who'd arrived to take a statement. After the policewoman had left, taking Hetty's diary and the originals of James's letters, Sabina had pleaded exhaustion and gone back to bed. It had been an emotionally draining evening for everyone and no one had had much sleep.

Anna picked up James's first letter. She and Jake had skim-read them all last night, but she felt she needed to read them through again while there were fewer distractions. Though he had sent money for Hetty's daughter every month for sixteen years, James had written to her only a dozen or so times in all. At no time, even in the very first letters, did he seem to picture himself addressing a small child. It was more as if he was unburdening himself to the adult he imagined that Iona would one day become. Maybe he had never seriously believed the letters would ever reach her? Perhaps he'd sent them off the same way a desperate castaway entrusts a message to a bottle, throwing it into the sea to sink or float? Anna suspected the letters had been written at low moments when James's guilt, and the crippling silence Tallis had imposed upon the Six, had become too much to bear.

With the help of the letters she and Jake had been able to piece together more of Hetty's story. In fact, Hetty had confided in James almost as soon as she knew she was expecting a baby, which sounded to be surprisingly far along in the pregnancy. At first, he assumed she'd told him because he was the father of her child and immediately declared that he would give up everything, his place at Oxford, his dreams of being a historian and a writer, to look after them both.

Hetty had told James that she didn't need him or anyone to take care of her. He wasn't the father and she wasn't going to keep this baby. Her ex-stepmother, Maeve, was arranging for her to have the baby in Switzerland. Hetty and Maeve had agreed that Hetty's father must never find out; which seemed strange, Anna thought, given that he seemed to go around impregnating females like some randy old stallion.

James said Hetty had expressed relief that her child wasn't due to be born till the long summer holidays. She could give birth then go back to start her final year at Oxford as if nothing had happened.

'*I told her this was wrong,*' James wrote to the young Iona.

I told her, 'You can't have a baby, a small living, breathing person with a soul, and carry on as if nothing's happened!' I said I didn't care whose damn baby you were. I'd stand by her and marry her and we could bring you up together. Hetty said that was insane. She said I would only end up resenting and hating her. Besides, she wasn't ready to settle down with a husband and a child. She didn't feel like enough of a grown-up. 'How can I raise a child, when I don't even know who I am?' I begged and pleaded with her to change her mind. I said I could be grown up enough for the two of us.

If I could go back in time to that day, Iona, I swear I would beg and plead harder, because I would know that I wasn't just begging for your life but for Hetty's.

After she came back nobody seemed to see the change in her but me.

That wasn't entirely true, Anna thought. Isadora had half sensed a difference in Hetty, but since Hetty hadn't directly confided in her, she had no way of understanding the trauma her friend had been through. She returned to James's letter.

Your mother was still beautiful, possibly even more beautiful, but there was something slightly frenetic about her now. She was like a light that shone too brightly and it scared me. I didn't know how to reach her. I kept remembering that night when we lay together in her bed and my fear that I'd lost her forever seemed like the cruellest thing anyone had ever had to bear. I was young and selfish and I related everything back to my own happiness. I didn't know what I know now, that the cruellest thing was seeing your mother cold and white on that hotel floor, knowing that I'd ended the life of the person I loved most in the world.

Anna took a gulp of her cooling coffee. *Love,* she thought, and had an involuntary flashback to her surprise awakening at six that morning: when she opened her eyes to find herself lying on Isadora's sofa, with her head resting on Jake's chest. Despite their cramped conditions he'd appeared to be sound asleep.

She had felt such a bewildering mix of pleasure and fear that for a few moments she couldn't seem to move, just stayed where she was in Jake's arms, feeling his strong heartbeat, listening to his slow, even breathing, as she mentally paged through the events of the previous evening.

She'd gone back to Isadora's with Bonnie. They had all eaten crackers and cheese. Somewhere around two a.m., Sabina had gone up to bed. Mindful of their promise to her father, Jake and Anna had sat up playing Scrabble from a battered set Anna had found on a dusty bottom shelf. Sitting side by side on the sofa with the Oxford dictionary between them, in between some gentle wrangling about proper and improper words, they

222

had talked in that spacey unfocused way of people who have had far too little sleep.

Jake had told Anna he'd started reading the book she'd brought him for Christmas. 'I knew dogs were amazing,' he'd told her. 'But this book gives you the science *behind* canine amazingness. I've always been nuts about dogs. When I was a little kid I used to fantasize about finding my own version of Lassie and just setting off with her on adventures!'

'You did find her. Eventually,' Anna had reminded him. 'You found Bonnie. She definitely has her Lassie moments! She found Naomi's body if you remember.'

Jake had nodded. 'I'd never thought of it like that. She had more than a few Lassie moments in Afghanistan now I think about it.' And he'd told her of the time Bonnie had led him and his men to where an injured comrade was lying half buried under rubble. Somehow this had led on to Jake's memory of another dog-related adventure story he had loved as a boy. 'One time after I met Mimi, she took me to a yard sale and she bought me an ancient hard-backed copy of *The Call of the Wild*, by Jack London. Ever read it?' Anna had shaken her head. 'It's about sled dogs in Alaska,' he'd explained. 'Man, I literally loved that book to death! I read it so many times, it fell apart.'

At some point, they'd both become too tired to even string a coherent sentence together, and she and Jake must have crashed out next to each other on the sofa. She wished Bonnie and Hero could tell her exactly what had happened next. Had Jake consciously moved to hold her against

223

his chest? Or had they just naturally drifted towards each other in their sleep as the dogs lay snoring at their feet?

Softly disengaging herself, she'd left Jake sleeping. She'd let Hero and Bonnie out into the garden and gone to wake herself up with a long hot shower. Later, she'd come downstairs to find a barefoot Jake in the kitchen making coffee. When she walked in he'd seemed exactly the same as always. Did he know that Anna had slept in his arms? It was impossible to tell. He must have slept extremely deeply, because the peaceful rhythm of his breathing hadn't changed, not even when she'd had to free a strand of her hair that had become entangled in the metal strap of his wrist watch. Anna could still feel the surprisingly painful tweak to her scalp mixed with the sweetness of intimacy.

Her phone beeped. She had a message from Tansy.

Back at yrs. Crashed at L & N's. LG still not talking. Thought I'd do a big cook up for Isadora so no worries when she comes home. xxx

Anna checked the time. There were still a couple of hours to go before she could visit Isadora. She had packed nightwear and toiletries for her and added a couple of novels that she'd found by Isadora's bed. She'd also taken an entire series of photos of Hero on her phone to prove that Isadora's little dog had survived her owner's ordeal unscathed.

Suddenly feeling chilly, Anna got up to close the window. There were still no sounds from upstairs so she continued to reread James's letters. Last night, she'd told Sabina, 'It isn't true that

224

none of Hetty's friends helped her. None of her friends *knew* – except for James Lowell, and he offered to give up everything to marry her and take on her child!'

'You think he loved her?' Sabina's face had registered disgust. 'James didn't love Hetty! He was like her *stalker*!'

James had become obsessed with Hetty, Anna thought as she read, but she didn't think it was in a weird stalkery way, it was more like a frantic last-ditch need to make things right again between him and Hetty – also to make things right *for* Hetty. His letters showed that he'd become increasingly worried about her. She appeared to have lost all interest in her studies. She missed tutorials, handed essays in late and if James said anything she just shrugged and laughed. 'Will the world be a better place if I read *Beowulf*? No! Will I be a better wiser person? No! I will just have wasted precious hours of my one and only life that I am never going to get back!' She was constantly disappearing off to London. James didn't know if it was to do with Tallis or to meet someone he only ever referred to as 'A'. He was secretly terrified that Hetty had met someone who appealed to her more than James and would be finally lost to him for ever.

One afternoon, he'd bumped into her on the High. Seizing his chance, he'd asked if he could buy her a drink. They'd found a quiet corner in the Turf and it seemed to James that they were suddenly talking together almost as freely as they had in the early days of the Six. It struck him that Hetty looked happier than she'd seemed for a long time. Encouraged by her sunny mood he reached for her hand and told her that he loved her and would never stop loving her as long as he lived.

To my dismay, Hetty hastily pulled away. 'But you have to stop, darling,' she told me. 'Oh, dearest James, I really am so enormously fond of you. I just can't love you in the way you need. The fact is, I've met someone.'

She didn't seem to notice that she had shattered my heart into pieces, she just went on to tell me about this someone, an American. Sam was reliable, steady, all the things she used to think so unglamorous. She said what she loved about him most was that he was so quiet and ordinary. 'He makes me feel peaceful, James. I never met a man who made me feel peaceful before. He doesn't play games. I am so sick and tired of all these games.' She said after tomorrow she was breaking off all contact with Tallis. She'd agreed to meet someone in London at the Palmeira Hotel, her last ever assignment for our handler. Then she was going shopping for a suit to wear for her first meeting with Sam's mother. 'Isn't that just the most hilarious thing you ever heard?' she said, laughing. 'I'm going to be a proper grown up, and I'm going to be quietly ordinary and have a house with a picket fence. I can't tell you what a relief it is!'

226

If James was devastated by the news that Hetty had fallen in love with someone else, he was doubly devastated by her hymn to Sam's ordinariness. *I'd always worried that I was too quiet and ordinary for your mother*, he wrote. *If she'd said my rival was exciting and witty and wild I'd have understood, but this just felt – wrong.* Anna thought of James's extraordinary beauty as a young man and how Hetty had impulsively seduced him. She remembered Isadora saying that those first golden months with Hetty and the other members of the Six had a quality of Shakespeare's *Midsummer's Night's Dream*. Except that Shakespeare's play ended with a fairy blessing and all confusion happily resolved. But the confusion Tallis had set in motion was still reverberating through people's lives fifty years later.

James described how he'd caught the mid-morning train to London, downing several beers in the buffet car and several more in the bar of Hetty's hotel until he'd finally summoned the courage to go up to her room. At this point James's handwriting became shaky and harder to read. He hadn't really thought about how his big intervention was going to work out and was horrified when Hetty immediately tried to slam the door in his face. Fuelled with desperation and far too many beers, he forced his way into her room. He told Hetty that he couldn't let her go off and marry some numbskull Yank who required her to wear a two-piece suit to meet his mother. 'I was quite drunk by this time and probably said a lot of things best left unsaid.'

James said he remembered what happened next in the way people recall nightmares.

In nightmares, people behave like ugly distorted versions of themselves. More and more hideous events keep on unfolding and you get swept along with them like a matchstick caught up in the tide, helpless to prevent the final horror.'

Hetty said I had to leave, right now this minute. I refused. She told me that she hadn't wanted to be cruel but I was being so ridiculous I'd left her no choice but to tell me the truth. She'd taken me to bed because she'd felt sorry for me, that was all. It was one night and it had meant absolutely nothing and I had no right following her around like some whiny little puppy. She started pushing me towards the door, yelling that I was stupid and immature, that I was trying to ruin her life. I said I was there to stop her ruining her life. She said I had no right, no right, no right. She was screaming the words into my face as she kept shoving and hammering at my chest. I tried to push her away and I must have pushed too hard because I somehow caught her off balance, and she fell striking her head on the corner of the marble-topped coffee table. The screaming stopped, everything stopped and there was this terrible silence and Hetty was just lying crumpled on the *floor, not moving, blood pooling around her head.*

I must not have closed the door properly, because next minute Tallis walked in. He saw Hetty lying there and me standing over her. He said, 'What have you done?' I said, 'I think I've hurt her.' Tallis knelt down, feeling for her pulse and then he shook his head. He said, 'You've killed her.' His voice had absolutely no expression. I thought I was going to black out. Tallis said something like, 'This is no time to be sensitive, James. We have to keep our heads,' or something equally stiff-upper-lip. He said I was to get the first train back to Oxford. He said I wasn't to say a word to anyone about what had happened and he would handle everything.

I was in shock, Iona. I was numb, and so I simply did what he said. I went back to my college and I felt so blank and empty, it felt as if nothing was real. Sometimes even now I wonder if it was all just a bad dream, that none of it really happened. Then in the newspapers they said your mother was found strangled, but when I left her she was already dead. I still feel sick with shame and horror when I think of what Tallis must have had to do to cover up my crime.

Iona, I need to tell you that there isn't a day that goes by that I don't think about your mother. I know the money I send you can't make up for what I did, but maybe it will smooth your path in life just a little. I have told you my story now and I am in your hands. I am leaving the next move up to you, just do what you think is right.

Anna laid down James's final, most harrowing letter, feeling as if she was emerging from the pages of some dark and brooding novel. She thought of the professor as she'd seen him last, talking to a student in the college gardens. Everyone had spoken of James Lowell's gentleness, his humility. But what had Isadora said? 'He burned, Anna. He *burned.*' Poor man, she thought, how had he borne so much guilt? How could he go on to live a normal life, let himself fall in love again, after such a catastrophic end to his first love? Part of him had died with Hetty.

Anna decided she would risk a quick trip to the kitchen. She made a fresh pot of espresso in Isadora's dented metal pot and rinsed out her cup, still thinking about what she'd read. For the first time she wondered how much the other members of the Six had known about what had happened to Hetty? Had they guessed the unsavoury nature of the work she was doing for Tallis? Isadora had. James seemed to have had his suspicions, though he'd never spelled it out. Had Piers? Had Robert? Anna remembered Catherine's oddly cool behaviour towards Isadora. Catherine definitely knew something, something that Isadora's other friends hadn't been party to. Anna had a bad feeling that it had to do with Tallis.

She returned to her chair with her coffee, puzzling over Isadora's enigmatic handler. He was the joker in the pack, she thought. Nobody seemed to know who he was or who he worked for, or what his true agenda was, yet he had somehow got into these young people's heads, exploiting not just their weaknesses and character flaws but their youthful ideals.

Her thoughts went back to Catherine. Anna had not liked the little she'd seen of Sister Mary Catherine, and she wasn't sure if she'd have liked her in her undergraduate incarnation as Catherine Hetherington. Catherine was the member of the Six that Anna had the least sense of. She had infiltrated alleged communist groups for Tallis, gone on shared jaunts in Piers's London taxi and danced all night at the May Ball, relishing being young and free. If Robert was to be believed, Catherine had also had a lot of sex though apparently not with Robert. Now she was a nun. What had happened in Catherine's life to cause her to make that leap?

Anna stood up. She felt her heart thumping in her throat. It had just occurred to her that as one of the only two survivors of the Six, Catherine could also be in danger. Anna was horrified that she had not realized this before. Had she pictured Catherine as immune by virtue of being a nun, not part of the real world? OK, that might present quite a challenge to a possible attacker, assuming that Catherine lived in an enclosed order, but it wouldn't be impossible if you were filled with

231

sufficient hate. The person who had attacked Isadora and battered James to a bloody pulp had more than enough hate.

After a few seconds dithering, Anna pulled out her phone and called Liam's mobile but it went straight to voicemail. She left a slightly incoherent message, explaining that Catherine had also been part of Isadora's group and suggesting that the police should go and talk to her. She hung up knowing she hadn't properly communicated her fears for Catherine.

At some point Anna must have moved to stand by the window. For a while she watched the antics of three acrobatic little birds clinging to the bird feeder. She felt she should be doing more, but what? How the hell did you trace a nun?

'You ask an investigative journalist, you idiot!' Anna answered herself out loud. Tim Freemantle had managed to find Max Strauli when she had only found the deadest of dead ends.

She found her phone, punched in Tim's number and waited edgily for him to pick up. It felt imperative to find and speak to Catherine *now*; not only to warn her but to get some answers. Maybe Catherine didn't know any more about Hetty and James's murders than Isadora. Maybe Anna was clutching desperately at straws. Even so she had to try.

Why wasn't Tim answering his phone? It belatedly dawned on her. *Shit, it's still Christmas. Cancel the call, Anna!* She had a vivid image of Tim in his mother's house, eating leftovers and deciding whether to answer. Perhaps it was a

genuine flash of telepathy because a moment later she heard Tim's voice through a babble of TV and piping little voices. 'Anna, *thank* you,' he said fervently.

'For what?' Anna said surprised.

'You've saved me from watching my little twin nieces' *Barbie Tinkerbell* movie. They make me sing along to all the songs! It's like they're inducting me into their insidious Barbie cult! So what can I do for you?'

'I need you to find someone for me,' she said. 'It's quite urgent.'

Tim took his phone into another room, away from the sounds of loudly warbling little girls, and Anna told him the few details she knew of Catherine Hetherington's life. 'Can't promise anything obviously,' he said, 'but if I do succeed in turning up some info, I'd like to go with you, if that's OK? There's something I really need to talk to you about.'

'Tim, I thought I'd explained . . .'

'This isn't about your family's murders. It's something else,' Tim reassured her. 'I'll be in touch just as soon as I find anything.'

Before she could thank him, he'd gone.

Seventeen

Next morning, Anna woke in her own bed in Park Town. She'd left Jake holding the fort at Isadora's until Sabina's father arrived. It was by no means certain yet if Sabina was going to return to London with him. But at the very least she and her dad needed to have a long and hopefully therapeutic talk. Jake had said he thought that Iona's daughter needed an advocate, someone to stand by her and/or calm things down if things got too emotional with her dad. Anna thought Jake would be the perfect person.

But though Jake had stayed in Summertown, it quickly became apparent that Anna hadn't spent the night alone. Feeling a soft tickling sensation on her cheek, she opened her eyes to find Hero peering inscrutably into her face. '*No!*' she protested. 'You can sleep in my room, but I draw the line at sharing my bed with you.' At the sound of Anna's voice, Bonnie looked up from her basket, with a soft grumbling sound. The meaning of this sound depended on context. If Bonnie grumbled when she was being brushed it meant she was relaxed and happy. On this occasion, it was like a very gentle first cousin to a growl.

It was strange how dogs were able to communicate their feelings, Anna thought. Unlike humans, their features didn't really change, yet Bonnie's expression seemed not so much disapproving as resigned. *What can you do?* her soulful brown eyes seemed to say. *Isadora's in hospital. Hero's scared and homesick.*

'I know all that,' Anna told her. 'But I'm still not letting her share my bed!' As she firmly returned Hero to the floor it occurred to her that she had become a person who not only talked to her dog but had actual conversations with her.

After a late breakfast, she and Tansy decided

234

their first task was to take down their Christmas tree. 'It just feels wrong now after everything that's happened,' Tansy said.

Anna had stayed on at Isadora's until around midnight when Sabina went to bed, and had got home to find Tansy decanting home-cooked soups and casseroles into sealable containers to take over for when Isadora came out of hospital. Anna and Tansy had both visited her earlier in the day, staggering their visits so as not to tire her. Anna had gone first so Isadora had been able to tell an astonished Tansy who was the real writer of the anonymous letters.

Anna had only told Isadora the bare facts: that James had accidentally killed Hetty, confessing his crime in his letters to Hetty's mentally fragile daughter who had then filled her own daughter with thoughts of revenge.

Tansy had now read the photocopied letters. As she and Anna untangled strings of fairy lights, they kept going back to the tragic accident that had devastated so many lives. Like Isadora, Tansy found it almost impossible to believe that James had caused Hetty's death. 'I suppose in some weird old school-tie way Tallis thought he was protecting James by covering everything up,' she said. 'But if you ask me he made everything a million times worse.' She carefully unhooked a large iridescent bauble. 'I know it was terrible what happened to Hetty, but if James had gone straight to the police and confessed – OK, he might have gone to prison for a few years, but he wouldn't have lived the rest of his life in the shadow of this – this crippling secret!'

'I think you could be right.' Anna began to wrap an identical bauble in white tissue. 'Isadora's really something, isn't she?' she said in a sudden segue.

'You mean, when you told her about Sabina and the letters?'

'Yes! She must have spent about sixty seconds being distraught that she hadn't suspected that Hetty had been pregnant. Then she was all, "But this is *wonderful*! This is like my second chance, Anna! Hetty's granddaughter is living in my house. Oh, this is *extraordinary*, it's *glorious*! I feel as if I'm living in an Agatha Christie novel. I can hardly take it in!"'

'You know what she said to me? "Well, you know, Tansy, some of those letters were *quite* poetic in places. Sabina has obviously been doing some *extremely* esoteric reading!"' Tansy darted a grin at Anna. 'I had to look up "esoteric" on my phone. I thought it meant the same as "erotic".'

'It's possible to be both, I believe,' Anna said straight-faced.

Tansy sat down on the arm of a chair, still clutching her unwrapped bauble. 'I might have missed my chance at being esoteric with my lovely Liam though.'

'Lovely Liam's still not talking?' Anna said sympathetically.

Tansy shook her head forlornly. 'To be fair, I wouldn't talk to me if I was him either.' Her forehead puckered and she began to look vaguely around the room. 'I think I can hear your phone.'

'It's in the kitchen.' Anna ran downstairs,

praying, *Let it be Tim, let it be Tim*, then had to go hunting frantically for her phone. She found it in the wrong pocket in her bag, micro-seconds before it stopped ringing. Tim's name had come up on her screen. 'Hello,' she said breathlessly.

'Hi, I've found your nun!' Tim sounded pleased with himself.

'You've found her already?'

'You said it was urgent,' he said. 'So I pulled out all the stops.'

'Tim, thanks so much. Is she very far away?'

'No, just a few miles outside Oxford.'

Tim had located Catherine at a convent not far from Woodstock, called the Little Sisters of Mercy. 'I thought I'd come and pick you up in ten minutes or so, if that's OK?'

'That would be wonderful,' Anna told him.

She ran to her room to change out of her jeans and generally tidy herself up then ran back to Tansy to explain.

'You are going detecting in a convent without *me*, one of the original dog-walking detectives?' Tansy's tone made it clear she wasn't entirely joking.

'I am on this occasion,' Anna said apologetically. She saw a car pull up outside. 'Tim's here, I've got to go!'

'I'll just walk the dogs then, shall I?' Tansy called after her. 'It's not like I have a life or a boyfriend or anything!'

'Just like old times,' Tim said as Anna clicked her safety belt into place. He seemed nervous now they were actually together in the car.

'Old times?' Anna said.

'How can you not remember us sneaking up your parents' loft ladder to investigate the Mysterious Noises from the Attic!'

'Oh, my God, yes! And it turned out to be some poor bird that had got trapped under the eaves!'

'You say "poor bird", now. At the time, you totally freaked out! There you were in your ninja outfit, brandishing your Dad's torch, ready to confront who knows what – and suddenly you were shrieking like a girl!'

'Yes, because when birds get scared they fly around erratically and poo everywhere!' she said, laughing. 'I didn't want a bird pooing in my hair! Besides, in case it's escaped your notice, I *am* a girl. What was your excuse for screaming your head off and flapping your hands?'

She saw some of the tension leave Tim's face. He gave her an openly affectionate grin. 'It's good to see you, Anna.'

'Ditto!' she said smiling. 'Very good, actually.'

'Anyway, unlike our noises in the attic mystery, the Fates seem to be on our side with this one. Though Sister Mary Catherine sleeps in the Mother House or whatever they call it, she works shifts in the adjoining hospice. She'll be there this afternoon – so that's where we're going.'

'A hospice?' Anna felt a flicker of dread. Wasn't a hospice somewhere people went to die? 'You can't just walk in there though, surely? You have to have a valid reason?'

'It's all under control,' Tim reassured her. 'I also rang the hospice and I've given us a cover

238

story. I told them we're looking for somewhere to provide respite care for our sick grandfather. He's being cared for at home but sometimes his relatives need a break.'

'So who did you say we were? Husband and wife?'

Tim looked startled. 'No! I told them we were brother and sister obviously!'

His ill-concealed dismay amused Anna, because she understood exactly how he felt. She had always seen Tim as the more congenial and less annoying brother who happened to go home to a different house. 'Why are *we* making arrangements for our grandfather though?' she asked. 'Where are our parents?'

'Oh, bugger! Good question!' Tim thought for a moment. 'How about teaching in Dubai? Two-year contract? Uncaring bastards!' he added with a grin.

'Makes you wonder really, how you and I turned out so nice,' Anna said.

Up ahead the lights turned red and Tim began to slow. 'On the phone, you said you thought Catherine might be in danger. Do you think you could fill me in on the backstory? I'm assuming there has to be quite a meaty backstory?'

'It's an extremely complicated one,' she said. 'It starts back in the mid-nineteen sixties.'

'It's OK. We have time,' he said.

Tim was a good listener, stopping her now and then to make sure he'd grasped the essentials. 'So the anonymous letters and diaries were in fact quite separate from these attacks?' he said. 'Just a good old-fashioned red herring?'

'As it turns out,' Anna said.

'But you believe your friend Isadora was attacked by the same person who murdered James Lowell?'

'Not just me,' she said. 'The police are starting to think the same way. At least that's the impression I got from a friend in the police. I don't know for sure, as Liam still hasn't got back to me.'

Tim gave her an amused look. 'But you didn't think you should just wait for the cops to get up to speed?'

She shook her head.

'Once a ninja always a ninja,' he said with a grin.

The convent was set behind high brick walls clearly visible from the road. But the actual turn-off was so well hidden that Tim had to swerve off at the last minute, causing the driver behind them to sound his horn. Through the trees, Anna caught glimpses of mellow red-brick buildings. She had imagined that the hospice would be situated in an extension of the convent, but Tim swung his car between a pair of gates and drove up to the first of several extremely stylish single-storey buildings, obviously purpose-built. A sign outside read *Mercy Hospice*.

'If I look like I'm about to start singing "Climb Every Mountain", please feel free to punch me,' Tim said, as he got out of the car and Anna surprised herself with a giggle.

They went inside and reported to the softly spoken nun at the desk. She picked up a phone and told someone of their arrival. 'Sister Mary

Frances will be here in a few moments to take you around,' she told them.

While they waited, Anna and Tim stood looking out into a small sheltered garden. Anna could see pretty painted birdhouses and a trellis with winter flowering jasmine. If you had to go somewhere to die, Anna thought, Mercy Hospice was a good place.

Sister Mary Frances, a small white-haired nun who looked to be somewhere in her seventies, arrived to show them around. She wore the same neutral Marks and Spencer style of clothes as Sister Mary Catherine and the nun at the desk. The only outward sign of her spiritual vocation was the simple wooden crucifix on a chain around her neck. 'Welcome to our beautiful new hospice,' she said warmly. 'It's only eighteen months old and we are all extremely proud of it. We put in a bid for funding and then all the sisters prayed until their eyes practically popped out – and, as you see, our prayers were answered!' She explained that local supporters had worked additional miracles to raise the remaining revenue necessary to realize the sisters' vision.

'Now let me show you the kind of bedroom your grandfather could expect to stay in if he comes here for respite care,' Sister Mary Frances said, bustling ahead and opening a door. 'We had one dear lady here say it was like a boutique hotel! I don't know what in the world one of those is, but I assume it was meant as a compliment!'

They looked around the pleasant room with its windows that opened out on to trees and water.

The nun showed them the state-of-the-art bathroom facilities and Tim solemnly experimented with the taps. They followed her to the hospice kitchen where two cheerful nuns were preparing vegetable soups and juices. 'We do our best to use locally sourced ingredients,' Sister Mary Frances explained. 'Fresh, well-cooked food can make a big difference to a patient's well-being.' She gave a little shrug. 'But we also have to be realists. When your time is running out, it's not so much about vitamins, but more about what tickles your fancy.' She gave them a mischievous smile, 'What I'm trying to say is, if your grandfather wants one of Mr Kipling's cakes, he can have one!'

Anna had almost started to believe in her and Tim's fictional sick grandfather, when Tim said, smiling, 'Thank you so much for showing us around. You've certainly set my mind at rest. How about you, Anna?'

'Oh, I feel just the same,' Anna said. 'Now we just need to talk to Granny.'

'Oh, you should have brought her with you!' exclaimed the nun.

'I know and I wish we had,' Tim said. 'But we'll tell her everything you've told us. By the way,' he added, 'is Sister Mary Catherine still here? She was so wonderful to our aunt during her last weeks.'

'Oh, so you have been here before then?' Sister Mary Frances looked puzzled.

'Not in this building,' Anna said quickly. 'Our aunt was in the old hospice. And Sister Mary Catherine took such wonderful care of her.'

'Well, I'm sure she'd love to see you,' Sister Mary Frances said. 'At the moment she's in the lounge, trying to fix the DVD player. She's our go-to girl for all things technical!' She gave her warm laugh. 'She's just through here.'

The lounge turned out to be a communal hub for patients and relatives. There looked to be seven or eight people standing around the TV set, arguing about which film they were going to watch if the sister ever managed to fix the player. As they walked in, a woman whose advanced illness had turned her papery yellow, was saying, 'Don't put the poor sister under pressure!'

'I'm not putting her under pressure,' objected a teenage girl with a transparent nasal tube. 'I just asked if I could have a try!'

'Hush, all of you rabble!' Sister Mary Frances said cheerfully. 'I've brought some visitors for you, Sister. God bless you both,' she told Anna and Tim, 'and we will look forward to hearing from you about your dear grandfather very soon.' She whisked out of the room.

Anna saw the exact moment that Catherine recognized her. A strange expression came into the nun's eyes, almost of relief. 'Could we have a word in private?' Anna asked her.

She half expected Catherine to invent some excuse, but she only said in a neutral voice, 'It'll probably be a bit quieter in the corridor.'

They followed her to an alcove that looked out on to another small enclosed garden. This one had a bench and a stone statue of a woman that Anna assumed to be the Virgin Mary.

'You're Isadora's friend,' Catherine said. 'You were at James Lowell's wake.'

'Yes, I'm Anna. This is my friend Tim.' Anna took a breath and cut straight to the chase. 'Have the police been in touch?'

Catherine shook her head, looking mildly perplexed. 'No. Why?'

'You don't know what's been happening, then?' Anna took another sharper breath. 'This is probably going to sound crazy, but I think you could be in danger.'

A woman emerged out of a door, obviously in tears. A man, possibly her husband, immediately followed her out. 'I just can't bear to see her so frail,' the woman wept. 'I can't bear that we're going to lose her for ever.'

Not wanting to eavesdrop, they quickly moved on down the corridor stopping outside the pristine little kitchen that Sister Mary Frances had told them was for the use of relatives. 'Is that why you came?' Catherine said. 'Because you think I'm in danger?' Her voice had an edge of surprise, almost disappointment, as if she'd imagined they'd come for some entirely different reason.

'Someone attacked Isadora on Christmas Day,' Anna said.

Seeing Catherine's eyes widen, Anna said quickly. 'She's recovering now. But she'll have to be in hospital for a few days. Her consultant was worried about her heart.'

'And now you think someone might try to hurt me – here in the hospice?' Catherine sounded disbelieving. 'Who'd want to harm me?'

'Someone who knows something about the

Oxford Six,' Anna said bluntly and had the secret satisfaction of seeing Catherine flinch. 'The trouble is, I don't know exactly *what* they know. It's all such a tangle of secrets and lies. But someone somewhere still remembers you all, and whoever they are, they've already attacked at least twice.'

'You think this was the same person who killed James?' Catherine rubbed absently at her arms as if she felt cold. 'Secrets and lies,' she repeated. For the first time, she properly met Anna's eyes. 'Yes, you're right,' she said abruptly. 'There have been too many.'

Anna said, 'You see, I can't figure out if it's to do with James and what happened to Hetty's baby—'

'Hetty's *baby*?' Catherine interrupted, astonished. 'Hetty didn't have a baby!'

'She had a daughter at the end of her second year,' Anna told her. 'She went to Switzerland, gave birth in the summer holidays, then came back to Oxford and carried on as normal, except nothing was ever normal again for any of you after that, was it?'

Catherine shook her head. 'I didn't know.' Her eyes were suddenly bright with tears. 'I really wish I had. It explains so much about Hetty that I never understood at the time.'

A woman walked past them into the kitchen. She took a plastic container from the refrigerator, placed it in the microwave and began pressing buttons. Then she went to the sink and very noisily filled a kettle.

A small girl dressed like a Disney princess

came running down the corridor holding a helium balloon on a silver string. She disappeared into one of the rooms, shouting, 'I'm back, you can all sing it now!' and Anna heard enthusiastic voices start to sing 'Happy Birthday'.

'That's Zoe's little sister,' Catherine said. 'It's Zoe's eighth birthday today.' She gave a self-conscious laugh. 'We're not having much luck with our quiet talk, are we?'

'Why did you lie about seeing Tallis at the wake?' The words were out of Anna's mouth before she'd thought. 'Both Robert and Isadora saw him. You fobbed Isadora off and I want to know why.'

Again that look of relief came into Catherine's eyes. 'I always knew someone would come and ask me about him one day. When you walked in just now I thought that's why you'd come.'

Anna felt adrenalin flash through her. 'Do you know where he is?'

A sudden steely resolve came into Catherine's eyes. She set off along the corridor at a fast clip, not checking to see if they were following. Tim shot a startled glance at Anna. They caught up with Catherine just as she stopped outside a door. She knocked softly, then pushed the door open so that Anna could see inside.

The room was an almost exact replica of the one they'd viewed with Sister Mary Frances. An oxygen cylinder stood behind the bed, trailing wires. On the bed was a pair of black leather gloves and a familiar black fedora.

Beside the bed, looking back at Anna, unsurprised, was an elegant old man in a wheelchair.

246

Eighteen

'Visitors, what a pleasant surprise! Please do come in.'

Tallis could have had no idea who Anna was or why she was here, yet he'd instantly taken command, the gracious host.

He was quicker-witted than Anna. Her dismay at finding Isadora's former handler here in the hospice threw her off balance, making her lose all her social graces. She only knew that she felt an instant visceral dislike for this man. If Tim hadn't been standing just behind her, she might have taken a step backwards.

'Kitty will find us an extra chair, won't you?' Tallis added without looking at Catherine.

'I'll get a chair,' Tim said at once.

'The room next door is empty,' Catherine said. 'You can borrow one from there.'

'Maybe you could make us some tea then, Kitty?' Tallis said.

Kitty. The condescending pet-name told Anna everything about his relationship with Catherine Hetherington. Here was the critical missing piece of the puzzle, a part that Isadora had never suspected.

'Thanks, but we didn't come for tea,' Anna said bluntly. She didn't care if she was being rude.

'It's fine, honestly.' Catherine shot her an almost pleading look. 'I'm sure we could all do with a cup.'

247

Tim returned with the chair. Catherine moved towards the door, presumably to make their tea, but at the last minute she turned to Tallis and words burst from her as if she couldn't hold them back a moment longer. 'This is when it stops, Matthew! Today is when it stops, and these people are my witnesses!'

Tallis's expression of detached amusement didn't flicker, but Anna could feel his suppressed fury. 'Oh, Kitty, my love, don't be so tedious,' he said in a bored voice. 'We're both too old for these kinds of dramas.'

'It's *over*.' Catherine's voice was low and insistent. 'I *need* it to be over – for both our sakes.' She quietly closed the door leaving Anna and Tim alone with Tallis.

It was one of the most surreal moments of Anna's life. Though her gut instincts warned her against this arrogant old man, she was ashamed to find herself feeling slightly giddy; she was actually in the same room as the near-legendary figure of Isadora's and Hetty's stories.

Tallis gave Anna his ironic smile. 'I'm afraid you rather have the advantage. It appears you know who I am. Unfortunately Kitty forgot to introduce us.'

'I'm Anna Hopkins,' Anna said, not moving to shake hands.

'Tim Freemantle,' Tim said, also not moving.

'And I assume you are Anna's young man?' Tallis said.

'No, I'm her friend,' Tim said curtly.

Tallis shot him an intrigued look. Anna thought he was going to pass some comment, but he just

248

said softly, 'Ah. Yes, I see,' and returned his attention to Anna. 'I hope you've had an enjoyable Christmas, Anna?'

'Actually, no I haven't!' Anna flashed back. She'd had enough of Tallis's game that they were all having a civilized tea party. 'My friend was attacked outside her house. I believe you knew her, Isadora Salzman?' The little colour Tallis had left drained from his face. He began to wheeze, clearly struggling to get air into his lungs.

Anna was horrified. She'd just wanted to shock Tallis out of his complacency. She hadn't meant to kill him. She flew to unhook his oxygen tube as Catherine arrived back with the tray. Seeing Tallis fighting for breath she said calmly, 'I'll do that, Anna. He'll be fine in a few minutes.'

Not wishing to be voyeurs, Anna and Tim went to stand at the window while Catherine helped the obviously humiliated Tallis to draw oxygen into his lungs. 'This happens all the time,' Catherine said over her shoulder. 'He's got advanced emphysema. He comes in every few weeks for respite care.'

Anna heard her murmur reassuringly to Tallis until the crisis had passed. Then she heard Catherine ask in an undertone, 'Have you told them yet?'

Tallis shook his head. 'Waiting. For you,' he managed to gasp out.

Catherine simply looked at him. There was so much history in that look, so much hurt and disappointment. Then she lifted her chin, and Anna saw the return of her earlier resolve. 'Then I'll simply have to tell them myself.'

Catherine set about pouring tea, adding milk and sugar according to people's preferences. 'I've asked that we shouldn't be disturbed,' she told them. She seemed surprisingly composed. It wasn't the false calm she'd shown at James's wake. This felt more as if she'd made her peace with whatever was going to follow. She glanced once at Tallis, as if to confirm that she intended to go through with this, then she said, 'Of all the many shameful things I have done in this life, the one which distresses me the most is that I allowed James Lowell to die still believing that he killed Hetty.'

Anna felt herself go very still. 'But that wasn't true?'

'I believe the technical term for what I did is "the perversion of justice",' Catherine said. Tallis made an inarticulate sound of protest. She ignored him and continued talking.

'At the time, I convinced myself, as people who commit terrible crimes so often do, that I'd had no choice. But as the years passed, the burden of my sin became increasingly . . .' Catherine paused to search for the right word – '*unendurable*. Once, in my thirties, I tried to kill myself, but I was found just in time. It occurred to me then that God had intervened to spare me. I thought that since I couldn't confess my sin to anyone' – she gave an involuntary glance at Tallis – 'I could maybe find a way to atone. First, I trained as a nurse and then, after long soul-searching, I took holy orders. For many years, I worked overseas. But no matter how hard I worked or how many lives I saved, my guilt at my part in covering up Hetty's murder refused to diminish.' She briefly closed her eyes as if she felt her guilt as a physical force, dragging and pulling. 'And so I came back here to Oxfordshire, to the Little Sisters of Mercy. The day I started work in the hospice – the old hospice – Tallis was brought in. It felt like some cruel divine joke, as if God had walked me around in a great big circle and brought me face-to-face with my own inescapable vileness and stupidity! All those years, all that struggle and here I was right back where I'd started.'

Oh, my God, Anna thought, *you still loved him.*

Catherine saw Anna's expression and misunderstood. 'I've shocked you,' she said. 'You think I'm some kind of monster.' She gave a bleak little laugh. 'I sometimes feel that way myself.'

'Actually, I'm confused,' Anna said. 'I still don't know what you and Tallis did and I don't understand what happened to Hetty or why.'

Catherine's eyes went to Tallis. 'Tell her, Matthew. Tell Anna why Hetty had to die.'

'Don't do this,' he told her. 'Let the dead stay dead, and the past stay past.'

'The past *is never* past.' Tim was suddenly angry. 'People are still being hurt – someone has been killed – because of whatever you and Catherine and the others did back then.'

'*Tell* them,' Catherine insisted to Tallis.

His bland expression had become a fixed mask. 'You can't expect young people to understand. Those were different times. Too much was at stake.'

'*You* had too much at stake,' Catherine almost

251

snapped. She turned back to Anna. 'Hetty found out that Tallis had been using her, as part of a honeytrap.'

'Kitty, *stop* this!' Tallis almost barked the words. 'Before you go too far.'

Anna found herself imagining telling Tansy that a nun had used the term 'honeytrap'.

'I am no longer yours to control, Matthew.' Catherine drew herself up in her chair. 'And I will go just as far as I think necessary.'

'You were saying Hetty found out she'd been used,' Anna reminded her.

'Yes. She was furious. Worse than furious, she was sickened and ashamed. She'd started working for him in the belief that she was part of something noble, helping to save the world.' Once again she gave Anna that bleak smile. 'When she'd only been helping Tallis to help Tallis.'

'How about you?' Tim asked Catherine. 'Did you want to save the world?'

She shook her head. 'Nothing so noble. I just wanted Tallis. I wanted him from the first time I saw him. He had this way of making me feel so absolutely – *essential*. I'd never been essential to anyone. It was like a drug – as you knew it would be,' she said to Tallis.

'Kitty, I don't know why you're dredging up all this ancient history in front of these young people. You're embarrassing yourself.' Tallis was attempting to sound authoritative but he was beginning to look trapped.

'I'm not embarrassed, Matthew. I'm finally telling the truth, something I should have done decades ago. Then maybe I could have had a real

252

life instead of this – charade.' For the first time Catherine's voice became unsteady. She turned to Anna. 'I'm sure Isadora has told you how persuasive Tallis was in those days?'

Anna heard Isadora saying, *I'd have followed him through fire.*

Catherine took a sip from her cup. 'He said when we had enough money we'd go away together, maybe South America; somewhere we could make a fresh start.'

'A fresh start based on murdering one of your best friends?' Anna suggested.

Catherine blinked. She seemed horrified. 'No, this was before – before what happened in the hotel.' She seemed to lose her thread. 'I honestly didn't know about Hetty's baby. I didn't know she'd had a child . . .' Her calm had deserted her. She looked around the room in a kind of panic as if she might try to escape.

Tallis seized his chance. 'You see? You are just upsetting yourself, my love.' He patted her knee. 'You were always more fragile than the others. Sometimes I think you imagined things that—'

Throwing him a disgusted look, Tim simply talked over him. 'What happened at the hotel?' he asked Catherine. His voice, professional but friendly, seemed to bring her back to herself.

'Hetty told Tallis she was breaking off with him. She said she'd known criminals who were more honest. Tallis pretended to have these high ideals but he was out for whatever he could get. He asked me to meet him in this bedsit that he and I used sometimes. He was almost hysterical. "She's going to blow everything sky high. She's

253

going to expose me." I'd never seen him so out of control. It was the first time I'd ever felt that I was the stronger person.'

Until now, Anna thought.

'Eventually, I was able to calm him down. He started mocking Hetty for being so naive. She'd accused him of being a criminal, yet some ridiculous code of ethics made her feel she had to follow through on her last commitment for him before she went off into the sunset with her American.'

'What was her last commitment?' Anna asked.

Catherine looked away. 'She had to meet a man at the Palmeira Hotel in Chelsea.'

'Someone Tallis needed to keep sweet?' Tim said.

Catherine nodded. 'Sometimes it was just dinner or being some foreign delegate's plus one at some society party.'

'But sometimes men expected more?' Anna suggested.

'I don't think Hetty minded that too much at the start. I think it just felt like a part she was playing, a part in a thrilling spy movie. It was a strange time for young women,' Catherine said. 'The rules were changing but nobody quite knew what the new rules were supposed to be.'

Catherine told them that Hetty had gone up to her room at the Palmeira to wait for Tallis's man to show up. In fact, Tallis had already fixed him up with someone else, a girl he judged a safer bet than a disillusioned Hetty who was on the verge of leaving Tallis and England forever.

'I don't think Matthew ever planned to kill

Hetty.' Catherine threw a look at a grim-faced Tallis. 'He just wanted to frighten her enough to ensure her silence.'

'But James Lowell got in the way?' Anna said.

'I don't know what made James follow her to the hotel that day. But everyone knew he loved Hetty. It's possible he went to beg her not to go away with this American.'

Catherine said Tallis had told her to wait in the hotel bar while he went up to talk to Hetty.

'So I waited and I waited then in the mirror I suddenly caught sight of James hurriedly leaving the hotel. I was sure Matthew hadn't said anything about James coming. I had this terrible feeling – that something had gone wrong. I didn't know what to do, so I just went on waiting. Maybe fifteen minutes or so later, the barman called me to the phone. It was Matthew telling me to go up to Hetty's room. I took the lift up to her floor, and he pulled me inside before I had a chance to knock. Right away I saw Hetty lying on the floor. I'd never seen a dead body but I immediately knew she was dead. Matthew said I just had to stay calm and do exactly what he said and everything would be all right. He said there had been an accident. James had got upset and there had been some kind of scuffle and Hetty had hit her head and lost consciousness. Then, after James had left, she'd started to come round. Matthew said he'd only had a few crucial seconds to decide what he should do. He decided this was his one shot at saving everything he and I had worked for together.'

Catherine raised her eyes to meet Anna's. 'He strangled her.'

Tallis drew a sharp hissing breath.

'He said he'd done that so the police would think it was some unsavoury sexual shenanigans gone wrong. He said I had to help him dispose of – the body. He said it was the only way we'd be able to be together.'

Tallis opened his mouth, but didn't say whatever he'd been going to say.

'It was the kind of ludicrous scenario only a completely deluded young woman could believe,' Catherine said. 'You never really meant to run away to South America with me, did you, Matthew? You can tell the truth about that at least.'

'No.' Tallis had hardly moved his lips. 'I never meant to run away with you to South America or anywhere.' He didn't seem contrite so much as coldly furious that his former lover had exacted this admission.

'You see! The first glimmer of truth. There might be hope for you yet!' Tears stood in Catherine's eyes. 'Now tell them what you made me do.'

Tallis threw up his hands. 'All right, I'll tell them! I told her to take the sheet off the bed then I made her help me wrap the body in it. Luckily for us, Hetty had bought a ridiculously outsize suitcase for her travels. We took her things out and' – he gestured – 'put her in.'

'I'd never realized how small and slight she was.' Tears spilled down Catherine's cheeks and she quickly brushed them away. 'That night we sneaked out with the case and took it down to the river. Matthew said it would be high tide.

Then we just bundled her into the water and watched her disappear.' She shuddered as if she was suddenly back beside the Thames, watching as the water sucked Hetty's body down into the dark.

She turned back to Anna. 'That's what happened. That's what I allowed myself to be made a party to. My justification, believe it or not, was that I deserved to be happy with the man I loved.' She gave a despairing laugh. 'I told you I was a monster.'

'Are you happy now, Kitty?' Tallis said savagely. 'Do you feel righteous and cleansed now that you've dragged us both so pointlessly through the mud? And it *was* pointless!' He turned aggressively to Anna. 'The police won't dare to lay a finger on me.'

She was disgusted. Tallis had taken one life that they knew of, and had blighted countless others, including Iona's and Sabina's. The damage he'd caused still went on and on, spreading like ripples in a pool. Yet he showed no sign of remorse. He still believed he could operate outside normal human laws and be protected by his mysterious 'people'.

Anna was half out of her seat when Tim said, 'Anna came here because she thought she should warn Catherine that she might be in danger. From what Catherine's just told us, you're an extremely dangerous and unprincipled man. But, if you'll excuse me saying' – he shot a look at the angry old man gripping the arms of his wheelchair – 'I can't see you physically attacking Isadora or James, unless you paid someone else to do it.'

257

Tallis went to speak but Tim quickly held up his hand. 'And you obviously need Catherine far more than she now needs you.'

'Thank you for reminding me of my complete dependency,' Tallis said drily.

'I thought it was time someone did,' Tim told him. 'But my point is that there's still something very significant that we're missing.'

Tim was right, Anna thought. Catherine had supplied a crucial missing piece of the puzzle, but they were no nearer to finding out who had killed James.

'Matthew and I have some thoughts about that.' Catherine sounded hesitant. 'There was someone we all knew at that time, someone who might have a grudge against the Six and Matthew.' She glanced at Tallis and he gave a reluctant nod.

'His name was Alec Faber,' he said. 'His father was a prominent civil servant at the Foreign Office. Alec had come down from Oxford, and was starting out in the lower echelons of the FO. He was also a heavy gambler, and generally into shortcuts. This meant he was often strapped for cash. Through his father, Alec had access to all kinds of sensitive information. We received a tip-off that he might be selling secrets to the Soviets via an unlikely little left-wing group in Oxford. To my surprise, this turned out to be true, but I kept that interesting discovery to myself.'

Anna sat back in her chair. She remembered Isadora's story of finding a distraught Hetty in her room. *It's not about politics, it's about money.* 'You were blackmailing this man?'

'Can we just scroll back a bit?' Tim asked Tallis. 'Your department – I'm guessing MI5? – was working day and night to stop the flow of sensitive information going to the Soviets, but you were actually *profiting* from it?'

Tallis shrugged. 'Alec and I both profited from it. I also had other ways of "keeping him sweet" as one of you so charmingly put it.'

'Hetty,' Anna said.

'Alec liked her. In fact, he became besotted by her, which initially worked in my favour.' He shot them a humourless smile. 'But then one evening he had a whisky-sodden crisis of conscience and let it slip to Hetty that he'd been giving me money and why. Hetty, being Hetty, came and confronted me. I thought she was threatening to expose me, so when the accident happened I took the chance to be rid of her.'

'Now tell them the rest, Matthew,' Catherine said.

Tallis gave an irritated sigh. 'I don't know why you're so sold on confession, Kitty, my love. It really is *terribly* tedious.' He rubbed his gnarled hands over his face and Anna remembered her first glimpse of him in the memorial gardens and how she'd imagined he might be an actor or maybe a jazz musician. Despite the advanced state of his illness, Tallis still felt compelled to perform.

'The rest, Matthew,' Catherine insisted.

He passed his hand over his thinning white hair. 'I could see everything blowing up in my face, so I made what you'd call a pre-emptive strike and reported Alec's activities to my superiors. The scandal was hushed up of course, or it was hushed up as much as possible. The country was still reeling from the Profumo–Keeler affair, not to mention the Philby scandal,' he explained. 'Her Majesty's Government couldn't afford to be seen to have another rotten apple in the barrel.'

'What happened to Alec Faber?' Tim said.

Anna heard someone knocking softly on the door.

'He lost everything,' Catherine said, before Tallis could speak. 'His family disowned him, just cast him out. Overnight he became a – pariah.' She swallowed. 'He lived on the street for a few years. I saw him a few times in Hackney with his dog on a piece of string. Then he disappeared. I always hoped it was because he'd somehow got his life back together. But if you're looking for someone with a valid reason to hate us . . .' Her sentence trailed away.

The person knocked again, more forcefully this time. 'Is Sister Mary Catherine in here?' a young and distinctly annoyed voice demanded. Anna suspected it was the girl with the nasal tube. Catherine still hadn't fixed the DVD player.

'I'll be with you in a moment,' Catherine called. 'Go back and wait for me.'

She drew a breath, clasping her hands in front of her chest. For a moment, she was a nun again. 'I'd already decided that I would go to the police,' she told them, 'whatever the consequences. But now that you've heard my story, I've left myself no choice, which I find strangely liberating.' She gave Tallis a wistful smile. 'You owe me this,

Matthew, don't you think?' She accompanied them to the door, white-faced and resolute. Tallis had wheeled himself over to the window, turning his back on all of them, the only power he had left.

'Jesus Christ,' Tim said as soon as he and Anna were back in his car. 'I'm exhausted. I hate to think how you must feel.'

Anna managed a tired smile. 'Was it worse than sitting through your little nieces' Barbie movie?'

'That's a tough one.' Tim said, turning the key in the ignition. 'My nieces are terrifyingly Machiavellian, but unlike Matthew Tallis they'll presumably grow out of it.'

She patted his knee. 'Thanks for coming. It made a big difference that you were there.'

'You'd have done the same for me. We always had each other's backs, didn't we?' Tim gave her a fleeting smile. 'I think, in the circumstances, I'll save my other news for later.'

Anna had forgotten about Tim's mysterious news.

'I promise it's nothing to do with spies or murder. I'll come over some time, if that's OK?'

Anna felt too emotionally blasted to do more than nod. She wondered vaguely how Jake was getting on with Sabina and her dad. God, but she was shattered. Hopefully it was just lack of sleep catching up and she wasn't going down with something.

All I want right now, she thought, *is to be back at home with Bonnie*. Instead of this thought comforting her, she found her mind turning to the disgraced young civil servant whose life Tallis had helped to destroy, living out on the street in all weathers, despised and reviled by everyone except his dog.

Nineteen

'And Catherine just sat everyone down and *confessed* to helping this handler guy conceal the murder? She helped to cover it up, the *nun*?' Wearing an oversize grey sweater with skinny jeans, her hair still wet from the shower, Sabina paced Isadora's kitchen, as she struggled to absorb this startling development. 'Oh, my God!' she said, obviously struck by a disturbing new thought. 'Another fucking psycho nun!'

'I wouldn't describe Catherine as psycho,' Anna said.

'Oh? So how *would* you describe her?'

Mark Bingham, Sabina's dad, came through the door like a man hoping to pick a fight. He'd been out to fetch something from his car, for the third or fourth time in the half hour since Anna had arrived at Isadora's, in between checking his laptop and his phone. Anna had started to wonder if Mark might have some kind of condition. He certainly had an alarming surplus of nervous energy. Anna, who also wasn't great at sitting still, had initially felt sympathy. Now she just wished he'd jump in his car and drive back to London taking his jittery vibes with him.

'Obviously I didn't know Catherine when she was young.' Anna was trying not to sound confrontational. 'But the woman I met yesterday has been to hell and back. She knows what a terrible thing she did and she's willing to face the consequences.'

'And that makes it all right does it?' Mark said in a jeering tone.

Jake turned around from Isadora's cooker where he was making French toast, closely watched by Bonnie who had developed a passion for anything egg-related. 'Anna didn't say that made it all right,' he said mildly. 'She was suggesting that people shouldn't fling the psycho label around. As a rule, psychopaths and socio-paths aren't capable of remorse.'

Sabina's father made an irritated huffing sound, but subsided into a chair and fished out his phone to check his messages. Anna wondered what had made Sabina's mother fall so much in love with this man that she'd moved countries to be with him. She supposed Mark was quite good-looking, if you like men who look like sulky boys.

Jake piled the last pieces of French toast on to to a large platter and brought them to the table, along with a plate of crispy bacon rashers.

'I'll grab the maple syrup,' Sabina said, and went to fetch it.

Mark Bingham put his phone down beside his plate and went to help himself to a piece of puffy golden-brown French toast. He seemed to be having difficulty spearing it with his fork. For the first time Anna properly noticed the bandage wrapped around the fingers of his right hand.

'Oh, what did you do to your poor hand?' she asked with a solicitousness she didn't really feel.

'Just a silly accident,' he said, without looking up, clearly reluctant to go into it.

Anna could feel Jake carefully not reacting. He obviously had his own suspicions as to how Mark might have hurt his hand. Judging from what Anna had seen so far, Mark Bingham only had two settings: aggrieved and aggressive. He'd told her he was on medication for high blood pressure and she wasn't surprised. Jake had been amazing, Anna thought, stepping in to support Sabina and now playing host to her bizarre father.

When she arrived at Isadora's with the dogs, Jake had opened the front door, wearing jeans and a dark blue sweater, his reading glasses on his head and the book she'd bought him in his hand. His first words to her were, 'Did you know dogs can smell food even when it's *inside* the refrigerator! I mean, that's like a superpower!'

Anna could still feel that little flicker of happiness inside as she sat eating her share of the brunch Jake had cooked for everybody. He liked her present. He really, *really* liked it.

Sabina carefully drizzled maple syrup over her toast. 'You make good French toast,' she told Jake.

He gave her a humorous salute. 'Thank you, ma'am.'

'You put vanilla in,' Anna commented.

Jake raised a surprised eyebrow. 'You don't use vanilla when you make it?'

'No, never!' Anna slid him a grin. 'But I shall from now on. It's delicious!'

'So – what happens next,' Sabina asked. 'I mean, about Catherine and Tallis?'

Thanks to Liam Goodhart, who was once again talking to Tansy, Anna was able to tell Sabina that Catherine had followed through with her resolution to confess her part in Hetty's murder to the police. She and Tallis had been taken down to Thames Valley Police headquarters for questioning.

'I'm glad,' Sabina said, but Anna noticed that she sounded far less venomous than before. Sabina was going to need to rethink everything she knew about her family's history, Anna thought. All her life, James had been a pantomime villain to boo and hiss, the man who'd murdered Hetty Vallier then sent guilt money to her orphaned little girl. Like so often, real life had turned out not to be that simple.

Having silently devoured his breakfast, Sabina's dad was once again fiddling with his phone, checking for new messages or updates, or anything that would take him out of this room, Anna thought. 'So have you packed your bags, Sabs?' he asked his daughter. 'I need to get back to the office.' He gave his hostile laugh. 'Those bills won't pay themselves.'

'Actually . . .' Sabina sounded tentative. 'I've kind of changed my mind about coming back with you. I think I'm going to stay here.'

His face darkened. 'You seriously intend to stay with this woman after she turned her back on your grandmother at her time of greatest need?'

Sabina looked flustered. 'Dad, we don't know for sure if that's what happened. Anna said

Isadora didn't even *know* Hetty was having Mum.'

'They're friends! Of course she's going to bloody back her up.' Hearing Mark's raised voice Bonnie came out from under the table, deliberately interposing herself between him and Anna. She didn't growl but the corner of her lip lifted very slightly.

'Dad, please, I don't want to have a fight.' Sabina gave his uninjured hand a loving little pat. 'I really appreciate you coming up to see me and I promise I'll come to visit soon. But I think I ought to stay here for now.' She deliberately met his eyes, willing him to understand. 'Ms Salzman is going to need someone to be here when she comes out of the hospital. I can, you know, walk Hero and stuff. That's, if she'll let me.' She shot a shame-faced look at Anna.

'I'm sure she'll be incredibly grateful.' Anna said. She was touched. Sabina had obviously done some soul-searching and decided to try to make it up to Isadora for her earlier behaviour.

Mark stood up, his features suffused with rage. 'Well, that's unusually forgiving of you, Sabina. Extremely . . .' He seemed to be searching for a suitably hurtful word. '*Christian*,' he finished triumphantly. 'I wonder what your poor mother would think about your wonderfully Christian behaviour, if she were here.'

'Dad, please don't be like this—' Sabina started, but her father carried on like he hadn't heard her.

'Your mother should have been the love of my *life*, Sabina.' His voice quivered with emotion. 'She was so beautiful, so perfect. I never saw anyone so perfect. But she was *broken* inside, absolutely broken by her experiences in that orphanage. If you ask me, Hetty's so-called friends deserve everything that's happened and more. I've got nothing but contempt for the whole pack of them!'

Anna avoided Jake's eyes. She suspected they were thinking the same thing. Mark Bingham's moral outrage seemed a bit misplaced for a man who had left his young child in the sole care of her 'absolutely broken' mother.

Not long afterwards, she and Jake stood in the doorway with Bonnie, watching Sabina and her father say their goodbyes through his car window. Sabina had wrapped herself in the pale pashmina she'd worn the first time Anna saw her, but the biting wind kept briskly unwrapping it.

'Well, ain't he a real charmer?' Jake's voice took on its most southern intonation.

'I'd assumed it was Sabina's mother who'd poisoned her mind against Isadora and her friends,' Anna said. 'Now I'm wondering if it was Mark.'

'"Your mother should have been the love of my life",' Jake quoted. 'You have to hope he hasn't passed that delightful piece of info on to his current wife!'

'Bonnie *really* didn't like him,' Anna said. Hero didn't like anyone much except Isadora, but until recent unfortunate events Bonnie had always been a people dog.

Jake shook his head. 'Reminded me too much of my old man.'

Anna glanced at him. 'Really?'

'Hell, yeah! Same self-pity, same rage, every-thing is always someone else's fault. Of course, he was also a drunk which obviously didn't improve him any.'

Jake never talked much about his parents. He had told her a bit about Aunt Mimi, the neighbour who had intuited some goodness in him and allowed him to walk her dog, the first Bonnie. Anna would have liked to ask Jake about his mother, but Sabina was slowly walking back up to the house, her blonde hair whipping across her face.

'It's downright eerie how much that girl looks like Hetty, isn't it?' Jake commented. 'I saw it straight off. She was breaking her heart about what had happened to Isadora and I thought, *I know you!* Then it dawned on me who I'd confused her with. So I said, '"Are you a relative of Hetty Vallier?" And she fell to pieces!'

Anna hadn't thought to question how Sabina came to confess her authorship of the anonymous letters to Jake within minutes of meeting him. Now she could see exactly how it had come about. Sabina had just found Isadora unconscious and bleeding. She must have been traumatized, also feeling extremely guilty; all her defences would have been down. Then Jake brought up the family resemblance and Sabina must have thought the game was up.

'Sabina,' she said, as the three of them walked back into the house. 'I'm going to visit Isadora later. Would you like to come?'

Sabina seemed thrown. 'I – I don't know,' she stammered. 'Don't you think it might upset her?'

Anna smilingly shook her head. 'She's longing to meet you! Well, obviously she's met you, but she feels as if she hasn't really, because she didn't actually know who you were!'

Sabina looked as if she might cry again. 'I don't think I'd want to see me,' she said tearfully. 'I hurt her. I wanted to give her a little taste of what my mum had to suffer, and I did and now I feel *so* bad.'

'The thing you need to understand about Isadora is that she's a tough cookie. Isadora's been through things we'll never know, but she tries not to let those things dictate how she lives her life. Give her a choice between love and hate and she'll always—' Anna had a sudden vivid memory of a wrathful Isadora brandishing a bottle of Bombay Sapphire and swiftly corrected what she'd been going to say, 'and nine times out of ten she'll choose love.'

'I don't really feel like I deserve to be loved,' Sabina said in a small voice.

'I don't think you get a choice!' Anna told her. 'You're Hetty's granddaughter. Isadora can't *help* but love you! Just come with me and you'll see.'

In fact, twenty minutes after their arrival by Isadora's bedside, Anna and Jake slipped Sabina her taxi fare and discreetly excused themselves. This was a special moment for both Isadora and Sabina and it felt right that it should be private.

On the short car journey back to Park Town, Hero started panting, possibly wondering which house she was being taken back to. For a dog that disliked all forms of change, she must be completely out of her comfort zone, Anna thought.

This was the first chance she and Jake had had to talk about her and Tim's experiences at Mercy Hospice, so with a small panting dog for her soundtrack, Anna filled him in, as she drove. When she'd finished Jake gave a soft whistle. 'That was some confession. Not an easy thing to have to hear.'

'No,' she said. 'And there was Tallis, apparently not giving a shit about what he'd done. That was hard too.'

'I've been trying to picture the moment when the elderly nun opened the door to reveal her secret lover. Exactly what you want to find behind your Advent calendar – a rogue agent in a wheelchair!'

Anna laughed. 'I suppose it was quite a moment!' She briefly took her eyes off the road. 'You think that's what he was? A rogue agent?'

Jake shrugged. 'Agents get used to walking on the shady side of the street. They use fake names, swap identities, play people off against each other. Whatever gets results. Unfortunately with some of them it gets to be a habit – a compulsion even. It sounds like that's what happened to Tallis. At some point, he decided he needn't answer to any authority but himself.'

As they parked outside Anna's house Hero began to whine. Anna wasn't sure if it was anticipation or protest. Jake smiled at Anna. 'That was really sweet back there at the hospital. Isadora and Sabina will be good for each other.'

Anna thought back to the scene they'd just left. Isadora tentatively taking on the role of substitute grandmother, Sabina shyly responding to Isadora's warm overtures.

'I think so too,' Anna said. 'Sabina is overdue some love in her life. I know Iona loves her but she's so damaged I suspect Sabina has ended up parenting her most of the time.'

'So anyway,' Jake said, very obviously changing the subject. 'Before we go inside your house, there's something I've been wanting to say to you.'

His expression gave no clue to what this mysterious something might be so she just said cautiously, 'OK?'

He nodded. 'I wanted to say that I am seriously impressed with your British self-control.'

Anna suddenly felt slightly too warm. 'You are?'

'Hell, yeah! I'd have had the gift wrap ripped off in a heartbeat. In fact, I believe I did! But so far as I know yours is still waiting to be opened?'

'Oh, you're talking about my *present*!' Anna could feel herself getting flustered. 'It's honestly not that I don't want to. But you said to wait until I was alone, and then Isadora got attacked, and there was all the business with Sabina, not to mention the hospice.'

'And hearing Catherine confess to concealing a murder.' Jake gave Anna a wry smile. 'It's been quite a crowded few days, hasn't it?'

'It has and this is probably going to sound really silly. But it feels like – like the lovely sparkly Christmas boat has sailed away till next year now, and I don't – well, I didn't want to just open it like an afterthought, if that makes any sense?' *Shut up, Anna, you're embarrassing yourself.* She remembered disentangling her hair from his watch strap. She remembered waking in his arms, hearing the slow steady ebb and flow of his breath.

'You wanted it to be special,' Jake suggested. Anna could feel his eyes on her. She swallowed, afraid that she'd already given away too much.

He thought for a moment. 'OK, then, so how about we make a new plan? I have really always been more of a New Year man; fresh starts, new hopes. How about opening my present on New Year's Eve?'

She smiled at him. 'I think I like that plan.'

They let the dogs out of the jeep and went into Anna's flat.

They found Tansy downstairs on the small kitchen sofa texting feverishly. She looked up, said, 'Just let me send this!' then put her phone down on the sofa arm and said, 'So how's Isadora?'

'She seems much better. All being well they'll let her out tomorrow. We left her with Sabina,' Anna added.

'Sabina went to visit her?' Tansy's eyes widened. 'Is that the first time Isadora's seen her since it came out about the letters?' Anna nodded. 'That was really brave of Sabina,' Tansy conceded.

'She is brave,' Anna said. 'She's a surprisingly OK person, considering her parentage.'

'Anna met Sabina's father,' Jake explained. 'She wasn't overly impressed.'

'I only had to put up with him for an hour,' Anna told Tansy. 'I don't know how Jake coped.'

He laughed. 'I was in the military, don't forget. If I let myself get wound up by every creep who crossed my path, I'd have been in trouble!'

Tansy uncurled from the sofa. 'Do you guys want coffee?'

'Always,' Anna said smiling.

Sensing that a treat of some kind was on offer, Hero was immediately alert. 'I know what you want, you greedy little dog, you want cheese,' Tansy told her. Hero gave a short sharp bark. 'Yes, you're a greedy little cheese-eating goblin dog, and you are going to be *so* happy tomorrow when Isadora gets out of hospital!'

Anna watched Tansy cut tiny cubes of cheese for both the dogs, her denim dungarees tucked into brightly coloured slipper socks. She seemed so at home that Anna had to remind herself that she wasn't a permanent fixture.

Tansy poured water into the coffee maker and switched it on. 'I just heard from Liam. Catherine and Tallis have been taken into custody. The police formally charged Tallis with Hetty Vallier's murder and Catherine with perverting the course of justice and preventing the burial of a body.'

Anna took a few moments to let this sink in. It was doubtful if Tallis would survive until the case was brought to trial, but it seemed likely that Catherine would have to spend the rest of her life in prison. It was a sad ending for Isadora's old friend, who must have started out with so many hopes and dreams. But the most important thing, obviously, was that Hetty's murderer had finally been found. The toxic secret that had blighted so many lives was finally going to be brought out into the light. 'I'm glad,' Anna told Tansy. 'It's been a long time coming.'

'Any further leads about the attacks?' Jake asked.

Tansy shook her head. 'None.'

'I'm not sure how much credibility I'd give anything Tallis says,' Anna said, 'but he and Catherine both mentioned someone from the Oxford Six days who they thought might be nurturing a grudge.'

Tansy made a face. 'It doesn't seem very likely. If you've got a murderous grudge, why wait fifty years? I mean, that's, like, *serious* festering! Wouldn't you be more likely to attack while your grievance was still fresh?'

'The trouble with amateur detecting is you start suspecting everyone,' Anna said. 'I was starting to have my suspicions about Sabina's dad!'

'I'd bet good money he got that injured hand aiming a punch at someone or something,' Jake said.

'*I* might be a suspect,' Tansy said cheerfully. 'You never know.'

Anna laughed. 'Tansy, you couldn't even swat a fly! You can't even eat a sausage unless it's an accredited happy sausage!'

'Or maybe that's just what I *let* you think!' Tansy gave them her most sinister smile. 'Maybe I have mysterious blackouts, like characters have in soap operas, and keep running amok but afterwards I totally can't remember!'

'You're in a suspiciously good mood, Tansy Lavelle,' Anna said accusingly. 'You wouldn't be back on lovey-dovey terms with Sergeant Goodhart by any chance?'

Tansy looked demurely at her fingernails which

had been freshly repainted with rainbows. 'Maybe,' she said. 'Maybe just a little bit lovey-dovey. Helped by the fact that Liam was forced to confess to a most heinous act!'

'What on earth did he do?' Anna was prepared to be shocked, though it was hard to imagine the upright Liam doing anything terribly heinous.

'He secretly posted my fucking Christmas card to my dad, didn't he!' Tansy had assumed an expression of extreme outrage.

'He *didn't*!' Anna said.

'He did. Even worse, he lied when I told him I thought it must have been thrown away by accident. I said I thought it was a sign from the universe that Frankie wasn't supposed to be part of my life.'

'What a shitbag!' Anna couldn't help laughing.

'I know! I was all set to kill him, until I calmed down and realized what it meant.'

Anna was lost. 'What did it mean?'

Tansy gave her a beatific smile. 'He accepts me! He accepts everything about me. My past, my dodgy criminal dad. How can I stay mad with him after that?'

They sat chatting over coffee, mulling over the events of the past few days. After a while, Anna realized she was flagging. She enjoyed having Tansy for her flatmate. She loved that Jake had magically become part of her life. But she'd been in close proximity with other people, it felt, for days now without respite, and she was talked out.

'I'm going to take the dogs out before it gets dark,' she said abruptly.

Bonnie and Hero immediately came to sit by

her feet having learned that the words 'dogs' and 'out' used in conjunction generally referred to them.

Jake just gave Anna a grin. 'OK, have a nice walk.'

'Say hi to Mr Darcy if you see him,' Tansy said. 'Mind if I look through your Ottolenghi cookbook while you're gone? I fancy cooking something lovely and veggie tonight.' She puffed out her cheeks. 'That night I crashed at Leo and Nick's they fed me so much Christmas food, I feel like I might start sweating pork fat out of my pores!'

'I'll be your *sous* chef if you like,' Anna heard Jake say as she ran upstairs to get her coat, followed by two excited dogs.

Outside the house, Anna took a welcome lungful of cold winter air and found herself mentally adding one more item to her growing list of *Good Reasons to Own a Dog*. When you have a dog, you can say, 'I need to go out and walk Fido now', and nobody thinks you're strange. Whereas saying 'I urgently need to be by myself in order to process some of this weird shit that's been happening' made you sound as if you were somewhere on the spectrum. Except, with Jake and Tansy, she thought she probably could say, 'I need time to myself, bye!' and they'd just say, 'OK, see you when you've decompressed!'

She'd almost reached the end of her street, when she saw Tim walking towards her. His face was unusually grim, as if he was about to perform some unpleasant duty.

She tried to hide her dismay. 'Hi. Were you coming to see me?'

'I was actually. I really need to talk to you. Sorry if it isn't a good time?'

Anna had a brief struggle with herself. Tim had proved that he was still her friend. After years of radio silence from Anna he had leapt into action on her behalf. He had not only tracked down Catherine, he had gone with Anna to see her at the hospice. There had been very little in it for him that Anna could see. And whatever it was Tim needed to say, it was terribly important to him, she could feel it.

Instead of answering, she handed over Hero's lead. 'Here,' she said. 'We're going to Port Meadow.' Hero immediately craned around to glower at this new interloper.

'That's Isadora's dog, Hero,' Anna said.

'From *Much Ado*, right?' Tim said.

Anna just nodded.

'She doesn't seem too impressed with me,' Tim said, as they continued down the street.

'Hero doesn't really do "impressed",' Anna said. 'She's more into "quietly appalled".'

'Or even "comically aghast",' Tim suggested, as Isadora's little dog fixed him with her glassy brown stare.

By the time they reached Port Meadow, the midwinter sun was slowly slipping down towards the tops of the trees. They let themselves and the dogs in through the wooden gate. The bitter winds of the morning had dropped and the meadow, with its faintly rising mist, looked and felt calm and peaceful. Anna unclipped Bonnie's lead but decided they should keep Hero on hers. She could easily imagine the little dog taking off across fields and major roads, following some mysterious canine GPS as she stoically made her way back to her beloved Isadora.

'I'm glad you've got a dog. You always wanted one.' Tim's voice sounded strained.

'How amazing that you should remember that,' Anna said. 'I only remembered after I'd actually adopted Bonnie.'

'I remember all kinds of things.' Tim quickly looked around, making sure there was no one within earshot. He took a sharp in-breath. 'I've got something quite big to tell you. I almost feel like you should be sitting down in case I . . . oh, shit!' he said angrily. 'I had this all planned out and now I'm going to make a total bollocks of it!'

Anna touched his arm. 'Who cares if you make a total bollocks of whatever it is? Just say it! Neither of us is going to die from it, Tim.'

'I'm your brother,' he said harshly.

She froze in the middle of the path. For a moment she couldn't move or even think. It was clearly impossible, so why didn't it feel like a lie?

'Say that again,' she managed at last.

'Now you see why you should be sitting down.' Tim sounded despairing. 'I knew I should wait. It's just I've known about this for over two years and I—'

'*How*?' she interrupted. 'How can you possibly be my brother?' Even as she asked the question, something inside told her that Tim was telling the truth.

He took another sharp breath. 'Chris had an affair with your mum, with Julia.' Tim had always called his parents by their first names. It was part of their laid-back style of parenting. 'Your mum and dad were going through a bad patch and . . .' He gave an unhappy shrug. 'I'm sure I don't need to spell it out.'

'You're saying Chris is actually *my* dad – he's *both* our dads?'

Across the meadow, Anna recognized the familiar figures of Blossom and her owner. She could see bare winter trees with a red-gold sun starting to slip behind them. '*Holy fuck!*' she whispered, then gave a slightly hysterical laugh. 'You're absolutely sure?'

Tim nodded, embarrassed. 'I read his diary.'

'You read his *diary*! Shit, Tim!' Hero and Bonnie were staring up at her, sensing something was going on. 'Something must have tipped you off though?' Anna said. 'You didn't just wake up one morning and decide to go poking around in your dad's private life?'

He looked horrified. 'Of course not! Jane asked me to do it.'

'Your *mum* asked you to spy on your own dad?' Anna felt a flash of dismay. 'Did she have suspicions about my mum?'

Tim shook his head. They had resumed their walk, keeping their voices low. 'This was only about two years ago. Chris's behaviour had become a bit – erratic. Jane said she never knew which version of my dad was going to come home from work. One minute he was bad tempered, the next weepy. Then there was a

279

period when he'd vanish for hours without explanation. Jane tried to get him to tell her what was wrong but he insisted nothing was. She was scared he might be having some kind of breakdown. She was genuinely worried for him. So she asked me to investigate.' He yanked Hero back on her lead and Isadora's dog gave him a huffy look. 'She really pulls, doesn't she?'

'Like an express train,' Anna said. 'She's better in a harness but I left it at Isadora's.'

Tim resumed his story. 'So one day when my dad was at work, or supposedly at work, I went through his study looking for anything that might shed some light on his alarming weirdness. In the process, I came across one of his old diaries from the mid-eighties. Inside was a letter from your mum, breaking off their affair. "We have to stop this before too many people get hurt, but you will still get to see your beautiful daughter, et cetera, et cetera."'

Anna was still reeling. 'Did you tell your mum?'

'No!' Tim was horrified. 'How am I going to tell her something like that? She and your mum were always such close friends!'

'What about your dad? Does he know you know?'

He shook his head. 'It's not just cowardice. I found out what was wrong with him. He'd had a cancer scare and was having a hard time facing up to it.'

'You told your mum about that presumably.'

'Of course, and as it turned out it was a false alarm, but then it just got harder and harder to

280

confront him about, you know, my secret half-sister.'

Though he had put invisible air quotes around the words, Anna felt a little thrill. She was Tim's sister. Everything she knew about herself had blown up in her face, leaving her with this one extraordinary fact. 'But you intend to?' she said. 'Confront him, I mean?'

'That's one reason I needed to talk to you, Anna, to find out what you want to do. I know this must feel like a lot to take in. I've had two years to get used to the idea.'

The rising mist made the figures of distant walkers seem to be moving ankle-deep through dry ice. It was like a dream, or the cover of a fantasy novel, yet Anna felt more real than she'd ever felt in her life.

As she and Tim continued to talk, her mind was working overtime. She remembered her mother's hyper-vigilance about never leaving Anna and Tim alone after they'd hit puberty. They had seen this as one more example of bizarre adult behaviour. There was never the slightest risk of romantic involvement between her and Tim. It would have been like when Anna was eleven years old and decided to get in some practice at kissing by experimentally kissing her own arm. *It's like we've always known,* she thought.

So many things were starting to make sense. Though Anna had been the eldest child in her family, she'd never been through that period of being her parents' little princess. She'd always been the difficult cuckoo in the nest. She'd sensed that something was wrong and had always assumed that this something must be her. She'd loved her dad, but she'd never felt particularly loved *by* him, not in the way she longed for and needed. Her mum, on the other hand, had loved her but it hadn't been an accepting kind of love. Anna had always felt as if her mother was silently criticising everything she did – everything she *was*. It got so she couldn't be in the same room with her mum for ten minutes without wanting to scream from the tension.

It wasn't my fault, Anna thought suddenly, and it felt like an immense weight rolling away. It had never *ever* been her fault. She had just been a confused little girl caught up in a situation that she wasn't remotely equipped to understand.

'Did you ever suspect anything was going on?' she asked Tim.

'I wouldn't say I *suspected*,' he said. 'I do remember walking in on them once and feeling some kind of – I don't know – odd vibe.'

'Was it at that farmhouse in Pembrokeshire?' Anna said.

'Yes,' he said, surprised.

'I remember that too.' Anna immediately flashed back to that puzzling midsummer's evening. She and Tim had been nine and eight years old respectively. It was their first evening at a dilapidated farmhouse their parents had trustingly rented unseen. Anna and Tim had been exploring outside and had gone rushing back into the kitchen to tell the adults about the stream they'd found at the bottom of the garden. At the moment that Tim and Anna burst in, Chris and Julia were not

282

touching each other, but there had been a strange electricity in the air that had made the children stop in the doorway. Anna's mother's eyes had been red and swollen as if she'd been crying. Anna had immediately wanted to run back outside into the honeysuckle-scented evening and away from that ominous kitchen with its smell of drains mixed with a more potent reek that Anna's father had decided must be damp.

The true source of the smell was discovered next morning when Tim's mum went downstairs to make breakfast and discovered an enormous rat sitting calmly on the kitchen table and two more in the larder feasting on the bread and cheeses they'd brought with them. Within the hour, both families had packed up and left and somehow the horror of the rats had eclipsed that bewildering moment in the kitchen. Anna had just stored it away as one more of those inexplicable childhood memories.

'Does your brother know?' Anna asked. Tim had had an annoying younger brother called Rob, presumably the father of the Machiavellian little girls.

Tim shook his head. 'He moved to Vancouver a few years ago. He and his wife just came over for Christmas so we could finally meet the twins. The truth is, Rob and I never did have a great deal to say to each other. Maybe the time will come when I feel I have to tell him, but right now it doesn't seem right to upset his picture of our dad, you know?'

'So you've had to carry this all by yourself,' Anna said.

'Obviously I told Anjali,' he said. 'But the person I was really desperate to tell was you! Now you know why I was so keen to get in touch,' he added wryly. 'I needed my big sis for backup.'

Anna saw a familiar figure approaching through the now almost knee-deep mist. It was the man with the elderly spaniel. As they drew level, the little spaniel hobbled right up to Bonnie, wagging her tail. Anna's dog immediately responded to her friendly overtures, sniffing the old spaniel all over, wagging her own feathery white tail the whole time. Hero, however, went stiff-legged with suspicion and wanted nothing to do with this intruder.

'Now, Meg,' the man said quietly. 'Don't make a nuisance of yourself.'

'She's fine honestly,' Anna reassured him. 'Hero's just a bit touchy at the moment.'

'And why shouldn't she be touchy if she likes?' he said with a smile. 'Dogs have their preferences just like we do.'

Anna smiled and agreed, expecting Meg's owner to go on his way, but he lingered on the path. 'I've seen you before at Walsingham College. Do you work there?' His manner was tentative, almost shy.

'Yes, I work in the admin office,' she told him.

'Then you've probably seen me working in the gardens.' He gave her a shy smile, and for the first time she put two and two together.

'Of course – I'm so sorry! I probably didn't recognize you without your lovely dog!' This must be the mysterious Roop whose dog Tate

284

had coveted. Anna had seen him several times at work in the gardens but failed to make the connection. 'You must have thought I was so rude,' she said. But she'd already seen his expression soften at the words 'lovely dog', and knew she'd been forgiven. She could feel Tim amusedly watching this exchange, and realized that she'd been performing, just slightly, for his benefit.

'These days I'm better at identifying people by their dog than by their faces.' Roop had a faint Oxfordshire burr. 'My eyesight isn't what it was, that's for sure!' She saw now that he had the weather-beaten appearance of someone who'd spent most of their life out of doors.

'Well, now I shall know who to thank for Walsingham's fabulous roses when summer comes,' she said. 'I'm Anna, by the way.'

He shook her outstretched hand. 'People call me Roop.' He gave a curious glance at Tim.

'This is my brother, Tim,' Anna said for the first time in her life. She would have liked to tell the world. Aglow with her new knowledge she felt giddy, almost euphoric.

'Are both these dogs yours?' Roop's voice was quiet as if he didn't get to use it much.

'The little one belongs to a friend,' Anna said. 'Bonnie, the White Shepherd, is mine.'

'Beautiful dog,' Roop said. 'She looks young still.'

'I don't know how old she is,' Anna admitted. 'She was a rescue dog.'

'Meg's getting old now.' Roop looked down at his dog with a sort of pained affection. 'She can't walk very far these days but she's such a stoic

285

old girl. I think she only comes out with me to keep me company. She doesn't want to let me down.' Hearing her name, Meg had come to sit at his feet. Anna had never thought of old dogs as beautiful, but Meg's face had so much nobility and character it seemed as if her whole heart was shining out of her eyes.

One day soon this wonderful old dog would go for her last walk, Anna thought, and Roop would be left alone. Her own overflowing happiness made her want to reach out to this gentle and unassuming man. 'I've just discovered a really brilliant book about dogs,' she told him. 'You might like it. It's called—'

Roop interrupted her with an apologetic laugh. 'Don't bother telling me, because I'm not going to remember. My short-term memory has jumped ship along with my eyesight!'

'You could put it in your mobile,' Tim suggested.

He smilingly shook his head. 'Don't have one. I can't stand those things.'

'Why don't I drop off a note for you then?' Anna said. 'It honestly won't be any trouble.'

Roop looked surprised and pleased. 'All right, if you're sure? I've got one of the gardener's cottages. Turn left past the Buttery, keep going until you see the sign to the Apothecary's Garden. Mine's the first cottage next to the gate.'

'I'll pop it in next time I come in to work,' she promised.

'I'll look forward to it,' he said. 'You can tell me all about your beautiful dog.'

Tim watched them slowly vanish into the mist. 'Nice guy. Really sweet old dog.'

Anna said, 'So now tell me how you met – sorry, I've forgotten your wife's name.'

Tim smiled. 'She's called Anjali.'

'So tell me how you met Anjali.'

Twenty

Anna almost never had her car radio on for short journeys, but when she got into the driver's seat on New Year's Eve, some impulse made her turn on a local music station. Immediately the bluesy opening chords of one of her favourite golden oldies filled the car.

To spare her neighbours, Anna waited until she'd reached the end of her crescent before turning up the music and joining in with the Rolling Stones' raucous chorus. 'Ti–i–ime is on my side! Yes, it is!'

Lucky Isadora, she thought, having these kinds of songs for her soundtrack. Imagine being hit by that tsunami of youthful optimism every time you switched on the radio. No wonder Isadora's generation believed they had the power to change the world.

As she headed towards Summertown, singing along with Mick Jagger, Anna saw a bright sickle moon sail out from between the clouds and was suddenly filled with almost painfully sweet emotion. *I'm happy*, she thought astonished. The word didn't seem anything like big enough. She wasn't just happy. She was grateful, hopeful, in

287

love with her life. It was New Year's Eve and Anna had places to go and people to celebrate with.

Beneath the Stones' guitars she heard the festive chink of bottles. Anna had chilled two miniature bottles of champagne, now tucked into the foot-well on the passenger side. It had become a tradition for Anna and her grandfather to spend New Year's Eve together. Next year, depending on how things developed, she might take Jake, but this year she'd wanted it to be just her and her granddad. One day soon she'd have to tell him that his daughter, Julia, had had an affair with the husband of one of her best friends, an affair that had resulted in Anna. But she didn't want to complicate their New Year's celebration by telling him tonight. She would stay with her grandfather as long as his energy levels would allow then go on to Isadora's.

Isadora was out of hospital now. Still on strong medication, with a visibly black eye, and her right arm in a cast, she had not felt up to appearing at a friend's glitzy fancy-dress party. 'I did contemplate getting an eye patch and going as Long John Silver,' she'd told Anna and Tansy last time they were over. 'But I'm afraid I lack the necessary *chutzpah*.'

Tansy and Liam had originally planned to meet up with friends in London, but neither of them wanted to abandon Isadora on New Year's Eve when she'd just got out of hospital. 'Isadora is still quite fragile after what happened,' Tansy had told Anna. 'Even a normal New Year can be a horrible time to be on your own, but knowing

288

that guy is still out there . . .' So Tansy had called Isadora to suggest they should all go over to her house and make a proper party of it. Her suggestion had immediately cheered Isadora up.

'Jake and Liam can be my two hunky bodyguards!' she'd suggested much to Tansy's amusement. Jake had already gone over to Isadora's with Bonnie to help Liam and Tansy with preparations.

The Stones track gave way to an old reggae number. In Anna's current buoyant mood, it was impossible not to see Jimmy Cliff's song as a personal message. Like the singer she and her friends could see everything more clearly now. They finally had answers to some of the questions that had been plaguing them. They knew who had really killed Hetty Vallier. They knew who had sent the anonymous letters, and they knew that the sender was not the same person who had attacked James and Isadora, but the granddaughter of Isadora's murdered friend.

Anna thought it reflected well on both Sabina and Isadora that they'd managed to put this rather bumpy start behind them. Isadora's first words to Sabina when Anna took her to visit Isadora in hospital were 'Darling, they say to understand all is to forgive all and I absolutely understand how much you must have hated us.' Sabina had been so overcome that she'd cried. She hadn't expected forgiveness and understanding. Anna had the feeling Hetty's granddaughter had never really seen herself as a person in her own right, just an instrument of familial vengeance.

Sabina was still a little too polite around

Isadora, but from time to time when Isadora was telling one of her more outrageous stories, Anna and Tansy had noticed a distinctly star-struck expression on the young girl's face. 'Wait till Isadora's had a couple of drinks and lets it slip she once had a moment with Mick Jagger!' Tansy had murmured to Anna.

'You think Sabina will be shocked?' Anna had whispered back.

Tansy had been astonished. 'Are you mad? She'll be in *awe*!'

Anna drove in through the gates of her grandfather's retirement home and turned off the engine. Though it was still early, most of the windows of Bramley Lodge were dark, except for some lights in reception. Anna took the champagne out of the footwell, stuck an ice-cold bottle in either pocket of her parka, and went in.

As usual the temperature inside was subtropical. The young woman on the reception desk was dressed for summer in a thin cotton dress and cropped leggings. She looked up reluctantly from watching a cute puppy video on her phone and said, 'Oh, hello. Do go through. Mr Ottaway is expecting you.'

Anna felt her shoes sinking into the soft carpet as she made her way down the corridor. Muted sounds from radios or TVs came from a couple of the rooms she passed, but most of the residents seemed to have turned in for the night. Her grandfather's room was at the back overlooking the garden. Through his door she could hear a woman singing the blues. She knocked loudly enough for him to hear her through Billie Holiday, assuming he had his hearing aid in. 'Can I come in?' she called and heard his delighted laugh.

'You're here! Wonderful!'

Anna let herself into his colourful and chaotic apartment. George Ottaway's rooms resembled absolutely nobody's idea of an almost ninety-year-old man's living space.

She caught her grandfather in the middle of tinkering with an arrangement for his latest still life: a crumpled white cloth, a bowl of nuts and an old blue-rimmed plate on which he placed a pomegranate cut in half to show glistening pink seeds. Tomorrow he'd be at his easel as soon as it was light. Each time she visited she'd find new vibrantly painted canvasses carelessly propped against walls or pieces of furniture. Uncertain whether any were still wet she took care not to brush against them as she went over to kiss him.

'Does the music bother you?' he asked her.

'No, I like it.'

'I'd just been listening to one of those ghastly New Year's news roundups,' he explained. 'Just catastrophe piled on catastrophe. So I decided I'd listen to Billie instead.'

'Good call,' Anna told him. She smilingly produced the bottles out of her pockets. 'Ta-da!'

'Just when I thought things couldn't get any better!' he said.

She placed the misted-over bottles on his coffee table. 'I'd better take off my coat, before I expire from heat exhaustion.' Anna peeled off her parka to reveal a delicate claret-red lace and crêpe de Chine blouse. The neck with its small covered buttons was high, but the lace panel that made up the front part of the yoke and the long lacy sleeves were so whisper-light they were barely there at all.

'Pretty top,' her grandfather said. 'That colour suits you.'

'Thank you!' Anna gave him a twirl. 'Temperley London. I got it in a sale.'

'That's what your grandmother always used to say,' he said with a grin. 'I never believed her either.'

Anna went into his tiny galley kitchen and came back with two champagne flutes she'd bought him the previous year. 'I'll hold the glasses, you open the bottles.' She had a moment's doubt. 'I'm sorry, this looks mean. I should have bought a full-sized bottle.'

He shook his head laughing. 'At my age a full-sized bottle might be fatal!'

'Grandpa!' she protested.

'It's true! This way, we can have all the theatrics and bubbles without the hangover! Glad they still use corks though. Not much drama in a screw top!'

'Just hush and pop the corks,' she teased.

He started to laugh then his expression became wistful. 'You know you looked just like your mother when you said that.'

Anna felt a guilty pang. Her grandfather had survived so many losses, his daughter and three of his grandchildren, and more recently his wife; and now she had to tell him something about his beloved only child that was sure to shatter him to his very foundations.

Her grandfather efficiently popped both corks

and filled their glasses. She held his for him until he was settled in his favourite armchair. 'Did I upset you when I said you look like your mother?' he asked anxiously.

She shook her head. He didn't miss a thing. 'It didn't upset me. I liked it.' The words just popped out but Anna realized they were true. Once she'd have been appalled at the idea that she bore any resemblance to her mum. She raised her glass. 'Happy New Year, Grandpa!'

'Happy New Year,' he echoed. 'Here's to a new start and fresh hope for our world.'

Anna took a sip of her champagne. 'So have you made any resolutions?' Before her grandfather could open his mouth she said, 'I think your first resolution should be to show your paintings in an exhibition.'

'Oh, that's your resolution for me, is it?' he said with gentle irony.

'Tansy's gallery has open exhibitions,' she reminded him. 'She's already told Gerry, the owner, about you.'

'Anna, I'm just a dabbler! I'm not nearly good enough yet to merit that kind of exposure.'

'Stop it, Grandpa! You absolutely are! I've shown Tansy some photos of your paintings that I took on my phone and she and Gerry would like to come and visit.'

Her grandfather looked first astonished then slightly alarmed. 'Well, I suppose there's no harm in that,' he conceded eventually. There was a brief lull in which they both found themselves captivated by Billie Holiday singing 'The Very Thought of You'. Then her grandfather said, 'So now we've settled on what *my* resolution ought to be, what about yours? What are you going to do next year to set the world on fire?'

Anna watched the tiny champagne bubbles rise in her glass. Resolutions were about making improvements to your life. Still glowing from the discovery that Tim was her brother, Anna didn't feel there was anything in her life that urgently needed improving. But it was only fair to keep her grandfather company, so she said, 'I should probably get my act together and finish decorating my bedroom.'

He made a face. 'A New Year's resolution should get your heart racing. I don't think interior decoration really fits the bill, does it?'

Feeling cornered, Anna said the first thing that came into her head. 'I suppose I might think about looking around for a new job. I enjoy working with Kirsty, but I don't really want to end my days in admin.' *Being bullied by Nadine's fucking Post-its*, she added silently.

'What do you *think* you'd like to do?' he asked.

'Stop asking me scary questions!' she said laughing. 'I have no idea.'

'Scary, but, I'd suggest, ultimately liberating?' He looked at her mischievously over the top of his glasses.

'OK, here's the deal,' she told him. 'I'll give some serious thought to your scary questions and you give serious thought to putting your paintings in an exhibition!'

Around ten she could see her grandfather starting to tire and rose to leave.

294

'I hope you're off to meet your American beau?' he asked.

'"My beau?"' she said. 'You make me feel like I should be wearing a bonnet! But yes, I'm joining Jake and the others at Isadora's. First, though, I'm going into town to buy some very exclusive gin!'

'Exclusive or expensive?'

'I should think both!'

Anna figured she just had time to pop to the Holly Bush to buy a bottle of the special gin Jake had hoped to sample at the German market. In the car, she quickly texted him to let him know she'd be at Isadora's soon.

The Banbury Road was eerily free from traffic. Now and then she saw groups of young people carrying bottles, heading to some party or other. Occasionally a lone firework went streaking up into the sky. She parked up on St Giles and hurried down towards the Cornmarket. It was a cold clear night. Shivering, she wrapped Tansy's scarf around her more closely. She could feel the winter chill penetrating her parka and the new lace top she'd worn partly for Jake (though she'd deny this if asked), but mostly for the new Anna who dared to dress in bright colours.

The Holly Bush was up a tiny hidden alleyway that branched off Brasenose Lane. This old four-teenth-century inn was reputedly once the haunt of cutpurses and other unsavoury medieval characters. Anna wondered what the cutpurses would have thought of the braying north Oxford males who had invaded their local.

The queues at the bar were so long that she almost changed her mind. But she pictured Jake's surprise and pleasure when she presented him with the bottle and stood her ground. At last she handed over her card to pay for what turned out to be an eye-wateringly expensive purchase. Fighting her way back towards the door she almost collided with Roop, the gardener, also carrying a bottle.

They both laughed with surprise.

'Hello,' she said. 'Is this your local?'

'God, no,' he said. 'I hate pubs. Full of red-faced men shouting contradictory opinions.' He held the door open for her and followed her out. 'So you're on your way to a party, I expect?'

'Nothing so grand,' she said with a smile. 'I'm just going to spend the evening with friends.'

He held up his bottle. 'As you see I'm also ready to see in the New Year.'

'You and Meg,' she said.

'Yes, just me and my old Meg.' A wistful look came into his eyes. 'You wouldn't like to come and have a quick drink before you meet your friends? You could write down that book title for me.'

As Anna hesitated, a group of young, loud-voiced men came out of the pub, barging into Roop almost knocking him over. He didn't comment on their behaviour, just quickly recovered his balance, and said, 'Sorry, I shouldn't have asked. Your friends will be waiting.'

She consulted her watch. Anna couldn't help being slightly intrigued by Roop. In a way she felt they were kindred spirits. 'Oh, I'm sure I've got time to squeeze in a quick drink,' she told him, smiling. 'In fact, I'd like to!'

'Well, my evening is looking up!' Roop gave her his shy laugh.

They set off towards Walsingham College. She'd expected they'd go in via the Porter's Lodge. Instead Roop turned down a narrow side lane and stopped at what looked like a kind of service entrance. He punched some numbers into a security pad and let her in.

She'd never used this particular entrance to the college and in the dark it took a moment to get her bearings. Seeing her hesitate, Roop said, 'We'll go this way; unless you want to bump into a lot of drunk CEOs and their wives.'

'I'd forgotten about that.' Walsingham College had taken to renting out their Great Hall along with their Michelin-star chef, for various functions. 'The Harry Potter effect', Paul called it. A well-known tech company had arranged to hold their big New Year's Eve bash there.

Roop set off down a path Anna could hardly see. Compared to the Great Hall, with its big and probably extremely boozy party, this part of the college felt silent and empty.

She heard Roop click his tongue. 'Those bloody security lights are a bit slow coming on.' The words had barely left his mouth when a pale flare of light illuminated the familiar approach to the Buttery. He laughed. 'They do say the key to comedy is good timing!'

Anna followed Roop through an arch that took them down another of the college's covered walkways, their feet echoing in the silence. She could make out dim shapes of trees and shrubs. The college gardens were far more extensive than she'd realized. She'd never taken time to explore, she thought, just picked up her post and headed straight to the admin offices.

Eventually they reached the elaborate wrought-iron gate that led into the Apothecary's Garden. Anna remembered Roop mentioning it as a landmark.

'Ever been inside?' he asked.

'I'm ashamed to say I haven't.'

'Not much to look at now, but come and take a look in summer. We've got a seventeenth-century knot garden with all the old medicinal plants. It's like bee and butterfly heaven. This is my place,' he added and Anna saw that they'd arrived at the first of two tiny semi-detached cottages. She followed him up the path. 'Come in,' he said. 'Hopefully the fire will still be alight.'

If possible the cottage seemed even smaller on the inside. Small but unusual and quite lovely, Anna thought. Everything was in the same subdued palette of blues and greens, including the dozen or so framed paintings on the wall that Roop had designated for his art gallery. Two other walls were fitted with floor-to-ceiling book-shelves, filled to bursting with books, mostly hardbacks. There were further piles of books at each end of the one small battered sofa. Meg, Roop's old spaniel, was in possession of the only armchair. She didn't move to greet them but gave a slightly guilty wag of her tail.

'Meg! You know that's not your chair,' Roop said mock-sternly. 'Dogs!' he said to Anna. 'Give them an inch!' He went to throw a couple of logs on the fire. The room with its uncarpeted stone flags was not particularly warm but it seemed rude to keep her coat on, so she took it off, keeping on her scarf as a comforting extra layer, and slipped her phone into a trouser pocket in case Jake called.

'I always love that smell of wood fires.' Anna could hear herself making polite conversation.

'We get a free supply of logs. Goes with the cottage,' he explained. 'Sit anywhere you like. Sorry, I should have said.'

Since Meg was occupying the armchair there was a choice of a small sofa or one of two blue-painted kitchen chairs on either side of Roop's table. Anna took one of the chairs. The small gate-legged table was partially covered with a pale tablecloth embroidered with flowers and leaves formed in tiny cross-stitch. 'This looks Chinese,' Anna said.

'Does it? I think I got it from a car boot. Pretty much all my furnishings came from charity shops or car boots.'

'"Upcycling", people call that now,' she said with a smile.

'Necessity, I call it.' Roop's smile faded. 'Sorry, Anna, you must think I'm a terrible host. Bit out of practice. Would you like a proper drink, or would you prefer to just have a cup of tea? I don't mean to be plying you with drink!' He looked flustered as if he'd only just realized the implications of inviting her back. 'I haven't got much of a selection. I've got whiskey. Someone gave me a bottle of ginger wine. Disgusting stuff in my opinion; only good for making Whiskey Macs but you need ginger ale for that. I do have a very pleasant dry sherry.'

'I'll have a glass of dry sherry then,' Anna said. 'Have you got a piece of paper? I can write down the book title for you.' Roop found her an old envelope and a pen and watched her write it down. 'I'll ask them to get it in for me at the library,' he said.

'It's a really good book,' she said.

'I've always loved dogs,' Roop confided. 'I wasn't a very assiduous reader as a boy but if anyone gave me a book with a dog or a horse in it, I'd be awake all night reading under my covers! It was a great day when I discovered Jack London,' he added. 'Ever read him?'

She shook her head. 'But my friend Jake raves about *The Call of the Wild.*'

Roop gave a delighted laugh. 'He has good taste. It has everything a boy needs in a book: the Gold Rush, Alaska, sled dogs. I must have read it a thousand times and it never gets stale.' He shook his head. 'I'll stop talking now and organize our drinks.'

She could see him through the half-open door, moving about the tiny green-painted kitchen. She heard him briefly running taps, possibly rinsing glasses. 'We can still talk,' he called. 'Tell me about your dog. You said she was a rescue dog?'

'Yes, Jake, the friend I was telling you about, rescued her in Afghanistan. She'd survived a bomb blast and god knows what else. She's still got lots of tiny scars.' She didn't tell him that Jake had had to coax a badly injured Bonnie away from the body of the small boy she'd been guarding (he'd told Anna he'd had to bribe her with chicken sandwiches), so that the child's body could be taken away for burial.

'I've got some Japanese cracker type things somewhere,' Roop said. 'They're not unpleasant, if you want to risk them?' He began hunting through the kitchen cupboard.

Anna was starting to feel too much like a Jane Austen character sitting on the straight-backed kitchen chair, so she wandered over to investigate Roop's bookshelves. She was touched to see a battered copy of Jack London's *The Call of the Wild* crammed in with several other well-thumbed books that she guessed had formed his childhood reading. She thought of Jake finding his treasured copy of the same book in a yard sale, and reading it until it finally fell to pieces. She opened it to the flyleaf where someone had glued an old-fashioned bookplate, smiling to herself when she saw that the young owner had laboriously written his name and address exactly as she remembered doing when she was small; probably Jake had done the same.

Alec Rupert Faber, The Old Manor, Laundry Lane, Bruisyard, Saxmundham, Suffolk, England, Europe, the World, the Universe . . .

Her eye went back to the name. Alec Rupert Faber. Rupert. Roop.

The young man from the Foreign Office whose life had been ruined by the Oxford Six.

Roop came in with their drinks and a plate of Japanese crackers on a tray.

'You changed your name.' The words seemed

301

to speak themselves and Anna should probably have regretted them the instant they were out of her mouth. She could have closed the book and pretended not to have seen. She could have had her drink and left, and she might have, if she hadn't seen Isadora bleeding and bruised in her hospital bed.

'Sorry?' Roop didn't seem to understand.

Anna swallowed against a wave of nausea, as the full horror of her situation started to sink in. 'This is getting to be a really bad habit,' she said half to herself.

'Habit?' Roop's expression was growing puzzled.

'Drinking with murderers,' Anna explained. Her voice sounded strange in her ears. She wasn't visibly shaking, not yet, but she could feel tiny vibrations of fear starting deep within her muscles. 'I know who you are,' she said. 'You're Alec Faber.'

His smile vanished. It wasn't just his expression that changed, it was as if, by saying his true name, Anna had broken a spell, allowing James Lowell's killer to throw off shy softly spoken Roop like a tired old coat.

'That's unfortunate. For you, that is.' Alec Faber occupied space more confidently than Roop. He looked taller and straighter and several years younger. Even his faint hint of an Oxfordshire burr had vanished. Alec Faber's real voice was more obviously educated and nothing like so warm.

'My friends will come looking for me,' Anna told him, swallowing down her panic. Roop had told her he didn't know anything about mobile phones. She hoped Alec Faber didn't either. Surreptitiously slipping her hand into her trouser pocket, she swished her finger across the screen of her mobile to unlock it and dialled the last number she'd called: Jake's. He would hear everything she and Roop – Alec – said; if the call went through.

'By the time your friends come, if they come, it'll be too late.' Alec reached behind the worn tapestry cushion on Meg's armchair and withdrew an ancient-looking pistol. Anna was so astonished that she almost laughed.

'Do they sell guns in charity shops now?' she asked, for Jake's benefit.

'Get moving,' Alec told her.

'What are you going to do to me?' she asked.

'I'm going to take you with me,' he said.

He was taking her hostage. He had a gun. He could take her anywhere he wanted.

'I knew the police would be sniffing around soon,' he said. 'I'm just advancing my plans, that's all.'

'You're going to leave the country?' she said.

'In a way.' Pressing the gun into the small of her back, Alec Faber pushed her towards the door.

She tried to turn back. 'My coat.'

'You won't need it.' He shoved her out into the night.

Anna glanced back to see Alec's little spaniel watching her master's departure with a bewildered expression. 'Aren't you going to take your dog?' she asked. But it seemed that Roop's dog had been abandoned along with his harmless gardener's persona because he snapped, 'Just walk!'

Nervous about stumbling with a loaded gun at her back, Anna obeyed. She remembered that guns had safety catches, but was Roop's on or off? They were retracing their steps back to the Buttery. The security lights flared and she had a wild hope that some hard-working research fellow might look up from his or her books in time to see the startling tableau of a man pointing a gun at a woman. But then the lights died and she was alone with a killer in the dark. Apart from her and Roop's breathing, everything inside the college walls was silent. Outside the college, the city seemed to be having one big riotous party. Anna could hear yells and shrieks of laughter, and at least three clashing sets of music as the New Year celebrations got into full swing.

'Where are we going?' Anna asked.

'To see the fireworks,' he told her.

Alec's words triggered a new surge of adrenaline. 'Why waste time with fireworks, if you're just going to leave?' she asked. But she was afraid she already knew the answer. *You're leaving the country? In a way.* Alec Faber was taking her somewhere so he could kill them both.

He answered her question with a grim laugh. 'Why? Because I've been a bloody failure all my life and you've given me my chance to go out in one final blaze of glory!' She felt the barrel of his gun pushing painfully into her spine through the fragile fabric of her blouse.

They had arrived at the cloisters by the college chapel. In the darkness, Anna could make out the outline of a door. Reaching past her, Alec pulled it open, revealing only a deeper, more impenetrable darkness. Afraid, Anna stopped in her tracks. Anything could be in there. A dungeon. A bottomless well. 'Climb!' he ordered.

'I can't see,' she protested.

Again he reached past her and clicked a switch. A harsh yellow light fell on the first five or six narrow steps. The walls were rough-hewn stone. A sharp bend hid the rest of the staircase from view. 'Climb!' he repeated, in a harsher voice.

'I'm not very good at heights,' she said, hoping against hope that Jake could hear.

'You won't be up there long.' Alec's voice was cold.

She felt another twist of terror. The crude stone steps had been designed for medieval feet. Anna had to turn hers to the side so as not to lose her footing. Medieval people must have had thigh muscles like mountain goats, she thought.

As she climbed, she had a mental image of Meg anxiously looking up from the chair as her master disappeared from her life for ever. It was stupid, but part of her still believed that Alec was the impostor and Roop was the real authentic person. Roop, she thought, would have been incapable of abandoning his old dog.

She thought of her grandfather and of Tim and his wife, Anjali, who she'd planned to meet after New Year. She pictured Tansy and Isadora clinking glasses, while she climbed with a murderer's breath behind her, and his gun pressing into her back. As it turned out it wasn't Isadora who needed hunky bodyguards but Anna.

305

Jake might not have his phone switched on. Even if he had overheard her and Alec's conversation, what were the chances anyone could find her in time? Jake didn't know the college. There's no way he could know where Alec was taking her. She daren't risk saying something obvious like, 'Oh, my God, you're taking me up to the roof!' in case her captor realized what she was doing and shot her. All she could do was try to buy some time.

'I don't understand why you're doing this,' she said. 'I assume you're planning to kill us both and I don't even know why.'

They had reached the top of the stairs. There was a small door at the top, hardly more than a hatchway. 'Go through,' Alec ordered.

She leaned her weight against the door and it opened letting in bitterly cold air. Anna clambered out shakily on to a mercifully flat piece of roof. 'How will it change things if I tell you why?' Alec had appeared beside her.

'You implied that you don't want your life to be meaningless,' she said. '"Going out in a blaze of glory", I think you said? Well, I'd prefer my *death* not to be meaningless.'

Antiquated stone chimneys rose up on either side of them, bristling with electrical antennae. Anna felt the bitter cold striking up through her slipper-like shoes. Directly in front of them were steeply sloping Italianate roof tiles. There had once been iron safety railings between the flat and sloping parts of the roof, but several railings had corroded away. Anna vaguely remembered memos going back and forth to the maintenance department. As a temporary measure, someone had put traffic cones and a stretch of red-and-white tape warning people to keep away. Anna risked a dizzying glance over the edge and felt sick at the sight of mellow stone buildings turned red-gold by the orange street lights and much, *much* too far down. 'I don't get why you think your life was such a failure,' she said.

Alec gave a bitter laugh. 'You liked poor old Roop.'

She didn't deny it. 'Tell me you didn't like him, just a bit?'

'Do you know who I was?' he demanded. 'Do you have any idea who I was supposed to be?'

Anna wanted to say, *I was supposed to have two parents and three living breathing siblings.* Aloud she said, 'I know you lived in a manor house.'

'That house was supposed to be mine,' he said. 'The house, the estate, another house and a loch in Scotland.' He gestured with the gun. 'All gone to my younger brother.'

She thought of the tiny gardener's cottage, carefully furnished, Anna had imagined lovingly furnished, from car boots and charity shops. 'Someone told me they saw you living on the street.'

'Did they?' he said, without much interest.

Alec had gradually moved out from behind her while they'd been talking. He was directly in front of Anna now, pointing his gun at her chest and blocking her terrifying view of the gap in the railings. Logic told Anna that she was standing on a completely flat surface, yet she felt as if her thin-soled shoes were being pulled ever closer to the edge of the roof.

'Did you have to live like that for very long?'

'Long enough.' Alec jammed his free hand in his pocket. Anna and Alec were both shivering violently now.

'She saw you with a dog on a piece of string. Was that Meg?'

He looked at her and she saw cold anger in his face. 'Don't try to make me be Roop.' His anger scared her, but she knew she had to keep him talking.

'I don't think I understand why you had to be Roop in the first place.'

'Necessity,' he said. 'Matthew Tallis and his little cohorts stitched me up between them, then he reported my unpatriotic activities to my superiors – but you know all about that.'

'I know some of it,' she said.

'They hushed it up, but obviously the Foreign Office heard about it and consequently so did my father. In a single day, I lost everything that made up my life. I lost my job. My parents disinherited me, told me they never wanted to see or hear from me again. I lost my fiancée . . .'

'Fiancée?' Anna said surprised. 'I thought you were in love with Hetty Vallier?'

'What's that got to do with anything?' he said so sharply that she knew Hetty was a sore point even fifty years later.

'So you lost everything and so you decided to come back to Oxford to take your revenge?' Her mouth was so dry with fear it felt stuffed with cotton wool.

'No!' he said. 'Not how you're making it sound. I was living on the streets for – I don't actually know how long. I started out with all the right Boy Scout intentions, used public washrooms to keep clean, stayed more or less sober, but after a few years and a lot more knocks I started drinking. It was the only way I could get through the nights. Then one summer's day I was sitting on my piece of cardboard and I saw Robert Keane, walking towards me, all suntanned from his latest holiday, his suit jacket thrown over his shoulder. I'd been beaten up a few nights previously so I wasn't looking particularly pretty, but he recognized me at once. Robert was stunned. I could see it in his face then, what I'd become. He took out his wallet and peeled off some notes. He said, "There's a men's hostel just around the corner. This ought to get you a bed and a hot meal for a couple of nights. Clean yourself up, Alec. Dry yourself out and I promise I'll be in touch.'

Anna thought of Robert's self-portrait as a homeless down and out. She thought of how he'd ended up ruined, on the verge of bankruptcy. Had that been guilt over Alec Faber?

Alec's voice had grown bitter. 'I was tempted to just blow his fucking money on the horses. I used to be a gambler, did you know that? But Robert had left me with this ridiculous little ray of hope. He was going to get in touch. I thought maybe he was going to offer me a job. I don't really know what I thought. But I went to the hostel like he said. I cleaned myself up. I stayed off the booze. I had a shave and cut my hair, and caught up on some sleep. And on the second morning I came down to find a package waiting at the desk.' Alec gave a mirthless laugh. 'Inside, I found five hundred pounds in cash, and a set of car keys with directions to a garage.'

Anna could tell from Alec's disgusted expression that Robert's attempt to get him back on his feet had only rubbed more salt into his wounds.

'I got there to find he'd already had the van filled with petrol. He'd left a message on the passenger seat full of some bullshit about hoping I could make a fresh start. A fresh start on five hundred quid, plus a clapped-out old van! *Is that all he thinks I'm worth now?* I thought. Well, I suppose he's right. And I got in the car with Meg and I just drove. It was terrifying! I hadn't driven for years. And it was like all the times I drove to Oxford to those meetings, hoping I could sneak some time alone with Hetty. I just came straight here like a tired old dog finding its way home. I wasn't even that old, but I *felt* old. I felt finished.'

'You didn't come here to find James?' Anna said, surprised.

'I didn't plan any of it. I was just surviving day to day. At nights I slept in my van. By day, I started hiring myself out as a jobbing gardener. I'd always enjoyed gardening. I used to help our gardener at Bruisyard. I worked privately for a few years, eventually got myself a bedsit, then a job came up here at Walsingham with a cottage.' He turned to Anna. 'I never set out to be Roop.

310

He emerged out of necessity, a sound, straight-forward bloke. The kind of man who was content to spend his life mowing grass and spreading muck.'

The kind of man who was kind to his dog, Anna thought.

'I'd been working there a few months when I saw James Lowell sauntering across the quad like some saintly old professor in a book – and this – choking rage just welled up. You know when people say they saw red? I'd always assumed that meant you still saw the world normally but coloured red.' His voice became tight. 'You can't see anything. You go blind. There's nothing left but red. I had to make him pay. I didn't have a choice.'

'Professor Lowell didn't recognize you?'

'Of course he didn't bloody recognize me!' Alec almost spat out the words. 'College gardeners are just part of the scenery, didn't you know!'

'And Isadora?' she said. 'How did you know who she was? I thought she didn't usually go to the town meetings?'

'I'd seen her from a distance out and about with Hetty,' he said. 'Hetty wasn't always very discreet. She didn't really fancy me, but some-times I think she forgot we weren't really lovers and told me things I wasn't supposed to know. I knew all their names and little bits and pieces about their lives. Obviously, once I knew I was in trouble I made it my business to ferret out everything I could about the Six or whatever they called themselves. Then after my sighting of James, I did some research online.'

311

He saw her surprised expression.

'I can use a computer, you know! Gardeners do have opposable thumbs. I couldn't seem to find Catherine, but I found out that Isadora was still in Oxford. Then the day of James's funeral I saw her outside smoking, all dressed up in her funeral finery – and it was the same as when I saw James. Those people destroyed me. They destroyed everything that made up my life. They had no fucking *right* to be still walking around as if I was just nothing, just some piece of dirt they could step over!'

Alec was talking himself into a rage. His confessions hadn't purged him of his demons. They had simply psyched him up so he could carry out his threat. 'I'm glad you're coming with me.' Anna saw Alec's eyes glitter in the dark. 'I'm so sick and tired of being alone, I'm sick of being trapped inside Roop. Nobody sees me. You didn't see me. Those fuckers coming out of the pub didn't see me, I'm no one now!'

Anna heard a church clock start to strike. Others followed in a cacophony of chiming. At the same moment, celebratory fireworks exploded over their heads. Anna heard cheers and a ragged chorus of 'Auld Lang Syne' from a nearby bar, and a faint persistent barking as someone's dog protested at the noise.

'It's time.' Alec's voice was softly menacing now as he slowly closed the space between them. Anna would never see Bonnie again, would never kiss Jake, her grandfather would lose his last living relation. *Please don't let me die*, she begged the god she didn't believe in.

312

Explosions of gold, silver and violet stars filled the sky; each starburst falling back to reveal thousands of new and brighter stars. It was beautiful, like some kind of cosmic unfolding. Even Alec glanced up, just for a moment but a moment was all that Anna needed.

She dived for his gun but he hung on, cursing. He was far stronger than she'd realized and despite her martial arts training, she couldn't break his hold. They struggled for possession of his weapon, as the bangs and multicoloured flashes continued over their heads. As they fought, Anna felt her scarf slip from around her neck. She saw it go floating over the edge of the roof like a banner and disappear into the dark. The scarf made her think of Tansy and she redoubled her efforts to wrestle the gun from Alec's hands. She was terrified of falling, terrified the gun would go off in her face. She tried to bring up her knee, but Alec got in a vicious kick before she could finish the move.

Scared to loosen her grip on the gun, Anna hooked her foot around his ankle to unbalance him. Alec staggered backwards. The gun fell from his hand as he flailed, attempting to regain his footing. But their fight had moved him too close to the railings. To Anna's horror his back foot slipped through the gap and he went over the edge.

She dropped to her knees, grabbing on to his hands. 'Hold on!' she told him. 'I can pull you back up.' She was trying to convince herself as much as Alec. He was a heavy muscular man, and she could feel herself gradually being dragged over with him.

'Just let go,' he begged her. 'Can't you see I want to die?'

The flat surface of the roof didn't allow her any purchase. She needed to dig in her toes so she could brace herself against his weight, but her stupid shoes kept slipping. The pain in her hands and wrists was agonising. 'Nobody needs to die,' she told him angrily. 'What's so wrong with your life? Robert gave you a fresh start. How many people get that? Plus, if you die, who's going to look after that poor dog?'

'I am not fucking Roop!' he hissed at her.

'You are to me!' she yelled. Common sense told her she only had two choices: to let Alec Faber fall or be pulled over the edge with him. But how could you just let someone fall to his death if there was even the slightest chance you could save him?

Her arms felt as if they were being torn out of their sockets. The sheer muscular strain involved in holding on to him was causing Anna's vision to blur. Her heart thundered in her ears, and somewhere in the distance, there was a sound like a dog's distressed keening. Tiny lights started flashing behind her eyes. The adrenaline was making her light-headed, making her feel like she was hallucinating.

Suddenly she breathed in the smell of soap and clean linen. A heartbeat later she felt strong arms grasping her from behind. She almost sobbed with grief and longing. That's what happened in the moments before you died. You saw and heard and felt all the things you were going to miss the most.

Her strength had already given out yet she must be summoning reserves from somewhere because she was still somehow grimly hanging on to Alec even as he was frantically trying to loosen her grip. Anna couldn't see any trace of Roop or anything human now in those cold baleful eyes, yet deep within her, she still felt it was her responsibility to keep him alive. Perhaps he realized that, because he gave her a sudden chilling smile. 'I lied to you Anna,' he told her through gritted teeth. 'I always knew who you were.'

She felt her heart stop.

'Dominic Scott-Neville is my brother's godchild,' Alec ground out. 'And if you think I'm a monster, then Dominic is the fucking devil!' With the last of his strength, he prised his fingers loose and fell backwards into the blackness below.

Anna was still staring numbly at the empty space where Alec Faber had been when she felt herself being pulled back from the edge of the roof. Someone tried to help her to her feet, but she collapsed back on to her knees. Her would-be rescuer crouched down beside her. She heard a voice say, 'It's OK, kid. You're OK.'

Dizzy and disorientated, she peered at him through tiny pulsars of light. 'Jake?' she said disbelievingly. 'Are you really—?' He didn't let her finish her sentence. Gathering her into his arms, Jake kissed her with so much determination that Anna had no choice but to believe that he was real. If she had still harboured any doubts, the arrival of a rapturous White Shepherd was final proof. 'Oh, my God, *Bonnie!*' Uttering little moans and whimpers of relief, Anna's dog immediately set about squeezing herself in between her two beloved humans, managing to get in a couple of licks at Anna's cheek.

For a timeless moment, the two humans and their dog clung to each other as a last few sporadic fireworks lit up the city skyline.

'Jesus,' Jake said fervently when he finally released Anna from his embrace. 'I'm never doing that again! Not the kissing part,' he added hastily. He was holding her against his chest as if he would never let her go.

'I thought I was going to die,' she managed through her shivers. 'But you found me.'

She could hear police sirens wailing up the High.

'To be fair, it was Bonnie who found you,' Jake admitted. 'You should seriously consider changing her name to "Lassie". Honey, you're freezing.' He took off his jacket and wrapped it around her shoulders.

A moment later, Liam clambered out to join them on the roof, obviously out of breath. 'Oh, thank Christ, you found her!' His voice was sharp with relief. 'She's OK?'

Jake just nodded. 'She's OK!' He didn't seem able to take his eyes off Anna. 'First, we'll get you off this roof,' he told her. 'Then, I'll tell you how we found you, me and Bonnie.'

Twenty-One

A week later

The first soft flakes began drifting down as Anna drove her grandfather and his artist friend Desmond to the Orangery, Isadora's friend's bistro on the Woodstock Road. By the time everyone had ordered their starters, it was snowing in earnest.

There were ten of them seated at the long table; Anna and Jake, Tansy and Liam, Tim and his pregnant wife Anjali, Anna's grandfather and Desmond, and Hetty Vallier's granddaughter, Sabina. Isadora had been persuaded to sit at the head of the table (not that she'd needed too much persuading, Anna had noticed), since they were all here at her invitation.

Isadora waited until everyone had a glass of whatever they were drinking, then gave an imperious ding on her own glass to get their attention. 'I'll admit that I organized this belated New Year's celebration with a distinct sense that we might be tempting fate! As all of you know by now, Christmas Day didn't quite work out how we'd expected.' She gave a rueful glance at her wrist which was still in plaster. 'And New Year's Eve – well, I'm sure we'd all prefer not to dwell on how that might have ended.' Her gaze went to rest on Anna. 'It's almost impossible for me to believe now that just a few months ago I didn't know Anna or Tansy. We were drawn together in dreadful circumstances, and we've gone through more dramatic times since then and I owe them both, and Liam and Jake, an immense debt.'

'No, you don't,' Tansy said at once.

'But I do, my darling!' Isadora insisted. 'I never could have survived it without you all and it's also partly through you that another wonderful girl has come into my life.' She bestowed a fond smile on Hetty's granddaughter. Sabina, looking fresh as a flower in the dress her adopted grandmother had bought her, did her best to appear cool and enigmatic but couldn't hide her pleasure.

Isadora took a breath. 'I learned, painfully young, that this world can be a dark and terrifying place. My father once told me that all we ever really have are moments, and that moments like these with the people we care about' – at this point her voice developed a distinct wobble – 'are precious and to be treasured.'

'This woman is determined to make me cry!' Tansy protested.

'There is nothing wrong with tears!' Isadora said, swiftly brushing away her own. 'So here's my toast for us all. May the Fates allow us to enjoy this small celebration without any taint of murder, mayhem or last-minute roof-top rescues!'

'Amen!' Jake and Desmond said simultaneously and everyone raised their glasses.

'You heard the lady!' Liam called to Anna. 'No roof-top rescues until after dessert!'

'I'll try my best,' she promised.

Outside snow continued to fall. Maybe she was having some kind of delayed reaction to her New Year's Eve brush with death, but Anna felt cocooned in a state of near bliss. As a small girl she'd once been the proud owner of a snow globe and had secret fantasies of being able to go into the tiny perfect world inside. Just now, with the sparkling cold outside the windows and the warmth and companionship inside, she felt as if she was coming close to achieving her wish.

Towards the end of their meal, the table, with its burned-down candles, half-empty bottles and smeared and sticky dessert plates, looked like one of George Ottaway's paintings brought to life. Desmond was the only one who hadn't finished eating. 'Because I talk so much!' he explained unapologetically. Anna guessed he was in his late fifties, but his long dreadlocks and the wicked twinkle in his eyes made him seem ageless.

Bonnie and Hero lay companionably by the French doors, watching the softly tumbling snowflakes. Since Isadora's lunch was being held in a private room, the Orangery's owners had agreed to her request that the dogs should be allowed to join the celebrations.

At last Desmond laid down his spoon and carefully wiped his mouth on his linen napkin. 'That was a wonderful meal,' he told Isadora. 'I feel blessed that Anna and George asked me to be part of your special occasion.' Anna was pleased she'd thought to ask Isadora to include him. He'd been a lively lunch companion, sparring humorously with the younger men, as well as keeping her grandfather company, and flirting light-heartedly with Isadora as if they'd known each other all their lives.

In a lull between courses, Anna had overheard her grandfather talking to Tim. 'It's wonderful to see you two together again. It feels almost like old times. I remember one of my first sketches was of you and Anna on the beach at Holkham.' During this exchange, Tim's wife, Anjali, had concentrated especially hard on her dessert. Anjali knew the truth, of course, as did all Anna's friends.

It wasn't just simple cowardice that had prevented her from telling her grandfather. Anna thought he needed – they *both* needed – some time to recover before she dropped yet another bombshell.

Her memory of the moments immediately following her rescue mostly consisted of disconnected snapshots. She had a blurry recollection of being checked over by paramedics in the back of the ambulance while a concerned Jake waited, crouching beside Bonnie. She remembered Liam driving them all back to Isadora's. She remembered Tansy solicitously piling on quilts, cracking jokes about the Princess and the Pea as Anna shivered and shook. She must have slept at some point though because she remembered waking herself up with a great gasp of fear and hearing someone say quietly, 'You're OK, kid. You're going to be OK.' She'd opened her eyes to see a dog-tired Jake sitting beside her bed. Isadora told her later that he'd kept watch over her through what remained of the night. 'Rationally, he knew Alec Faber was dead. But he wasn't taking any chances.'

It wasn't until the following day that Anna began properly piecing together the sequence of events that had led to her miraculous rescue.

Jake had got her call. He'd heard everything and immediately tried to call the police. 'But of course it was New Year's Eve. We didn't have a prayer of getting through. It was obvious there was no time to lose, so Liam said he'd drive us. We were just leaving the house and Bonnie came hurtling out after us like she'd been fired from a cannon. We tried to make her stay, but she just started barking like crazy.'

'Bonnie *barked*?' Anna had said in awe. Bonnie almost never barked, except very occasionally in one of her more action-packed dreams.

'Barking that rapidly escalated to ear-splitting howls,' he'd said ruefully. 'We didn't have time to take her back inside and we couldn't leave her yowling on Isadora's drive so we were pretty much forced to take her along. It wasn't like we'd planned to use her as our search-and-rescue dog!' Jake had given Anna his lopsided grin. 'Then off we went. Man, I thought I could drive but Liam is something else! Went streaking down the Banbury Road and into the city centre, drove us right up to the porter's lodge and flashed his Thames Valley ID at some sleepy young guy.'

'That was probably Tate,' Anna had told him.

'Used to be a soldier right?' Jake had asked. 'Thought so. Guy was on his feet in a heartbeat. All we knew was that Faber was taking you up on some roof somewhere. Tate helped us narrow

321

down the possibilities. He couldn't leave the lodge because they still had some big party going on, so Liam went one way, Bonnie and I went the other. Then all at once Bonnie got this look, exactly how she'd looked in Afghanistan that time; like, *beyond* focused! Running around, nose glued to the ground, nostrils working overtime. And I'm thinking, *Is she genuinely on to something, or is she just picking up on my terror pheromones*, you know? Then, all at once, she pounced.' Jake had shaken his head. 'I wish you'd seen her! It was beautiful how she did it, so fast and precise, and when I looked she had your scarf hanging out of her jaws and you could see she was so damn pleased with herself! I stuffed your scarf into my pocket and she took me straight to that tower with the nightmare stairs.' He'd passed his hand across his eyes trying to banish the memory. 'Like I said, we should seriously think about changing that dog's name.'

'Not a chance,' Anna had told him. 'Bonnie is Bonnie.'

Someone touched her lightly on the shoulder, pulling her back to the Orangery's dining room. She glanced up and saw Tim. 'We're taking off in a few minutes,' he told her. 'Anjali's getting tired.' He dropped his voice as he added, 'Plus, I thought I'd come and check how my big sister's doing.'

She smiled up at him. 'I'm fine. I'm ridiculously excited about being an aunt.' They'd agreed to wait a while before talking to Chris. (Anna still found it hard to think of him as her father and wondered if she ever would.) Tim was about to become a dad and Anna was contemplating a possible life change of her own. She slid a glance at Jake, who was smiling at something her grandfather had said.

'Have you found anything out about Dominic?' she asked Tim, lowering her voice. She'd called Tim to tell him about her terrifying New Year's Eve adventure and reported what Alec Faber had told her just before he fell. 'I've pretty much exhausted all my abilities.'

Tim shook his head. 'I haven't come up with anything yet. But I'll get there, Anna, and that's a promise.'

'I feel like I haven't really talked to Anjali properly,' she said.

'Don't worry about it,' Tim told her. 'You're both a bit shy of each other, that's all. We've got our whole lives ahead of us to sort that out.'

Tim and Anjali left. Jake came over to suggest taking the dogs into the garden before they drove home. Anna glanced across at her grandfather and saw him in animated conversation with Desmond. 'OK,' she agreed.

'Did you bring your present as per instructions?' Jake asked.

'I did. It's in my bag,' Anna said with a grin. 'Shall I prepare to be amazed?'

'After *this* much build-up?' Jake shook his head a little ruefully. 'I'd have to lasso a shooting star now to have a hope of impressing you! No, kid, I'd just like to put that whole ill-conceived surprise element behind me now, and move on!'

They fetched their coats and took Bonnie out into the snowy garden. Hero had firmly refused

323

to leave the warmth of the dining room. It was still snowing so Anna and Jake went to shelter under a pergola where a dense tangle of evergreens had formed a natural roof. They stood side by side, hands almost touching, as they watched their dog happily snuffling around in the snow. Anna thought of how he'd stayed by her bed all night and how he'd been shocked into finally kissing her up on the college roof. 'You don't need to lasso a shooting star, Jake McCaffrey,' she told him softly. 'I already find you sufficiently amazing.'

Jake gave her a quick, searching glance. 'Are you saying I already passed the test?' His voice was slightly husky.

She deliberately met his eyes. 'What do you think?'

'I think you should open my damn present,' he told her with a grin.

Anna took the package out of her bag, and began rather self-consciously peeling off the sticky tape from one end. She slid out a shallow rectangular cardboard box, about seven inches by five. 'I should probably mention that I'm really terrible at surprises?' she confessed with a nervous laugh.

'I'd say you're quite good at them,' Jake said, straight-faced. 'You constantly surprise me, that's for sure! Go on, kid, put us both out of our misery and open the box.'

Anna cautiously lifted the lid. Inside the box was something flat, carefully wrapped in white tissue. 'This is like pass the parcel!' she protested.

Jake was looking decidedly nervous now. 'Keep

going,' he ordered. 'Before I decide this is a really bad idea and snatch it back!'

Anna removed the top layer of tissue and found herself looking at a photograph in a simple solid silver frame. The photograph showed a proudly smiling little boy – Anna guessed no more than six years old – dressed in a waistcoat and baggy trousers and an embroidered cotton prayer cap. He was kneeling on a piece of dusty ground with his arms around what Anna initially took for a snow-white wolf cub. For a moment, she didn't understand what she was seeing. Then she looked more closely at the cub's alert, intelligent eyes.

'Oh, my God,' she whispered. 'Is that Bonnie?'

Jake nodded. 'And that's the little boy she tried to save.'

'How ever did you get hold of this photo?'

'It's quite a story! It always bothered me that I never knew who Bonnie really belonged to,' Jake explained. 'After that roadside bomb went off it was pure mayhem. Then by the time things had calmed down, the kid's family had decamped somewhere, nobody seemed to know where. But I kept on putting the word out and a couple of weeks ago, I got lucky and my contact finally tracked them down. The family is in Pakistan now, and they very kindly sent me this picture of their little boy with our Bonnie.'

Anna was still looking at the photograph. 'What was his name?'

'Emal,' Jake said. 'Looks like a nice little kid, doesn't he?'

She was too moved for words. Jake hadn't just given her a glimpse of Bonnie's past history; he'd given her a glimpse into his world, his former life.

Jake swallowed. 'Kind of a morbid choice for a Christmas present, right?'

She quickly shook her head. 'Not to me. I mean, it's tragic and wrong how Emal died, but this photo is perfect. He looks so happy with Bonnie.' She glanced at Jake. 'What did Emal's family call her? Do you know?'

He gave her his here-and-gone-again smile. 'They called her Farishta. In Pashto, it means "angel".'

'No,' Anna said in disbelief. This new piece of the ongoing mystery that was Bonnie made her break into goosebumps.

'I know,' Jake said. 'And that was *before* she found you up on the roof! How Emal's family acquired her in the first place is probably a story for another time though,' he added with a grin.

'Thank you,' she told him. 'You couldn't have given me anything better.'

Anna was carefully stowing the photograph back in her bag, as Isadora and Tansy came out to join them. 'I'm leaving you girls to chat,' Jake said. 'Me and Bonnie have a date with some snow.' He began to pretend-stalk Bonnie, who immediately dropped flat on to her belly, recognizing the opening moves of a well-loved game.

Isadora and Tansy went to stand on either side of Anna beneath the sheltering honeysuckle.

'That was a fabulous lunch,' Anna told Isadora. 'Thanks so much for getting us all together.'

'I needed to thank you all,' Isadora said. 'I

wanted us to have a lovely time together before we have to dive back into the fray.'

'What fray? What's happening?' Tansy looked anxious.

'Robert's funeral is next week,' Isadora said. 'I'm absolutely dreading it. I had to meet up with his ex-wife and children. I know Robert wasn't perfect but he deserved better than those cold, grasping people.'

'Did you know Alec Faber's getting cremated next week?' Anna asked her.

Liam had told them the service was scheduled for the early-morning slot, the time normally reserved for public-health-funded funerals, what used to be referred to as a pauper's funeral.

Isadora nodded. 'Tansy told me. Is there really no one from Alec's family who's going to attend?'

Anna shook her head. 'After Tallis reported him to his superiors, they cut him off. After that, Alec's life just unravelled.'

'You almost sound sorry for him.' Tansy said. 'He killed James and left Isadora unconscious and bleeding on her drive. And he would have killed *you*, Anna, if Jake and Liam hadn't got to you in time.'

Anna shook her head. 'I'm not sorry for Alec, but I can't help feeling bad for Roop.'

Tansy looked exasperated. 'Anna, you do know Roop wasn't real? He was just some character Alec Faber invented so he didn't have to own up to all the dodgy dealings he'd got up to in the past.'

Anna didn't feel up to explaining her feeling that Roop had not just been real, he'd been Alec's

327

last shot at being a decent person. It distressed her that Alec Faber had killed that gentle man; no, not Alec, she corrected herself, but the dark distillation of rage that he had finally become.

'And he abandoned his poor old dog,' Tansy added.

'Actually, I have a recent update on Roop's dog,' Anna told her friends. 'I had to pop into college on the way to pick up Desmond and guess who I saw in the porter's lodge curled up in her smart new basket?'

Tansy's face lit up. 'Meg?'

Anna nodded. 'Looking surprisingly content.'

'Oh, my God, that's *so* sweet!' Tansy clapped her hands. 'The porters decided to adopt her!'

'Tate decided to adopt her,' Anna corrected her. 'But while I was there, both he and Boswell were fussing over her like two mother hens. Someone told Boswell about some special supplement that might help her joints. I have a feeling Roop's Meg might be getting a whole new lease of life!'

'I'm thankful some good has come out of all of this however small,' Isadora said soberly.

The three women fell silent for a moment. Once again Anna found herself thinking of the destruction Matthew Tallis had brought about, for reasons that only he would ever know. Isadora was the only one of the Six who had survived relatively unscathed.

Isadora slipped an arm through Anna's and Anna could smell her familiar musky perfume. 'The police brought back Hetty's diary,' she said. 'I forced myself to read it finally. I read it all.'

'I'm glad,' Anna said.

'So am I.' Isadora swallowed. 'She said I was her heart's friend. She really did want to tell me about her baby. And I've decided I got it wrong about her and Sam. It was hideous how Hetty died, but at least she died knowing she was loved.'

'I'm glad about that too,' Anna said. Her eyes had strayed to Jake who had started to mould a handful of snow into a snowball.

'So I'm guessing your New Year resolution is to stay away from murderous psychopaths?' Tansy said giving Anna a quick hug.

'That is definitely one of my more important resolutions,' Anna said.

Tansy took hold of her free arm. 'You do realize that you were actually saved by my dog-walking detective scarf? Clever dogs and ex-Navy SEALS were entirely incidental. It was all down to my magic pink scarf. If I was you, I wouldn't take it off except to wash it!'

'Good idea,' Anna said. 'It will be my scarf of invincibility.'

Jake hurled the snowball at Bonnie, who caught it with an audible snap of her jaws, then stood open-mouthed, incredulous at finding her solid-looking prize turned to icy mush.

Tansy burst out laughing. She quickly pulled her phone out of her pocket. 'Jake, get her to do it again and I'll film it!'

Anna's dog fixed her intense brown eyes on Jake as she gathered herself for another doomed attempt to catch a ball composed of hundreds of thousands of compressed snowflakes.

Isadora's father was right, Anna thought. The world was a dark and terrifying place where monsters and devils of all kinds waited in the shadows, and this wasn't something which was likely to change any time soon. But there were also fragile moments like these, each one as fleeting and unrepeatable as the starry white flakes falling through the air.